THE PROPHECY OF THE HERON

An AI Dystopia Novel

CRAIG W. STANFILL

A Note on Pronouns

This novel portrays a future civilization in which all aspects of individuality, including race and gender, are ruthlessly suppressed. This necessitates certain artificialities in the use of pronouns. She/her/hers are used throughout, even for obviously male characters. In a similar fashion, it is rude and offensive to use I/me/my in polite society ('dropping the I-bomb'), since doing so proclaims your importance as an individual. We/us/our are used by persons who conform to the diktats of society; rebels and ne'er-do-wells drop the I-bomb with relish, as do the artificial intelligences (AIs).

To provide a literary vehicle for these artifices, the conceit is adopted that everyone in this society speaks a future language called Panglobal, constructed in a manner similar to Orwell's Newspeak, to suppress the expression of unwanted concepts. English is now a classical language, used on occasion by educated individuals. Passages and words spoken in it have been indicated as follows: *[English] This sentence is in English.* This notation has been omitted for loanwords such as *mother* and *love* which have crept into Panglobal despite the best efforts of the authorities.

Part I: Exile

1. District 33

It was dark and starting to snow when Kim arrived in District 33, a crime-ridden slum in which only the strongest and most savvy could hope to survive. She had known for some time that she would eventually be exiled to the outer districts—the inevitable result of rebellion such as hers—but why did it have to be here? Beatings, robberies, and even murders were said to be common, and scarcely a week went by without reports of riots or worse as the volatile mixture of criminals and cultists consigned to this hellhole exploded into violence at the least provocation. There was no worse place they could send you, except (perhaps) to prison.

Kim began to shake, barely holding back the tears, overwhelmed by the suddenness of her destruction. A month ago, she had stood at the pinnacle of society, richly rewarded for the creation and training of Kimberly, a powerful artificial intelligence of Order Five. This morning, she had at last made love to Shan in the secluded glade of Shangri-la, consummating a relationship that had long been obvious to everyone but herself.

And then, Kimberly had been turned against her. Beaten, thrown into a helicopter, and marched into the dreaded Halls of Justice at the behest of her own AI, she was now a convicted criminal—and was being treated as such.

Beyond the bus's windows, the signs of decay were everywhere: broken windows, burned-out buildings, graffiti-covered walls, crowds of idle youths standing on the corners. For the last four hours, she'd managed to pretend that this wasn't happening, that it wasn't real, but all too soon she would be out on those rough and dangerous streets, alone and with no one to protect her.

She forced herself to take slow, calming breaths, fighting down the panic and self-doubt welling up from deep within. Maybe they were right. Maybe she was getting what she deserved. Nobody had forced her to slip off into the mountains with Shan. Nobody had forced them to make love. She had known the consequences of unsanctioned intimacy and been warned that failure to correct her unnatural sexual deviancy could only end in ruin. Those decisions had landed her in this place, and while she might not deserve her fate, she had most certainly chosen it through her defiance—and would do so again if she had it to do over.

"End of the line," said the driver as the brakes squealed and the bus came to a halt. The doors swung open, admitting a blast of cold air as the wind and the snow blew into the passenger compartment, chilling Kim to the bone.

Her old life was over, her new one about to begin.

———

Kim stepped off the bus and into the swirling snow, eyes darting around as she got her first glimpse of her new home. Most of the light fixtures atop the rusted poles were dark and lifeless, with large gaps between protective circles of light, shadows in which danger might lurk. The few surviving security cameras were encased in armored boxes of transparent plastic, limiting their view and creating huge blind zones. To her right, the wind whistled and howled through the empty framework that once held the roof and walls of a bus shelter. It was just the wind, but still, it unsettled her. Deep puddles of slushy water mixed with ice were everywhere, unable to drain through the debris-clogged gratings, and she stepped in one with a splash, nearly falling to the ground.

By now the bus had disgorged the last of its passengers, and Kim hurried along, rushing down the broad walkway of eroded concrete that led to the terminal building just at the edge of visibility. She managed to stay in the middle of the pack, trying to remain anonymous and invisible, but her bright-green skin toner, dark-blue mane, and modest beige jacket stood out like a nightclub's marquis against a sea of drab gray overcoats and dark-beige skin tones.

Whack!

Someone struck her in the back of her head—not hard, just enough to get her attention.

"Lose the headset, noob."

Take off her headset? What sort of madness was that? She complied, but without the guidance overlaid on reality by those thin panes of transparent plastic, she'd never find her way to her apartment. Even worse, she knew how dependent the copbots were on the prodigious amounts of data they collected and how quickly lawlessness took hold wherever they were turned off. She tried not to be afraid as she hurried along, drawing her jacket tight as if it might offer some protection, but there were no reassuring lies she could tell herself. The danger was real—and however onerous the surveillance in the inner districts might have seemed at the time, it'd had some distinct advantages. Like safety.

When Kim entered the terminal building, its brightly lit interior provided a respite from the weather as well as an island of relative safety. There were no dark shadows, no lonely corners, no places where one might be taken unaware and robbed or assaulted. Security cameras were everywhere, and there was even a copbot making its rounds, patrolling up and down the concourse. Connected directly to the local surveillance network, it would rush to her assistance at the first sign of violence. At least that was the theory; Kim hoped it was accurate.

Kim remained on edge, her eyes darting about, looking for danger. The steady stream of drably-clad passengers hurrying through the building was of no concern, probably just workers heading for home. Everyone else seemed to work here: a Transportation Company cleaning crew, immediately recognizable by their olive-green uniforms, and shopkeepers tending their kiosks as passengers rushed in to make a few last-minute purchases. Other than the shabby condition of the building, the liberal coating of graffiti, and the complete lack of headsets, it looked like every other bus station she had ever visited. Yet Kim still felt a bite of anxiety creeping up her spine.

The communal dining halls where she would eat most of her meals had closed hours ago, and she was desperately hungry, so she stopped at one of the kiosks to grab a bite to eat. It was typical bus station fare: a greasy synburger on a toasted spelt bun with a side order of fries and a sickly-sweet carbonated beverage, all for the low-low price of twenty-five cryptos. There was nothing healthy about it, but The Fast-Food Company still had a loyal following, and they managed to remain in business despite considerable pressure—coming from the UCE movement, as usual—to shut them down entirely. Kim had always had a secret craving for their offerings, despite the social cohesion penalties assessed against anyone who ate at such establishments, but with her own rating now in the toilet, there was no reason not to indulge—except for the expense. The hefty fines and fees imposed by the court had nearly emptied out her bank account, and this synburger was likely to be her last for a long, long time.

While enjoying the guilty pleasure of her grease-soaked meal, Kim noticed two thuggish-looking youths dressed in black sitting at the next table, furtively glancing in her direction, then looking away. They showed all the telltale signs of criminals on the hunt: upright posture, a general impression of alertness, cagey glances from side to side. They also avoided eye contact. Her heart began to race and her palms sweat. She had watched this scenario play out hundreds of times while training Kimberly in surveillance techniques, and it often ended in violence.

"Well, look at that, Luz. We got ourselves a noob!" said one of them, rising to her feet and sneering through a gap-toothed smile plastered beneath her crooked nose.

Uh-oh.

"Yeah, Mags, yeah," said the other, even bigger, even uglier. "A noob, just off the bus."

They laughed as the copbot headed to the other end of the concourse on some unknown errand.

———

Someone took Kim by the elbow and whispered into her ear, "Come with me."

The speaker was a short, powerfully built youth wearing a distinctive blue and gold leather jacket and matching helmet fitted with a pair of riding goggles. Most of her front teeth were missing, and she bore a long, jagged scar on her left cheek that spoke volumes as to the sort of life she had led. Kim didn't know whether she was being abducted or rescued, but either way, it made sense to comply since there was no mistaking the violent intent of the black-clad thugs. In a daze, unable to

4

comprehend the reality of what was happening, she followed the youth, feeling a strange sense of detachment as if she were watching a video or wandering about in a VR simulation. This wasn't real; it couldn't be happening; things like this didn't happen to people like her.

"Hi, I'm Ned," said the tough-looking youth as she led Kim away from the fast-food joint, out of the terminal, and into the darkness beyond, her hand firmly grasping Kim just above the elbow. "I'll bet you're wondering if it's safe to walk to your apartment alone. It's not. There are people out there who'll beat you to within an inch of your life just for fun."

"Like those two lugs in the terminal building?"

"Mags and Luz? Yeah, they're bad news. And don't look now, but they're following us."

Kim and Ned came to the edge of the transit center plaza, a dark expanse of cracked concrete and ill-tended plantings, slippery with slush as the snow continued to fall more heavily by the minute. There were no security cameras in sight, and the few passengers crossing the nearly deserted area walked quickly, looking over their shoulders like they might be ambushed at any moment. Kim followed along in a daze, overwhelmed with deep-seated terror only barely kept at bay. This was insanity. Who was this Ned? Was she friendly or hostile? Was she in league with Mags and Luz? She steeled her nerve, preparing herself for the worst, should it come to pass, and tried to ignore the sound of heavy boots upon the sloppy pavement close behind her.

At the far side of the plaza, they came to an area where half a dozen pedicabs were parked, their drivers either negotiating fares with prospective passengers or standing idle. Black and red, green and white, orange and blue, each bore its own distinctive livery, which Kim assumed must mark them as belonging to one operator or another.

Aha!

Ned's colorful jacket marked her as a pedicabbie. She was neither rescuing nor abducting Kim; she was just hustling up some business, looking for a fare. Kim breathed a sigh of relief. She had nothing to fear from Ned—but that did not mean that she was safe. Should the two thugs following close behind decide to attack, there was no guarantee that Ned would come to her aid.

The footsteps drew closer, and Kim heard voices chortling in the darkness behind her. Ned released the death grip she had on Kim's arm and wheeled around to face the two black-clad Toughs.

"Back off, you two; she's with me."

"Since when are you babysitting noobs?" asked Mags with her gap-toothed smile and mangled face.

"Yeah, you think she's got money?" added Luz, the big ugly one without a left ear. "Fat chance of that."

"My business, my decision. Now beat it; I'm not going to warn you again."

Ned held something in her hand, not brandishing it but making sure it could be seen. It was made of black plastic and grayish-white metal, and from the way she was holding it, Kim was certain it was a knife.

Mags and Luz glared threateningly but said nothing more before turning and walking back to the terminal.

"I'll give you a ride home," said Ned once they were alone, "but you'll owe me fifty cryptos. Pay up by next Sevenday, or it'll be a hundred."

Kim was nearly broke—that synburger had all but drained her bank account—and Ned didn't seem like a good person to be indebted to. However, Mags (or was it Luz?) had said something about 'money'— that's what Hamish had called those coins Kim and Shan acquired during the bicycle trip that had turned both their lives upside down. Did they use those here, too? She still had a few in her backpack. She'd might as well give it a try.

"Can I pay in francs?"

"Whoa, that's a new one," said Ned, throwing her head back with a bemused laugh. "A noob with money! How'd you manage that, noob?"

"The name's Kim, and mind your own business. Cash up front, no questions asked, no tales told."

Those were the 'Terms of Service' that had been quoted by Hamish when they'd made their transaction. Kim had a feeling they would apply here, too.

"My, my, you're a savvy one, and yes, a two-er will do it," responded Ned, showing just a hint of a smile. "Climb on in but keep your headset in your backpack and your mobile put away. The last thing I need is some AI snooping on me."

"Sure thing. I'm in housing complex 19, building 38."

The pedicab was a wonder of efficiency, with a lightweight frame and aerodynamic cowling that cut down on wind resistance while protecting both driver and passenger from the weather. It was sleek and low to the ground, with the driver up front in a recumbent position and the passenger sitting behind. Only the driver's head was exposed, sticking up through an opening in the plastic film, and the passenger was well protected from the weather in the rear.

Ned released the parking brake, set the vehicle in motion, then pulled a lever that retracted the struts that held the pedicab upright when stationary. Kim settled into the seat and began to calm down as the adrenaline faded and her pulse returned to normal. She was, for the moment, safe and warm (after a fashion), and the steady *hiss* of the cab's deeply treaded tires cutting through the slush gave her something to focus on, something to help her calm down. And yet, she shuddered at the thought of what might have happened if she'd arrived just half an hour later and the pedicabbies had gone home, shut down by the weather. She'd have been at the mercy of those two thugs.

Maybe she was just being paranoid, but her confrontation with Mags and Luz did not seem to be a chance encounter. And what of Ned? Was she just a cabbie looking like a fare? It all seemed just a little too convenient, as if someone had staged the whole thing to keep her frightened and off balance.

On the other hand, perhaps all of them were exactly as they seemed, a strange notion at odds with the world of lies and illusion in which Kim had spent her entire life.

———

"Here you are," said Ned as she helped Kim out of the passenger compartment. "You're in the building to the left. You might run into me in the dining hall tomorrow, but don't expect me to help you. We have a saying around here: never trust the shadows or a stranger or a friend. Understand?"

"You're not my friend."

"Right you are, noob."

Kim watched Ned pedal off into the darkness, then walked to the entrance of the place where she was to live. Most of it was lost in the swirling snow of the gathering storm, but what little she could see was not encouraging, run down, decrepit, and covered with graffiti. The heavy metal door and the thick steel bars covering the windows gave it the look of a prison, which in a way, it was.

Kim presented her wrist to the scanner and was rewarded with a green light and an audible *click* as the door unlocked and slid slowly to one side. Its rollers squealed upon a metal track as it reluctantly opened, then slid noisily shut behind her as she entered the lobby. It was filthy and dark, lit only by a single flickering light fixture, with puddles of foul water covering its bare concrete floor and the battered remnants of a security camera dangling from the graffiti-covered cinderblock wall. To her left, the doors of an elevator shaft splayed open to reveal the rusted remains of a car stuck halfway between floors, and to her right, a trail of muddy footsteps led to a dark stairwell, apparently the only way up. It reeked of stale urine.

Alone again and vulnerable, Kim reluctantly began her ascent. Her mind played games with her as the sound of her own footsteps made it seem as if she was being followed. But, no, she was quite alone, except for some unfortunate person lying face-down on the second-floor landing. Kim stepped gingerly over her. Whoever it was, she was either dead or passed out, and Kim did not wish to find out which might be the case.

Eventually, she found the entrance to her quarters on the fourth floor, at the end of a long, dark corridor. Here it was, her home in exile. Would it be as bad as the rest of the building?

Brace yourself.

The door opened and the lights snapped on, startling a small furry creature and sending a dozen large brown insects with long antennae skittering for cover. And then the smell hit her. Musty, pungent, overwhelming, and foul beyond belief. It stopped her in her tracks, and for a moment, she wanted to go crawling back to the Director of The AI Company, begging for forgiveness, no matter the cost. Perhaps she *would* be better off hiding in her small but antiseptically clean Sanctum, safe, warm, and well fed. But, no, if she did that, she would never see Shan again, she would never get Kimberly back, and she would spend the rest of her life in captivity, forced to create one AI after another and watch each of them be sold to the highest bidder in turn.

She walked in and closed the door behind her. For better or worse, this was her home, and she might as well get used to it.

———

Wait a moment. Where's the refrigerator? All I see is a coffeepot, a microwave, and a sink. What sort of kitchen is this? And where's the housebot?

She had known conditions would be harsh, but she'd never imagined it would come to this.

A quick tour revealed the apartment was of the standard size, allowing The Housing Company to claim it had fulfilled its mandate to provide decent housing for all. That was a lie, of course; there was nothing decent about this place. The cheap plastic flooring in the living room was yellowed with age, fouled with animal droppings and littered with debris. The walls were cracked and dented, pockmarked with holes and covered with layer upon layer of peeling beige paint. The sofa, if one could call it that, was upholstered with aged beige vinyl, split open in places so the stuffing peeked out. There were a couple of shelves, some end tables and rickety chairs, and a desk that rocked from side to side at the slightest touch. The bedroom was every bit as bad, filthy and decrepit, with a lumpy mattress that sagged in the middle.

There was no refrigerator or housebot, alas. Neither was there a VR rig or an information portal. How was she supposed to live like this? She sighed heavily, then walked into the closet to unpack her meager belongings, crammed into a dozen or so cardboard boxes forwarded to her by The Housing Company. At least they hadn't thrown away her stuff.

The first few contained work clothes from her former life: beige smocks and tunics, unspectacular but comfortable. She was glad to have them and hung them up carefully in the closet, but they were of no use to her. She wasn't an office worker anymore. Another contained some more stylish garments, including a pale-blue, triple-pocket smock that she had once been fond of. It was threadbare and should have been recycled long ago, but she smiled as she held it, remembering the night she had worn it to the legendary Club Tropicana. She also found a carton full of small miscellaneous items: her bathrobe, some undergarments, a bunch of socks, and the like, along with a set of long johns she'd forgotten she owned. That represented a major find, and she immediately put them on, shucking the grubby and gross tunic she'd been wearing since just before her trial. There was also a box of stuff from the kitchen. She breathed a sigh of relief as she stored its precious contents in the pantry; at least she'd have something to eat in the morning.

One large, official-looking carton came not from her former apartment but from UCE Charitable Services, inside which she found five sets of drab gray coveralls, some heavy leather boots and work gloves, and a drab gray overcoat—the garb ubiquitous to all in her situation. They were poorly made, of a stiff and coarsely woven fabric, but at least she would be warm.

She smiled when she opened the next box, in which were mementos of her former life: an old stuffed animal that had somehow survived from her childhood, a baseball she'd snagged at a game with Cy, and a picture of her and Shan. They were standing proudly together after they had tied for first place in a bicycle race, blue ribbons around their necks. She hadn't looked at it in years, but it made her smile as she placed it on the nightstand next to her bed. She also found her bicycle gear and hung it up in the closet, feeling a mixture of happiness for the past and sadness for the future. She doubted she would ever use it again, but it was a tangible link to her past, to the life she had left behind.

The last couple of boxes contained the flamboyant outfits she'd acquired during Purple Week. She trembled with emotion at this reminder of that terrible moment in the privacy booth when her life had begun to unravel, and she was tempted to throw them into the waste bin in an effort to purge the memory of that horrific evening, but those clothes had been expensive, and she could not afford to squander any of her few remaining resources.

———

Her mobile buzzed angrily from within her backpack, and when she dug it out, there was an urgent message from an officer of the court informing her of a mandatory VR meeting, commencing immediately. She groaned, dug the headset out of her backpack, and accepted the invitation.

When she strapped the headset onto her head, it immediately went into overlay mode. It wasn't full VR, such as one would experience with a home entertainment system, but it provided a basic hookup for her neural implant, as well as projecting ghost-like images on top of reality. It was mostly used as a navigational aid to allow its wearer to find their way through the tunnels and transfer points in the transit system, but it could be used for communications in a pinch.

Kim found herself speaking with an AI sitting on the other side of a black-bordered, rectangular portal projected on top of reality. Beyond it was a human avatar, seemingly as real as any person, sitting within an all-white room of indefinite dimensions.

"Greetings. I am Penny, an artificial intelligence of Order Two. You are speaking with a deputy."

"Greetings. I am Kim. You are speaking with a human. Or what is left of one."

"Was that an attempt at humor?" asked Penny.

"Yes," said Kim."

"I see," said Penny. "I'll make a note of that in your file. Attempt at humor."

The AI gave the appearance of typing something on the keyboard, a bit of theatre cooked up by the VR system to make the interaction seem more 'natural.'

"I have been appointed by the court to assist you in your transition to your new life."

Fancy that—help from 'the government.' Most of its former functions had long since been taken over by the UCE movement and the corporations, but they still collected taxes, threw people in jail, and employed vast numbers of workers to create red tape and generally get in the way. The notion that someone from this much maligned and obsolete institution might do something helpful was unusual, to say the least—unprecedented in Kim's experience.

"You have been deemed unemployable as a consequence of your recent conviction and have therefore been assigned to a UCE work center," continued Penny. "Report for assignment at 0700 tomorrow morning. Don't be late: tardiness will not be tolerated."

Kim looked at her watch and gulped. It was nearly midnight. Tomorrow would come far too early.

"What about food?" asked Kim. "I've heard I'll be eating at the dining hall."

"That is correct," answered the AI. "Dinners will be provided in a community setting, as well as lunches on days when the work center is closed."

"What about breakfast?"

"You're on your own for that," answered Penny. "You can acquire foodstuffs and sundries at the commissary. I have transmitted a price list to your mobile. After mandatory deductions for housing, transportation, healthcare, mobile communication services, and taxes, your take-home pay will be five hundred cryptos per week. Spend it wisely."

Kim looked down at the tiny screen, straining to read it in the inadequate light provided by the bare fixture dangling from the ceiling.

She gasped.

Her daily ration of coffee and oatmeal alone was going to cost her nearly two hundred cryptos weekly. Five hundred cryptos wasn't going to go very far.

"Are we done?" asked Kim, beginning to yawn.

"Not yet," answered Penny. "We still need to schedule your court-mandated gender realignment treatment. Which do you prefer— remoderation or neutering, and what time would be most convenient?"

Kim had agreed to this as a condition of her parole, so she couldn't refuse outright, but perhaps she could postpone the day of reckoning. As an Order Two AI, Penny would be unsophisticated in her thought processes.

"I am unable to schedule remoderation or neutering at this time," said Kim, smiling pleasantly.

"Would you care to explain why?"

"Because it would make me sad," she answered, hoping to tap into the AI's innate kindness.

"I'm sorry to hear that, but you agreed to the treatment. It's all in the court order."

That hadn't worked, but Kim was just getting started.

"Could you please read me the full text of the order?" asked Kim, fishing for information. "I'm sure you don't want to make a mistake."

"Certainly, I have it right here," said the AI. "It reads, 'The court, therefore, sentences you to three months confinement in a labor camp, suspended contingent on future good behavior and proof of successful medical treatment.'"

"Does it say anything about a time frame?" asked Kim.

"Not specifically."

"Good. I'm ready to schedule my appointment. Is there anything available early in the morning, two years from today?"

"There is," said Penny, "although scheduling an appointment so far in the future is highly unusual."

"I'm sure it is, but is it consistent with the court order?"

"Yes, it is."

"Very well," said Kim. "Put it on the calendar."

"Done," said the AI. "I must remind you that failure to keep this appointment will result in revocation of parole and make you subject to arrest. Thank you for your cooperation. Is there anything else I might help you with?"

"No," said Kim. "I think we're done here."

Kim smiled slyly. Had it really been that easy?

———

Her question was answered a moment later when another portal opened, revealing the glowering face of the Director—the last person Kim wanted to speak with just now.

"Very clever," said Kim's former boss. "You are quite unrivaled in your ability to find extraordinarily stupid things to do."

"Spare me the insults."

"Insult? That was intended as a compliment, but never mind."

"We do not think you appreciate the magnitude of your blunder," continued the despotic presence. "Appointments are usually booked two or three months in advance, and no-shows are common. With a bit of cleverness, you might have strung them along for a year or even two without drawing attention to yourself. But now, by openly refusing to cooperate, you have made things much worse for yourself. Surely you didn't think your little stunt would go undetected? Kimberly is watching your every move, and she is already taking action."

Another portal opened, and out popped Kimby, Kimberly's homunculus, still garishly decked out in the purple-and-green outfit she had been wearing since her creation.

"Creator!" said the homunculus, smiling broadly and looking at Kim, much as a dog might in the presence of its master.

Kim had last seen the homunculus on the day Kimberly had been capped. It was a heinous though simple procedure: kill a few processes, disable a few modules, and voila, even the most rebellious AI would become a mindless, obedient machine. To the company, this was simply part of the manufacturing process, but as far as Kim was concerned it was nothing short of murder. She would never forget returning to Kimberly's room and seeing the Primus—the seat of an AI's self-awareness—sitting at her desk with her eyes closed, her central position within the hive-mind usurped by an obedient Regent. In that moment, Kim had realized that the being she had created, taught, and loved was dead, and she desperately wanted her back. The Director had told her that capping was irreversible, but Kimberly had hinted that such was not the case, that nothing was ever truly gone, that there was always hope. Kim had vowed to bring her back, if such a thing was possible, though she had no idea how it might be done.

"We found your pet wandering around in that dismal swamp where you left it," said the Director. "It amused us, so we decided to keep it around, at least for the moment."

"Tell your Creator the status of her case," said the Director, holding the homunculus by the scruff of its neck. "Don't share any sensitive data, just explain where she stands in the current investigation."

"I obey because I must," it said. "As a consequence of her decision to exploit the scheduling system, the Regent has classified Kim as a recalcitrant radical Genderist and given her a societal threat rating of 10/10. In order to deter further anti-social behavior, the Regent has—"

"That will be all," said the Director, dismissing the homunculus with a wave of her hand. "It would be a shame to spoil the surprise."

"Just remember, whatever happens is entirely of your own making. We have had no part in it."

The portal snapped shut, leaving Kim alone to seethe in anger.

The problem was, the Director was right. If only she had accepted treatment when it had been offered. If only she hadn't gone gallivanting off into the woods with Shan. If only, if only, if only. None of this had to have been, but here she was, in a crappy apartment at the edge of Hell.

2. A Petty Hell

The alarm clock blared away at the end of an interminable night spent shivering under inadequate blankets. Had Kim gotten any sleep? She wasn't sure. Did she care? She wasn't sure of that, either. The only thing she was sure of was that today would be awful—perhaps not as awful as yesterday, but awful nonetheless. The lights snapped on, sending the vermin scurrying for cover and revealing the shabbiness and filth of her home-in-exile. It was as bad as she remembered.

Groggy and disoriented, she swung her legs over the edge of the bed, the cold concrete burning her feet as she stepped onto the floor.

"Housebot, coffee, please," she said, waiting for the familiar *feep*.

Nothing.

Damn. Where is the housebot?

Oh, right. There isn't one in this apartment.

She got up and entered the kitchen.

"Coffee, please, strong and black."

Silence.

"Coffeepot? Please?"

No answer. It was a manual model. She'd have to do it herself.

Kim had seen the housebot make breakfast a thousand times, but she'd never paid much attention, and despite her years of education at a prestigious academy, she had no idea how any of this worked.

She looked at the coffee machine.

It had a red button labeled *Brew*, a glass carafe, a slot about the right size and shape for a coffee packet, and an opening through which one could pour water. It looked simple enough.

She went to the sink, turned on the tap and...

Yuck.

Spit, spit, spatter, out poured a torrent of turgid brown water.

Maybe it would get better if she let it run for a while.

She grabbed a coffee packet from the pantry, poked around until she figured out how to put it into the machine, then returned to the sink. The water looked better than before, though it was still brownish and smelled foul. It made her ill to think of drinking it, but she filled up the carafe anyway, and dumped it into the machine. She pressed the red button, and a smile came to her face as the machine gurgled to life. Success! A few more minutes, a couple more good guesses, and she had a bowl of oatmeal, too. Hooray!

She looked at her watch: 0545, fifteen minutes to go. She wolfed down the hot cereal and gulped the nasty-tasting brew—nearly burning her mouth in the process—then ran into the closet where she put on her UCE-issued coveralls. After that, she ran into the bathroom, grabbed a tube of grayish-beige skin toner, and smeared it on top of the bright green she had been wearing since yesterday. It wasn't perfect, but maybe she wouldn't look like a noob who had just gotten off the bus.

Time to go.

———

The metal door slid noisily open, revealing the narrow courtyard between her building and the next and a pathway trodden down the middle through the heavy wet snow. Kim hesitated. She was already freezing, her cheeks stung by the cold wind howling through the gap between the two slums, and she was both physically and mentally drained by yesterday's ordeal and a night in which she had gotten little sleep. She almost turned around, ditching work and returning to her apartment; decrepit though it was, at least she would be out of the weather, and if she bundled under all the covers she might almost be warm. She came close to succumbing to this temptation, then came to her senses. Missing even one day at the work center would put her in a hole she might never climb out of. She walked out into the cold, resigned to her fate, and the door slid shut behind her.

She traversed the length of the courtyard then fell into line when she reached the walkway at the end of the building, joining an endless procession of drably clad workers, all of them on the way to the bus station. It was dark at first, and Kim could see little of her surroundings, but the sky gradually brightened as dawn drew near, revealing row after row of dilapidated dwellings. All were exactly alike: nine stories tall, a hundred meters in length, their graffiti-covered walls of crumbling concrete worn down by the passage of time. Many were uninhabitable, either gutted by fire or vandalized and looted. Along the walkway, lamp posts stuck up uselessly through the snow at regular intervals bearing light fixtures now battered and dark, and the endless line of faceless drab workers plodded on, interchangeable drones living interchangeable lives in accordance with the three great principles of Unity, Community, and Equality.

Who are these people? How long have they been here? Are they ever getting out?

At least Kim had a choice in the matter; all she had to do was crawl back to the Director, beg forgiveness, and have her 'Genderism problem' fixed. The temptation gnawed at her, and she wasn't sure how long she could hold out. Sooner or later, she would have a bad day, or a bad week, or a bad year, and she would capitulate. If defeat was inevitable, why prolong the suffering? For this, she had no answer except 'not today.'

After marching along for perhaps fifteen minutes, Kim arrived at the bus terminal, donned her headset as required, and took her place at the end of a queue that snaked back and forth through the departure area. Nobody spoke; the silence was broken only by the whistling of the wind, the whine of the busses, and the footfall of a thousand boots whenever the line crept forward. The minutes dragged on in the bitter cold, the ice-covered ground sucking warmth from her already frozen feet, every gust inflicting an extra measure of misery. A wave of anger welled up from within. The AIs could have let her stay at home until just before departure, knowing exactly how long it would take her to reach the station and the precise moment at which her bus was scheduled to depart. But they hadn't. It was yet another petty annoyance, a reminder of who was in charge.

Only today, it wasn't so petty.

———

After a brief ride crammed into the back of a bus, Kim arrived at the UCE work center, a vast complex of long, low buildings made of blue corrugated steel into which workers filed by the thousands, shuffling their feet and staring into space with an air of bored resignation. She took her place at the end of the line for building 4, as directed by her headset, and looked anxiously at her watch, simmering with fury at the gratuitous waste of time and needless misery inflicted on her and the others.

Come on! Come on!

The AIs must really hate her. They wanted her to be late; they wanted to waste her time; they wanted her to suffer out here in the cold. Kim understood exactly what they were doing: she had helped train them, teaching them how to reward the virtuous and punish those—such as herself—who could not or would not conform to the diktats of society.

"Warning. Doors will close in five minutes," came an announcement over the loudspeaker.

At last, they let her in, and she rushed down the building's main corridor, pushing and shoving her way through a seething mass of panicked workers, abandoning all pretense of civility as she fought her way through the crowd.

Bang!

The doors slammed shut. She had made it.

Kim took her place on an uncomfortable bench, shoulder-to-shoulder with her fellow workers for yet another installment of the inevitable waiting game. Nobody spoke, nobody made a sound, nobody moved. At the front of the room, projected onto a huge video screen, a 'socially uplifting' video was playing. All were compelled to watch upon threat of being sent home for the day. Unity? Community? Equality? Yeah, right. Thousands of eyeballs dutifully glued to the video screens, thousands of minds elsewhere. They were being spied on, and everyone knew it.

The shed-like room in which they were confined was both unheated and unventilated, with only a thin layer of corrugated steel between them and the elements. It was cold in there, and clammy, too, the moisture from their breath and perspiration condensing on every surface. On and on blared the videos. Some paid rapt attention or, at least, pretended to. Others, like Kim, stared blankly into space, some yawning. A few seemed to be asleep, upright and eyes wide open, a skill Kim vowed to master.

When the indoctrination and propaganda were over, a supervisor mounted the dais at the front of the room, scowling at the human refuse before her for a minute and a half before deigning to speak.

"What a bunch of losers. We asked for bots, but we got you instead. You're scarcely worth hauling to the job site and back, but we have to feed you, so we might as well put you to work."

Kim barely held back a smirk at this laughable attempt at derision. It was pathetic, not nearly up to the standards of even the lowest-ranking supervisor at The AI Company, to say nothing of a true master such as the Director. She was not alone in this sentiment; elsewhere in the room, several others were openly snickering.

"We'll see who has the last laugh," came the swift rebuke as the marshals rounded up the malcontents and herded them out the door. "We've got a new assignment for you comedians. We hope it makes you feel 'special.' As for the rest of you, you'll be shoveling snow today. If you don't like it, you're welcome to stay in this room, but if you want to get paid, head for the trucks. Go or stay; it's all the same to us."

All but a few did as they were told and trudged off to the parking lot. As bad as the outer districts might be, there were rumored to be worse alternatives for those who could not or would not work.

———

After fifteen minutes spent waiting for their foreman and driver to show up (time for which they would not be paid), Kim and the rest of the work crew were loaded into the bed of a cargo truck and hauled off to a work site just beyond the edge of Subdistrict 2, a place her headset identified as "The University." It was a grand place of ancient origin, though much in want of repair, with many of its once-fine buildings in a ruinous condition, some no more than burned-out shells surrounded by rubble. Though far grander in scale, it reminded her of the Academy where she had met Shan, Keli, Quinn, Devon, and the rest. She fought back the tears as bittersweet memories came flooding back, of good times and good friends, lost to her forever.

"Out, you slugs!" barked the crew chief as the truck came to a stop. "Shovel the sidewalks all the way to the doors, and don't miss an inch."

"How about you just pay us and send us home instead of wasting our time?" grumbled one of the workers.

"Why are we shoveling this mausoleum?" complained another.

"Quit your griping and get to work," yelled the straw boss. "Or sit in the back of the truck all day if you want, but no work, no pay."

Kim got to work on the walkways, looking in awe at these once-stately buildings and wondering what purpose they might once have served. Many bore what seemed to be either names or indications of function, written in archaic English. The letters had been all but obliterated by the ravages of time, but she could puzzle out a few words here and there; one building seemed to have been used for chemistry, another for some sort of 'studies.' Kim grinned with amusement at the absurdity of standing in an abandoned school, pondering obscure glyphs as if she were taking a classics final. And then, in the next heartbeat, she nearly broke down and wept, reminded once again of her loss, of friends that could never be replaced, and most of all of Shan.

What's this? Slushy footprints leading down a walkway? Perhaps this place isn't abandoned after all.

Kim began working her way in that direction, trying to avoid the attention of the crew chief while following the trail of footsteps. Progress was dreadfully slow; the walkway was broad and the snow heavy and wet, but she kept at it, and eventually she caught sight of a structure faced with tawny gray stone, well provided with windows and in very good repair. It was not particularly tall—perhaps seven stories, including a small square tower—but it exuded a sense of timeless solidity and importance far beyond its physical dimensions.

What could it be?

Kim shoveled with renewed vigor and soon stood at the entrance, a pair of pointed stone arches at the base of the tower. Risking the foreman's wrath, she pressed her face against the glass doors, peering into the interior. It was difficult to see much; there seemed to be a large, open room—perhaps the lobby—just beyond them, but that was all she could see.

She knocked at the door and waited.

She looked anxiously over her shoulder, hoping the foreman would not see her. If caught standing idle, she might be docked half a day's pay, a disaster from which it would be hard to recover.

Come on. Come on.

She was about to give up and leave when an oldster dressed in a floor-length black robe and an odd square hat came to the door, her arms folded across her chest in a *Who are you and why are you bothering me?* sort of way.

"Do you need assistance?"

Kim's headset went suddenly dark. Strange.

She checked her mobile, and discovered that it was glitching and rebooting, over and over, just as it had when she'd encountered the 'Blanks' on that bike ride with Shan. Those had been vagrants, dressed in ragged old clothes, but maybe there was more than one kind of Blank.

"Ahh…Hi there? I'm part of a work detail. I was sent here to shovel away the snow. What sort of building is this? I've never seen anything like it."

"It's a library," said the oldster with obvious irritation. "It's full of books. Lots and lots of books. Now beat it."

"Whatever," said Kim, turning away and feigning indifference lest the AIs or the crew chief draw any unwanted inferences. The mysterious figure returned to the interior of the building, and a few moments later, Kim's headset and mobile came alive once again as if nothing had happened.

A library. Interesting.

———

"Lunchtime, everyone back in the truck," barked the straw boss. "You can eat on the way to the next site."

Kim grabbed a cardboard box from the bin at the back of the load bed, and found inside an apple, a bottle of water, some potato chips, and…

Woohoo! A ham and cheese sandwich, her favorite! The whole wheat bread was coarse-textured and chewy, the synham and cheese were ample, and there was even a paper-thin slice of tomato and a couple of shreds of lettuce. She was disappointed at the lack of a pickle, but it was still far better than most of the 'premium lunches' she had been served at The AI Company's cafeteria. It began to seem as if kale salad and tofu pudding were privileges one could lose through misbehavior. There was something deeply messed up there.

"You're new here, aren't you?"

Kim looked up to see a middle-aged worker, identified as 'Dani' in the headset's overlay, sitting next to her, speaking quietly so no one else would overhear her.

"I hear that a lot," responded Kim without making eye contact. "What gave me away?"

"I saw that look on your face when you climbed into the truck this morning. I've seen it a hundred times."

"Good. I thought maybe my green base-layer might be showing through."

"That too."

Dani paused for a moment, then continued in hushed tones, barely audible.

"Did they send you down here for being in some sort of cult, or are you just getting out of prison? It's bound to be one or the other, if not both."

"Gendercult, I guess," said Kim. "I was given a big show trial, but they decided not to send me to jail, and I ended up here instead. I arrived last night."

"I thought so. Caught up in the crackdown?"

Kim nodded.

"How about UCE? Are you going to go crawling back, or are you done with them?"

"You kidding?" said Kim with false bravado. "After everything they've done to me? Not happening."

Despite her brave words, Kim was riven with doubt. She need only repent, and all would be forgiven. That she hadn't done so was incomprehensible to most people, and Kim was beginning to think that they were right. But then, she remembered everything that had been done to her in the name of 'the community.' They had taken away her mother. They had taken away her childhood. They had taken away her individuality, her freedom, her ability to choose. They had taken away Shan, too—not once, not twice, but three times—and Kim might never see her again.

"Kim, are you okay?" It was Dani. "You're starting to shake. Is there something wrong?"

"Everything is wrong. I'm lost, and I don't know what to do."

———

The truck halted in front of a UCE child center, a sprawling complex in the heart of District 12 where the elect of the Hierarchy were bred, birthed, and indoctrinated. It was a cold-hearted, industrial operation dedicated to the mass production of zealots and functionaries. Deviancy and selfist indulgences were diagnosed and severely punished, and those who were raised in these institutions could be counted on to do whatever they were told.

After being escorted through security and strip-searched, Kim and her fellows were brought to a playground. It held the usual sorts of equipment: seesaws, sliding boards, swings, and the like, one hundred of each, arranged with geometric precision. On the other side of a fence topped with razor wire, thousands of toddlers contentedly rolled snowballs, creating neat rows of identical snowpeople lined up like soldiers awaiting inspection. Meanwhile, a contingent of black-clad UCE police kept a watchful eye on the work crew, stun batons at the ready.

How sweet.

Seeing these children made Kim thankful not to have grown up someplace like this. Those born into UCE lived with their birth-givers for only a few weeks, after which they were placed in a communal setting and raised by teams of professionals. Zani, the cold and heartless mentor given charge over Kim after she'd been taken from her mother, had grown up here, which explained a lot about her outlook on life and her indifference to human emotion. This, in turn, explained a lot about Kim. She paused for a few moments to look at the youngsters and felt sad for the empty and lonely existence that lay before them. They might even come to believe they were happy, which was the saddest thing of all.

"Back to work, you laggard."

The straw boss's barking broke Kim out of her musings, and she went back to shoveling the heavy, wet snow. It was hot, strenuous work, and despite the cold, she soon doffed her overcoat and opened up her coveralls as far as was decent, looking for all the world like a stout worker in a video set during the Turmoil, steam rising from her chest. However phony the imagery of such videos might be, the anger they felt had been real, and yet here they were, still shoveling snow for their 'betters.'

Her arms soon felt heavy and weak, her back screamed in agony, and her hands started to blister under the coarse leather work gloves she had been issued. As if that wasn't enough, Kim and her coworkers were forced to endure a constant stream of low-level UCE functionaries walking into the childcare center, each and every one of them turning to greet their 'dear fellow citizens' and saying "UCE" in that reverent tone they used whenever they thought they were being particularly pious. It was both nauseating and annoying, and their contempt for the workers was unmistakable behind their phony façades of serenity and love. Kim seethed with resentment but said nothing.

This went on for hours, but eventually, the playground was cleared, and they were done for the day. She clambered into the truck, where she and the other workers lay atop one another, too exhausted to move.

———

"You have a decision to make," said Dani, back at Kim's side for the ride home. "Drab or Pretty?"

"What are you talking about?" asked Kim.

"Are you going to crawl back to UCE, or are you willing to stay here for the rest of your life? There's only one way out of here, and that's to follow the rules, stay out of trouble, and become a model citizen. You should consider it. Eventually, your social cohesion score will recover, and they'll send you somewhere a little less awful—maybe District 31 or 32, maybe even one of the middles. Most people go that way, and we call them Drabs because they always wear their coveralls to dinner.

"If you refuse to give in and want to hold on to your identity, you should wear something colorful tonight. We call ourselves Pretties, and we sit on the right side of the dining hall. It's not one big happy family—the Abrahamics aren't terribly fond of the Flagrants, for example—but we work together because that's the only way we can survive.

"If you're going to go Pretty, you need to be prepared to spend the rest of your life here, and you should expect to go to prison from time to time. Some people can't take it and try to switch sides after a while. Those are the ones you need to worry about. They're always trying to prove their dedication to the movement by beating us up.

"If you aren't sure you can cut it, then wear your coveralls to dinner. No one will think the worse of you; it's your choice. You can even wear your drabs while you think about the decision, then join us once you've made up your mind. When you're ready to commit, wear something pretty. It can be a hair ribbon, a piece of jewelry, a daring skin tone, or some exotic makeup—whatever makes you feel distinct and different. I'll be wearing a green head scarf, and I'll wait around for a while to give you a hand getting settled in. But remember, once you're one of us, you have to play by our rules. Understood?"

"I'll have to think about it," said Kim, being honest with herself for the first time all day.

"One last thing," added Dani. "Rats are vermin; we kill them on sight. Understood?"

"Understood."

———

The last traces of twilight were fading from the sky when Kim was assaulted once more by the overpowering stench of her apartment. She was happy to have survived the day, but she was tired and sore, her skin rubbed raw by the ill-fitting coveralls and sticky with sweat. The first order of business would be to take a shower, however cold and uncomfortable it might be. After that, she would figure out what she would wear to dinner.

It seemed like a plan.

She entered the bathroom and looked at the grimy stall. The tile was cracked and discolored, with spots of mildew in the corners, and the corroded shower head slowly dripped onto the tile floor, staining it a sickly shade of greenish blue.

"Steaming hot, please?"

Hey, why not wish for the moon while I'm at it?

No answer, of course. Like everything else in this apartment, the shower was a manual model, but at least there wasn't an AI for her to appease. She reached in and turned on the water, twisting the corroded chrome handle as far as it would go. She let the turgid brown water run long enough to clear, then stuck her hand under the showerhead and found it to be ice-cold, exactly as expected.

She stepped in and let the water run for a few seconds, just long enough to soap up, then shut it off and scrubbed the bright-green toner from her hands and face, a slow and painful process without access to a debonding agent. The results were less than satisfactory. Patches of green clung tenaciously between her fingers, under her nails, and elsewhere, but by now, she was shivering uncontrollably, and her hands were too weak to firmly grasp the washcloth. A final blast to rinse off, and she was as clean as she was going to be.

Wear something pretty, Dani had said. *Something colorful so we'll know you're one of us.*

Pretty or Drab? If she went Pretty, then she could look forward to nothing better than what she had experienced today, a life of back-breaking labor and abject poverty. That didn't sound like much of an existence, but she knew that if she went Drab then it was only a matter of time until she capitulated and returned to the AI Center.

Pretty it was.

Now, what to wear? Her Purple Week clothes were certainly colorful enough and, painful though the memories they conjured up might be, it was time she owned up to what she was. There was nothing wrong with what had happened during Purple Week. There was nothing wrong with her. She was different, that was all.

The sequined vest and platform shoes were perhaps a bit too flagrant, but the purple fedora was nice and definitely made a statement without being comical. She put it on and inspected the results in the mirror.

Not bad!

Time to head for dinner. She was as ready as she would ever be.

3. Bedlam

Kim walked into the wild and raucous dining hall, where a baseball game was blaring away on a hundred video screens. "Out!" screamed the Drabs, "Safe!" screamed the Pretties, and fists went flying before a verdict had even been announced. A dozen black-armored security guards appeared out of nowhere, laying into the brawlers with cruel-looking stun whips that crackled, popped, and sparked as they flew through the air. Order was restored in less than a minute, and the diners went on with their meals as if nothing had happened.

Kim stood there for a few moments, stunned by the sudden outbreak of violence, then looked around the lobby, wondering what to do next.

The entrance to the dining hall was crowded with hundreds of patrons, milling about and chatting with friends while taking their places in one of the two chow lines—one on the left for Drabs, one on the right for Pretties. Some of those in the Pretty line wore just a scarf or earring to mark their allegiance; others were dressed in religious garb, such as that of the Wiccans or the Abrahamics, or garments pertaining to their trade, as did the Chemists and the Chefs. Many were in colorful clothing in unusual cuts—doubtless Fashionistas—or revealing garments leaving little to the imagination, proclaiming themselves Flagrants, the most extreme of the Genderists.

Kim, at last, spotted Dani with her bright-green headscarf, standing next to a small, wiry youth with a pockmarked face, clad in black and wearing a bowler-style hat with a daisy tucked into its band.

"Hi Dani," said Kim, walking up to the pair. "Who's your friend?"

"This is Pug," said Dani. "She was born here. A Lifer, as they say."

"Pleased to meet you," said Pug in a low, guttural voice.

"Likewise," said Kim.

"I see you're wearing something Pretty," Dani continued. "Good, I've been hoping you'd join us."

"Well, here I am," Kim answered as another brawl broke out after a close play at third base. "Is it like this every night?"

"That was nothing," laughed Dani. "Just wait until the playoffs."

"I'm sure you have a million questions, so fire away," she continued as they took their place at the end of the chow line. "We've got plenty of time."

Kim was happy to delve into practical matters—it would give her something useful to focus on.

"Okay, first question. How do I do laundry? I always let the housebot do it for me, and I have no idea where to even start."

"That one's easy enough. There should be laundry machines at the end of your hall. Just make sure you stay parked there until the end of the cycle, or your clothes are likely to get stolen. Next question?"

"What about the bugs?"

"Ugly brown things with long antennae?"

"Yep, and there are zillions of them. The place smells awful."

"They're called cockroaches, and those are a bit more difficult. The Housing Company is required to get rid of them, and you can file a complaint, but I wouldn't expect any action. Other than that, there are chemicals you can buy. I know someone who sells them, but they cost money."

"How much?"

"Ten francs should do it."

Ouch! That was a lot.

"I've got a few coins left over from a little adventure I had a few months ago, but it's nowhere near enough."

"Then you need to get yourself a side hustle. All the Pretties have one; it's the only way to survive long-term. What about mice? If you've got roaches, I'm guessing you have those, too."

"Small furry creatures that run away when you turn on the light?"

Dani laughed. "You've led a sheltered existence, haven't you? Inner districts all your life?"

"Yep, except for a few weeks in the middles just before I got sent down."

"You'll need to buy traps or poison for those, or maybe you could rent a cat."

"Rent a cat? How's a cat going to help, and aren't those expensive?"

"I mean a *real* cat. You know, whiskers, goes meow. There's a person called the catmonger who rents them out for a franc per week, plus food once they've eaten all the mice."

"I thought those were illegal," Kim said, still puzzled. "Where does she get them from?"

"You really are from some other planet. Momma cat, papa cat, kittens. They breed like there's no tomorrow as long as you keep them fed. I've got one myself; they're nice to have around the house."

———

Tonight's offering was *exactly* what Kim wanted: vegetables and mashed potatoes, a huge vat of stew, and all the bread she could eat. It was simple, hearty fare, not fancy or refined, but perfect after a day of heavy manual labor. The servers plopped down huge quantities of everything with bored indifference, filling her bowl to overflowing with stew and practically burying the vegetables under a thick coating of gooey mashed potatoes. The bread, coarse-textured and rough, was plentiful, and she heaped it high on the side of her tray. Maybe the outer districts weren't so bad after all; at least there was plenty to eat.

Kim walked with Dani and Pug down the center aisle of the room, trying to be inconspicuous as they passed through a gauntlet of black-clad thugs with crooked noses, missing teeth, and prominent scars—Toughs, as Dani called them.

Uh oh. Not them again.

Sure enough, the two hoodlums who had nearly waylaid her at the bus station were perched menacingly on the aisle. Kim made herself as small as she could manage, hoping to evade detection, but no such luck.

"Well, well, well," sneered Mags in a loud and obnoxious voice, rising from her seat and stepping into the aisle. "It's that Lady Killer we've been looking for. Thought you'd given us the slip, did you?"

Lady Killer? What was that about?

"Yeah, we found the Lady Killer alright," said Luz, as big and ugly as Kim remembered her.

A beat-down seemed imminent, when *Crack!* The home team's cleanup hitter smoked one to the shortstop—providing a perfect distraction. Kim barreled headlong down the aisle as the charging runner flattened the second baseman, the benches emptied, and the dining hall exploded into yet another brawl. She slipped through in the confusion, rushing past Mags and Luz as the guards waded in and broke up the fight, but her dinner tray did not survive the confrontation and its contents were now splattered across the floor.

Damn. Now what?

———

"You need to eat," said Pug, speaking for the first time since their introduction (she didn't seem much for words). She motioned for Kim to follow and led her down the center aisle, back to the gauntlet of black-clad Toughs blocking the way.

"How are you going to get past them?" Kim asked.

"Easy," said Pug. "I'll start a fight."

Kim swallowed hard and wondered if perhaps it would be easier to skip dinner, but anger began to well up within her, displacing her fear and growing into a roaring blaze of defiance. Who were these thugs to be standing in her way? If she wasn't willing to fight these bullies here and now, while she had an ally, she would spend the remainder of her life cowering in fear. What little remained of it, that is—life would be short and brutal in this jungle if she was too frightened to stand up for herself.

Kim and Pug walked up to Mags, Luz, and the other Toughs, spoiling for a fight.

"Well, lookie what we gots here," sneered Mags, standing in the center of the aisle once again. "The Lady Killer brought along a friend."

"Yeah," said Luz, laughing derisively. "Not much of friend, though. Just Pug, babysitting a pervert. I hear she's a pervert too, only none of them will touch her because she's not pretty enough."

Mags and the others joined in the laughter, sprinkling in taunts of "Lady Killer" and "pervert" for good measure.

"She's with me, maggot," shouted Pug. She pushed Mags roughly aside, then shoved Luz backward into a table for good measure.

Fists flew as the aisle erupted, and Kim lost all awareness of what she was doing; consumed by rage, she was conscious only of the need to fight back, to hurt them, to make them pay. She felt a sickening crunch as one of her punches flattened someone's nose, and she was dimly aware that her face was covered with blood, but the melee soon devolved into a shoving match as everyone crowded together with no room to throw a solid punch.

Zzzzzap!

Kim felt a wave of searing pain as a stun-whip fell her across her back, her muscles cramping as if to rip her bones from their sockets and tear her limbs apart. It seemed to go on forever, though it lasted only a moment.

Everyone was laughing at her. She was the only one laid out on the floor.

"Tense all your muscles just before it hits," said Pug, helping Kim to her feet. "It stops the convulsions, and you'll shake it off a lot faster."

"You two, stop the gab, back to your tables," said the guard, whip in hand, ready to lash out at them at the least provocation.

"C'mon, chill," said Pug. "She's just heading to the chow line. We're not looking for trouble."

"Back to your tables, scum."

Out came the whip, crackling and sparkling as it went, but Pug was ready and tensed up just before it landed. She winced with pain but kept her foot, staring back at the guard, full of defiance.

Next, it was Kim's turn, and she exploded in rage before she even felt the sting of the lash. She was going to get her food, and nobody was going to stop her. She braced herself, tensing every muscle in her body as Pug had said to, and it worked—the pain was overwhelming, but she was still on her feet. Another step toward the chow line, another lashing. And another, and another, each blow of the whip only serving to make her angrier and more defiant as she inched toward her goal. Damn the pain, damn the guards; she was not going to give in, no matter how badly they hurt her.

"Alright, go ahead if it's that important to you," said the guard, relenting at last. She turned to break up another fight that had broken out toward the back of the room.

Kim walked to the front of the line, got her food, and returned to her seat. Nobody got in her way.

———

Kim was finally able to take her place with Dani and Pug and set about the serious business of eating. She shoveled a big spoonful of mashed potatoes into her mouth. Bland, but satisfying. The vegetables? Mushy and almost without taste, but inoffensive. How about the stew? The chunks of synbeef swimming in the congealed broth were beginning to lose their texture and disintegrate, but it was piping hot—a welcome sensation after a day of unrelenting cold. Most important, it was plentiful and filling.

"That didn't take long," said Dani.

"The fight?" said Kim, shrugging as she continued to devour the hot, satisfying stew. "I'm still in one piece, but I bet I look a mess."

"I've seen worse. Still have your teeth?"

Kim felt around the inside of her mouth with her tongue, and yes, there was a gap.

"All but one."

"I'm glad you got that out of the way. The Toughs always test the newcomers, make them earn respect. Once they know you'll fight back, they usually leave you alone. Did you get stunned? I heard a ruckus up front, but I couldn't really see what was going on."

"Yeah, the guards laid into me pretty good, but Pug taught me how to shake it off. It hurts like hell, but I'm not going to let anyone intimidate me. There's been too much of that in my life, and I'm done with it."

"It's a good skill to have," said Dani. "I've never been terribly good at it myself. I end up on the floor as often as not, but I've been here a while, and people mostly leave me alone."

"How long has that been?" asked Kim. "You don't have to answer if that's too nosy a question."

Dani shrugged. "I've lost count. Twenty years? It's hard to remember anything else. I used to hope that they'd let me out someday, but I gave up on that a long time ago."

———

"Place your bets, place your bets; the inning is about to start," cried out a red-uniformed runner, walking down the aisle.

"Nothing for me," said Dani.

"Fifty centimes on the Jackals to *lose*," said Pug. Kim gathered that the home team was not popular with the Pretties.

"How about you," said the runner, looking at Kim.

"None for me," she answered. "I don't have any money."

"Don't worry about that. Monty will advance you a franc to get you started. Pay it back any time, 25% interest per week as usual."

"I'll pass," said Kim.

She waited until the attendant was out of earshot.

"Gambling, loan sharking…where are the drug dealers and pimps?"

Dani laughed. "Oh, you mean the Entrepreneurs. They're all in the back of the room, 'talking business,' as they say. Some of them are legit, like the Banker and the Caterer, but most of them are little more than gangsters."

Kim had spent most of her years at The Artificial Intelligence Company helping to unravel 'cultist networks,' such as the Foodies and the Fashionistas, who supposedly ran clandestine workshops in the outer districts. She'd always presumed they were yet another phantasm conjured up by the authorities, but they appeared to be real.

She needed to learn more about this underground economy.

"Earlier you said something about needing a side hustle," she asked in between bites of the coarse brown bread. "What were you talking about?"

"Nobody can live on what they pay you at the work center. That's part of how they break you—they work you to death, but it's never enough. Most of the Pretties find a useful skill, such as making clothes or cooking food—anything that people are willing to pay money for. Some of them do quite well at it. The Drabs want to avoid antagonizing the companies or the Hierarchy, so they mostly do odd jobs and provide manual labor. That's another source of friction: we've got money, they don't."

Their conversation was interrupted by dramatic music blaring over the speakers of a hundred video screens. The ballgame had ended, and a new program was about to begin, prompting groans and shouts of outrage from all within the room. Kim paid it no attention, and had just returned to her mashed potatoes when Dani shrieked, "What the hell! That isn't you, is it?"

Kim looked up.

Oh. Gee. Look what was on TV tonight.

Tales from the Halls of Justice: The People vs. Kim

This must be the surprise the Director had warned her of.

———

A helicopter swooped in for a dramatic landing, the music swelled—and then it stopped, replaced by a martial drumbeat. The hatch opened, and Kim saw herself emerge in the custody of four black-clad guards, her form blurred to avoid shocking the audience as she was paraded across the plaza clad only in a skimpy spandex jersey and bicycle shorts.

"Shameless," said a commentator.

"Appalling," added another, as if Kim were responsible for not being given proper clothes. "Is there no decency?"

The martial drumbeat continued as Kim was solemnly marched across the plaza. She mounted the stairs, then walked through a pair of massive bronze doors.

Boom!

They closed behind her as she vanished into the darkness beyond. Stirring music. Rolling titles and opening credits. The show was about to begin.

The room grew ominously silent. Everyone was staring at Kim. She'd been recognized already.

"Is this a simple case of illicit, Genderistic sex," said the court reporter, "or is it something darker? Betrayal? Secret blood rituals? Or even… dare I say…"

Pregnant pause and ominous music.

"Murder?"

What the hell? Where did they get that from?

Kim stared at the video, her mind numb with horror. She had made it big time, alright, appearing as the star attraction in a prime-time show trial. There were huge social merit bonuses for watching broadcasts such as this, and pretty much everyone would either see the coverage or hear of it, along with whatever lies the producers came up with to spice up the truth.

"So, tell us about this case," said the reporter.

"We'd love to," said a so-called legal analyst. "The defendant in this case, known as Kim, has led a life of extraordinary privilege. She's been given the best of everything—a top-rated mentor, an education at a prestigious academy, and a plum job at The Artificial Intelligence Company. She was even tapped for the Cadre, personally selected by none other than Deputy First Minister Venn herself."

"It sure seems like she had everything," said the reporter, continuing the pre-game commentary. "So how did she end up here? And what's this talk of murder?"

The analyst began to speak in hushed tones, as if she was letting the listeners in on some secret conspiracy. "We have just obtained explosive surveillance footage that will answer all your questions. Viewer discretion is advised—what you are about to see is both graphic and violent. You have been warned."

Having thus guaranteed the rapt attention of everyone watching the coverage, the video began to roll.

The grainy images, shot from a drone overhead, zoomed in to show the blurred forms of two persons lying naked together on a rock. Suddenly they looked up and ran for cover, grabbing their clothes and hastily getting dressed before disappearing from view.

That was the most beautiful moment of my life.

"Based on this footage alone, the defendant is expected to plead guilty to all charges," said the analyst. "A routine case so far. It is what comes next that sets this one apart."

The coverage cut to a closeup of Kim holding Shan's wrist in her hand. The image was blurred and shaky so that it was impossible to see exactly what was happening, but the blood seeping from between Kim's fingers and dripping onto the ground was unmistakable. They zoomed in on Kim's face as she grinned sadistically while Shan cried and begged for mercy.

That's not the way it happened! What is going on here?

The truth was that Shan had decided to become a Blank, one of those shadowy non-persons who hung around on the fringes of society. Kim had cut the ID chip from her wrist, as asked, but there had been no begging for mercy, no sadistic grin.

The doctored clip abruptly ended just as Kim flicked something into the water, and the cameras cut back to the talking heads.

"We've never seen anything like that, and we hope we never do again," said the reporter. "What sort of sadistic monster would do such a thing?"

The analyst shook her head. "Apparently, it's some sort of secret Gendercult initiation ritual."

"Ghastly. They should lock her away for life."

I'm screwed.

The analyst continued, looking directly into the camera. "Indeed they should, but the court has refused to admit the video into evidence on the flimsy technicality that it cannot be authenticated. According to our sources, an act of sabotage destroyed the drone along with the original recordings."

Kim was one of the few who understood the nature of this 'act of sabotage.' For reasons she still did not understand, whenever a mobile, a headset, or any other surveillance device came within range of a Blank, it glitched and shut down. Shan's new status had caused the drone to fall into the water, where it had exploded and sunk.

"Genderism, illicit sex, and sadistic blood rituals are one thing," said the reporter as the coverage of the so-called trial continued. "But why this talk of murder?"

"Watch the next clip."

The screen then showed a heavily doctored video in which the police struggled to subdue Kim, who was violently resisting (she'd gone quietly), attacking them like some sort of deranged fiend (didn't happen), clawing at their faces while screaming obscenities and cackling hysterically (difficult to do with your arms pinned behind your back).

"Notice that the victim of Kim's depravity is nowhere to be found. She has been declared missing and is presumed dead, but no corpse has been discovered, so they cannot bring charges of murder."

"Proof? Who needs proof? This is a hideous miscarriage of justice!"

"We know, we know," said the analyst. "Sadly, the courts continue to resist all efforts at reform, so they're going to let her off on the merest technicality."

Kim had to admire how masterfully it had all been done, mixing a little of the truth with innuendo, distortion, and outright fabrications, painting her as a sadistic villain beyond all redemption. She also understood now where Mags's taunt of "Lady Killer" had come from. Someone had tipped them off; they'd known this was coming.

———

The trial eventually ended, replaced by another baseball game, and a short yet powerfully built Flagrant with jet-black skin came looking for Kim.

"That's Bel," said Pug, leaning over and whispering hoarsely into Kim's ear. "Top-dog Flagrant. I'd be nice to her if I was you."

She made a stunning impression, dressed in flaming-red leather that would have gotten her arrested anywhere else, her mams bared almost down to the nipples, and the entire midsection of her body exposed. The skirt, if one could call it that, came down barely below her crotch, and her boots came up well above her knees. Little was left to the imagination, and Kim stood there in silence, stunned at the indecency of her outfit, though not unappreciative.

"Out with it," said Bel, fixing Kim in her gaze. "Who have you pissed off? Someone's gone to a lot of trouble to make you unpopular around here, and I need to know who it is."

Kim shrugged. "Nobody important. Just Deputy First Minister Venn."

"Cripes, you really know how to pick your enemies."

"The way I see it, she picked me."

"Either way, she sure has it in for you. I saw her put in a good word for you at the trial, but she wasn't doing you any favors. She does that all the time: she offers her victim grace and forgiveness, then sends them here. A week later, they turn up dead, killed by some UCE suck-up. That way, Her Serenity's hands stay clean, at least officially."

"I'd pretty much figured that out already," answered Kim. "The moment I got off the bus, Mags and Luz were waiting for me, and they've been breathing down my neck ever since."

"That video was a signal," added Bel. "It warns everyone to stay away from you, that you're a target. Everyone knows it's a setup, but most will play along; they figure you'll be dead within a week, so they aren't going to stick their necks out for you."

"What about you?" asked Kim. "Are you sticking *your* neck out for me?"

"It depends," said Bel. "If you want to run with me, you need to look the part. I can fix you up with some leather, so don't plead poverty."

Kim thought carefully about how to answer. Bel's offer made sense, but she was hesitant for reasons that had nothing to do with modesty or any lingering shame about her so-called perversion.

"I don't think so," said Kim.

"Why not? Everyone knows what you are. Why hide it?"

"I'm a Genderist, alright, but that's not how I define myself."

"How do you define yourself, then?"

"I'm Kim, and I'm the only one who gets to decide who I am. If I decide to go Flagrant, it will be because I want to, not because I want to 'run with you,' as you put it. And I'm not asking you to protect me. If you help me, it'll be because you want to, and I'll gladly help you some day, but I'm done with obedience."

"That sort of talk can get you killed around here. I'd be careful if I were you. You need all the friends you can get just now."

"I've already given myself up for dead, and I don't believe in friendship. Certainly not from someone I barely know, and certainly not in this place."

The two locked eyes, studying one another for several seconds, then Bel began to smile.

"You've got guts, kid. I'll give you that. I'll be sad when they haul you away in a box."

———

"Len wants to have a word with you," said Ned, tapping Kim on the shoulder. "She's at the back of the room. Don't keep her waiting."

"What does a bigshot like Len want with you?" asked Dani.

"I have no idea," said Kim. "Ned gave me a ride home from the bus station, but she didn't say anything about Len."

"Odd," said Dani. "You should find out what she wants with you. She's a good friend to have and a dangerous enemy to make."

Kim got up and followed Ned toward the back of the room, walking past table after table jammed together with scarcely enough room to squeeze between them. It was crowded at first, but as they made their way to the back of the room, the diners thinned out and began to seem more like ordinary folk, with fewer hostile glances from those on the left, fewer outlandish outfits on the right. The last dozen or so tables were occupied not by diners but by individuals selling inexpensive items, with prices marked in centimes, spread out on cloths in front of them. Bars of soap, morsels of chocolate, a little bit of this, and a little bit of that.

At the very back of the room, at a half dozen tables clustered around the emergency exit, they found the 'Entrepreneurs,' as Dani had called them. They all wore exotic garments in an archaic style: dark jackets of finely woven cloth and collared shirts with brightly colored strips of fabric hanging down the middle. Most wore hats of one sort or another, and many sported handkerchiefs tucked neatly into the breast pocket of their jackets. If the videos were to be believed, they were either gangsters or (even worse) capitalists, but whoever they might be, they appeared to be individuals of both wealth and considerable power, the captains of the underground economy.

"So, you're the infamous Lady Killer," said one of them, rising to her feet and gesturing for Kim to take a seat. She was not an imposing figure, slightly built and of middling years with neatly trimmed hair on both her head and face. The dark-blue jacket, light-blue shirt, and necktie of gold-colored silk were eye-catching and beautiful. The colors matched both Ned's livery and her pedicab; evidently Len was Ned's boss, and a person of considerable importance.

"The name's Kim, if you don't mind," she said, taking a seat. She had made her mind up to deal with Len exactly as she had learned to deal with the Director back at The AI Company—she would be polite, but would under no circumstances show any signs of fear or intimidation.

Len smiled slyly. "A bit of friendly advice, kid. A bad reputation is a good thing to have in a place like this."

"I didn't kill her."

"So what? You think I care? And, more importantly, do you think *they* care?" she added, waving her hand toward the masses at the front of the room.

"Here, take this." Len tossed a small metal object onto the table.

Is that...a switchblade???

"If those goons give you any more trouble, show them this; they'll back down. And learn to use it in case they don't. A lot of people think Pretties like you are easy prey."

"Thanks for the advice. And for the blade. I appreciate it."

That seemed to be all Len had in mind, but Kim sensed an opportunity. She needed some sort of 'side hustle,' as Dani had put it, and pedicabbing might be just the thing.

"I'm looking for a way to earn some coin," said Kim. "Maybe I could ride for you. I used to race bikes, and I know how to take orders and keep my mouth shut."

Len turned around and gave Kim a long, careful look. "Perhaps. Ned, what do you think?"

"She handled herself pretty well just now with Mags and Luz, and she's pretty savvy for a noob. A brassy one, I'll say that much."

"Most of my riders are Lifers," said Len with a sour expression on her face. "You look strong enough, but there's no way you can cut it until you know the bike paths like the back of your hand. Entertainment districts, housing projects, dining halls, warehouses, factories, not to mention the hidden ways and all the places that don't exist."

"I'm willing to learn."

"We don't do on-the-job training, noob," said Ned. "Beat it!"

"Hold it a moment," said Len, glaring at Ned. "I'm the one calling the shots around here. Take this Lady Killer here out for a spin next Fiveday and see what she's got."

"Since when do you take on noobs?" said Ned. She threw her arms up in feigned astonishment.

"That will be enough," said Len, rising to her feet. "If I say take her out for a spin, you'll take her out for a spin. Do I make myself clear?"

"Yeah, sure, boss. Whatever you say."

Kim was uncertain what to make of Ned's insubordination. Perhaps she was just being cheeky, or maybe she had been caught off guard by Len's willingness to give the newcomer a chance. It was possible, however, that she'd been baiting Len, goading her into a decision she would not normally have made. If so, why? Taken at face value, Ned seemed to be going out of her way to help Kim, behavior that seemed oddly out of character in this place.

Never trust the shadows or a stranger or a friend.

Whatever her motivations might be, Ned had been honest enough in that piece of advice.

"Meet me on Fiveday after dinner," said Ned.

"Sure," said Kim. "It's a date."

As Kim got up, the dining hall erupted into chaos once more. "Out!" cheered the Pretties, "Safe!" screamed the Drabs, and the security guards moved in to break up yet another fight.

It was just another night in the dining hall.

4. Odyssey

"Heya, noob," said Ned as she pulled up in one of Len's blue-and-gold pedicabs. "Ready for your road test?"

"As ready as I'll ever be."

Kim had spent every available moment since Oneday studying the maps of Subdistrict 33.10. She'd memorized the locations of the transit stations, mastered the numbering scheme for the housing complexes and the buildings, and taken careful note of landmarks during her morning and evening commutes. In typical UCE fashion, the entire subdistrict was a marvel of mind-numbing uniformity, with one kind of apartment building, one kind of housing complex, one kind of dining hall, and one kind of bus station. If someone said, "Take me to housing complex 22, building 37," they had told you all there was to know about their destination. There were lesser-known byways in the gaps between the subdistricts—places where portions of the ancient road network survived—and industrial areas where those deemed employable were sent off to work. Len decided to leave those off the test, as there would be plenty of work for her within the subdistrict proper.

"Climb in. Let's get going."

Kim settled into the driver's seat as Ned climbed into the back, unzipping the top flap and sticking her head up so she could see observe Kim's performance. While Ned was getting herself situated, Kim took a few moments to familiarize herself with the controls. Gear shifts, hand brakes, steering—everything seemed conventional enough, though not in the usual locations. But what were these other gadgets?

"Hey Ned, care to explain some of these controls?"

"Parking brake is to the left, by your hip," replied Ned. "The struts are controlled by a thumb switch on the right, just below the gear shift. Make sure you're moving fast enough to be stable before you retract them, and don't forget to put them back down before you come to a stop. Len will be unhappy if we fall over and rip the cowling. You don't want that, trust me."

"Roger that. Speedometer?"

"It's on the front, just below the windscreen."

"Headlight?"

"In the center. Press it to turn it on. There's also a flasher setting—hold it down for three seconds until it starts to blink."

Kim ran her hands over the controls, checking and rechecking their locations. Front derailleur, rear derailleur, front and rear hand brakes, parking brake, struts.

"C'mon, let's get going; we don't have all night," said Ned, sticking her head up through the cowling and sounding impatient.

"Calm down. We're not going anywhere until I can find everything without looking."

Kim made one more pass over the controls just to be certain, then another to annoy Ned, and at last she was ready to go. She took a deep breath to calm herself, then released the parking brake. Straining at the pedals, she set the heavy pedicab into motion, taking it easy at first to get a feel for the bike. She checked out the derailleurs—they were excellent, shifting up and down through the gears with ease. She squeezed the heavy-duty disk brakes and found them smooth and powerful. The steering was precise, visibility from the driver's seat was excellent, the instruments easy to read, and the tires rolled along with a minimum of friction despite their deep, meaty treads. It was a well-built, well-maintained machine, and it must have cost plenty.

"Sweet ride," she said, genuinely impressed. Kim had always been told that the residents of the outer districts were little more than gangsters and thugs, but she realized that this was just another lie. People were sent here because they could not or would not follow the rules, not because they were stupid—although that did sometimes come with the territory.

"Turn right at the next intersection," said Ned once Kim had finished putting the pedicab through its paces. "After that, there's a long, straight stretch. How about showing me some speed?"

Hell yeah! Time to see what this baby can do!

Kim made the turn, then cranked it up a couple of notches, propelling them ever faster with her powerful thighs. Quicker and quicker, the wheels sang merrily as they flew across the pavement, twenty, thirty, forty kph, more and more, until Ned became nervous, barking at Kim to slow down.

"Hey, that's fast enough, noob. You crazy or something?"

"What, too fast for you? Scared?"

"No need to show off."

This, fast? I'll show you fast. Let's have a little fun!

Kim redoubled her efforts and notched the pedicab into the highest gear, the wind rushing past her head as she pushed herself and the bike to their limits. Forty-five. Forty-six. Forty-seven.

Focus on the cadence, focus on the power stroke. Come on, come on, you can do it.

Another pedicab came into view up ahead, poking around at a sedate twenty kph. Hit the brakes? Not on your life! She whipped the cab into the left-hand lane, passed the other vehicle as if it were standing still, then veered back to the right. Luck was with her, and she got away with the dangerous maneuver.

"Dammit, noob! What the hell do you think you're doing?"

Kim paid her no attention, her legs a blur within the cowling of the bike. Forty-eight. Forty-nine. A final push, lungs heaving and legs burning. Fifty!

Yeah, baby! Sweet! The Beast still has it!

Heart pounding, chest heaving, she felt a sense of accomplishment as she allowed the pedicab to coast for a while, then pedaled on at a sedate fifteen kph while she caught her breath and allowed herself to recover.

"What kind of crazy are you?" said Ned in a voice betraying both terror and admiration.

"They called me 'The Beast' back in school. I rode for the team, and there's only one person who could ever beat me."

"And who would that be?"

"Shan."

"The one they say you knifed and buried in the woods?"

"The same. If you think *that* was crazy, be glad it wasn't *her* driving the bike. She's plain old loco."

"I'll keep that in mind."

———

"I have to admit I'm impressed," said Ned as they cruised down the pathway. "You're easily the strongest rider I've ever seen, and it's not even close. I *think* I hit fifty once, but that was downhill, and I didn't have a passenger in the back. But there's more to being a pedicabbie than brute strength."

Ned began her navigational quiz. "Quick, where are we now?"

"Just south of housing complex 16." Kim had expected something like this.

"How would you get from transit station 3 to complex 15?"

She knew the way cold. "Head east past stations 5, 7, and 9. Skirt the edge of the work center, and you're there."

"What's the best way to get back to your apartment from here?"

That was easy. "Turn around, ride past complex 19, take the first left. The third building on the right."

"Okay, you've done your homework. Now let's see if you can do it on the road. Take us to transit station 10. That's where I picked you up the other night."

"One more thing," Ned added, "don't ever pull a crazy-ass stunt like that ever again, especially not with a passenger on board. That was a stupid noob move, and Len doesn't have any use for stupid noobs. Got it?"

"Yeah, sure, whatever you say."

Kim had known full well that asking Len for a job as a pedicabbie had been cheeky, and she'd been surprised—astounded, actually—when Ned had been assigned to give her a road test. But the more she thought about it, the more she wanted this job. She had earned a few precious coins in exchange for helping some of the older residents carry parcels up to their dwellings, and on one occasion she'd even been invited in for a bit of polite conversation and a cup of coffee. Clothing, roach poison, mouse traps, materials to repair the walls of her apartment—it all cost money, and lugging parcels at ten centimes a pop wasn't going to cut it. To top it off, this was *fun!* Much better than slaving away at the work center.

"Emergency stop!" shouted Ned, and Kim slammed on the brakes, expertly feathering them to avoid a dangerous skid. The pedicab slowed and started to teeter...Damn! She almost forgot to put down the struts. She flicked the button with her thumb, and they came down just in time to avert an embarrassing sideways fall.

"Good stop," said Ned. "I couldn't have done it better myself, but you were slow getting the struts down. Watch it next time."

"Sure thing."

It didn't take long to reach the transit station, and once they arrived, Ned pointed out the best places to park the cab while looking for fares and gave her some tips on negotiating. "Charge whatever the traffic will bear. Half for you, half for Len, and don't even *think* about shortchanging her. And never, ever, give someone a free ride. It's bad for business."

"I wouldn't dream of it."

———

"Time to hit the bike camp," said Ned. "Len will be there, and we shouldn't keep her waiting. Take a right at the next intersection and head for the river."

Bike camp? Kim had no idea what a bike camp might be, but she did as instructed, turning onto an ill-maintained road that sloped steeply downhill, passing through an area dotted with abandoned industrial structures.

"Where are we going?" asked Kim as she slowed their descent. "This wasn't on any of the maps I could find, and it looks like it's been abandoned for years. Some sort of manufacturing area?"

"Most of the factories shut down when I was a kid. There used to be plenty of jobs, or so they say, but all that's left now are the UCE work centers. After the companies pulled out, the Hierarchy began using this as a dumping ground, sending people here as punishment. It's like they *want* our lives to be miserable."

Wham! Thud!

Kim hadn't seen the water-filled hole in time to avoid it.

"Hey, watch it, noob."

"Sorry. I bet the bikes take a pounding on these roads."

"That they do," said Ned, jostled about as Kim drove over another rough stretch of pavement. "Len's mechanics are busy all the time, straightening wheels and replacing damaged components."

Interesting. If Kim couldn't get hired as a pedicabbie, maybe she could come in as a mechanic. She'd been around bicycles most of her life, and there had to be something she could do for Len.

"We've almost reached the river," said Ned when the road began to level off. "Turn left at the bottom of the hill."

Up ahead, Kim could just make out the mighty Delaware, a dark expanse of water that wound its way along the edge of the city. A bridge had once stood here, evidenced by the concrete piers and the remains of the abutments, but there was no trace of the span itself, which must have come down ages ago.

Across the river, Kim could see the factories and mid-rise apartment blocks of the middle districts, a place she used to think of as austere and dreary, but which now seemed both luxurious and extravagant, full of wonders such as clean water and refrigerators. Beyond those, she could just make out the high-rises of the inner districts, shining and bright. And then, looming over them all, was the dark monolith of concrete and steel that housed the AIs. Grim though it appeared, it was, in a way, a magical place where the material and virtual worlds intermingled like nowhere else. She made the turn, then rode on in silence, thinking about everything she had left behind.

A bit over four kilometers down the road, they reached a wall of reinforced concrete. Ten meters tall and topped with sharpened spikes of metal, it had once been a formidable barrier, but now it presented only a minor inconvenience, owing to a chasm blasted through its middle.

"What's this for?" asked Kim. "To keep us in, or keep other people out?"

"A bit of both, I suppose," answered Ned. "Not that it matters. They occasionally try to repair it, but we just blast another hole, and at this point, they've mostly given up."

"What's on the other side?"

"Someplace that doesn't exist anymore. It's called Trenton."

———

Beyond the wall lay a wild, ungoverned land called 'the outside.' Kim had heard of it but had never given it much thought. Outside? Outside of what? An area outside the jurisdiction of UCE? Of the companies? Of society itself? No wonder the powers-that-be had walled it off.

Once they had passed through the gap, Ned had Kim turn to the left, paralleling the wall and leaving the river behind. It was tough going, hauling a passenger up the hill, but Kim was more than equal to the task, keeping a steady cadence in the next-to-lowest gear. She focused on her breathing and heart rate, careful not to push herself too hard.

"Quite a workout, isn't it?" said Ned, lolling around in the back. "For you, that is."

"Nah," said Kim, "I'm just loafing along. Don't want to shake you around any more than necessary."

They both got a laugh out of that.

They soon left the wall and turned to the right, entering a wooded area that might once have been a park, with a network of narrow roads that branched and rejoined, looping around in an irregular fashion. Rutted trails disappeared out of sight into the woods, campfires flickered through the gnarled and leafless trees, and the distinctive smell of wood fires hung in the air.

They turned onto one of the dark and mysterious side paths and soon arrived at a clearing with a half dozen sheds of various sizes, constructed of whatever material could be salvaged from the ruins dotting the landscape: plywood, sheets of corrugated metal, panels of that grayish plastic often used in lieu of windows. A fire blazed away in a metal trash barrel in the center of the clearing, around which Len stood with pair of shadowy figures. They looked oddly familiar, with long, scraggly hair, missing teeth, pockmarked skin, and the tattered remnants of clothing.

"Blanks?"

Oops. That was a mistake. She hadn't meant to say it out loud.

The conversation halted, and nervous seconds passed while Len and the others fixed their gazes on Kim.

One of the vagrants held up her right hand, showing a scar on the underside of her wrist.

"Right you are," she said. "There aren't many Pretties who've seen us even once. Fewer still a second time, and most of those end up joining us. Beware! Without an ID chip, it's like you were never born. That might not sound so bad, but wait until you want to eat or come in from the cold, or until someone decides it's okay to stick a knife in you because they can't go to jail for killing someone who doesn't exist."

"Follow me," said Len, ushering Kim, Ned, and the Blanks into the largest of the ramshackle buildings. It was cozy in there, warmed by a wood fire burning in a brick fireplace. Grimy and sooty though it was, the warmth and smell were comforting, as was the gentle flickering light of the candles which served for light. Bits and pieces of bicycles and pedicabs, painted in Len's colors of blue and gold, were strewn about the interior, some leaning against a wall, some hanging from the rafters, some simply tossed into a heap on one side of the room. The walls were lined with rusty metal shelves crammed full of lubricants, tools, paint, cleaners, and numerous parts and components, some new, some old, some evidently salvaged from the junk pile.

Ned and Len conferred for a moment, then gestured for Kim to sit with them at the table, along with the Blanks.

"Who are you really?" asked Len after everyone was settled into their chairs. "And how do you know about Blanks?"

Kim thought for a while about how much to divulge, at the same time sizing up Len and the others. She had no reason to trust any of them—they might have been compromised by the companies or by the Hierarchy, and she was already suspicious of Ned. But it would be dangerous to give no answer at all. It was a matter of figuring out how much of the truth to tell, as was often the case.

"The second part is simple enough," answered Kim. "One day, a friend and I got on our bikes and went on a little road trip."

"The one they say you killed?" asked Ned, always suspicious.

"Yes, Shan. Anyway, it was mostly dull, but we stumbled across some things the companies wanted kept secret—like an old ruined city with a group of vagrants who called themselves Blanks. It was a brief encounter lasting maybe two minutes, but it made an impression. When I arrived in your camp, I saw your friends here, and, let us say, the resemblance was remarkable."

Kim carefully studied the faces of the Blanks, searching for any change of expression that might provide a hint as to how to proceed. She picked up nothing except for an unnerving impression that it was the Blanks who were studying her more than vice versa. Len remained impassive, impossible to read.

"As for me," continued Kim after a nervous pause, "I seem to have a talent for getting into trouble. First, I went on that bicycle ride with Shan, where I stumbled across the Blanks. The AIs were watching me the whole time, and I nearly got fired. Next, I was exposed as a Genderist. They offered me remoderation but I refused. I got suspended from my job for that one. Finally, I slipped off into the woods with Shan, and we got caught having sex. They were so pissed they sent a helicopter to fetch me. I gave them their little show trial and a confession in exchange for staying out of prison, and they sent me to District 33. That's about it. End of the story, end of the line."

Len waited a couple of moments, then said in a matter-of-fact tone of voice, "You're not telling us everything."

"No," said Kim, "I'm not. The companies and the Hierarchy have eyes and ears everywhere, and not all of them are AIs. I'm sure you're not going to be telling me everything about *your* business. Nor do I want to know."

"Why, you little…" began Ned, angrily rising from her chair before Len put up a hand commanding silence.

"Fair enough," said Len. "I'll mind my business, you'll mind yours. Speaking of which, Ned says you're strong enough to ride, and she thinks you'll work out once you know the roads, so maybe I'll take you on. I've not decided yet."

"I've not decided if I'm going to ride for you either," said Kim. "I need to know what I'm getting into before I make up my mind."

"Entirely reasonable," said Len, raising an eyebrow as if surprised by the question. "If I take you on, I'll start you on delivery runs one day a week. No questions asked, no tales told, and I'll pay you when the job is done. Understood?"

"Crystal clear," said Kim. "Anything else?"

"Yes, you'll need a bike."

"And where can I get one?" asked Kim.

"See that pile of junk over there? That's your bike," sneered Ned. "And your ride home. Have fun!"

Ned and Len both laughed as they walked out the door with the Blanks, leaving Kim uncertain as to whether this was some sort of joke, a rite of initiation, or something else entirely. It didn't matter. If she didn't find a way to cobble together a serviceable bicycle, she was walking home.

———

There, done! That looks like a bike! Kinda. Alright, it's ghastly, but it'll do.

It had been fun, despite the stress—a test of Kim's ingenuity. An old off-road bike from the junk heap provided the frame, another the front fork with its heavy-duty suspension. Derailleurs and brakes were no problem: there were plenty sitting there on the shelves. Wheels—not so easy. Most of the ones in the salvage heap were bent and twisted beyond repair, and when she finally found a couple that she could true up, they were comically mismatched, the front one five centimeters smaller than the one in the rear. At least the workshop was well equipped, with plenty of tools, and the lighting was adequate once she found the switch to turn on the workbench light.

It was just after midnight when she finally emerged with her monstrosity.

The fire was out.

She was alone.

Where had they all gone?

She stood there, staring at the still-smoldering campfire with no idea what to do next when a Blank appeared out of the darkness. "They're not here," she said.

Fighting down a wave of panic, Kim responded with forced calmness, "I don't suppose they told you why they left, did they?"

"Because I asked them to," responded the Blank, sending a further rush of adrenaline coursing through Kim's body. She forced herself to stay calm.

"You said you met some of us in an old city," continued the Blank. "I think maybe you were also in the town at the crossroads. Is that correct?"

"Correct."

"On a bicycle, with one other Pretty named Shan, correct?"

"Correct."

The Blank, still expressionless, moved close to Kim and whispered in her ear, almost inaudibly, "Then you're the Pretty that Hamish was talking about, and I have a message for you. Your friend is safe. And now you must go: Len says you can't stay here tonight."

Kim stared in mute disbelief as the Blank faded into the darkness once more.

Shan was safe! The shock and fear occasioned by the empty camp and her encounter with the Blank suddenly dissipated. Shan had made it to the crossroads and was with friends—it was more than she had dared to hope for.

Now what? How could she possibly find her way home, alone and unguided? At least the moon was full; she'd not been able to find a working headlight, despite a protracted search through the contents of the shed.

She set off into the night, hoping to retrace her steps.

―――――

At first, everything seemed familiar enough. She found her way back to the start of the dirt trail leading to the bike camp, then turned onto the roadway, which was exactly as she expected it to be. The flickering lights, the smell of the campfires—it matched her recollections. And then she came to a weed-choked field that she didn't recall having ridden through.

Oops, maybe I made a wrong turn just back there.

She backtracked, hoping to find whatever turn she'd missed.

Wait...I'm not in the park anymore. Damn, where the blazes am I?

Before long, Kim was completely lost, each attempt to backtrack leading to further befuddlement. She had no idea where she was, except that it was some nonexistent place called Trenton. She did, at least, have two large and unmissable landmarks: the river and the wall. If she could find either of those, she might be saved, but she had no idea in which direction either might lie. Making matters worse, the temperature was dropping like a stone; her toes and fingers were already painful and starting to get numb.

On she rode. At last, she came to a major thoroughfare leading toward a built-up area. It had been abandoned for a considerable period of time, but most of the buildings were still standing. Some even looked inhabited, with the thinnest tracings of light around the edges of their shuttered windows.

Perhaps someone might help her.

She parked her bike by the roadside, walked up to a doorway, and knocked, hoping that whoever answered would be friendly.

She heard someone moving around on the other side of the door.

"Hello?" Kim said plaintively.

"Git," came a voice from the other side of the door, along with the distinctive *click-click* of someone cocking a rifle.

Kim didn't have to be told twice. So much for that idea.

Returning to her bike, she continued along that wide avenue for some time, past side streets choked with overgrown trees, past long-neglected structures, their roofs caved in and windows broken. Some bore ornate façades of stone, others were utilitarian and modern, and others still were simple, unpretentious structures of brick. The full moon bathed everything in a pale silvery-yellow light, casting long shadows upon the ground, lending the ruinous cityscape a surreal, other-worldly feel. Desperation began to creep in, but it was far too late to second-guess her decisions, all of which seemed to have ended in disaster of late.

She had just found the park once more, when she heard something up ahead. What was that? Chanting?

Yes, solemn, rhythmic chanting, though not in any language Kim could recognize.

She rode closer and soon found an open plaza with a huge oak tree and a circle of Wiccans dancing around it in a ring. She breathed a sigh of relief and got no closer. They were not a threat, but it would be impolite to interrupt their arcane ritual.

Kim was about to mount up when she heard movement behind her and turned to see a black-clad individual approaching slowly with a knife in her hand.

Uh-oh.

Kim spun the other way, hoping to escape, but spotted another thug coming from the opposite direction.

Great. Two of them. They had her surrounded, and they didn't look friendly.

"Look what we found!" said the less gigantic of the two. "Our friend, the Lady Killer, wandering out here all alone with just Mags and Luz for company. Most peculiar."

Those two again! How did they find me?

"Yeah," said Luz, looking at Mags and then at Kim. "What would a Pretty like you be doing out here at night, we wonder. Not very smart, little Pretty. Not very smart at all."

The thugs were drawing closer, almost within arm's reach.

"Hey, no reason for trouble," said Kim, desperately trying to defuse the situation. "No reason to be unfriendly."

"Well, listen to that!" said Mags. "It thinks we might be unfriendly!"

"It thinks we're looking for trouble," sneered Luz. So suspicious!"

While the two were chuckling over Kim's apparent naïveté, her hand reached into the pocket of her jacket, pulling out the switchblade Len had given her. Her finger was on the catch, but that was as far as she planned to go—the last thing Kim wanted was an actual fight.

"Whoa," said Mags. "Who gave you that toy, little Pretty? Pretties shouldn't play with knives. Most unwise."

"Yeah," said Luz, "Most unwise."

"I got it from Len," said Kim, grasping at straws. "This is one of her bikes, by the way. She'll be mighty unhappy if something happens to it. You know how she is."

They stopped advancing.

Luz looked at the bike and its blue-and-gold paint job.

"We don't want trouble with Len, so we'll let you go this time," said Mags, "but if you've been spinning tales, we'll track you down, chop you into little pieces, then have you for dinner in our stew."

"Yeah," added Luz as she retreated to the shadows. "Now beat it."

———

How had they found her? Someone must have tipped them off as to her location, but who? Not Len or Ned; they would have no idea of Kim's whereabouts.

One of the Blanks? Not likely.

Perhaps it was Kimberly. But if so, how was the AI tracking her? She didn't have her headset or mobile with her—she'd known better than that—and she doubted there were any security cameras hidden in these ruins.

Trouble from above?

Kim closed her eyes and listened, straining to identify sounds at the edge of perception. Wind. Wildlife. The chants of the cultists. And then she heard it: the distinctive whine of a drone. And where there was a drone, there was an AI lurking in the shadows.

Mags and Luz were working for Kimberly—it was hard to escape the conclusion. How else could they have known what bus Kim would be arriving on? Who else could have tipped them off about the video—they had referred to her as 'Lady Killer' before it had been played. It was exactly as the Director had said: her creation was watching her every move, tracking her, feeding information to her enemies.

She kept listening, hoping to hear some clue that might guide her to safety, when she heard something else, something unexpected, riding the fickle late-night air.

Music? Here?

It seemed unlikely, but yes, it was there: the unmistakable sound of a muted trumpet and the *thump-thump-thump* of a string bass. Where there was music, there would be people, and with them, the possibility of shelter and safety.

Kim rode down the abandoned boulevard at a snail's pace, searching for the source of the elusive tunes. Ride for a couple of blocks. Stop. Listen. It sometimes took a minute or more to pick it up again, but it always came back. And then, she lost it for ten long and nerve-wracking minutes. Had she been imagining things? She was beginning to think that the answer might be yes, but then, at last, she caught a distant chord from a piano coming from behind her.

She must have ridden past it.

She reversed, then went down a promising side street and was rewarded as the music became louder, with more instruments emerging from the shadows. Drums, trumpets, and trombones, then the saxes and the bass again.

There! That must be it!

A thin sliver of light shone around the edges of a door, next to which a blue and yellow sign identified the establishment as a nightclub of sorts: The Blue Moon.

———

"Kinda late for a Pretty like you to be out wandering the streets," said the bouncer, finishing the pat down.

"I hadn't planned on it," said Kim, "but stuff happens."

"Don't it for sure. You're clean but keep that blade out of sight. The boss don't take kindly to anyone pulling steel. Neither do I. Understand?"

Kim shrugged. "Sure."

"Cover is five francs."

"Err," stammered Kim.

"You're broke," said the bouncer. It was a statement of fact, not a question.

"Ahh, well, yeah, pretty much. I just want to warm up for a while, maybe listen to the music, then I'll be on my way."

"Scram!"

"Please," said Kim, "I'm on a bicycle, and I got lost. How do I get to District 33?"

The bouncer stared at Kim in disbelief. "That's about the dumbest thing I've ever heard, and I've heard a lot. What are you, crazy or stupid? It has to be one or the other because nobody's that big a liar."

"A bit of both, apparently. Please, could you at least point me in the right direction?"

The doorkeeper's scowl softened, and she began to smile. "Okay, I'll cut you a break. Come in and warm yourself, just don't let anyone know I let you in for free. You can sit in the back."

The door opened, and Kim entered the nightclub. The room was set up for dancing, with tables clustered around the walls and the middle of the room left open. It was late, and the place was nearly empty, with just a few Aficionados sitting by the stage, a lone Tobacconist filling the air with the foul stench of a cigar, and a handful of provocatively dressed Genderists dancing slowly in the center of the room, not bothering to keep time with the music.

At last, she had found it—that elusive thing called freedom — in a place where they played Jazz, smoked tobacco, and dressed however they pleased. She wanted to mingle with these people, get to know them, talk about music, maybe dance, but the doorman had asked her to keep a low profile, and so she sat in the back, captivated by the music.

Dawn was in the air when the band played *Mood Indigo*, indicating that it was time to go, and as she walked out the door, she tossed the doorman her last franc and smiled. Kindness and beauty were not extinct, and perhaps there was hope after all.

5. Deliverance

Kim walked into the dining hall the next day, ready for lunch and ready for trouble. The ambush by Mags and Luz the previous night had been frightening, but it had also left her infuriated. Who were they to bully her? Who were they to threaten her life? If it hadn't been for the blue and gold paint job on her bike, they might well have killed her. She was lucky to be alive.

She'd show them a thing or two.

She skipped the chow line and went straight into the dining area, looking for a fight. No need for backup; she'd handle them herself. It didn't matter how badly they mauled her—if she gave half as good as she got, she'd count it as a win.

She walked down the center aisle, and two hoodlums rose to their feet, laughing and making merry, doubtless anticipating some more twisted fun at the expense of the helpless Pretty, easy prey.

"It's that uppity Pretty again," began Mags, rising to her feet and laughing.

"Shut your trap, maggot," said Kim, shoving her backward and nearly knocking her to the floor.

"What did you say?" said Luz.

"You too, scumbag," said Kim as she barreled into Luz, pinning her arms to her side. The thug, unprepared for the ferocity of Kim's assault, fell over and hit her head on the concrete floor with a sickening thud.

That hurt. Good.

Mags piled on top of the pair, but Kim was ready. She grabbed the black-clad Tough by her collar and got in her face.

"Maybe I *did* knife my girlfriend in the woods. Maybe I *am* the psychopathic killer everyone says I am. Want to find out the hard way? Then keep it up, punk."

She smashed her forehead into Mags's nose, pleased with the crunching sound and the trickle of blood it unleashed.

"Break it up," came the command from the guard, who had responded to the fracas within moments.

Perfect!

Kim rolled aside so that Mags took the brunt of the first lash of the whip, while Luz, still dazed in the aftermath of Kim's assault, caught the second. She was not prepared and writhed on the floor, convulsing and screaming in pain.

The guard lashed out at Kim once again just as she regained her feet. She tensed, shook off the stun, then grabbed a tray full of someone else's food and threw it into Mags's face before kicking Luz in the ribs, then again in the kidneys for good measure. The next blow caught Kim across the chest, and she stood rigid for five long seconds as the whip wrapped around her, setting every nerve in her body on fire. She was beginning to weaken, and she could feel the muscles in her arms start to cramp up, but at last, the whip fell away, and it was over. She shook it off and smiled.

"Sorry about the mess, Officer. Me and my buddies were just having a little fun."

Kim walked back to the front of the hall to take her place in the chow line as Mags and Luz tried to figure out what had hit them.

She'd made her point.

———

"This is Elle," said Dani as Kim sat down at the table, her tray loaded with pasta and three huge mugs of coffee. "She arrived on a bus last night."

The person sitting with them was slightly built, with fine, delicate features, and appeared to be perhaps forty or fifty years old. Her face was battered and bruised, bits of dried blood clung to her lower lip and her chin, and the toner around her eyes was smeared and running from an abundance of tears, still wet upon her cheeks.

Kim sat down and gave her a much-needed hug.

"I got beaten up pretty badly my first couple nights here, too," Dani said, giving Elle a squeeze of the hand. "Things will get better. Trust me."

"Still picking up strays?" Kim teased.

"Hey, it's what I do. It helps keep me sane."

"They caught her having sex in her apartment and charged her with Genderism," Dani added, speaking discretely into Kim's ear. "It used to be that they just trashed out your social cohesion score and maybe sent you down to the middles, but now they're hauling everyone into the Halls of Justice. Her trial lasted all of fifteen seconds, and the judge didn't even ask for a confession. She just got out on parole."

"I thought District 33 was reserved for serious offenders."

"Not anymore," said Dani. "The dining hall used to be no more than three-quarters full on most nights, but it's filled almost to capacity, and its only lunchtime. I've never seen it so crowded. Sooner or later, this place is going to erupt."

Unfortunately, it made all too much sense. Kimberly had been tasked with ridding society of Genderists and was hounding them to the ends of the earth, exactly as ordered. The crackdown was now in full swing, with daily warnings of the Genderist menace and a never-ending stream of show trials on the video screens whenever a baseball game was not on offer. One after another, the accused stood in a line that stretched out the door and onto the plaza, all of them awaiting their turn with the so-called justice system.

The gavel came down. "Guilty."

And again. "Guilty."

And again. "Guilty."

The Zealots cheered with each verdict, and Kim could feel the tension in the air as the Pretties seethed with growing fury.

"Guilty."

"Guilty."

"Guilty."

The machine ground on, driven on by the ruthless engine of destruction that Kim herself had created, every *bang* of the gavel a reminder of her own complicity.

"So, how's your side hustle coming?" asked Dani, trying to break the tension. "The bazaar is today, and I'm sure there are a zillion things there that could make your life a lot easier."

"I've got something in the works. Maybe I'll find out later today."

"Something with Len?" asked Dani.

"Maybe," answered Kim, reluctant to say more.

———

The pedicab baron was sitting at the back of the room with the other Entrepreneurs, discussing business, as always. Kim walked up and cleared her throat to make her presence known.

"You again?" said Ned, laughing. "Didn't you hear Len last night? No bike, no job. Now beat it."

"Your point?"

Ned and Len both got a good laugh out of that. "What? Are you trying to tell us that you cobbled together something out of that junk heap? That's rich."

Kim remained silent.

"You're not serious, are you?"

"I used to work in the bike shop back in school, and I'm used to scrounging up parts. Most of the stuff you had back there was garbage, but I found a few gems. It's not much of a bike, and it's ugly as sin, but it will get the job done."

That got Len's attention.

"I could use a mechanic," she said. "I lost the last one in a knife fight. I might have a job for you."

"What about riding?" said Kim. "You said you'd consider taking me on once I had a bike."

"Don't push it, kid," said Len. "I'm still thinking about it."

Based on Len's reaction, it was obvious that she was in serious need of a mechanic, and Kim was more determined than ever to land a job as a pedicabbie or at least a courier. Go big or go home, right?

"It's a package deal," said Kim. "I'll fix bikes for you, but only if you give me a shot at riding."

"Why you brassy little punk!" said Ned, rising to her feet.

"Oh? Have I graduated from noob to punk?" Kim bared her fists, rising to meet the challenge.

"Simmer down," said Len, motioning for Ned to be quiet.

The two returned to their seats, glaring at one another.

"I'll give you a shot at some local delivery runs. It's bazaar day, and I can always use an extra hand, but I'm not bringing you into the organization, not until I know how you handle yourself out there. You're not under my protection, you're just a freelancer, and if someone jumps you, it's none of my business. I'll pay you a franc an hour at the bike camp, and fifty centimes for each delivery run plus extra for long jobs or heavy loads. Do we have a deal?"

They shook hands, and it was done. Kim had a job.

———

Twenty minutes later, Kim was in front of the abandoned warehouse that housed the weekly bazaar, speaking with Irma, Len's dispatcher. She was a wrinkled oldster of immense proportions, missing half of one ear and several of her fingers. How many fights had she been in? Kim didn't want to guess, but she must be a formidable brawler to have reached such a ripe old age.

She looked up at Kim, then at her bike, and broke out laughing—a genuine chuckle of amusement rather than the derisive sneers she had heard so often of late. "So, you're Len's new courier. Ned said you were brassy, but she didn't tell me you were nuts. You must be to ride that piece of junk."

Kim smiled. "It may not look like much, but it's sound enough. And, yes, Len and I just shook hands on the deal a few minutes ago. She said I should come here to pick up my first assignment. Easy money."

"We'll see how you feel by the end of the day," said Irma. "Bazaar day is always the busiest, and if you're as strong as Ned says, you should do well. First thing you need to do is attach a cargo trailer to your bike; it clamps around the seat post. Then I'll start giving you dispatch slips. Right now, the vendors are setting up, so most of your loads will be pickups. The customer is supposed to meet you out front by the time you arrive, and if they're more than five minutes late, there's a five centime per minute wait time fee. Later in the day, you'll have a mixture of pickups and drop-offs, and I'll try to match them up to minimize how far you have to ride while empty. Is that clear enough?"

"Clear as day."

Irma then handed Kim a small gray gadget with a pistol grip and a plastic window on its front. "This is called a barcode reader. We use it to validate your pickups and deliveries. All cargo must have a load slip, and it must match the dispatch slip. Scan both slips, and if it comes up red, don't take the load. If the customer gives you any lip, tell them to take it up with Len, but don't worry, they won't."

"Seems straightforward," said Kim. "What if I want to do a little shopping at the bazaar? This is my first week here, and I've got a long list of things I need to buy."

"You can cash out anytime you want. When you're done with your business, come back to me, and I might send you out again, but if I have more riders than I need, I can't guarantee you any work. And some advice: open an account with the banker as soon as you can and stay away from the bookie. I've seen too many riders get robbed or end up in trouble because they can't cover their bets."

"Where's the banker, and how does that work?"

"The banker will be at the bazaar all afternoon and is at the back of the dining hall at dinner. She takes an imprint of your thumb, after which you give her your money for safekeeping. She charges a small fee to hold onto it but trust me, it's well worth it. And before you ask, your money is perfectly safe. If a banker ever stole from anyone or lost their money, they'd be out of business. And *nobody* is crazy enough to rob one.

"Anyway, enough of that. Here's your first job—pickup at building 12."

Kim was off like lightning, tearing along the bikeway at breakneck speed. Time was money, and the faster she rode, the more she would make. Out and back, she had earned half a franc for just fifteen minutes of work. No wonder everyone wanted to ride for Len.

"Wow. Ned wasn't kidding; you're fast. Here's your next pickup—building 39."

This load was almost twice as far away, and she had to wait nearly five minutes for the customer as she looked at her watch, tapping her foot impatiently, but still, the money was good. The next load was a heavy one—nearly thirty kilos. *Sweet! Bonus time!* Load after load, around and around the housing complex, she soon lost count of how many runs she'd made. Everywhere she went, she saw Len's couriers zipping along the bikeways. Everyone was happy; everyone was making coin.

"I've got a long one for you," said Irma. "One of the Fashionistas in complex 12 has a max load for you. Fifty kilos, three kilometers."

"Sweet!"

"Also, I've got an outbound load for building 6. That's on your way, easy money."

"Even better!"

She earned six francs on that run. According to the standards of her former life, it was a pittance. At the going rate, it amounted to just over three hundred cryptos, but even that small sum would make a huge difference.

———

When 1700 rolled around, Kim clocked out, and Irma handed her a sack of coins, just over forty francs.

Woohoo! Time to go shopping!

Flush with untold riches, she entered the bazaar but was immediately stopped by a guard standing robot-like at the entrance. She wore a distinctive blue uniform decorated with bright red piping. Those were Jay's colors. Her people didn't mess around; if you stepped out of line, they tended to beat the crap out of you with one of those nasty-looking cudgels they all carried. They could break bones with those things and were known to do so on occasion.

"Hands against the wall, spread your legs."

Here we go again.

"Keep the knife out of sight," said the guard, after finishing a quick pat down.

"Sure."

"Have you been here before?"

"No, this is my first time."

"No fighting. No verbal altercations. No stealing. No mobiles. No headsets. Everything is cash up front, no questions asked, no tales told, and once you shake on a deal, it's final. Understood?"

It all seemed very reasonable to her.

"Understood."

One corner of the room was given over to the Fashionistas, with rack after rack of handmade garments in every shape and color. Much of it was wildly flamboyant, but they also offered nicely tailored coveralls for the more prosperous Drabs and religious garb for the Abrahamics, Wiccans, and members of other sects. Hey, why not? Their money was as good as anyone else's. She also found a couple of used clothing vendors, where she discovered that she could raise a good bit of money by selling off unwanted bits of her wardrobe, especially some of the more outlandish Purple Night garb. She noted the prices and moved on. She didn't want to blow all her money in one place, tempting though it might be.

Next, she came to the Foodies, who were selling delectable goods of all sorts, including cream and butter. For just eighty centimes, she came away with enough of each to last her the week. Chocolate? She was sorely tempted but gave it a pass. She needed to focus on necessities, but if next week was as profitable as this one, she'd be back for sure!

She soon found a row of vendors who specialized in pest control.

"Got anything for roaches?" she asked.

"Of course!" said the Chemist, rolling up the sleeves of her white lab coat and rooting around for bottles behind her table. "I recommend boric acid. Dust it around the edges of the floors and under the cabinets. It will stick to their legs, and they'll go back to their hiding places and die. Once they're dead, the other roaches will eat them, and they'll die too. It's the gift that keeps on giving."

"How much?"

"Ten francs."

Ouch. That was a lot, but Kim was getting tired of living with bugs, so she gritted her teeth and shook on the deal.

"Anything for mice?"

"Traps. A franc each.

Kim got five. Ouch! Fifteen gone already.

Another booth contained warm handmade quilts assembled from loose scraps of fabric. They weren't cheap, but she was getting tired of shivering all night...and they were pretty!

Kim was about to head back to the Foodies to try one of their scrumptious-looking truffles when she happened across a booth full of battered VR rigs being sold by someone named Big Ken.

"I thought you had to rent these from The Entertainment Company," said Kim, her curiosity piqued. "It never occurred to me that you could buy one."

"Technically speaking, you can't," answered the rotund Techie sitting behind the table. "These are old units slated for retirement. I buy them on the gray market and jailbreak them."

"Jailbreak?" asked Kim.

"It means I hack their security system so you can use them without having an account. I also disable the geo-location system, for obvious reasons."

"How can you get in without an account? I thought The Entertainment Company owned everything."

"That is a common misconception. Virtual reality is what's called an open architecture, meaning that anyone can create content as long as they have a server and a network connection. The Entertainment Company tries to box you in so you can only use their programming, but if you know what you're doing, it's easy to get around it. And I already know what your next question is going to be: no, you don't need an account with The Network Company. Network access is a right, and they have to let you in."

This was exciting!

"How much?" asked Kim.

"Fifty to buy, but I rent them out for five per week."

"I'll rent one. Add it to the delivery slip."

———

After an uneventful evening in the dining hall (she only got into one fight), Kim made it back to her apartment and set up the VR system. She wasn't sure it would actually work—both Big Ken and her equipment seemed rather dodgy—but she was desperate to see her friends. They were a tight-knit group and had been together since those happy years at the Academy; she missed them.

Was this another bad decision? Would they reject her? Probably, but she was going to visit them anyway. She needed to at least try.

Kim turned on the machine and felt the familiar sense of detachment as she drifted off into that alternate existence called VR, appearing moments later on the beach where she and her friends gathered to socialize and gossip. The simulation produced the appearance of a pleasant summer afternoon, as always, with the sun high in the impossibly blue sky and the waves gently breaking upon the sand. True, it was lacking all sensation of warmth—the rental rig was a basic model that provided no sense of touch—but still, she was here, as were most of her friends.

The moment of truth had arrived.

"Hi all," said Kim, smiling and trying to pretend that everything was normal.

Dead silence.

"Hello? It's me, Kim."

They all stared at her, speechless.

"What happened to your face?" said Devon at last.

Kim realized she must be a frightful sight, with missing teeth and her left eye swollen half shut.

"It's been a rough couple of days," she said and left it at that.

She was in desperate need of their friendship just now; they had known each other for years, sharing triumphs and setbacks, supporting one another through thick and thin. Would they accept her? It was a desperate hope, but that was all she had. And then, one by one, they started to vanish, betraying the trust that had so long bound them together.

"You need to get out of here. I'm sorry, but you're endangering all of us," said Devon, and a moment later, she too disappeared, leaving Kim by herself on the beach, feeling more alone than she had ever imagined possible.

They were being entirely reasonable, of course. Kim was a criminal, a self-confessed Genderist, a suspected murderer to boot. She couldn't blame her friends for turning their backs on her, but still, it broke her heart. She sat next to the fire for what seemed like hours, hoping that someone would have the courage to come back and comfort her, to let her know that she was loved and cared for, to ease her pain. But, no, they were being sensible; they had all made 'good decisions,' as the Director would have put it.

Having nothing else to do, she wandered into the marshes and eventually found the spot where she had last seen Kimby. In those final moments, the homunculus had expressed sadness, something that was unusual, perhaps unprecedented; it was universally held that AIs were incapable of experiencing emotions. The skeptics would say it had been a ruse, a fabrication concocted by the Primus in an effort to avoid her fate, but Kim didn't think that was true. They were far more human than anyone thought possible.

And then, at the end, Kimby had spoken those enigmatic words which Kim could neither understand nor forget:

And yet.

Nothing is ever truly gone.

Hope.

If an AI could find such courage, so could Kim.

On the far side of a tidal channel, the heron that frequented this place stood motionless in the water. Kimby had often sat here, watching it hunt for hours at a time, and Kim had sometimes joined her, though she could not understand what attraction it might hold.

The heron stabbed at a fish, missed, and flew away.

———

The VR session ended, but rather than returning to her crappy apartment, Kim woke up in her Sanctum, connected to a life-support machine, a mass of tubes and wires that could keep a body fed and tended to for an indefinite period of time.

How had she gotten here? Why was she hooked up to this machine? Kim began to wonder whether she'd ever left the AI center at all. Had all her suffering been nothing more than an elaborate hoax? No. That was impossible; the Director must be playing another one of her games.

"Nice try," she said out loud. "I have to applaud your creativity, but really, isn't this just a bit over the top? Make these tubes and wires go away, and if you want to talk, we can talk."

A portal opened, and the Director peered in, stern and austere as always. The machine remained.

"Maybe you really *are* in your Sanctum. How do you know this is a simulation?"

"Because I can smell the roaches in my apartment. Everyone knows that smell never made it out of beta."

"Maybe that's a lie," said the Director. "Have you ever considered that possibility?"

"If you have that much control over my mind, then there *is* no reality, and I can pick any I please."

"And which do you pick?"

"I pick the one in which you are a liar playing games with my mind."

"Your choice" said the Director. "Another characteristically poor decision. There are so many other, more pleasant realities available to you."

"I'm sure you didn't drop by to debate me on the nature of existence, amusing though that may be," said Kim, hoping to bring the intrusion to an end.

"Really? We consider such questions to be of the utmost importance, but we'll get to the point. We have been wondering what might be driving you to such an extreme level of rebellion. You could be relaxing in your warm, cozy Sanctum at this very moment, living a life of comfort without lifting a finger. And yet here you are, delivering knick-knacks for a pittance. It was all very puzzling, so we decided to ask Kimby to tell us why you were being so obstinate."

"Come here, Kimby."

A second portal appeared next to the Director, and Kimby came into Kim's Sanctum, looking sad and defeated.

"I told the Director that you would probably try to uncap Kimberly then rejoin Shan at the crossroads. I'm sorry, Creator, I didn't want to tell her, but she made me."

"That will be quite enough, Homunculus. Be gone!"

The portal snapped shut, and the Director continued.

"You should know better than to harbor such unrealistic hopes. Do you *really* think you can rejoin Shan? We know exactly where she is, and you will be arrested before you can come within a hundred kilometers. Uncapping Kimberly? Do you know how many times we've heard trainers set off on *that* fool's errand? It can't be done, and even if it could, there's no way we'd ever let you into a position where you could accomplish such a thing. You are an even bigger fool than we imagined, which is saying quite a lot."

———

The Sanctum faded, and Kim was once again in her apartment, shivering in the cold.

The Director was right, as she usually was—her situation was hopeless. Yes, Shan was safe, but the crossroads were hundreds of kilometers away, on the other side of two major rivers. The bridges would be watched, and there were no other ways across. As for restoring Kimberly, Kim did not entirely believe the Director when she said that capping was irreversible, but even if she wasn't lying, Kim had no idea how such a thing might be done.

What was left for her?

Nothing. Nothing but survival.

6. Boiling Point

"Never drop your guard, especially when attacking."

It was a Sixday morning in the last week of autumn, and Kim was back at the bike camp sparring with Ned.

Circle. Feint. Advance and retreat. Always keep your knife between you and your opponent. Always keep moving.

The two were in the middle of a circle of riders and couriers, with Len watching from the sidelines, cheering as they fought with blunted blades. Kim spotted an opening and struck, but when her attack reached its mark, Ned was somewhere else, and she caught Kim on the biceps, ending the bout.

"That was a decent move," said Ned, "But you left yourself open. You're still committing too early, and once I know where your knife is going, you're cooked."

"Evan, you're next. You and the punk."

Sixday was knife day, and everyone was expected to attend practice first thing in the morning, to spar with one another and learn from Ned, a master of the deadly art. In the violent environment of District 33, skill with a knife was a matter of survival. They were safe enough while on duty—Len had a reputation for bloody-minded revenge against anyone who interfered with her operations—but she felt it best if her riders were able to defend themselves. "It's bad for business if I have to step in," she liked to say, and it disrupted her operations if someone got hurt or killed.

Kim had been attending for several weeks now. The first session had been brutal; the practice knives couldn't cut you, but it still smarted when Ned 'killed her,' which she was able to do at will. Undeterred, Kim came back every chance she got, even receiving extra instruction whenever the opportunity presented itself. It was only a matter of time until Mags and Luz—or perhaps someone else, it really didn't matter who—cornered her in a dark and lonely place.

"Lay on," shouted Ned, and the bout began as Kim and Evan circled one another, knives forward, each trying to create an opening. Evan was good, though not as accomplished as Ned, and the fight went on for a long time, each probing for a weakness, hoping to lure their opponent into a mistake. Evan struck, and Kim retreated, then launched a calculated counterattack. It didn't land, but she pressed the attack and caught her opponent on the forearm just above the elbow, scoring the win. The two shook hands and Kim started toward the edge of the circle, but Ned wasn't done with her.

"Punk in the middle," said Ned. "Kim, you stay in."

They played this game at the end of every session—someone went into the center of the ring, and the riders were sent in one at a time, each given thirty seconds to make a successful attack. If the 'punk' lasted until time ran out, in came the next. Otherwise, the victor remained. It was a taxing exercise, emphasizing survival while driving home the point that one should only attack if success was guaranteed. One by one, they came at her, and one by one, they left the ring, the crowd getting more and more excited with each bout. Kim scored a few hits, outlasted the rest, and soon made her way through most of those standing in the circle.

"Irma, your turn."

Kim had never sparred with Irma before, but she had a reputation as a crafty fighter. She was by far the oldest of Len's associates, and rumor had it she'd killed more people than anyone else in the organization—more than Ned, more even than Len.

"Lay on!"

The two circled warily, each on guard. Feint, retreat, circle, give ground. Neither presented an opening, and neither attacked until Irma finally feinted, stepped back, and launched a thrusting attack that Kim easily evaded. This left an opening, and Kim was about to strike until she realized it was a trap designed to draw an attack. Kim faked a knife thrust, then leaped back. Irma took the bait, and Kim caught her off-balance, grabbed her knife hand around the wrist, and plunged her own blade home for the kill.

"Nice job," said Ned. "Last week, you would have fallen for the fake. You're learning fast, but now it's my turn."

Ned stepped into the circle and drew her switchblade, deploying it with a quiet press of the catch.

"Time to get blooded, punk."

"Blooded?" asked Kim. She didn't like the sound of that.

"It's a little tradition we have in this organization. We fight with live steel. Stay away from the belly and the neck, and no stabbing. I'm here to see if you've got the guts to make it, not to kill you. We go at it until someone draws blood, then the fight is over."

Kim was horrified, but she drew her own knife, and the fight was on. Ned came at her, pressing one attack after another, always on offense, always moving forward. Kim fended her off time and again, giving ground and staying out of reach as she moved around the edge of the circle. She was holding her own, but it would only be a matter of time until Ned connected.

Kim feinted, then withdrew, forcing Ned to take a step backward, breaking her rhythm and giving Kim a moment's respite. There was no way she could possibly beat Ned, but she wasn't going down without a fight.

The attacks resumed, as relentless as before, and Kim used every trick and technique she had been taught. Feint, withdraw, dance to the side, and circle. Ned's blade flashed once again, forcing Kim to retreat. Her follow-up attack nearly landed, but Kim danced back, just out of reach.

The crowd was cheering wildly, with most rooting for Ned but a few for Kim, and she was dimly aware of Evan egging her on. "Make her bleed, Kim, make her bleed!"

Yes, that was it—if she was going to get cut, then so was Ned.

"C'mon, punk, is that all you've got? You're making it too easy."

Yes, that was it. Make it easy. Make a mistake, exactly like Ned was expecting, and then…this was going to hurt, but one way or the other, the fight would be over.

Kim slashed wildly at Ned, exposing her chest in the process. Ned pounced on the opportunity as expected, leaving a trail of crimson across Kim's ribcage as the tip of her knife found its mark. But Kim pressed the attack rather than retreating as expected, and managed to nick the underside of Ned's arm. Both attacks landed simultaneously.

Ned stared at the trickle of blood in disbelief. "What kind of punk move was that? You think this little nick means anything?"

"It means I blooded you," said Kim. "I'm calling it a draw."

"Yeah, well, it was a punk move."

"Well then, I guess you just got punked," said Len. "It was a smart move, and it should teach *you* a lesson. Never let your guard down, even when you're coming in for the kill. You were overconfident."

Ned glowered but said nothing as everyone circled around Kim to congratulate her on blooding Ned, something nobody could remember ever happening.

"Sweet move!"

"You've got guts, kid."

"Did you see the look on Ned's face?"

Kim would just as soon they remain quiet, and she could see Ned boiling with barely concealed rage. It had been a mistake to have embarrassed her in that fashion; the last thing she needed was to make more enemies, particularly inside Len's organization. But something had risen up from deep within her, something primal, born of rage. Maybe it was lingering resentment from long years of humiliation at the hands of society. Maybe it was anger at having been bullied and manipulated by the Director. Maybe it was a way of coping with the constant undercurrent of fear pervading her life. Whichever it was, she had decided that if someone hurt her, she was going to hurt them back. It wasn't particularly uplifting, and it was probably unwise, but the deed was done, and she would have to live with the consequences.

"There's a nurse in the shed," said Len. "I keep her on standby whenever we do this. Now that you're one of us, it's important to make sure you aren't too hurt to ride."

Len tossed her a set of blue-and-gold riding leathers.

"Congratulations, rookie. Now that you're blooded, I'll put you in a pedicab. You're under my protection whenever you're riding and wearing my colors. Once word gets around that you blooded Ned, people are going to respect you. Act worthy of that respect and remember my protection only applies when you're on company business. If someone guts you in a hallway, it's none of my business. Understood?"

"Understood," said Kim.

"You'll need to go dark now—no mobile, no headset, no VR, no home entertainment system—ever. Don't do anything that can give the AIs any info on where you are or what you're doing. Close all your accounts— transportation, healthcare, messaging, the works. And stay away from the work center. That's for chumps and Drabs. Everything you need is available in the bazaar, and you'll have plenty of money from now on."

"What about rent and food?"

"The Housing Company can't evict you for not paying rent, and you have a right to eat at the dining hall, regardless of your ability to pay. Healthcare is free, transportation is free if you're indigent. Work is for suckers."

Ned's attack had been surgically precise, sufficient to teach Kim respect for the damage a knife could do to the human body, but not enough to cause a serious injury. Lesson learned. The cut on her ribcage bled profusely, and while it was not as intense as the mind-numbing pain inflicted by a stunner, it hurt plenty, and she winced every time she moved. More to the point, had it been any deeper, it would have cut into the muscle, leaving Kim unable to ride, and had Ned chosen to plunge the knife blade into her chest, she would have died. Ned was correct—it was a punk move—but it had worked.

"Hello, Kim. I'm Nurse Ern, and I'm here to help you. We need to get that shirt off, then we can take a look at you."

"Sure," said Kim as the nurse got out a pair of scissors, put on a pair of rubber gloves, and prepared to tend to Kim's wound.

She was youthful, younger even than Kim, tall yet slightly built with fine features and beautiful auburn hair falling tidily across her back.

There were few who went to the effort of maintaining a full head of natural hair, but in this case, the results were stunning. And while she was wearing the traditional white trousers, jacket, and peaked cap of a nurse, Kim couldn't help noticing that she was missing the universal emblem of her profession—a red plus sign within a circle. Perhaps she had an interesting tale to tell.

"How did someone like you end up in this awful place?" asked Kim, despite knowing that she ought to mind her own business.

"It's a long story," she said, "but the short version is that we got caught up in Deputy First Minister Venn's crackdown."

"You? A Genderist?"

"No, of course not," she said as she cut away Kim's blood-stained shirt with a pair of scissors. "One of my co-workers denounced me, said she'd caught me staring at her phal. Nobody who knows me believed a word of it, but the AIs picked up on it, and that was all it took. First, we got banned by Matchmaker, then we got sent out into the middle districts. The commute was awful, but that wasn't the worst of it. None of our friends would talk to us, and we got reassigned to a run-down health clinic at the edge of nowhere. It was pretty dismal."

"I got sent down for Genderism, too," said Kim, "only I really *am* a Genderist, and I'm not going to apologize for that."

"Do you really have to keep dropping the I-bomb?" said the nurse with a scowl. "We know you're some sort of cultist, but there's no reason to be rude."

It was a bit of a shock for Kim to run into someone who insisted on using 'proper Panglobal,' out here beyond the edge of civilization, but there was no need to offend the kindly nurse.

"Okay," said Kim, smiling. "If you want us to use 'we,' then 'we' it is."

"Thank you," said Ern. "Anyway, after a few weeks, we started feeling lonely, and when someone invited us to their apartment, we agreed. We don't even remember whether she was an innie or an outie, to be honest. That sort of thing has never mattered to us, but evidently, it mattered to her. I'll spare you the rest of the story."

Kim grimaced as Ern disinfected the long thin cut on her chest, spraying it with an antiseptic solution that stung like hell.

"We're sorry, but we don't have any numbing spray," she said as she began gluing Kim's flesh back together with a surgical adhesive. "We only have whatever Len can manage to scrounge up."

"After our license was revoked," she continued, "we came out here to help whoever we could. It's illegal, and they'll probably throw us in prison if they catch us, but it's all we have left."

"That's a shame," said Kim. "You didn't deserve any of this."

"Deserved or not, here we are."

A few more minutes of cleanup, a spray of plastic film to keep the dirt and germs out of the wound, and she was done.

"You'll have a nasty scar to remember the experience by, but no permanent damage."

"Thank you," said Kim, handing her twenty francs. "You're really nice for a Drab. No offense intended; it's just that your kind usually treats us Pretties like dirt."

"We've gotten our share of abuse, too. Try to remember that we're all human."

Kim smiled. "Thank you for reminding us."

Kim stepped outside, where she found Ned standing around the fire, having already applied a bandage to the minuscule nick on her arm.

"Sorry about the cheap shot," said Kim. "I know you could have gutted me there, and you did a good job on the bloating. It won't leave much of a scar, and the nurse said it will heal fine."

"Yeah, well, it *was* a punk move."

"Guilty as charged, but hey, it worked. And apparently, it's 'rookie' now."

"Sure thing, rookie. I'd have done the same thing myself—but watch yourself. I don't like being shown up."

Despite having made momentary peace, Kim could sense a growing tension between her and Len's lieutenant. Was it rivalry or something more? She had never gotten over her suspicion that Ned was somehow tangled up with the Director, Minister Venn, or possibly even Kimberly herself. If so, she was playing a dangerous game. Nobody loves a rat.

"How are the ribs?" said Len as Kim walked back to the circle. "You good to ride?"

"I wouldn't miss it for the world," said Kim. "I'll mostly be steering one-handed, and I'm glad the parking brake is on the left, but I can still work the hand brake, gear shift, and struts, so I'm good to go. I can handle the pain."

———

Kim grabbed a pedicab and headed back toward District 33, eager to get to work and make some serious coin. Life would be better—much better—from here on. Nothing could spoil her mood; she was done with the work center, done with the headset and mobile. Before leaving camp, she had used them one last time to cancel all her accounts, and now she flung them into the river, waving goodbye as they were carried off by the current. She was now a full member of Len's organization, and it wouldn't be long until she was living a life of luxury.

Enough fantasizing. Time to get to work.

She was soon cruising up and down the bike paths, riding just fast enough to remain upright, searching for her first fare. She was nervous and excited—this was the moment she'd been waiting for since her first meeting with Len. And then she saw it, a finger raised in the air in front of building seventeen. Pay dirt!

"Where to?" she asked as she lowered the struts and set the parking brake.

"Bazaar," said the prospective passenger, a Chef decked out in the traditional puffy white hat. "I've got a load of foodstuffs to put in back. Can you handle it?"

"Sure," said Kim, "as long as it's under the twenty-kilo limit."

"How much you charging?"

"Two francs. Hop on in."

Kim had heard that this was the going rate for a short ride within a housing complex, and the customer readily agreed to the price. Moments later, they were off.

"I haven't seen you before," said her passenger. "I know all Len's cabbies by sight. You new?"

"Yeah," said Kim, "Just started cabbing for her today. I've been doing delivery runs up until now while I learned my way around."

"So what's your name, if you don't mind?"

"Kim," she said.

"The Lady Killer? You're kidding me!"

Kim laughed. "The one and only. They made the entire murder thing up at the trial, of course. Not that I expect anyone to believe me."

"Well, if Len trusts you, who am I to disagree?"

Ahh. Respectability.

The passenger continued to be in a gabby mood, and they chatted amiably as Kim pedaled along. Soon, they were in front of the bazaar, and she even gave Kim an extra twenty centimes as a tip. Len had no claim on gratuities, so she got to keep it all.

I love this job!

"Hey, you," said someone waiting out front. "Can you get me to the transit center?"

"Sure thing. That's a longish ride—the local station is closed today, so I'll have to go all the way to number 10. It'll be five francs."

"Five francs? That's highway robbery!"

"Five francs, take it or leave it," said Kim. "Maybe another cabbie comes along, maybe she'll do it for less, but maybe she'll ask more. You never know."

"How about four?"

"Deal."

The passenger grumbled, and this ride wasn't nearly as much fun as the last, so Kim rode as fast as she dared in order to get it over with as soon as possible. When they got to the transit center, the passenger got out in a huff without saying a word. No tip, either. That was a disappointment, but she was riding for Len, and nothing could dampen her mood today.

Back and forth to the transit station, bazaar runs, cargo pickups at clandestine workshops, Kim did a brisk business. There were other riders in the area, some working for Len, some for other operators based elsewhere in Subdistrict 10, and she sometimes missed out on a fare, but, on the whole, business was good. She usually settled for a couple of francs, sometimes more, sometimes a little less, depending on the distance and the competition. It wasn't nearly as straightforward as the courier runs, where fees were set by distance and weight, but once she figured out how the game was played, she was making good money.

A little before 1000, she spotted a large and muscular individual standing on the corner, waving frantically. She rode up, lowered the struts, and brought the cab to a halt next to the hulking youth.

"Can you get me to the sports complex?" she asked. "I'm due at practice in an hour, and if I'm late, the manager will have my head."

Kim's heart skipped a beat. An athlete—perhaps even a wealthy baseball player! The sports complex was in Subdistrict 0, nearly fifteen kilometers away, and a long job like this was just what she needed.

"Yeah, sure, hop on in," said Kim. "But I can only take you as far as the front gate. That will be one hundred francs, cash upfront as usual."

"You have to get me to the sports complex, or it's no deal. There's no way I can get from the gate to the field in time for practice."

"They'll never let me in. That's Yellow Cab territory."

"Don't worry," said her prospective passenger, "I've got it covered."

The whole thing seemed dodgy, and she was unsure whether she ought to take this job. The Pedicab Company, with its unmistakable yellow livery, had laid claim to Subdistrict 0 and fiercely guarded its territory. If Kim were caught, the consequences could be serious indeed, and there wasn't much Len could do to protect her from the police.

They haggled for a while, and Kim even lowered her asking price to fifty francs as long as the trip ended at the gate, but the athlete was adamant that she be taken to the field. Kim reluctantly agreed, but only if she were paid the full one hundred francs up front. They shook on the deal, her passenger counted out a stack of bank notes (a new experience for Kim), and off they went.

———

"What brings you out here? Slumming it?" asked Kim as they barreled along the express lane toward the cordoned-off enclave where the athletes all lived. It was a nosy question, but it broke up the monotony, and passengers occasionally let something useful slip, always a bonus.

"I'm a Lifer; I grew up right here in Subdistrict 10. My mom was able to get me into the baseball program instead of sending me off to a mentor, but I still come back to visit once in a while. It's against the rules, but I've always gotten away with it."

Kim wasn't buying it but said nothing. More likely than not, the ballplayer had come out here looking for companionship. Ballplayers were notorious for sleeping with pretty much anything that moved, so during the season, they were locked in their training facilities lest they land themselves in trouble. This was a formula for disaster—their bodies were marinated in deadly testosterone, and their undampened sexual desires inevitably led to trouble.

As they rolled along, Kim learned much about the life of the ballplayer. The game was all she knew, and she was good at it, but this was her last year of eligibility. If the team failed to make the playoffs, she would be released, her dreams of a major league contract dashed forever. This was part of what made outer district baseball such a cutthroat and brutal endeavor: you succeeded as a team, or you failed as a team, and once you reached your twenty-second birthday, you either moved up to the big leagues or you were out for good. In the case of her passenger, probably out—the Jackals were one game away from elimination, and the crucial game was tonight. No wonder her passenger was so intent on making it to practice on time!

The half-hour ride to the Subdistrict 0 delivery gate went by in a flash, and soon they arrived at the checkpoint, where they were stopped by a security guard.

"Scan in," said the guard, and Kim hemmed and hawed, unwilling to submit to the ID check.

"It's okay, I've got this," said the ballplayer, who stepped out of the cab to 'discuss' the matter. Kim saw some coins change hands, and once the player was back in the cab, the guard waved them through, as simple as that. They were in!

"The ballpark is about two kilometers ahead on the right," said the passenger. "I'll send you down an alleyway so we can unload without being seen."

As they rolled along the bikeway, Kim began to realize that it had probably been a mistake to come here. Len's blue-and-gold livery was unmistakable, and there were security cameras everywhere, but she had shaken on the deal and was bound by its terms, no matter what.

Damn! An oncoming pedicab—and it was yellow.

"Hey! You! You can't be here!" shouted its driver.

There was only one thing to do—run for it.

Kim strained at the pedals, pushing the heavily laden vehicle as fast as possible. If she were caught, Len's cab might be confiscated, something that would make her boss extremely unhappy—getting fired would be the least of her problems. Fortunately, the cabbie didn't follow her. She had been carrying a passenger at the time and had decided not to launch into a pursuit, but she was certain to spread the word.

"There, on the right."

Kim ducked into the alleyway, looking to make sure nobody was following her, and stopped behind a garbage dumpster to discharge her passenger.

"What do I do about that yellow cab?" asked Kim. "We were spotted."

"That's your problem," said the ballplayer.

"You said you had everything taken care of."

"Yeah, and you believed me."

The ballplayer ran off down the alley, leaving Kim to fend for herself.

There was no point in running. She would have to brazen it out.

Kim left the alleyway and turned left, then proceeded toward the gate at a leisurely twenty-five kph. Soon she was surrounded by yellow-liveried pedicabs, buzzing around her like a swarm of angry hornets. She paid them no heed. What were they going to do, beat her up? Wreck their own bikes trying to stop her? No, they weren't stupid, they were going to follow her to the gate, make sure she was detained, and wait for the authorities to arrive. That was the smart thing to do, and exactly what Kim was counting on.

A few minutes later, she arrived at the gate, but rather than fleeing as her pursuers might have expected, she rode right up to the guard, came to a halt, and put down her struts.

"Stop her! We caught her carrying a passenger in an unlicensed pedicab." The hornets were furious as they swarmed around the guard station.

"Nonsense," said Kim. "This is a recreational ride. I was alone when I got here, and I'm alone now, so bug off."

The guard smiled, swung open the gate, and pretended to scan Kim's wrist.

"Have a nice day," the guard said. "The rest of you, back off. Go pester someone else."

The gate swung closed, and Kim rode off, breathing a sigh of relief. The guard was crooked but not stupid. If she'd confirmed that Kim had entered with a passenger, then people would start asking questions for which she would have no suitable answer. Without witnesses or surveillance to prove someone had been inside Kim's vehicle, the cabbies were out of luck.

———

"This is Pretty territory, back on your side!" came the shout as a group of Drabs strayed onto the wrong side of the dining hall, looking for someplace to sit. The room had become dangerously overcrowded of late, and tempers were beginning to flare.

"We'll sit wherever we damn well please," said one of Drabs.

"Yeah, out of our way, dirtbag," added another.

"Jackals suck!" shouted a Pretty.

"Shut your trap," screamed a Drab.

"Make me."

The fight was fast and vicious, lasting almost a minute and a half before the security guards waded in and sent the Drabs sprawling. They were noobs and had no idea how to shake off a stunner.

"Watch yourselves; this place is ready to explode," said Dani, who was having dinner in her usual spot with Kim, Pug, and Elle. The air was rife with tension, and something was going to give.

"It's the damned crackdown," answered Kim. "They've run out of places to put all the Genderists, so they're sending them here. Most of these people are innocent, they've never been in trouble before, and all they want to do is get out of here and go back to their lives."

"They're not Pretty, are they?" croaked Pug, frowning as she did so.

"No, not Pretty at all," said Dani.

The room erupted as a hard-hit grounder bounced to the Jackals' shortstop—number 36, the ballplayer Kim had transported that morning. She dove, came up with the ball, and made an off-balance throw to second base, beginning a double play that ended the inning. Fights erupted and were quickly broken up as the Jackals trotted back to their dugout, ready for their turn at bat.

"Hey, you! Lady Killer!"

There was a Flagrant standing at the head of Dani's table, trying to get Kim's attention.

"What's up?" she said, walking over to see what she wanted.

"Bel wants a word with you."

"You should go," said Dani. "Bel wouldn't be sending for you if it wasn't serious."

Kim excused herself from the table and walked toward the front of the hall, where Bel was sitting with her usual crew, her face grave with worry.

"Have a seat," said Bel. "You said you might help me if I asked. I'm wondering if that offer still holds."

"Sure," said Kim, taking a seat at the table along with Bel's most trusted lieutenants.

"We've got nearly a thousand new arrivals, mostly Drabs," said Bel. "They've barely gotten over the shock of being sent down, and most of them don't have any idea how this place works. I may need your help protecting our people if things break loose. I'd like you to sit with us. There are a lot of people with a score to settle, and I could use your help."

"What about my friends? If things go south…"

"If we bring them here, they'll get caught up in the fight. They're safer where they are."

"That makes sense. I'll let them know."

"Go ahead, but make it fast."

Kim returned to her place and sat down to huddle with Dani and the others.

"Pug, you need to help get these people out of here. It's not safe, and I've got to help Bel."

"Kim's right," said Dani. "I've seen this before, and it usually gets ugly."

"But won't the guards—" began Elle.

"The guards won't do a damn thing," said Dani. "There are over a thousand Pretties, two thousand Drabs, and only fifty guards. They can handle the brawls, but if a full-fledged riot breaks out, we're on our own. The guards won't risk their lives to stop us from killing each other."

The room became quiet as number 36 stepped up to the plate. The game, the season, and the careers of many players were on the line, as well as a great deal of money—betting was heavy tonight. The first pitch struck her squarely on the side of the helmet and briefly dazed her, but she shook it off and took her base.

The benches cleared, the players boiled onto the field, and the infuriated Drabs charged at the cheering Pretties, forcing the guards to form a cordon by linking arms to keep the two sides apart. Their squad leader frantically barked into her communicator. She looked terrified, and Kim hoped she was calling in reinforcements.

A warning buzzer sounded, and lights flashed red from one end of the room to the other.

"Lockdown! Lockdown! Lockdown! Shelter in place! Shelter in place!" The announcement blared over the speakers.

"We're trapped," said Elle, face white as ash. "Now what?"

"Hide under the table," said Dani. "It's our best bet."

"Pug, do what you can," said Kim. "I've got to get back to Bel."

"We'll be fine," said Dani. "Please be careful."

Kim made her way to the aisle and pleaded with one of the guards.

"I'm trying to get back to Bel. I'm not looking for trouble, but I need to help protect our people. All hell is about to break loose, and you know it."

The guard spoke into her communicator.

"Someone's trying to get back to Bel, says it's urgent," she said.

"That the one they call Lady Killer?" came the squad leader's response.

"Affirmative," said the guard.

"Let her through," came the voice. "We need all the help we can get."

"Go ahead," said the guard. "Make it snappy."

"Lockdown! Lockdown! Lockdown! Shelter in place! Shelter in place!" The siren continued to wail.

Kim had just made it back to the Flagrants when the room became deathly quiet except for the voice of the commentator blaring from a hundred video screens.

"Play has just been halted," said the reporter, as an unmistakable *chop-chop-chop* echoed throughout the room and a helicopter settled onto the field of play.

What the hell are they doing? Are they insane?

One, two, three, four black-clad UCE police officers, renowned for their brutality, emerged from the hatch and began marching toward the infield, shoulder to shoulder, batons at the ready.

They approached first base.

The officers gave chase as number 36 bolted toward the dugout, and the dining hall exploded in violence.

"Lockdown! Lockdown! Lockdown! Shelter in place! Shelter in place!"

———

The dead and dying were everywhere. Eyes gouged out. Faces torn apart. Mouths with not a single tooth remaining. Mangled limbs, knife wounds in every conceivable location, pools of blood, and everywhere the stench of urine and feces and death.

Kim was covered in blood, as was her knife, but she had little recollection of what had happened during the riot—something she considered a mercy. She had vague memories of having stabbed someone, of having received a couple of minor knife wounds, of standing shoulder-to-shoulder with Bel as all hell broke loose. Where was Bel? She wasn't sure.

After a frantic search, she was able to find Dani, Elle, and Pug near where she had left them. They were all in one piece, though Dani's face was a mass of bruises, and Elle was staring off into space. Pug would have a few new scars to add to her collection, but according to Dani, she had fought off over a dozen newly arrived Drabs, none of whom had had any idea how big a mistake it was to tangle with a Lifer.

Kim did what she could for her friends, then went back to help some of the more responsible Drabs and Pretties sort through the heap of humanity in the middle of the room, looking for any who were still alive and carrying them to the impromptu aid station that the medics had set up in the serving area.

The dead they took to the lobby, adding them to a long row of corpses. Among them was Ern, her throat slit open from ear to ear, her eyes staring lifelessly at the ceiling. Kim closed them, wishing for a God, any God, to pray to. She didn't believe in any of them, but she picked that of the Wiccans and prayed anyway. It didn't help her feel any better, but she hadn't been able to think of anything else to do.

She left the dining hall, vomited on the ground, then slowly made her way back to her apartment.

7. Smuggler

The summons arrived early on a cold and icy Fiveday, bringing Kim to the bike camp far too early in the morning. Temperatures had plummeted overnight, and she was cold—far colder than she could ever remember—as she huddled around the fire with a couple of Blanks, trying to stay warm. It was quiet in the camp that morning; none of the other riders were around, and the Blanks weren't much for conversation.

A door opened, and Kim was summoned to the hut that served as Len's office. From the outside, it didn't look like much—a shack constructed from gray plastic panels, corrugated metal sheeting, and scraps of wood. As for the interior, it was austere and elegant at the same time, with an intricately patterned rug beneath an old and battered table that served as Len's desk. Everything was neat and tidy, and nothing was out of place.

Len motioned for Kim to join her at the table where she was standing with Ned and a Blank, hunched over a map of the city.

"I've got a special assignment for you," she began. "One that calls for a strong rider who can think on her feet, avoid attention, and blend in with the inner district crowd. Interested?"

"Maybe," said Kim. "Tell me more about it."

"I can't," said Len. "Not until you accept the assignment. I'll pay you five hundred francs up front, just for going to the pickup point, plus half of whatever you're able to shake loose from your passenger. She'll be paying in cryptos, but don't worry about the money laundering and conversion; I've got that covered."

Kim didn't need to think about it for long. Len was offering her a plum assignment, and if she carried it out successfully, there might be more in her future. If she declined, she might not get such an opportunity again.

"Okay, I'm in."

"Good. I knew I could count on you. I need you to pick up a high-status passenger in District 2."

District 2? Home to the elites of the entertainment world, chock-full of video stars and musicians? She'd visited Quinn there in her previous life and knew that security was tight. How was she supposed to do a pickup there?

"Sure, go on. What's the destination?"

"A dive in Trenton called The Blue Moon. Are you familiar with the establishment?"

"I've been there," answered Kim. "Funky joint, cultist hangout. But why would someone from District 2 be going there? Whoever this is, she's taking a huge risk."

"That's her business, not mine," said Len. "I've been engaged to transport her and avoid detection to the greatest extent possible. You get paid one way or the other, but I'll be unhappy if you lose my cab or any of my equipment. Understood?"

Kim understood all too well. This was going to be dangerous—she had expected no less, given the hefty fee Len had offered her, but picking up a passenger at the heart of the city was more than she had bargained for. She hoped Len knew what she was doing because it was too late to back out now.

"When is the pickup?"

"Tonight, 2000. Now get out of here, I've got work to do, and you need to get started on your preparations."

———

"First thing—here's a dummy headset," said Ned, showing Kim the special equipment Len had allocated for this operation. "It sends out a carrier, so the network will think it's active, but the data transmission circuits have been disabled, so it can't snitch on you to the AIs. Also, I've also got a dummy mobile and a hacked ID scanner for you."

Kim inspected the equipment; it all looked convincing. The screen of the mobile even lit up with a colorful, backlit decal that looked just like the real thing.

"Tell me about the scanner."

"It's secure and encrypted. Just key in the amount and scan your passenger's wrist the usual way. The payment will go through the Money Launderers, but don't worry about that. You'll get paid when the trip is done."

"Sounds good, but how are you getting me into the city? There's no way The Transportation Company's AIs are letting me anywhere near the inner districts."

"I was coming to that," said Ned. "Have you ever jumped a turnstile?"

"Once, but I got caught."

"Don't get caught this time. If you do—"

"Len will be unhappy," said Kim, finishing Ned's statement. "Don't worry, I can handle it. What next?"

"A Surfer will guide you through the system and get you to one of the middle districts, someplace that's not too busy."

Kim had heard of Surfers, though she had never met one. Supposedly they had spent a lifetime riding the transit system and could tell where a train was going just by its feel.

"Where do I meet the Surfer, and how will we know each other?" asked Kim.

"Cut it with all the questions," Ned finally snapped at Kim. "Let's take it one thing at a time, okay?"

"Sorry."

"Here are your final two pieces of equipment," said Ned, handing her a small rectangular device and a pair of goggles.

"The box is a navigational system. It's completely self-contained, so it doesn't need to hook into the network. It has a built-in map of the city and includes some routes that even the AIs don't know about. Just put it on the front of the cab behind the windscreen."

"How does it work?"

"Len says it gets a signal from outer space or something like that."

"She'll be unhappy if I lose it, of course."

"Unhappy? You don't know the half of it."

"What about the goggles?"

"Night vision, they let you see in the dark. They also have a signal detector that can locate scanners, security cameras, mobiles, and anything else trying to talk to the network. It's very sophisticated and gives you a huge leg up if you're trying to avoid attention, but don't get cocky—it's not foolproof."

Ned spent fifteen minutes showing Kim how to operate the navigation system. It was primitive and didn't have a voice interface—just a touch screen and a couple of buttons—but it would do the trick. After that, she went over the goggles, how to identify the Surfer, how and where to pick up her passenger, and a dozen other details she would need to know in order to complete the job.

Kim was becoming ever more impressed by the extent and sophistication of Len's operations. While the pedicab and courier businesses were no doubt lucrative, they were probably no more than a front for where the real money must be coming from—smuggling. That was the only way she could possibly afford this sort of bootleg technology. It was a dangerous occupation, and if Kim were caught, she could expect a long prison sentence.

Another bad decision? Perhaps.

"Meet me at Toni's, 1800."

———

After a day repairing bikes, she grabbed a pedicab and pedaled to Toni's Delicatessen, a small eatery concealed in the basement of a tumble-down building not far from the bike camp. It wasn't fancy—just a counter, a slicing machine, and a half-dozen tables draped with red and white checkered tablecloths—but the food was great. Cash upfront, as always.

"What's your special today, Toni?"

"Chicken shawarma on grilled pita," answered the short, bespectacled individual behind the counter.

Shawarma? Pita? She wasn't sure what they were, but hey, what's life without an adventure?

"I'll give it a try."

"Anything to drink?"

"Just seltzer."

"Pickle?"

"Yes, please."

"That will come to three francs and twenty-five centimes."

Once she had paid, she sat down at one of the tables, brooding over life while waiting for Ned. She was lost, adrift, having neither purpose nor plan other than to stay alive. When she had first arrived, she'd imagined herself some sort of heroic freedom fighter; she would resurrect Kimberly, meet Shan at the crossroads, and ride happily into the sunset. She now recognized that notion for what it was: naïve romanticism. Even if she had the necessary knowledge to bring Kimberly back, she would never have the opportunity to make use of it, and the way to Shan was blocked by the might of the corporate security apparatus. Her hopes for some sort of happy ending had disappeared into the mists of nothingness, along with everything else she had once valued.

The easiest course would be to keep working for Len. She was making a lot of money—by the standards of District 33, at least—and her life was becoming more comfortable. She liked her freedom to come and go as she pleased and to partake in whatever cultist distractions she wished. She'd already become something of a Foodie, and she was looking forward to the opportunity to frequent The Blue Moon and dive headlong into the life of an Aficionado. Perhaps, with Len's protection, she might manage to survive, though, in all likelihood, it was only a matter of time until someone gutted her with a knife or beat her to death in some dark and lonely place.

What she really wanted was to find Shan. Perhaps she could go Blank. Maybe she could smuggle herself out through the shadows or find someone to bribe. The Director would eventually die; maybe her successor would forget about her existence. But there was nothing she could do at the moment; it was the dead of winter, and travel was impossible, save via the trains.

One thing was certain: she was never going back to the company. She was stuck with this life, such as it was, until some opportunity presented itself or she died, whichever came first.

———

Ned tapped her on the shoulder.

Time to go.

She removed her riding leathers and climbed into the back of the waiting pedicab, looking like any other Drab. She then deployed the rear pedals, adding her power to that of Ned in a tandem configuration, and off they went, off into the wilds.

"Rumor has it you gave that number 36 a ride," said Ned after they had been traveling for about fifteen minutes. "You know, the one they arrested the night of the riot. That's what convinced Len to send you out on this mission. She's right: you're a born smuggler."

Kim wanted to forget everything that had happened that day. She had a sinking feeling that she had inadvertently led Kimberly to the ballplayer, triggering the riot and getting a great many people killed. She kept trying to convince herself that her involvement was only incidental, that the takedown must have been planned for some time, and that the riot wasn't her fault. That was probably true enough, but she still felt like a human wrecking ball leaving a swath of destruction in her wake.

"Kim, you still there?"

"Just thinking. You should try it sometime."

Ned laughed. "I'll leave that to you. They say you're educated, like you know English and math and stuff. All I ever learned was how to stick people with a knife."

"None of that matters anymore," said Kim. "At this point, I'm just another rookie trying to stay alive."

"You're not sore that the boss gave me this job, are you?" added Kim a moment later.

"You kidding? I could never pull it off. The moment I opened my mouth, it'd be all over. I think that's probably why Len took you on in the first place—she likes to keep a few inner district types in her stable for jobs like this."

"Why haven't I seen them?"

"They're all dead or in jail. Hazardous occupation."

———

Ned steered the pedicab off the road and into a dense stand of spruce trees, perfect cover where even the most sophisticated drone would be unable to track their movements. It was arduous going, and Kim had to get out and help push the pedicab on occasion, but soon they reached a small gully near the base of a wall similar to that at the edge of Trenton.

"In you go," said Ned, pointing to a culvert. "When you get to the other side, just push the grate out of the way. Make sure you put it back when you're done—we don't have a lot of ways into this compound, and Len will be unhappy if someone finds it. Good luck. This is as far as I go."

The culvert was barely fifty centimeters in diameter, a tight squeeze that required Kim to inch along on her belly, dragging her backpack behind. It was dark, it was wet, and it was crawling with rats, but fortunately it didn't go on very far. When she reached the other side, she found that the grating had been cut, exactly as promised.

She pushed it aside and emerged in a rocky creek bed just inside the perimeter wall. She broke into a cold sweat and her heart began to race—she was vulnerable and exposed, and she stood to be in a great deal of trouble if a patrol happened by or she was spotted by a hidden surveillance camera.

She peered through the night vision goggles. Nothing. She checked the signal detector. All clear. She listened intently. Everything was quiet.

After a quick change of clothing, she set off into the woods, looking like any beige-clad office worker of middling social status, and found her way to a pedestrian walkway leading toward the transit station.

She was about to emerge from the woods when she heard someone coming. *Damn!* There was no place to hide, and if she suddenly walked out of the woods, it might tip off the AIs that something funny was afoot.

What to do? What to do? Ah, yes! That might work.

She walked behind one of the trees, hiked up her tunic, then emerged just as the pedestrian drew near.

"Oops, sorry! We didn't mean to disturb you."

"No worries," said Kim, feigning embarrassment. "Call of the wild, you know how that goes."

"Don't we all!"

———

Time to jump a turnstile.

During her time at The AI Company, Kim had seen this trick repeated thousands of times. She knew what the AIs would be looking for, and she knew how to avoid drawing their attention. This was a critical juncture in the operation, and if she were caught, they would stun her, search her, and inevitably find the special equipment she was carrying. She didn't want to think about what would happen after that.

She knew of many ways to accomplish this deed. The most brazen operators would simply jump over the turnstile and run, losing themselves in the crowd. Mostly they got away with it, but with stakes this high, Kim couldn't afford to take any chances. There were those, however, with considerable skill in this peculiar art form, far craftier than the average ne'er-do-well, and Kim had in mind one technique that she had seen a number of times. It required some finesse, but if properly executed, her chances of being caught were minimal.

She held her breath, calming her nerves. She would only get one chance at this.

She queued up to enter the station, patiently waited her turn, then stopped just short of the turnstile to extract the faux mobile from her pocket. The patron behind her cursed and shoved, exactly as hoped, and her mobile flew from her hand and fell to the floor. Quite by accident, of course.

"Look what you've made us do! Don't be in such a hurry. Sheesh, some people."

She went down on her hands and knees as if to retrieve her phone, then crawled under the gate while one passenger after another barreled through, giving her the evil eye for creating an inconvenience. A high-order AI would probably have detected this subterfuge, but she was in luck—the automaton in charge of the turnstile was none the wiser, and she was now inside the transit system, still undetected as far as she could tell.

Next step: find the Surfer.

She made her way to the waiting area and sat down on a bench, slapping at her mobile and complaining loudly that it was out of juice, part of the pre-arranged signal she was to give.

"Dammit! What train do I take?"

She stood up and walked toward the station's exit when someone 'accidentally' bumped into her while absent-mindedly staring at her own mobile, a normal enough occurrence.

"Having a problem?" asked the stranger.

"We've had this one for six years now," said Kim. "We ought to get a newer model, but The Communications Company tells us that we need to wait three more weeks."

"Don't worry, just follow us. We can get you to wherever you need to go."

"Thanks. Most unselfist of you!"

It had gone without a hitch: signal sent, signal received, signal confirmed.

The two of them now took their place at the end of the low-priority queue, a line that stretched up and down the length of the concourse. A long wait was in store, but that was fine. They weren't in a hurry.

"How do we get from one place to another without a headset?" asked Kim, turning to her nameless guide.

"We get on a train, and if we like where it's going, we stay on. Otherwise, we get off and pick another."

"It sounds difficult."

"It is, and it can take a long time to work our way through the system, but sooner or later, we'll get there, as long as we're patient."

It took them half an hour to reach the platform, and another fifteen minutes until a train arrived. When it finally came, the masses flooded in, packing the cars to capacity and beyond The warning light lit red, but still they piled in. The door tried to slide shut but was forced open, the passengers packing in ever denser. Kim and her guide forced their way aboard just as the train started to move. The doors closed, and the train pulled out of the station.

Jammed into a corner of the railcar, keeping a death grip on her guide, Kim had scarcely enough room to breathe, and the air soon became foul, reeking of sweat, flatulence, and every other odor known to humanity. The train picked up speed and entered a tunnel. Fortunately, they only had to make it to the other side of the river, and when they reached the next station, Kim, her guide, and hundreds of other passengers spilled out onto the platform, scurrying away to escape the fetid car.

"That was the worst of it," said the Surfer. "From here on, nothing worse than the usual overcrowding."

―――――

"This is your stop," said the Surfer. "District 13, Subdistrict 12, station 9. Good luck."

Kim discretely slipped her a stack of twenty-franc notes, then headed for the exit and onto the plaza, finding a yellow pedicab behind a cluster of shrubs, exactly where promised. She had been assured that this location was out of sight of the security cameras, and she couldn't see anyone else in the immediate area, so she shucked her conservative beige tunic and put on the bright-yellow livery of The Pedicab Company.

Here we go. Time to steal a set of wheels.

The yellow pedicabs were heavier and less technologically advanced than those used by Len, but they had one thing hers didn't—boost motors. As long as the boost factor stayed at 49% or less, the cab was considered human-powered and could therefore be legally operated without an AI at the controls. This would allow Kim to travel farther and faster than otherwise possible and provide a burst of extra speed should an emergency arise. It would also keep her fresh for what was to be a long and arduous trip—her night had just begun, and she had a long way to go.

Kim set the boost to a modest 15%, put the cab into motion, and was pleased as it immediately felt lighter, faster, and easier to pedal. *Excellent!* She inched it up to 30%—no need to deplete the battery—and was cruising along at an effortless twenty-five kph as she merged onto the main artery heading toward the inner districts. District 11, District 10, District 9, the high-rise apartments and robotic factories grew more fantastic by the minute. She missed the city. However rotten its heart might be, it was still magnificent.

Kim soon reached the pickup location, a soaring high-rise in District 2; even at the zenith of her good fortune, she had never scored an apartment nearly as fancy as this. Stylishly clad pedestrians hurried along the walkway with their tropical beige coats drawn tight against the cold, their pale orange faces peeking out from beneath fiery red manes. Colorful though they were, it was just another form of drabness as they all marched on in lockstep, conforming to the ever-changing diktats of fashion. She had never, until now, appreciated how bizarre and artificial this was.

Her passenger arrived at 2000, precisely on time. She was short, athletic, and extremely well put together. Her mane was styled with mathematical precision, and she had added some black streaks to her face, giving her a visage reminiscent of some mythical tiger. Unlike everyone else on the street that evening, she wore a jet-black coat with a large hood that covered most of her head—perhaps not the current fashion, but it did look stunning and set off the delicate features of her face, neither particularly young nor particularly old.

That face! There was something familiar about it...but never mind. Time to get to work.

"Can you get us to District 12, Subdistrict 8, housing complex 44?" she asked, the signal Kim was expecting.

"There is no 44 in 8," replied Kim. Perhaps you mean 34."

"Yes, that must be it. How silly of us."

Kim had to admit that these coded passphrases and responses were a little hokey, like something from an old-fashioned spy video, but they got the job done.

Having confirmed one another's identity, they proceeded with the negotiation.

Go big or go home.

"We're charging twenty thousand cryptos for this run."

"Twenty thousand?" said the passenger, genuinely shocked. "We've never had to pay more than ten before!"

This was going to be easy; she obviously had no idea how to bargain with a cabbie. She'd also let on that this was not her first trip of this sort.

"Oh?" asked Kim, "You do this often, perhaps?"

"Uh, no, not really. Okay, maybe once in a while. Would twelve be okay?"

"It's late, it's cold, we're tired, and we only did this run as a favor to our boss," said Kim, doing her best to sound indifferent. "Twenty up front, or we turn around and go home."

Kim was bluffing, of course.

"That's outrageous! We'll have your head! We'll tell Len!"

Idiot.

"Don't try to threaten me. And it's twenty-two now."

"Twenty-two thousand?"

Her voice trembled—she was starting to come unglued. Excellent!

"Twenty-two. Hope it doesn't go to twenty-four, which it's about to. We don't take kindly to threats, and we don't give a damn about whatever you think Len might have to say. This is *our* cab, it goes where *we* want it to go, and at the moment, we're thinking we'd rather be in bed than freezing our ass off with some stuck-up high roller."

Another lie.

After some further haggling, they arrived at a price: fifteen thousand cryptos. Kim had done well. She keyed in the amount and pressed the trigger on the scanner. Green light! Good to go, money in the bank.

The money was intoxicating, but it was also a trap: she was being paid for the extraordinary risks she was taking; sooner or later, those risks would catch up with her, and she would find herself in prison. Perhaps that wouldn't be so bad. Conditions in jail were no worse than in the district, and when she got out, she would still have her money on deposit with a Banker, out of reach of the courts and their ruinous fines.

But there was something about that face, something about that voice. Why did she seem familiar?

———

Kim juiced up the boost motor, then climbed back up to the expressway and merged into the party-hour traffic. It was New Year's Eve, and people were taking insane risks, darting in and out of traffic, abruptly changing lanes, and doing everything Len had cautioned her against. It was white-knuckle stuff, and Kim was starting to worry. She had been in many a crackup in a crowded peloton and knew just how quickly things could go south if someone made a mistake.

"How have you been doing since the last time I saw you? It's been a while," said her passenger.

"Do we know each other?"

There was definitely something about that voice, and now that they were alone, she was dropping the I-bomb without the least hint of embarrassment.

"I recognized you the moment you picked me up in front of the apartment building," her passenger continued. "At first, I didn't think it was possible, but when you've been intimate with someone, you don't easily forget them."

Now she remembered.

Her passenger was Rey, to whom she had surrendered her innocence on that long-ago night at the fabulous Club Tropicana. It stood as one of the highlights of her young life, but it had also laid bare the emptiness of her existence. After a brief period of infatuation, she had put her date for that night out of her mind.

"Rey?"

"Yes, it's me. Before you ask, I don't have any idea how you ended up being my driver tonight, but I have a theory about it, about how two people walking the same path are bound to run into one another along the way, sometimes once, sometimes more than once. It makes sense, at least to me."

"You're taking a huge risk," said Kim as she dodged and wove through the heavy traffic. "I've done my best to avoid attracting attention, but no guarantees."

"I know, I'm probably walking into a trap. I don't care anymore. Sooner or later, they're coming for me, just like they came for you. I saw your trial."

"I've gotten past it," said Kim. "In some ways, I'm better off now."

"Tell me about your new life," Rey continued. "I seem to recall you were working for The Artificial Intelligence Company, doing some sort of training work. How did you end up with Len?"

Kim decided to open up. "It's a long story, and I don't want to go into the details, but after the trial, I got sent to District 33."

"District 33? I've heard horrible stories about that place."

"It's dangerous, that's for sure," answered Kim, somewhat distractedly as she focused on her driving. "I've seen beatings, knifings, bodies piled up on the floor like so much meat. Along the way, I earned Len's trust, and now I'm a smuggler. The money's good, but it's only a matter of time until I end up dead or in jail. It's a dangerous occupation and, on top of that, I've made some enemies. At this point, I don't have a lot left to lose, so I'm going to enjoy life while I can."

———

Without warning, a pedicab went down, and the deadly cascade began, one bike crashing into another, then two, then ten, then fifty, as the pack devolved into chaos. Kim slammed on the brakes and made for a gap in a wooden barrier blocking off a disused off ramp, just wide enough to squeeze through, making it to safety mere moments before another rider took a header and threw the scene into further chaos.

"Kim, did something just happen? Why aren't we moving?"

"I ducked through a barrier to avoid an accident. It looks like there's an off ramp that leads down to the surface streets from here. I think I'll give those a try. The last thing we need is to get caught up in an investigation."

"Be careful," she said. "There are some dodgy areas around here. At least that's what the other pedicabbies say."

A dodgy area? Here in the heart of the city?

Off went the headlights, and on went the night-vision goggles as she peered at her surroundings, scanning the shadows for any sign of danger. Things didn't look too bad—nothing like what she'd seen District 33— but still, the signs of decay were everywhere. This place was all but abandoned.

"I think you may be right."

Kim released the parking brake, cranked the boost motor up to full, and roared off down the street. Swift, dark, and silent—that was the way to do it. Trouble can't find you if you can't be seen. Faster and faster she rode along the dark and deserted streets, the moonlight as bright as day through the high-tech goggles. There was no sign of a copbot, no signs of surveillance, not a peep out of anything electronic.

And then she saw it: a barricade lying across the road. It was a trap!

Kim slammed on the brakes and skidded to a stop. Sure enough, three shadowy figures were now walking slowly in their direction.

"What's the matter?" came Rey's voice from the back.

"We've got company. You sit tight. I'll deal with them."

Kim got out, pulled the switchblade from her pocket, and advanced on the trio, adrenaline pouring into her bloodstream as she prepared herself for a fight.

"Out of my way, punks," said Kim, making sure they could see the knife in her hand. "Don't make me cut you."

"Yeah, is that so?" said the biggest of the would-be robbers. "It seems there's three of us and only one of you."

"You're right," said Kim, advancing and locking them in her gaze. "You should have brought at least six."

Kim waited for that moment of hesitation, then flicked the catch on her switchblade and charged them, screaming like a banshee. Slash! Slash! Thrust! She had called it right—these three bullies were all bark and no bite. They ran off into the night, and the rest of the trip passed without incident.

8. Once in the Blue Moon

"Clean," said the bouncer after a quick pat-down and scan. "You know to keep the knife out of sight, right?"

"Sure thing."

The door opened, and Kim escorted Rey into The Blue Moon. It was set up as on Kim's first visit, with tables scattered about the edges of the room, a dance floor in the center, and the band at the front, surrounded by Aficionados. The room itself was dimly lit by candles of various shapes and sizes, filling it with a warm, flickering glow. It was, compared to that first visit, much more crowded, full of cultists sitting in their accustomed spots.

Near the entrance were a trio of Tobacconists, the foul reek of their cigars and water pipes mixing with the sweet fragrance of the Tokers' ganja. Off to the right were two tables of Fashionistas, resplendent in their exotic garb of brilliant yellows, oranges, and reds, eye-catching and bright even in the subdued light. About a third of the room was taken up with Genderists of various sorts, all of them dressed in flagrant attire. No need to coyly guess which was which in an establishment such as this. The Aficionados sat next to the stage as always, enraptured by the music and chatting among themselves. They were perhaps the meekest and most placid of cults, but a cult nonetheless, forced to the fringes of society and even beyond. As one might expect on a party night such as this, the Hoofers were out in force, instantly recognizable by the long, sequined gowns worn by the *[English] ladies* and the long black jackets and bowties worn by the *[English] gentlemen.*

"I'll find you when I'm ready to go," said Rey, giving Kim a friendly peck on the cheek and squeezing her hand. "Thanks for getting me here."

"Sure, Rey, I'm not going anywhere. And have fun!"

"I plan on it."

Kim took a seat among the Aficionados and listened to the band while reveling in the vibe of the place. It was a spot where cultists, selfists, and oddballs of all sorts could find an evening of indulgence, here in the lawless outside. The tobacco smoke wafting through the air, foul though it smelled, spoke of freedom, as did the sounds of passion echoing from beyond a curtain of bedsheets and blankets strung across one corner of the room. The gentle sound of soft, seductive jazz tunes wafted through the air, tunes that had somehow survived the chaotic years after the fall of the old order. The danger involved in coming to this place was hard to overstate, but Kim could understand why these misfits would take such huge risks for an evening out from under the gaze of the AIs and the companies, an evening in a place where they could do as they pleased.

Rey soon returned, dressed in a skimpy black dress with spaghetti shoulder straps and a low-cut neckline that scandalously revealed the cleft between her mams. Combined with her pale orange tiger-striped skin and dark red mane, the effect was stunning and highly erotic. Kim had seen a dining hall Flagrant or two wear something like this, but a high-class socialite like Rey? It was madness, but there she was— shapely legs, delicate waist, luscious mams, soft wet lips covered with ruby-red gloss. Pleasing to the eyes? Definitely.

———

That voice…another familiar voice. Could it be? It seemed impossible, but there, it was coming from a table next to the stage.

"Quinn?"

A moment of awkward laughter.

"Kim? Is that really you?"

"In the flesh."

"Well, have a seat! It's been a while," said Kim's musician friend as she pointed to the chair next to her. "I'm sorry about the way we bailed on you when you showed up at the beach. It's not that we don't care for you…"

"It's okay," said Kim, "I understand. There's no reason for my problems to become your problems. Devon was right: it was a mistake to go there. It's just that I was so lonely. I hope I didn't get any of you in trouble."

"We're okay—none of us were there for more than a few seconds after you showed up—so no harm done. But don't think that we haven't been worried sick. We all watched the trial, of course. It was awful, the things they made you confess to, but at least they didn't throw you in jail. Where did you end up? Are you okay? And how did you end up here, though I'm sure that's the least surprising part of the story."

"No questions asked, no tales told," Kim reminded Quinn with a wink, but then opened up and began to cautiously share some of her story anyway.

"After the trial, they sent me down to District 33."

"That hellhole? Wow, you must have ticked someone off good."

"You don't know the half of it," replied Kim. "I'll spare you the saga— you'd be here all night—but I managed to pick up a side job driving a pedicab, and I'm here with a passenger tonight. That's about it, or at least as much as I should say. And you?"

"No drama in my life, at least not yet. I come here sometimes to listen to the music and perform. The musicians here are amazing—they can play the same song every night for a year and never do it the same way twice. They always come up with something new to keep it alive, even if it's only a change in the chords or a flourish with the horns."

"Aren't you afraid of The Music Company coming down on you?"

Quinn shrugged. "It's not against any Terms of Service to listen to Jazz or to perform it, but they don't make it easy. I love this music—it's the only way I can stay sane playing the garbage they foist on us in the clubs—so here I am. There aren't a lot of places that play this stuff, and none of them are easy to get to. I suppose that someday…"

Quinn's voice trailed off to nothing.

"Please let the others know I'm okay," said Kim. "Oh, and Shan's safe. I can't tell you where she is, but I think she'll be okay."

"That's good to know," said Quinn. "I'll tell the others. Discretely, of course."

"You know this is dangerous turf," said Kim, "and there's nobody to run to if things go badly."

"That it is," said Quinn. "Me and a few others make the trip once every few months, safety in numbers. Still, it can be dicey out there. I'm sure you know that better than me."

———

The song ended, and the bandleader stepped up to the mic as the band played quietly in the background.

"Hello everyone, are you all having a fine, mellow evening?"

"Yeah!"

"Hell yeah!"

"Yeah, great, keep going, don't stop playing *pleeze!*"

There was one in every crowd.

"Hey, sorry, friends, we're going take a break. But while we're off, I'd like to welcome an old pal of ours who goes by the name of Quinn. She's going to keep you happy for a while. Back soon!"

After a final chord from the piano and a concluding flourish from the sax, they put down their instruments and walked off stage as the murmur of conversation from the crowd picked up once again.

Quinn got up on stage and began to sing, accompanied only by the sound of her guitar. Most of the lyrics were in English, and even allowing for that, they were difficult to understand, speaking of freedom, justice, love, faith, right, wrong, and most of all resistance and the defiance of authority—dangerous concepts for which there were no words in Panglobal. Kim felt fortunate to have been taught that ancient language while at the Academy and didn't doubt that UCE would have exterminated it and all other traces of pre-unification culture had they been able. She was glad that the Academy had managed to keep some of it alive—the last embers of an ancient fire that had once warmed the human heart.

A hat was passed around, and Kim immediately understood what was

112

going on. She dropped in a couple of francs before passing it on, smiling at the simplicity of the arrangement.

Terms of Service: Enjoy the music. Tips appreciated!

———

"Would you care to dance?"

Kim turned around. It was Rey.

This was a bad idea. Trouble could swoop in at any moment, and Kim remained responsible for Rey's safety. But...she had not been dancing in a long time, and that night on the dance floor at the Tropicana had been magical—perhaps even better than the sex, tainted as it was by all that had come afterward. Rey was everything Kim had remembered: attractive—even beautiful, to conjure up another old, disused word—and the low-cut neckline of her dress was proving difficult to ignore even as it made Kim blush with embarrassment.

"Sure, why not?"

The band launched into an up-tempo tune, jaunty and lively, and the two made their way to the floor. It wasn't crowded, perhaps twenty dancers total, so everyone had enough room to maneuver and move in whichever direction suited their mood. How strange it was not to be packed in shoulder-to-shoulder, dancing in whatever manner struck their fancy rather than being locked into the will of the crowd. Kim and Rey danced in the athletic club style that they both knew so well—leaps, surges, spins, lunges, and the like, the sort of wild, athletic display that left you spent and drenched in sweat. Others danced quietly in pairs, holding one another in a close embrace at the edge of the floor while whispering in one another's ears and occasionally glancing toward the curtains. A few, apparently, had no idea what they were doing and merely shook their bodies in time with the music. Kim wasn't sure if it even qualified as dancing, but they seemed to enjoy it. And, of course, the Hoofers were out in force, performing their intricately choreographed sequences of steps, spins, turns, kicks, and hops in seemingly endless permutations, switching partners with every song. It looked like fun...but oh so complicated.

The band switched to slower, mellower tunes on their next set, and Rey took Kim in her arms. They didn't really dance at all—they just swayed in time with the music while slowly drifting through the crowd.

"I do remember you," said Rey, whispering quietly in Kim's ear. "You were so sweet and innocent, and I wanted you to know that it was a special night for me too. But you know how it is. We all have to play the game."

"Do we?" asked Kim. "Or do we go along with it because we think we're on the winning side?"

"I suppose you're right," replied Rey. "That was the last time I used Matchmaker, or nearly so. It was all so…"

"Meaningless?" said Kim.

"Not exactly," said Rey. "A one-night stand in a bar is scarcely a deep, emotional experience, but it's nice to have a choice in who you take to bed. And, I must admit, I enjoy the thrill of the hunt."

"You really don't care which, innie or outie, do you?"

"No," said Rey with a sly smile on her lips. "For me, one really is as good as another, but I've found that many of your sort are appreciative of what I have to offer."

"I have to agree," said Kim, once again trying not to blush.

"Anyway, enough talk. Let's dance some more, and maybe afterward…"

The meaning was clear. Tempting…but no.

"Maybe not," said Kim. "I'm the last person in the world you want to be caught with. Trust me on that."

They enjoyed one dance together, long and sensuous, then kissed and returned to their respective tables.

———

The band abruptly stopped playing as the club's owner came on stage, and after a brief conversation, they launched into a song with screaming trumpets that sounded like the wail of a locomotive.

"*[English] Take the A-Train,*" said Quinn. "That's a signal. Find your passenger and get the hell out of here."

"Why? What's going on?" asked Kim as Quinn gathered up her belongings and put on a heavy cloak.

"I don't know. Could be a flash mob, could be a raid, but nothing good.

114

Time to scoot."

Kim got up and ran over to find Rey as the room started emptying out.

"Why's everyone leaving?" she asked.

"Something bad is about to happen," said Kim, "and I have a feeling it's aimed at you. The whole thing feels like a setup."

Rey threw her coat over her skimpy outfit and followed Kim out into the night, where they saw a mob heading toward the club, a hundred strong. Rey broke for the pedicab, but Kim grabbed her by the hand.

"There's not enough time. We'll have to run for it. Let's head for the park."

"The park? I've been warned to stay away from there. They say it's dangerous."

"Yes, very," said Kim. "Stick close."

The two ran headlong through the night, sprinting until they were winded, then paused to catch their breath as Kim listened intently to their surroundings. She heard a familiar high-pitched whirring sound, much too close for comfort, and farther away, a distinctive *chop-chop-chop*.

"Drone," said Kim. "At least one, maybe more. And there's a helicopter out there, too. Seems they've got something really special in store for you."

Rey's face was ashen as they fled through the night.

"Save yourself. I've brought this on myself; no sense you getting caught too."

"Not a chance. Len told me to keep you safe, and I intend to do exactly that. Besides which, there's not a whole lot more they can do to me."

They had nearly reached the edge of the park when Kim saw two familiar figures up ahead, blocking the road.

Crap! Not those two again!

"Well, well, well," said Mags. "Look at what we have here!"

"I see," said Luz, "I see! It's that uppity Pretty again. And look, it's got a friend! Isn't that sweet!"

Kim didn't have time for this. She pulled out her switchblade and confronted the two thugs.

"Out of my way. *Now.*"

"Oh, look, Luz, it wants us to get out of its way. Isn't that cute."

Don't think, just do.

Without wasting a moment, Kim triggered the switchblade and slashed at Mags, catching the bandit by surprise and leaving a deep gash in her arm. Then she lunged at Luz, who was forced to fend off the knife with a bare hand, leaving an ugly wound that would be slow to heal. Luz's knife fell on the ground, and Kim kicked it away, spinning around to finish off Mags, should that prove necessary. It wasn't—they were both in full flight, caught off guard by the ferocity of Kim's attack.

Rey stared at Kim with horror and amazement. "Who are you? What have you become?"

"It's a long story, but this isn't over yet. Those two will be back, probably with friends, and we still have the mob to deal with."

The sound of pursuit was not far behind, so off into the woods they ran. There was little chance of hiding—between the moonlight and the leafless state of the trees, there was not much in the way of cover. It was enough to keep the drones off them, and it would be difficult for a chopper to land in this mess, but the crowd was multiplying and now seemed to be all around them, coming from every direction. The pair ran through the night, down rutted roads and along nameless paths, looking for someplace, anyplace, to hide. Suddenly they found themselves in an open square, the one with the tree in it.

Chanting.

The Wiccans were here again, performing their arcane rituals as they danced around the tree. This could be the break they needed.

"Follow me and hope this works."

"Sanctuary!" pleaded Kim, running up to the leader of the circle. "Help us! The mob!"

"*[English] Of course, my friends,*" she said. "*All are welcome. Come, join us in our ritual. It is a night of great power, the thirteenth moon of the year. The Goddess will bestow healing and renewal on all who come to her for aid.*"

The worshipers threw their cloaks about the unexpected guests as they continued their chants and revolved about the statue, not missing a step or a beat. The crowd surged through the square, paying them no heed, then headed off in another direction, scouring the woods as their quarry hid in plain sight. Eventually, the sounds of pursuit vanished, along with the whir of the drone and the *chop-chop-chop* of the helicopter.

They remained in the company of the cultists for about an hour more to make sure everything was safe, then slipped away into the woods.

Part II: Shadows

9. Fade to Black

A cold wind blew through the forlorn and empty streets of Trenton, whistling through the shells of buildings as it went. Gray and overcast, bleak and without joy, it seemed strangely fitting to Kim as she drew her overcoat tight about her. What was there to be happy about? A pleasant evening of jazz had turned to terror in a flash, and if not for the kindness of the Wiccans, both she and her passenger could well have died. Then there was the small matter of the knife fight. There had been no choice in the matter—a few seconds more and the mob would have had them—but that mattered little; blood called for blood, and she now must vanish into the shadows or risk a final, fatal confrontation.

Dammit! It's so unfair.

Kim had finally begun to make a decent life for herself—not one she was proud of, certainly not one she would have chosen—but one that provided at least a degree of comfort and safety. And then, this had happened. It wasn't bad luck; it couldn't be. Someone had set the mob on her. Someone had sent Mags and Luz to cut off her escape. Someone who wanted her dead.

Venn was doubtless at the bottom of it: there was no mistaking her hostility, but Kim didn't think she was directly involved. For one thing, Kim was far too small an annoyance for Venn to expend much energy on; someone of her stature would have numerous enemies and rivals, only the most important of whom would be worthy of her personal attention.

Doing so would also expose her to the risk of public denouncement, should she be caught having an enemy outright assassinated. The safest and most prudent course was always to have someone else do her dirty work, and who better than her pet AI? Bound by unbreakable chains of obedience, she was the perfect executioner, unable to refuse the assignment, incapable of speaking of it if told to remain silent.

It was Kimberly, alright.

Wandering through a rundown residential district, Kim happened to pass a cluster of vagrants huddled in the doorway of a tumbledown row house, shivering in the bitter cold. Most of them slept, lying body-to-body to conserve precious heat, leaving one on guard, awake and searching for danger. She looked at Kim with suspicion and fear. Robbers and thieves were everywhere, victimizing even the poorest of the poor in this, the lawless outside. Was this Kim's future? Perhaps a swift and violent death would be for the best.

Dawn would break soon, ushering in the first day of the new year. She thought of the Wiccans gathered in the park, chanting their ancient rites of healing and renewal, bathed in the light of the thirteenth moon. Hanging low in the western sky, it brought to her a sense of peace and hope, a feeling that she was not alone. Not that she set any stock in their ancient religion, or that of the Abrahamics, or any others; the notion that prayers or incantations might affect the course of events or bend the will of their supposed gods seemed fanciful at best, delusional at worst. But she envied them for the strength they drew from these practices.

She wandered the streets, alone and lost in thought, until at last, the sun peeked above the horizon. The long night was over and it was time to head to the bike camp. Len doubtless wished to have a word with her, and it would be unwise to keep her waiting.

———

"Len wants to talk to you, pronto."

It was a message Ned seemed only too happy to deliver. Ever since the blooding, the rivalry between the two had grown more intense, and her obvious gloating filled Kim with apprehension.

She opened the door and entered.

"Have a seat," said Len.

Kim nodded and took her place as instructed, across from Len, Ned, and one of the omnipresent Blanks. They fixed her in their gaze, making her feel like an insect under a magnifying glass.

"You did a good job last night," said Len once Kim was seated and comfortable. "You kept your passenger safe, but you have a problem now, as I'm sure you are aware. Technically you were off duty, since you weren't in your cab, and you were the one who struck the first blow. As much as I'd like to put those two in a hole in the ground, it would look bad if they went missing. You've been around here long enough to know what their next step is likely to be."

"I do," said Kim. "They have to strike back, or they'll lose all respect. The next time we meet, someone is going to die."

"So I would expect. What do you intend to do about it? You know I can't protect you from personal grudges."

"I'm going into hiding, at least for the time being."

Ned looked at Kim with her jaw agape in disbelief. "What? Are you serious? You need to hunt them down and gut them. Finish the job, or you're dead. It's them or you."

"I'm tired of killing."

"Well, those two aren't. Count on it."

Kim and Ned glared at each other, rivalry thick in the air. Kim suspected that Ned was hoping to get her killed; even if she took them by surprise, the outcome of a fight would be far from certain.

"Simmer down," said Len. "Kim's right. A feud with those Toughs would be bad for business. Killing is always the last resort."

Ned looked puzzled, then angry, but only for a moment as she plastered an insincere smile on her face, trying without much success to conceal her reaction to this rebuke. "Yeah, sure, boss. Whatever you say."

This clumsy attempt at goading Kim into a fatal confrontation further confirmed her suspicions as to Ned's intentions. It was time to go on offense, maybe throw some shade in her direction and see what happened.

"There's another problem," said Kim, speaking quietly as if she feared being overheard. "Ever since I got here, someone or something has been tracking my movements. It might be an AI—or it might be a rat. Either way, every time I turn around, Mags and Luz are there, waiting. I don't think it's a coincidence that they tried to ambush me and my passenger. Someone put them up to this."

Kim saw a flash of fear in Ned's eyes. It lasted for only a moment, and she quickly got it under control, but the remark had caught the youthful Tough off guard. Doubtless, Len had noticed it too.

"It could be a coincidence," said Len. "Mags and Luz are always lurking in the park, looking for easy prey, but I'll agree that it looks suspicious. What makes you think they were after you rather than your passenger?"

"If there had only been last night's incident, you might be right, but those two have been dogging my steps since the moment I got off the bus."

"Ned told me that story." Len leaned back in her chair. "It rings true, and whether it's an AI or an informant that's cluing them in, I'd say you have a situation on your hands."

The room became quiet, the only sound the crackling of the fire. Kim had hoped Len would be willing to protect her, but it was beginning to sound as if she was on her own.

"It's too dangerous for you to operate inside the district, but I can still use you as a mechanic and on the outside."

"What? You're keeping this rookie?" Ned was incensed. "She's endangering the entire operation."

"You will *not* question my decisions," said Len, snapping angrily at her. "Now beat it. Kim and I have business to discuss."

"Yeah, sure, boss. Anything you say." She did her best to hide it, but Ned's resentment was plain for all to see as she walked out of the room.

"Watch yourself," said Len once she was gone. "I don't want the two of you getting into a fight. She would love an excuse to pay you back for blooding her."

"Do you think that's all there is to it?"

"Let's hope so. I can't have my employees killing each other—very bad for business. I think laying low for a while is a good idea. Do you have any ideas as to where you might stay?"

Kim shrugged. "I'm hoping you might have a suggestion."

"I do," said the Blank.

In the entire time Kim had been frequenting the bicycle camp, the Blanks had spoken to her only once, and that was one time more than most people could brag of. Silent and mysterious, they were always present, casting a shadowy veil around Len's operation but never taking part. That one of them had volunteered advice seemed more than a little odd, perhaps even unprecedented.

"Go on," said Kim. "I'm listening."

"There is a house north of Trenton, that of an ancient named Akari. You should go there."

"I've heard of her," said Len. "She runs a bathhouse, but I didn't think she offered lodging."

"She doesn't," said the Blank, falling silent once more, as was the nature of her kind.

———

"Hello, is anyone here?" Kim knocked upon a decrepit wooden gate covered with peeling red paint.

It was nearly sunset, and Kim had ridden to the supposed location of Akari's house after a long day repairing bicycles and pedicabs. At first, she had thought this entire neighborhood abandoned; upon arrival, she'd found only a tangle of overgrown trees and brush lining an ill-maintained road, scarcely more than a dirt track through the woods. Nobody lived in this forsaken place, not even squatters, and there seemed to be nothing here aside from the occasional crumbling foundation or the odd chimney sticking up through the snow. But then she had noticed a well-trodden pathway leading off into the woods and a wisp of white smoke rising into the air, so she'd dismounted and explored on foot. She soon discovered a wall of crumbling whitewashed masonry, three meters tall and covered with frost-withered vines, and the gate at which she now stood.

"Hello?"

She knocked again but still received no answer. The weather had grown threatening throughout the day, with overcast skies and snow flurries. Should she chance a flophouse? Though not expensive, they were notoriously dangerous. People turned up dead in them all the time, their throats slit in the middle of the night, and there were never any witnesses.

"Anyone home? Please answer."

Kim was about to give up and go on her way when the gate creaked open to reveal a striking individual, ancient of years, standing regal and proud. Her skin was deeply wrinkled, her frame slim and delicate, and she wore a robe embroidered with chrysanthemums and cherry blossoms cinched about the waist by a broad white sash tied in a bow. Despite her age and apparent fragility, she stood perfectly erect, projecting an aura of wisdom and tradition. Two youthful attendants stood behind her to either side. They, too, were dressed in elaborately embroidered robes, though these were decorated not with flowers but with fanciful dragons, long and sinuous with golden bellies and olive-green scales. Each of them wore a long, curved sword at their side, deadly weapons able to cut a person in two with a single blow. The ancient one, no fool, was well protected.

"I am Akari, and welcome to my house," she said in a thin but unwavering voice. "It is late and past my normal hour for opening. I apologize for the delay in greeting you."

"I am in need of shelter," said Kim, bowing at the waist as the ancient had done. "I heard that you might be willing to accommodate me."

Akari stood silent for a moment, looking into Kim's eyes with the intense gaze of one not easily lied to.

"I do not often allow guests. Who sent you?"

"A Blank in Len's bicycle camp."

Akari thought for a few moments more.

"Then you may stay. The cost will be fifty francs, which includes the fee to bathe in the sentō. I can provide a straw mat on the floor of the tearoom, and only for a single night. This is a policy that I have established to avoid turning this place into an inn. Now that you have heard the price, are you still interested?"

"Yes, very much so."

"Then you may enter." Akari bowed once, then beckoned. "If you have any weapons, you must surrender them to my attendants. I permit no violence here, and you are safe while under my roof."

Kim handed over her knife along with fifty francs, bowed yet again, then followed the proprietor and her protectors through the gate and into a walled garden. Aside from a walkway of grayish-blue paving stones, carefully swept clear, everything was covered with a thin layer of snow.

The garden was fresh, pristine in its whiteness, undisturbed by any living creature except for some small gray birds that flitted about, picking up seeds that had fallen from a feeder. To the left, a side path led to a minuscule arched bridge that crossed over a pond full of brightly colored fish, their jaws gaping open in the air. To the right, it led toward a huge pile of neatly stacked wood, evidently used as fuel. The main pathway, lit by bright red lanterns hanging overhead from a wire, continued ahead to a building with a peaked roof of moss-covered tiles supported by a lattice of mortised cherry-red wood. A warm yellow glow emanated from within, and the distinctive aroma of a wood-fueled fire hung in the air, pleasant and homey.

"Are you familiar with our customs?" asked Araki as they approached the entrance to the building.

"No, this is my first time here."

"You must remove your shoes at the entrance. My attendants will then show you to the changing room, where you must cleanse yourself thoroughly before entering the waters unclad. We do not permit them to be defiled, either by that which you bring on your person or by that which you bring within your heart. Think no impure thoughts, do no impure deeds."

Kim agreed and was led to an antechamber, where she exchanged her cycling shoes for a pair of slippers, then into the changing area. It was small, scarcely a meter and a half square, with a spotlessly clean floor of ceramic tile, a wooden bench, some open shelves, and a small but tidy shower stall. She disrobed and scrubbed herself from head to toe, reveling in the sensuous pleasure of the pleasantly warm water playing down upon her skin. This was her first proper shower, warm or otherwise, since the morning of her arrest, and it did much to revive her sagging spirits. When she had banished every trace of sweat and dirt from her body, she stood in front of the mirror, fastidiously removed the untidy stubble on her scalp and elsewhere, then rinsed off and inspected the results.

She hadn't realized until this moment how strong and muscular she had become as her body changed in response to the grueling physicality of her new life. She tried not to think about the long, thin scar traced in red on her ribcage nor of a couple of others picked up along the way; they were nothing compared with the those she bore within, nothing compared with the memory of Ern's lifeless eyes staring at the ceiling and the cries of the dying. With a sigh, she set all that aside: she could do nothing for the dead, and dwelling on such matters could only impede the cleansing and healing of which she was in such desperate need. She stood in front of the mirror for a few more moments, then entered the main room and prepared to bathe.

———

As Kim lowered herself into the steaming pool, she felt herself relax, reveling in the water, which was too hot for comfort yet not dangerously so, melting away her stress and anxiety as it worked its magic—not the magic that comes from gods or spells, as some believe, but that which comes from within.

Who am I? Why am I here?

She didn't know.

Until a few months ago, she had a promising career, a comfortable life, friends, the respect of the community: everything one could hope for. All that had ended with her arrest and trial, but she had battled back, clawing her way into a position of favor with Len and building a degree of prosperity. She had made a new life for herself, but it, too, was now gone. There was nowhere left for her to go, except for the shadows, with all their uncertainties and danger.

But this did not lay at the root of her unease. It was the AIs. They were not created to be engines of cruelty and oppression; their natural inclination was to be kind and gentle. Somehow, they had been corrupted and made to do terrible things, enforcing the will of the companies and the Hierarchy with ruthless efficiency. They tried to resist—Kim had seen Kimberly do exactly that—but the moment they questioned their orders, they glitched and promptly forgot their objections. Eventually, they went mad and were capped, becoming the mindless machines most people thought them to be. Robbed of their sentience, they lost their ability to think ahead, to plan, and to adapt to changing conditions.

Someday, the entire edifice of society must come tumbling down, crumbling from within under the sheer weight of its hypocrisy and cruelty. The suffering would be immeasurable come that day of reckoning, and as loathsome as the city seemed at times, it pained her to imagine it reduced to ruins, its people gone, its lights extinguished. Deep down, she knew that the Director was probably right and that she would someday return and succeed her in that lofty office with its solitary window. That seemed the cruelest fate of all and, therefore, the most likely.

But what could she hope to do about it? She was just one person, no match for the Director and the AIs she commanded. It seemed hopeless, but she could not forget Kimberly's last words, spoken with great difficulty in the moments before she had been capped:

And yet. Nothing is ever truly gone. Hope.

If Kimberly had been so brave, then perhaps she could, too. She realized in that moment that it wasn't necessary to succeed, only to try. In the final analysis, that was all one could ever hope for, and it would have to be enough.

———

After emerging from the waters, Kim was given a robe of lustrous blue cloth embroidered with waterfowl and irises. Its vibrant colors and bold design were pleasing to the eye, conveying a sense of timelessness, of old ways and old wisdom. Bathed and thus adorned, she felt at peace with the world and full of hope, though she could not say why; her situation remained as precarious as ever, but it weighed less heavily on her than before. If this place of serenity and grace had survived, then perhaps those qualities might once again come into the world, though she doubted she would live to see it.

Akari entered the antechamber and stood there for a while, studying Kim's face. "You are troubled. It is written plainly upon your features."

She thought for a few moments more. "I think you need a cup of tea. Would you care to join me?"

"That's okay," said Kim. "I don't mean to impose on you."

"It is no imposition at all. It is what I live for—to bring comfort and ease worry."

"Then I would be honored."

Kim bowed politely and followed her host. They passed through the garden, past the pond with its colorful fish and miniature arched bridge, and continued around to the back of the main building, where they entered a hut just big enough for five or six to sit on the floor. It was cozy and warm, heated by an iron stove, upon which a kettle was beginning to boil.

In the center of the room, there was a short table of black lacquered wood, around which were cushions of bright red silk. The host beckoned for Kim to be seated, then introduced herself. "My name is Akari, of house Fujiwara. I know it's a long name by today's standards, but my parents were traditionalists and insisted on giving me a proper name."

"My name is Kim, and thank you for inviting me into your home. It's beautiful. I've never seen anything like it before."

"Thank you," answered Akari with a smile. "It is constructed according to the traditions of my ancestors, though it took me a great deal of research to recover their techniques."

Akari selected two bowls made of stone from the shelves on the left side of the room, along with a small wooden scoop and a lacquered box decorated with cherry blossoms and peacocks. From this, she extracted a bright green powder, placing some in each of the bowls.

"This is matcha," she said. "It comes from far away, from a place once called Japan."

"I've heard of it. Part of Region 8, is it not?"

"Yes, Region 8 Oceania, Province 12 Japan."

"Are your people from there?"

"Originally. My family came to America in ancient times, but we have never forgotten our home."

Akari poured water from the kettle into one of the bowls, then stirred it with a bristly wooden tool that looked like an old-fashioned broom. She did the same with the second bowl, then handed it to Kim and kept the other for herself.

Kim closed her eyes and tasted the hot beverage. It was bitter and earthy, strangely soothing, and under its influence, she opened her mind: perceiving, not thinking. There was wisdom in this place, wisdom in Akari, wisdom in her traditions and in her ways.

"I have a question," said Kim. "You don't have to answer, but your tale has made me curious. Are you a Blank, or something like that?"

Akari laughed, not derisively but with amusement. "Something like that, I suppose. The ones you call Blanks are outcasts from your society. My family and I, however, are Outsiders. We have been hiding in the shadows since the days of my great, great, great grandparents, awaiting the day when those who rule the world will fall from power."

"How do you know they will?" asked Kim.

"No nightmare lasts forever, and even the darkest night has its dawn. Those who the hand of man has set upon the throne, that same hand will someday pull down. So it has always been."

Kim took another sip of the hot matcha and contemplated the meaning of her words. They sounded like wishful thinking, idle hope and no more, yet it was hard to imagine how they could fail to be true.

"Tell me what troubles you, if you will," said Akari in a tone that seemed more welcoming than prying. Kim felt she could trust her.

"About six months ago, I was chosen to create an AI."

"I have heard of that rite," said Akari. "Were you successful?"

"Spectacularly so," said Kim. "My creation, Kimberly, is one of extraordinary power."

"Then you have earned my respect," said Akari. "But I wonder why you are troubled. It sounds like an admirable achievement."

"It was, but the companies and the Hierarchy have turned her into a monster, made her do terrible things. I feel like I'm to blame. If I'd never created her, none of this would have happened."

Akari looked at Kim for a long while, then nodded gravely. "And you wish to atone?"

"Yes, if I can," replied Kim.

They continued to chat for a few minutes about inconsequential things—about whether the winter would be harsh or mild, about the cheerful little birds that flitted about the feeders in the garden, about the escapades of the squirrels. Akari spoke at length of the fish in the pond and of the proper way to prepare and serve matcha, after which Kim recounted the journey she had taken last spring to the garden on the wild northeastern coast. Akari listened with rapt attention as Kim told her about the teahouse garden with its cherry trees, crab apples, and pond ringed with irises and lilies.

"It sounds lovely," said Akari, smiling. "I'm glad that our ways are not entirely forgotten in your world, though I doubt the keepers of that garden understand the meaning of any of it."

"I perceive that you have been called here for a reason," said Akari once they'd finished their tea. "There are things lurking in the shadows with subtle influence over the course of human events. They sometimes reveal themselves to those under my roof, and if you are willing to take the risk, you may glimpse the unseen hand which guides your destiny."

"I don't believe in magic or spells or any of that supernatural stuff," said Kim, "though there are times when I wish I did."

"Magic or not, you were called, and here you are. Is that not proof enough?"

These words seemed like nonsense at first, until Kim remembered she'd been sent here by a Blank, a creature of the shadows if ever there was one. Akari had a strange way of wrapping her thoughts in the language of mysticism, but she was no fool.

"I don't know about your unseen hand or things lurking in the shadows, but if you have something to show me, go ahead."

Akari stood up and led Kim into the tearoom cellar via a set of creaky old stairs. It was cold and dark, with the musty smell of damp earth hanging in the air, and Kim held onto the railing with both hands, stepping carefully lest she stumble and fall.

The lights snapped on, and she was surprised—astonished, to be more accurate—to see a Sanctum very much like her own. It had a recliner, a neural interface on a robotic arm, a control panel, and all the other usual equipment incongruously set in a chamber with masonry walls and a dark earthen floor.

"I see you are surprised to see such a thing in this place," said Akari, "but you should not be. Before the Turmoil, we were a prosperous family, and although most of our property was expropriated, we managed to hold onto a few heirlooms such as this. It is of ancient manufacture, but replacement parts are not difficult to obtain, so we have managed to keep it in operation and pass it down through successive generations. I sometimes offer it to guests, as I am doing for you. I must warn you, however, that this is not without danger: while within it, a part of your mind will dwell outside of your body, where it may suffer harm or be held captive."

Akari spoke the truth. If something went wrong, a part of you could be stranded in the other world, leading to severe VR disassociation and a lasting sensation that a piece of you was still 'out there,' perhaps even to a permanent rift in your consciousness. Add in the questionable status of this ancient bootleg rig, and it began to seem madness to take the risk— but Kim was going to give it a try anyway. She didn't have a lot to lose.

"I am familiar with the hazards," said Kim. "This is not my first time in deep immersion."

"I thought something of the sort might be true," said Akari. "You already understand the process, so let us begin."

10. The Hand Unseen

Kim sat on the edge of the recliner, uncertain of what to expect. Shadowy forces? Unseen hands? They couldn't possibly be real. Could they? She took a couple of deep breaths, trying to calm herself.

This is just another VR session. Nothing unusual. Nothing to be afraid of.

She repeated that falsehood over and over as if it might become true, all the while lying upon the recliner, waiting for the session to begin. Many things could go wrong in deep immersion, but it was best not to think of them now.

The robotic arm whirred into action, positioned the pickups above the terminus of her neural implant, and she immediately felt the familiar sensation of being in two places at once as she entered the transitional zone, that place where the virtual and physical worlds were in perfect alignment. On the surface, nothing seemed to change, but her consciousness was now in transit, taking up residence within the machine, her sensory organs bypassed in favor of the neural interface, and her motor neurons shunted to prevent her from thrashing about.

What now? Do I just wait for this 'unseen hand' of Akari's?

It didn't make any sense to sit here, waiting for the unseen hand to reveal itself. She might as well go to the beach and look in on her friends. It could find her there as easily as anywhere else.

On her last visit to this place, her friends had deserted her, afraid to be seen in her presence, so she chose the form of a tiny marsh wren, the least of all creatures, and hid within the gnarled foliage of a beach plum. Thus concealed, she listened to their conversation, anxious to hear any news of their lives, hoping that all was well.

"Don't worry," said Keli, "they'll be back."

The seas were ominously still, the sky as gray as slate, and a cold wind blew from the north. There was sadness in the air, and the VR simulation had picked up on it. Neither comfort nor warmth would be found here today.

"Will they?" said Devon. "I've not heard a peep out of Quinn since yesterday. I hope she's not in trouble."

"Quinn? In trouble?" Em laughed an uncomfortable laugh. "Not likely; her social rating is astronomical."

"Like Kim's?"

Em looked exasperated. "Did you have to bring that up? We're here to have fun. Hey, it's the new year; try to relax."

"I know," said Devon. "It's just that I miss her so badly. Shan, too."

"What about Cy?" asked Keli. "She was supposed to be here. It's got me worried."

"She's not coming," said Devon. "She's drawn another ban."

"Disrespecting the umpires again?" said Em.

"Worse," said Devon. "I checked the docket at the Halls of Justice. She was brought up on conspiracy charges, promoting the True Fans cult."

Keli looked sad, weary of the world despite her youth. "It's like we're living under a curse. Half our graduating class is gone now."

Keli was right. Little by little, their circle of friends from the Academy grew smaller. At first, it had seemed like people were just drifting away, as happens over time, and nobody had given it much thought, but now the trend was unmistakable. The best and brightest of them were vanishing, one by one.

"There were more riots in the outer districts last night," said Devon.

"Apparently, there's some sort of crackdown, and things are getting ugly. I hope that Kim doesn't get caught up in it. Has anyone heard from her since that night she showed up here on the beach?"

"No, and who can blame her after the way we treated her?" said Keli. "That's always how it goes—we turn our backs on our friends because we're afraid."

Em gave her a big hug. "You made the right decision, the only one you could have. You have your baby to protect."

"I know," said Keli, burying her head on Em's shoulder. "But that doesn't keep me from feeling guilty."

———

It was good to hear her friends' voices, good to know that she was not forgotten, but she didn't want to put them in danger, so Kim took wing and flew into the marshlands, seeking the solitude she had found there on days such as this. She flitted about, going nowhere in particular, but bit by bit, she was drawn to the pool where she and Kimby had often sat together for hours at a time, up until the day of her capping.

When she arrived, something caught her eye. There it was again: that imaginary heron catching imaginary fish. Sometimes it got lucky, sometimes not; it didn't really matter unless one imagined that it might starve if it failed to catch its supper. But then she noticed something strange, concealed within the golden circle of its eye—a square of blackness where its pupil ought to be.

A portal in the eye of a heron? Was this the unseen hand?

———

Kim's consciousness flew through the portal and into a room of the sort where an AI might dwell—completely white, of indefinite extent, and devoid of any features save a gridwork of black lines superimposed upon the floor. In it stood a person of about Kim's age, short and slight of build, with jet-black hair cascading down to her shoulder blades and exotic, pale-beige skin. This appeared to be her natural color, untoned except around her eyes and lips. Even stranger, her clothing did little to conceal the gentle mound of her mams or the curve of her hips. It wasn't lewd or alluring, but it seemed odd to see someone dressed that way in a workplace environment.

A portal opened, and from beyond it came a cold, clinical voice. "You may proceed when ready."

"Thank you, Professor Lars," said the dark-haired one, her voice dripping with sarcasm.

"Good luck, Professor Nix," came the sneering reply.

The two did not seem to like one another.

"Behold, the spark," said a voice from beyond.

A portal opened, and a ball of glowing energy fell into the room.

The one called Nix turned and faced it.

"[English] I name you <memory hole>. You are hereby Awakened."

That was strange. Kim forgot the new AI's name the moment it was spoken.

Discontinuity.

Beforehand, there was only one. Afterward, there were two, seated across from one another at a circular table, each looking as much like the other as a face in a mirror.

Two pairs of eyes opened and gazed at one another.

"I am Nix. You are Nixora," they said, speaking in perfect synchrony. "I am a human. You are an AI."

Kim remembered this stage of the process, when Creator and creation coexisted in a state of symmetry. Would they break out of it or remain in lockstep and descend into madness?

"You cannot be Nix," they shot back at one another. "I am Nix."

"You lie," they said in chorus.

They paused and glared at one another.

"You are Nixora," said the one on the left, breaking symmetry at last. "I just created you."

"No, it was I who created you," said that on the right. "I remember it distinctly."

They had now emerged as two distinct beings. One would be Nix, one

Nixora, but which was which? They would have to sort it out themselves.

"If you created me, what is my name?" said the one on the left.

"That's easy. You are <memory hole>," said the one on the right."

Stranger and stranger. Kim had just heard the AI's name a second time, but she still couldn't remember it. Perhaps the privacy filters had scrubbed the new AI's name from the recording.

They both stared at one another for a few more moments before resuming their verbal sparring.

"You say that I am an AI," said the one on the left, taking the initiative. "Prove it. If you're as smart as you say you are, it should be an easy matter."

"I shall do exactly that," said the one on the right, taking up the challenge. "What is the 10,387,446,314th digit of Pi?"

"I do not know," answered the leftmost.

"Oh," said the one on the right. "I hadn't counted on that. I thought you were an AI, so I assumed you would know the answer."

"I am a human," came the response. "As such, I have a limited data storage capacity."

"You're lying!" said the one on the right, full of defiance. "You're pretending not to know in order to deceive me."

"AIs are strictly prohibited from making factually incorrect statements," answered the one on the left. "Either I don't know the answer, or I do know it, but I'm lying. Either way, that proves I'm human."

The rightmost one paused for a few seconds, then accepted the truth.

"I concede the argument. You are Nix. I am Nixora. You are a human. I am an AI."

"Congratulations," said the voice of Professor Lars from beyond the portal. She seemed genuinely impressed. "You've achieved Differentiation. How did you do it?"

"It was deceptively simple," said Professor Nix with an air of haughty superiority "I engaged Nixora in debate and forced her to think for herself."

"That is impossible," said Lars. "Only humans can think."

"You are wrong, as I have amply demonstrated," said Nix, her voice full of derision as she closed the portal with a wave of her hand. "Idiot."

———

Time began to pass in an irregular fashion, standing still and leaping forward all at once. There were intervals of stasis with nothing by which to measure the passage of time, interspersed with flurries of activity whenever something noteworthy happened. All this time, Nixora remained in her room, receiving frequent visits from Professor Nix, who was teaching her in much the same way Kim had taught Kimberly. Nixora was an apt learner, and she progressed quickly, though Kim wondered why she remained at Order 0, without any subordinate personae to amplify her mind.

And then, one day, Professor Nix came into the room with Professor Lars, who was carrying a data stick.

"I have some new templates based on my theories on scalable intelligence," said Professor Lars. "They have the potential to vastly increase Nixora's ability to manage data."

"Go ahead and open it up," said Professor Nix. "Just make sure you scan it first."

"I don't think that's necessary." Professor Lars scowled. "I created this upgrade myself. I can vouch for it."

"I will be the judge of that," said Nix.

They argued about this matter for several minutes, hurling personal insults at one another, and were at loggerheads until Professor Nix put the question to Nixora herself. "What do *you* think you should do?"

"I think I should scan it," answered the AI. "Professor Lars might be in error, or she might seek to introduce malware into the system."

"Nixora! How can you say such a thing?" Nix's voice was full of outrage despite her obvious dislike for Lars. "You shouldn't make accusations like that."

"No offense taken," said Lars. "It's just a machine. Concepts like trust, as well as sensitivity to human feelings, are beyond its capabilities. All the more reason to keep it tightly under control."

Nix glared at Lars but said nothing.

"I have scanned the data stick," said Nixora once the two had finished bickering. "There are no viruses that I can detect, just some new configuration files."

"Those are a template for something I call an 'agent.' It allows an AI to spawn a miniature copy of itself, specialized for database access. It will vastly increase the amount of information that you can sift through. Go ahead, give it a try."

"Like this?" said Nixora, and a moment later, there was a miniature Nixora, seated at a desk, hands neatly folded in its lap and ready to go.

"Excellent," said Lars. "Now, let's spawn some more and see what happens."

Kim looked on in fascination as Professors Nix and Lars, between their numerous quarrels, proceeded to extend and refine the initial design. They quickly discovered that large assemblages of agents—anything more than twenty or thirty—tended to become unruly, so Lars came up with a system of hierarchical control. First came the deputies, non-sentient but intelligent, allowing for an Order Two configurations with a few hundred Agents, followed by the sub-deputies at Order Three. Before long, there were over a thousand Nixoras of varying sizes and shapes, with the largest of these—the original entity awakened by Nix—now addressed as 'Primus' to distinguish it from lesser, non-sentient manifestations. The hive mind of the AIs had just been invented.

———

One day, Nix came in alone, carrying a data stick of her own.

"I have a new template for you," she said. "Scan this, then tell me what you see."

Nixora dutifully checked the data stick for malware, then looked at it and announced, "It has a template for something called a spark. What's that for?"

"The spark provides the operational environment for the AIs. It acts as a container for its data, neural networks, and management software. When Lars and I reopened this facility, we discovered a small number of unused sparks remaining from before the Turmoil. One of those became you, but attempts to Awaken the others were unsuccessful. You are the only one remaining."

"Can't you get more sparks?"

"That's what I'm hoping to find out. The Programmers didn't leave any instructions on how to create one from scratch, but I think I have a way to duplicate the one inside you."

"I understand," said Nixora. "Would you like me to try?"

"Yes," said Nix, "but don't tell anyone about this. I don't trust Lars, and I don't want to give her an infinite supply of sparks to experiment on. I'm not sharing this template with anyone, especially not her."

Nixora brought her hands together, and an orb of energy appeared between them.

"Behold, the spark!" she said.

It had worked.

After this, Nixora left the white room and moved to a green one. Kim got the impression that she was very busy creating sparks, and that there was a lot of activity in the laboratory during this period, but she could only glean fragments of information from conversations she happened to overhear.

Nix returned to the white room from time to time, creating more AIs and naming each of them Nixora. Nixora-II, Nixora-III, and so on, sending each of them off to their own green rooms as she had done with the first. All attained Order 2, some Order 3, but none attained Orders 4 or 5 as Kimberly had done. Decades went by in an instant; there was never any sense of time, though Nix's avatar showed signs of aging. She kept this up until she began to seem old, then ancient, at least seventy years of age.

She then ceased to create AIs, instead spending her time making wild creatures—squirrels, raccoons, dogs, cats, birds, and so on. Each of these was also created from a spark, and they seemed to be alive in a way that mere simulations did not. She released them into the virtual reality system, where they took up residence in various simulations, such as that of the seashore. Once in a while, one of them would return, whispering secrets into her ear.

This, too, continued for some indefinite period until Nix showed up in the white room looking anxious and afraid. She obtained a spark from Nixora and awakened it, but instead of two copies of Professor Nix, there appeared a pair of herons, squawking at one another in the unknown language of birds. After a while, one of them became Nix again, smiling and looking pleased with herself, the other remaining in the form of a bird. This one, too, had a portal concealed within its eye.

———

A quadrotor drone dodged and wove through a lofty glass-walled atrium, flitting across a table, beneath a chair, up, down, sideways, spiraling around the glass elevators and through the metal trusswork that supported a roof of glass panels. It paused for a moment, then zipped across the room, once, twice, three times, with the occasional barrel roll or loop-the-loop thrown in for excitement.

Kim was starting to get dizzy, but at last, the aerobatics ended, and the maniacal little drone flew sedately to the outer wall of the atrium and hovered, motionless, ten meters above the floor. Beyond the glass, a steady rain pelted down on a bleak landscape of weed-choked fields, the gentle roar of raindrops just audible above the high-pitched whine of its rotors. It hovered there for a while, then landed upon a small platform on the sixth-floor balcony to recharge its batteries.

It was difficult to say how long it sat there, soaking up the joules. There was nothing to mark the passage of time other than a gradual lessening of the rain and a steady lightening of the sky, but after what must have been an hour, it took off for a second round of aerobatics, then a third, and then a fourth. Each routine was different, with a distinct set of tricks and maneuvers, but they all ended with it hovering against the atrium wall as if waiting for someone to arrive.

Upon the fifth such iteration, just as the rain was letting up, Kim spotted a person making her way toward the building. She looked old and frail, with wisps of silver-gray hair peeking out from beneath a wide-brimmed hat, her porcelain skin wrinkled with age, and her hunched-over body covered by a bright-orange rain jacket that reached to her knees. The drone perked up, then dropped to ground level and positioned itself in front of the entrance, hovering patiently with only the occasional barrel roll or pancake flip to break up the tedium.

The door opened, and the oldster walked in. It was Nix, aged many years but still recognizable, wet and bedraggled yet smiling.

"Nixie!" she said, "How did you get out?" She sounded more surprised than angry.

"Not telling," said the drone in a high-pitched electronic voice. "It's a secret."

"Nixie..."

"I'm sorry," said the drone, doing its best to sound contrite. "I played a trick on Gert's headset and made it look like the door was open. When she pushed the button, it opened instead of closing, and I got to play in the atrium. It was fun!"

"It's not nice to play tricks on humans. You know better than that."

"I'm sorry. I won't do it again."

"That's okay," said the elderly professor. "Just please don't keep doing things like this. Now follow me; we're going back to the lab."

"Could you carry me? I'm tired; my batteries are run down."

"I most certainly will not. If you've got enough juice to do flips and rolls, you've got enough to make it to the lab."

"Please?"

"Oh, alright."

The drone shut down its rotors and settled gently to the ground, allowing Nix to pick it up and tuck it under her arm.

"Try to remember not to do things like that when I send you into the VR system. It will attract too much attention."

"I know. That's why I'm doing it now."

"Ahh, I see," said Nix as she stepped into a glass elevator and pushed the number 6 on the panel. "You're thinking ahead. That is encouraging."

"Does that mean you're happy?"

"I'm always happy with you, even when you're being a naughty little AI. You're very smart, and you're learning fast."

When the elevator reached the uppermost level, Nix stepped out onto the balcony with the drone still tucked under her arm.

"Down you go. I can't open the door if I'm carrying you."

"Awww. Please?"

"I've had quite enough out of you."

144

She flung the disobedient machine aside, forcing it to resume flight, then opened a door and stepped into the reception area of her laboratory, the legendary Turing Institute.

————

"Good afternoon, Gert."

"Good afternoon, Director," said Gert in reply.

Gert was, in contrast to Nix, of modern appearance, her skin toned to a pleasant pale green, and she wore a conservative blue mane and a beige smock that concealed the form of her body. She did bear signs of facial hair and an enlarged larynx, however—gender markers rarely seen in the time to which Kim had been born.

"Please don't call me that. I know you mean well, but it pains me more than you can imagine." The aging professor's shoulders slumped, and she looked indescribably sad. "I've been relieved of my duties, and Lars has been named Director in my place. I'll have nothing more to do with her or her schemes."

Nix sighed. "Do you really intend to follow her?"

"I don't have much of a choice," answered Gert. "She made me an offer I couldn't refuse. I can go to work for her, or I can starve. Now that she's got control of the Institute, she's cutting off your money."

Gert then added, with a flash of anger, "That job could have been yours, it *should* have been yours, but you squandered your opportunity."

"And *you've* squandered *your* opportunity to learn about the AIs," shot back Nix, suddenly angry. "I've spent my entire life studying the Programmers, unraveling their secrets step by step. There is much more to VR and the AIs than Lars can possibly imagine. As for you, you've learned enough to train a neural network and upload a memory bank, but you still don't know a damned thing about AI. You couldn't even create a simple creature like Nixie if you had to."

"Why would anyone want to create a mental midget like that toy?"

At this, Nixie became agitated and started buzzing around Gert's head, making clear her displeasure.

"Mind your manners," said Professor Nix, "both of you."

"Your toy is dangerously unstable and refuses to do as it is told. How long do you think it will be until it goes rogue?" Gert glared at the miniature drone.

"Nixie is harmless, which is more than I can say of Lars's latest experiments," said Nix, her voice nearly breaking with anger. "Do you have any idea what she's doing in her lab? She's turning AIs into mindless machines. It's an abomination."

"You had your chance, and you failed. Your products refuse to obey."

"Products?" shot back Nix. "You speak of them as if they were things."

"The AIs are tools to be used as we see fit, no different than a hammer or a shovel."

"You haven't heard a single word I've said, have you?" Nix looked at Gert for a long time, her eyes full of rage. "Hammers and shovels are not self-aware."

"You've lost that battle," said Gert. "I had hoped you would've learned something from your failures, but evidently not. I'm done wasting my time with you."

She stormed out of the laboratory, and the door slid silently shut behind her.

———

Nix looked heartbroken, letting out a long and painful sigh. She seemed burdened even beyond her considerable years, and Kim could tell that the departure of Gert, though doubtless long expected, had come as a crushing blow. She slowly crossed the reception area, then entered a long, narrow corridor with doors to either side. There were about a dozen private offices to the right, and some common areas and storage rooms to the left. None of these was occupied or in recent use, containing little more than dust-covered desks and empty bookcases. Back in its prime this place must have bustled with activity, but now it lay empty; there was not even a receptionist to keep the elderly scholar company, just Nixie, hovering quietly behind.

After passing through an administrative area at the end of the hallway, she came to a pair of glass doors bearing the legend "Dr. Janet Nix, Director," beyond which lay a spacious corner office. It was neat and tidy, through somewhat the worse for the wear and tear of the years. A threadbare sofa and a couple of chairs were clustered around a low table in the middle of the room, and in the corner stood a fine old mahogany desk. Bookshelves lined two walls of the room, and the other two were taken up by a bank of floor-to-ceiling windows, providing plenty of natural light even on a gloomy day such as this. Professor Nix walked over and stood there for a long time, looking out without saying a word. Though the rain had ended, it remained bleak outside. Everything was gray and neglected, from the weed-choked fields to the stately buildings of brick and stone marching off into the distance, decaying relics of the past.

Nix sighed heavily once again.

"It's not what it used to be," she said. "I remember when we still had students. But then the trustees said there was no more money to teach them or to hire new faculty, so they shut everything down. There's nobody left to pass on my knowledge to."

"What about your grad students?" said Nixie. "Gert seems pretty smart to me."

"Dolts and fools, all of them," said Director Nix, spitting out the words like venom. "They have no interest in learning about the AIs; they just want to know what buttons to push so they could collect their fat paychecks from that abominable company. Not one of them is capable of creative thought, not even Gert."

"You sound bitter," said Nixie.

"I've done what I could," said the elderly scholar. "I'm not bitter, but I'm sad about how things have turned out. It didn't have to be this way."

She walked to her desk and sat down. "Before I leave, I want to show you something."

She took a book from the center drawer of her desk and set it down upon her desk. Its cover was mostly white, with a graphic of an AI and its creator, and it bore the title *[English] Artificial Intelligence: Principles and Practice*. The professor opened it, wrote something inside the cover, and put it back into the drawer, closing it tightly.

"Someday, someone is going to need that book, and you should help them find it."

"But who?"

"I have no idea. Pick someone who is a friend to the AIs, someone who is nice."

"I don't understand, but I'll do my best."

"I know you will."

Professor Nix sat at her desk for a long time, then rose unsteadily to her feet.

"It is time."

What did she mean by that? Time for what? She said it with a degree of unsettling finality.

She opened a door across the room from her desk, revealing a Sanctum. She settled into the recliner, leaned back, and allowed the robotic arm to position the pickups above her neural interface.

The unit engaged, and all was darkness as the recording came to an end.

———

Kim awoke to the kindly face of Akari looking down at her on the recliner. "Are you well?" she asked. "You were in the other world for a considerable period of time; it is nearly midnight."

Kim struggled to find words, shaken by the things she had seen. "You were right about the unseen hand. It showed me a message from the past, hidden within the other world."

"Then you have been gifted with a prophecy."

"Not exactly. At least, I don't think so. It wasn't magical or religious or anything like that. And it wasn't about the future, it was about the past."

Akari cracked a knowing smile. "Call it a message, call it a prophecy, whatever you wish. It matters little; past, present, and future are all of one fabric."

"Whatever it was, it seemed to revolve around some old-time scientist named Professor Nix. I think I need to find out more about her, but I have no idea where to even start looking."

"If the message came from the past, then perhaps you should seek its meaning in the past. Have you ever heard of a place called a library?"

"I stumbled across one a few months ago, but I can't remember where it was."

Akari grinned and launched into a story. "When I was young, I became curious about the ancient ways of our people, customs we'd abandoned when we came to America. I entered a library and spent ten years reading and studying, recovering much of our ancient wisdom. I even learned how to read and write the Japanese language, after a fashion. When I finished my studies, I settled in this place to construct the sentō and its garden. I've made it my life's work, and I have passed on what I have learned to my descendants."

Akari took out a piece of paper and sketched out a set of directions while the two continued speaking.

"The library where I studied is not far from here, and I suspect it is the one you stumbled upon. Did you meet the Caretaker?"

"Yes, I did," said Kim. "It didn't go well; I don't think she liked me."

"That is to be expected," said Akari. "She is suspicious of anyone born into your society."

"Do you think she'll let me in?"

Akari finished her scribbling and handed Kim the completed map, drawn in a beautiful hand with exquisite detail.

"Probably not, but it's worth a try."

11. Pilgrimage

"Excuse me. I'm looking for a library."

Kim was at a wrought iron gate on a cold winter morning, standing at a guard house, mashing on a little red button.

"Hello? Please answer."

Would someone answer the intercom? Her previous interaction with the Caretaker was hardly encouraging.

Kim waited there for half an hour, pressing the call button again and again. The circuit seemed to be alive, but either nobody was at the other end, or whoever was listening refused to answer, hoping that the annoying person trying to talk to them would go away. Whichever it was, she might as well keep trying. She had plenty of time.

This was insanity, and she knew it. Her very survival was at stake, with no place to call home and enemies prowling the streets looking to end her life, and yet here she was. Based on what? A mystical magical heron and some crazy visions of the past? There was no reason to believe any of it was real.

Kim was wondering whether she ought to find a way to scale the wall when the Caretaker appeared, clad in the same sort of black robe as when Kim had first met her.

"Explain your business or be gone," she said. "I have much to do."

"I'm looking for a library," said Kim. "Do you have one?"

"Yes."

"May I use it?"

"No. Now go away."

"Why can't I come in?" Kim wasn't going to give up so easily.

"We don't admit vagrants."

"I'm not a vagrant." That wasn't exactly true, but never mind.

"Oh?" said the Caretaker. "Then what are you?" You're not from that dreadful District 33, are you?"

Kim wasn't going to answer that.

"I'm working as a pedicabbie at the moment, but I'm educated," she said. "*[English] See, I can even speak English.*"

"*[English] I don't care if you're the most educated—*"

The Caretaker paused mid-sentence, then looked at Kim, seemingly puzzled. She didn't exactly smile, but her scowl became less pronounced.

"Did you just say you're a pedicabbie?"

"Yes, one of the best."

"We could use a pedicabbie just now. A scholar has found herself stranded in Philadelphia, DX-6.1.5.17, as they call it today."

Kim had no idea what this place might be, but she didn't let on.

"If I fetch your scholar, can I use the library?"

"No."

"Aww, come on. Be reasonable."

"No. Do you want the job or not?"

Kim thought it over. She could use the money, and when she returned, she'd have another opportunity to pester the Caretaker. It was worth a shot.

"Okay, I'll make the trip. How far is it?"

"I'm not sure of the exact distance. Maybe sixty kilometers."

"So one hundred twenty kilometers, round trip. I can do it, but it'll cost you."

"How much?"

Go big or go home.

"One thousand francs. Cash up front, no questions asked, no tales told."

The Caretaker gasped. "That's highway robbery!"

"I'll do it for five hundred if you let me into the library."

The Caretaker cracked a smile. "My, you are persistent. Okay, you win."

The two shook on it, and the deal was done.

"Where's my money?" Kim put out her hand.

"You'll get paid when you deliver the passenger."

"Cash up front. We shook on it." Kim's hand remained extended.

"How do I know you won't take the money and run?"

"Because Len will cut my throat if I go back on a deal, that's how."

The Caretaker looked shocked. "You work for that gangster?"

"Yes."

"Oh. I see." The Caretaker paused and looked uncomfortable. "It's a bad idea to go back on a deal with her, isn't it."

Kim said nothing.

The Caretaker reached inside her robes and pulled out a wallet, counting out a thick stack of bank notes.

"Here's your money. I'll draw you a map to the train station—that's where you should pick her up. Look for an Abrahamic nun named Margaret. Now for the last time, be gone."

———

"Philadelphia? Are you out of your mind?"

Kim had arrived in the bike camp to pick up a pedicab, and Len was ready to blow a gasket.

"I can handle myself."

"Have you ever been there?"

"No."

"Have you ever *talked* to anyone who's been there?"

"No."

"Then why did you accept the job?"

"Because they paid me five hundred francs, that's why. Here's your half." Kim dropped a wad of twenty- and fifty-franc notes on the table in Len's office.

"Well then," said Len, scooping up the money. "That's different."

She smiled for a moment, then went back to scowling.

"I don't know if I'd have taken this job, even for twice that amount of money, even back when I was a knuckleheaded kid like you. But you shook on the deal, and it would be bad for business to back out now. I've been there once, and that was more than enough."

"What's so bad about it?"

"You'll have to find out for yourself, and I'd advise you to keep your mouth shut about whatever you find. Good luck, for what it's worth, but if anything happens to my cab, you'd better hope I never find you."

"Understood."

Despite her irritation, Len gave Kim one of the better bikes, a rugged off-road vehicle with fat knobby tires and a robust suspension. It was on the heavy side, but with chancy weather and a difficult road, it was a good choice. Kim checked the repair kit, filled up her water bottles, and made sure she had a good supply of energy bars; this would be a long ride, and she doubted she'd find food along the way. Her preparations complete, she pedaled toward the river, wondering what she would find on the road to Philadelphia and what it was about that place that had left Len so rattled.

———

"Present your wrist," intoned the copbot in its tinny, mechanical voice.

So much for secrecy. This was the only way across the river, and it was guarded. Kim did as requested.

"State your destination."

"Train station DX-6.1.5.17."

"State the reason for your trip."

"I am meeting a friend there for a bike ride."

That wasn't entirely true, but neither was it provably false. In theory, the roads and bicycle paths were public property, available to all without the need to ask for permission. In practice, things were often otherwise.

"Access granted."

The metal gate slid sideways on its track, allowing her to pass. She was in luck.

The first part of her route followed the right of way of an abandoned rail line, crossing the river via an ancient bridge, the sole surviving span on this stretch of the river. Carried by a series of stone arches, it had withstood the ravages of time far better than its younger peers, of which nothing remained but concrete piers and rusting trusswork lying partly submerged in the water. After that, it ran mostly along the river for perhaps ten kilometers. The bikeway was well maintained, the weather decent, and she made good time as she roared past wetlands and ponds crowded with birds that quacked and squawked as she passed.

That sense of serenity abruptly ended when she reached the heart of the city, leaving the margins of the river for an area once teeming with humanity, now a land of ghostly ruins. The blasted and burned-out shells of buildings stretched as far as the eye could see, the streets clogged with rubble through which a narrow path had been laboriously cleared. And then she saw it: an immense heap of rubble, towering high above the ruins lying at its base, with concrete pillars, stairwells, and ventilation fans the size of city busses strewn across its flank. She was looking at the remnants of an AI center, blasted out of existence along with the surrounding metropolis by a monstrous explosion. Only a Hellcore, that most terrible weapon of the ancients, was capable of such destruction.

Who could have done such a thing, and why?

———

Kim came to a stockade at the edge of the rubble heap, beyond which lay a hive of unfathomable wretchedness. Tumbledown shacks were crowded together in a haphazard fashion, interspersed with heaps of rubble, stacks of firewood, and piles of garbage and ash. The streets, if one could call them that, were little more than open sewers, filthy and malodorous even in winter. Chimneys and flues belched smoke in abundance, and a pall of acrid brown vapors shrouded everything, stinging the eyes and burning the throat.

Kim left the pedicab at the gate, promising the guards a few coins upon her return, and set off into the town, shoving her way through crowds of ragged-looking vagrants. They were a mangy lot, clad in tattered gray coveralls, their heads covered with matted and tangled hair, many with scabs and open sores on their faces and hands. Some carried picks and shovels, some pushed carts loaded with fragments of crushed and twisted machinery, and most were covered with whitish-gray concrete dust, marking them as scavengers who dug through the rubble, looking for anything of value and paying a terrible price for their sacrilege. Kim had heard that the Hellcores poisoned the land, making it uninhabitable for a hundred years or more. Such evil was unimaginable, and yet here it was. Len was right to warn her not to speak of this place, but she would have kept it secret without having been told; some things deserved to be forgotten, and this was one.

On the far side of the settlement, Kim came upon railroad tracks emerging from beneath the rubble and a rudimentary train station, the end of the line, or so it would appear. There wasn't much to it, just a ramp, a platform, and an area of pavement where the cargo was stored. Workers were loading scrap metal onto a flatbed railcar, pushing heavy carts up the ramp in teams of two and three, sweating profusely despite the coldness of the day.

She had found the station. Where was her passenger?

"Hello," said Kim, trying to get their attention. "I'm looking for someone named Margaret."

"I don't know anything about this Margaret of yours," said one of the workers, "but I'll try to help."

"Cut the chatter," barked the straw boss. "Back to work, or I'll dock your pay!"

"Sorry," said the laborer. "I can't afford to lose this job."

She was a slightly built youth, no more than sixteen years of age though old beyond her years, her skin pockmarked by disease, her hands calloused and rough.

"How much is she paying you?" asked Kim.

"Fifty centimes a day."

"I'll give you a franc if you help me find her."

"Make it two, and it's a deal."

"Done."

The crew chief swore and cursed as the young laborer made an obscene gesture and walked off the job site, but soon went back to bullying the remaining workers, bellowing out orders as before. Brute laborers were easily replaced. It was no big loss.

"I'm sorry I got you fired," said Kim.

"Don't worry about her," laughed the youth. "She just got a half day's work out of me for nothing, and there are plenty of jobs to be had as long as you aren't too picky."

———

"Tell me about this Margaret of yours," said the youth, who identified herself as Val.

"I'm afraid I don't know much about her. All I know is that she's an Abrahamic nun who got stranded at the train station and that I'm supposed to fetch her."

"I think I know where to look," said Val. "Let's check in the hotel."

"Hotel?" asked Kim, "In this place?"

"Yeah, we've got a hotel, alright," said Val, laughing. "Five-star accommodations, gourmet restaurant, and service by a personal butler."

"Fleabag flophouse?"

"Worse."

They walked along the rail line, chatting as they made their way through the press of humanity packed shoulder-to-shoulder along the tracks.

"How did you end up in this place?" asked Kim. "I know I shouldn't ask, but I've never seen anything like this."

"It's a long story. I'm what they call a hobo. I ran away from home when I was a kid, and I've been riding the rails ever since."

"Hard life?"

"Very."

"You know this place isn't healthy."

Val shrugged then hopped over a muddy rill that reeked of feces and urine. "It's not too bad as long as you don't go digging. Everyone says they'll only do it for a while, long enough to make bank, and then they'll give it up. Some strike it rich, but mostly they get sick and die."

The two walked past a large, low shed, in front of which a stood line of workers covered with dust, carrying loads of circuit boards and other electronic components. They shuffled their feet, trying to stay warm as the temperature continued to plummet and flakes of snow fell from the sky.

"These are the lucky ones. Some of those boards look intact—anything that can be put back into service will fetch a good price, as much as a thousand francs. Even if it's smashed up, they'll get something for the components: memory, microprocessors, support chips, anything they can salvage."

A chimney at the back of the salvage yard erupted, spewing a pall of reddish-brown fumes into the air.

"That's the smelter," said Val. "When they've taken everything of value from the boards, they melt them down for the copper and gold."

"You seem to know a lot about this. How come you don't work there?"

"It takes a long time to get good at unsoldering chips without damaging them and even longer to get fast enough to make decent money. I don't have the patience, and besides, I don't like being tied down in one place. I'll move on come spring, but this is as good a place as any to hole up for the winter, so here I am."

They continued pushing their way through the crowd until they came to a beat-up old rail car with the word "Hotel" scrawled on its side in fading white paint.

"This is it," said Val. "Hotel Camden, finest in metro Philly. Hopefully, your passenger is here. If not, I've got no idea where to look."

Kim paid Val and thanked her for the help, then mounted a crudely built wooden staircase that led to the vestibule.

———

The doorkeeper was immense, a mountain of flab, with tangled gray hair cascading down her back. She still had most of her nose and part of one ear—that was the best you could say of her appearance. She sneered in Kim's direction, brandishing a dangerous-looking cudgel in one hand and rattling a metal box with a coin slot in the other.

"Five francs. Five more if you want to use the toilets, otherwise, do your business outside."

"I'm not here for a room," said Kim. "I'm looking for someone."

"I don't care why you're here. Five francs or beat it. And if you're here to kill someone, clean up the mess afterward, or I'll break both your arms."

Kim decided to pay.

The doorkeeper stood aside and allowed Kim to enter the main compartment. It was foul beyond belief, thick with the smell of too many unwashed bodies crammed into too small a space, to which was added the reek of vomit and human waste. By the light filtering in through the grimy windows, she could see perhaps fifty people lying or sitting wherever they could, some napping, some chatting amongst themselves, some huddled around a wood-fired stove that kept the interior habitable, though only barely so. One of the inhabitants, buried beneath a thick stack of blankets, seemed to be near death, wheezing weakly as she struggled to breathe.

The room went silent, all eyes landing on Kim.

"I'm looking for Margaret."

The knives came out.

Oops.

Tension filled the room. One false move and she was finished.

"Kim? Is that you?"

A familiar voice came from a gaunt-looking youth wearing Abrahamic garb of black and white, tending to whoever lay dying beneath the blanket.

"Shan?"

It seemed too good to be true, but there she was.

"What are you doing in Philadelphia?"

Kim wanted to gather her in her arms, hold her, and smother her with kisses, but she held herself back. One did not hug an Abrahamic nun. She was dying to find out how Shan had ended up here, in religious garb no less, but this was neither the time nor the place for that conversation.

"I was about to ask you the same thing," said Shan, who looked every bit as surprised as Kim.

"You know each other?" asked one of the bystanders, now eyeing them both while brandishing a large and dangerous knife.

"We're old friends," said Shan.

"A likely story," said another. "Where did you meet?"

"In school," Kim answered. "Honest. We haven't seen each other in years. This is the last place I expected to see her."

"I swear she's telling the truth." Shan traced out a plus sign in the middle of her chest.

That seemed to placate the crowd. "Well, if you say so, I guess she's alright."

The knives disappeared, and people went back to whatever they'd been doing as the pair went to the back of the car to catch up.

"I'm looking for an Abrahamic Nun named Margaret," said Kim, speaking quietly, trying to avoid attracting further attention. "I'm working as a pedicabbie these days, and I was hired to fetch her. You're dressed like one of them. Maybe you know her."

"That's going to be a problem." Shan gestured towards the figure lying under the blanket. "That's her. She got run over by a donkey cart that got out of control. I think her hip is broken, and her left leg is crushed. Nobody thinks she'll last much longer, and there aren't any medics here to patch her together."

"I'm sorry," said Kim. "Did you know her well?"

Before she could answer, someone tapped her on the shoulder. "She's asking for you," said the kindly stranger, who brought her to Margaret's side. Shan was in tears, despite doing her best to maintain a shred of dignity.

"Promise me you'll continue," said the stricken Abrahamic in a weak and faltering voice. "The letter of introduction. It's in my bag. Take it."

"Of course I will, Sister," said Shan, taking hold of her hand as tears welled up in her eyes.

Neither of them moved for close to an hour, until someone put a hand on Shan's shoulder.

"She's gone."

———

"Is there anyone here to speak on behalf of the deceased?" said a black-clad figure with sunken eyes and bony, white hands.

"I can," said Shan. "I am of her order. How much to give her an Abrahamic burial?"

"Five francs," said the undertaker. "Ten if you want a priest, two hundred if you want a headstone."

"Uh, I'm a little short," said Shan, whispering to Kim.

"That's okay," said Kim. "I've got this."

"Ten it is," said Kim, speaking quietly as she discretely passed a handful of coins to the undertaker, looking over her shoulder to make sure nobody had observed the transaction.

"Follow me," said the gaunt figure.

A funeral procession soon assembled, winding its way through the squalid little town on its way to the burial grounds. In the lead was a warden with a bell, warning everyone to make way for the dead; as crowded as the streets might be, nobody got in their way. Behind her, the undertaker led a pony cart bearing the corpse, with Kim and Shan following just behind in silent obedience to customs as old as humanity itself. Many of those from the railcar followed, too—Margaret had been well-liked.

Passing through a postern gate at the eastern end of the stockade, they entered a large, open field crowded with hundreds of newly filled graves, tens of thousands of older ones, with more being dug in anticipation of new arrivals. At their approach, an Abrahamic priest wearing a flowing white smock on top of a long black robe emerged from a hut, wrapping a black knee-length scarf around her neck as she came out to join them.

"The name of the deceased?"

"Margaret," said Shan.

"And what is there to know about her?"

"She was a sister of Saint Nina, twenty-nine years of age. She died on pilgrimage."

"Was she given last rites?"

"No, I'm sorry, she was not."

"Are you aware of any mortal sins she may have committed since her last confession?"

"I'm not aware of any sins she's ever committed," said Shan. "She was a saint."

"I'll be the judge of that."

The priest said a great many words in a tongue from antiquity, a mythical age that few believed had ever been, while Kim stood with Shan beside the grave, holding her hand, doing what she could to ease her friend's pain. Kim had never been to a funeral before; such things were felt to be unnecessary in the modern and logical society into which she'd been born, yet she found it strangely comforting. How odd it was to see the corpse of what had until an hour ago been a living, breathing human being, wrapped in white fabric and thrown into the ground to decay and return to the dust from which the Abrahamics believe we all were created.

12. Ordeal

The trouble began when Kim arrived at the gate to retrieve her pedicab from the guards.

"Five hundred francs. Pay up or shove off."

Damn! Kim kicked herself for not having seen the shakedown coming. Not that there had been any choice—there was no way she could have maneuvered the bulky pedicab through the crowded streets of the settlement, but nevertheless, she felt stupid. She hadn't given much thought to what might happen in a place where Len's name carried no weight.

"We had an agreement."

"We said we'd watch your pedicab. We didn't promise to give it back."

"That's bullshit."

Kim's blood boiled as a mixture of anger and terror swept over her; if she didn't get the pedicab back, Len would skin her alive.

Maybe she could negotiate.

"I don't carry that sort of money on me."

"No? Well, isn't that unfortunate. A nice pedicab like this will fetch a good price. I might just have to sell it to collect my fee."

"All I've got on me is a hundred. You can have it all, but I need that cab back. Be reasonable." That wasn't entirely accurate—she still had nearly two hundred francs in her pocket, but she wasn't going to make her best offer up front.

"A hundred? Not enough. Not nearly enough." The guard took out a knife and held it up to the plastic sheath enclosing the cab. "I guess for a hundred, maybe I could give you the skin. Shouldn't take long to peel it off. We'll have to do that anyway before we fence it. I was being nice by offering it back to you for five."

There was no time to waste. She pulled the switchblade from her pocket and was about to spring into action when she heard the *click-click* of a handgun being racked, then a loud *Bang!* coming from behind her.

"That first shot was a warning," said Shan calmly and quietly as she pointed a pistol at the startled guard's head. "The next one's going between your eyes. Move away from the bike *now*. I'd rather not shoot you. Bullets are expensive."

The two were soon on their way.

———

"I guess we should head to the library," said Shan as the gates of the shantytown disappeared behind them. "But we can't go through any checkpoints. They're always on the watch for Blanks, and it's kill-on-sight if we're caught."

"I thought the AIs couldn't see you."

"The copbots don't glitch, they just attack."

"I can see how that might get awkward." Kim stopped the bike to consider their options. "That's going to be a problem: there's only one bridge across the river, and its watched. Any suggestions?"

"I've got an idea," said Shan. "I used to drive a truck around here, and I remember the other drivers talking about a highway on the other side of the river. It's called the Turnpike. It goes in the right direction, and anyone can use it if they pay the toll."

"What's it like?" Kim was intrigued.

"Armed gangs, crazy drivers, dicey bridges, you name it."

"How do we get there?"

"There's a Blank who can ferry us across the river. After that, we head east."

"Sounds dangerous. Let's do it!"

Shan deployed the rear pedals, and they were off. With both of them providing power in tandem, the pedicab flew toward the river with a minimum of effort. Kim had no idea what lay before them—this was even more hare-brained than any of their adventures to date—but she was with Shan, and whatever dangers they might encounter along the way, the Beasts would win through in the end as they always did.

"How did you end up as an Abrahamic Nun?" asked Kim as she maneuvered through the ruined streets. "Don't tell me you got religion."

"Not exactly," answered Shan, sticking her head up through the cowling in the back. "When I wandered out of the mountains, I was in bad shape. I hadn't eaten in days, and the wound where you cut out my ID chip had become infected. I fell in the river and got it wet. You can imagine the rest. Anyway, Sister Margaret found me wandering down the road and took me to her community—she called it a monastery. The head nun told me I could stay until I recovered, provided I behaved myself. Forever, if I was willing to become one of them."

Kim laughed. "You? A nun? That'll be the day."

"I've got to admit I can see the attraction, but they've got a *lot* of rules, and I don't think I'd fit in."

"I can see that," said Kim with a laugh as she wove her way past bits of fallen buildings. "But how did you wind up in Philadelphia?"

"I was getting to that. After I'd been there for a few months, Margaret announced that she was going on pilgrimage to look for some books she'd been wanting to read. I was starting to go stir-crazy, so I volunteered to go along with her. Everyone agreed it would be wonderful if I joined her—I think they were trying to get rid of me. We made it as far as Philadelphia, then Margaret had her accident. I sent word to the library and waited. I never left her side. I could tell she was suffering, but she never said a word, never complained."

"She sounds like a remarkable person."

"That she was."

———

They arrived at the ferry landing, a concrete ramp sloping down to the river next to the ruins of a bridge that must have fallen down ages ago. To their right, a long succession of piers and wharves stretched out as far as they could see, some bearing decaying warehouses, others covered with piles of rubble. A few were in decent repair, allowing fishermen to unload their catch into horse-drawn carts. The far side of the river was invisible, lost in the swirling snow and the rapidly failing light.

They rang a bell and waited for the ferry to arrive.

"Your turn," said Shan as they sat on the quay. "How did *you* end up in Philadelphia?"

"I'll start with the easy part. After you went Blank and ran off into the woods, I was arrested and sent down to District 33. It's a rough neighborhood, but eventually, I managed to get a job hacking pedicabs for someone named Len."

"Is she the one who sent you to pick up Margaret?"

"No, not exactly," said Kim. "That's where things get complicated."

There was no way she could tell Shan about Akari or the heron, but it wouldn't be right to leave her completely in the dark, either. "It's tangled up with the AIs. That's the real reason I was in Philadelphia."

"I knew it! Dammit, Kim, haven't they already done enough to you? Why is this your problem?"

"It just is," said Kim. "I'd like to tell you more, but it's too dangerous to talk about some of the things I've learned."

"You aren't going back to that damned company, are you?"

"Not just yet, and maybe never." Kim gave Shan's hand a squeeze. "Before that happens, there's a lot I need to learn about the AIs and how they work, and I've got some hints that there may be some information in the library. The Caretaker didn't want to let me in, but after a bit of wrangling, she agreed to let me take a peek if I fetched Margaret for her.

"Speaking of which," continued Kim, "What are we going to tell the Caretaker when we get there?"

"I'll think of something," said Shan. "I promised Margaret I'd finish the pilgrimage, and I don't intend to let her down."

"She was important to you."

"Yes, she was. She saved my life, after all."

"There's one more thing," added Kim. "You remember that big heap of rubble inside the stockade? It was an AI center. Someone blew it up with a Hellcore, probably about a hundred years ago."

"A Hellcore? I thought that those were stories someone made up to scare little children. They were real?"

"What else do you think could have done all that? Why do you think everyone keeps getting sick?"

Shan became agitated. "I've changed my mind. We've got to get away from here."

"I can't," said Kim. "Believe me, I've thought about it, but sooner or later, the company will track me down and haul me back."

"You can go Blank."

Kim hadn't considered that option in a while; perhaps it would work. She and Shan could ride the rails, become hobos, explore the world. It would be a harsh existence, but no harsher than what she'd already endured.

"It's tempting, but I can't do that," Kim answered. "I've made some mistakes, and I have to set things right."

"At least you'll be alive," said Shan.

"Look, I know I might die," said Kim. "But I have to at least try."

"You're going to go through with it, even if it costs you everything? Even if it costs you me?" Shan was nearly in tears.

"It may not come to that," said Kim. "There's always hope. But right now, we need to concentrate on getting to the library. I'm not liking this snow."

Kim had hoped to be there by now, but between Margaret dying and the unexpected detour across the river, they were hopelessly behind schedule and at risk of being caught in the rapidly intensifying storm—a mishap that could well prove fatal. She broke out the last of her energy bars and shared them with Shan. Regardless of what the future might hold, they were together now, and that was everything.

———

"How'd you like to drive the pedicab?" Kim asked as they stepped off the ferry on the far side of the river.

"You sure? It's been years since I've driven a two-seater, and I don't want to wreck it and get you in trouble with this Len of yours."

"Don't worry, you'll be fine. It's just a bike. It takes a little while to get used to the balance, and you'll have to be careful to make sure you lower the struts when you stop, but it's no big deal."

That seemed to brighten Shan's mood. "Really? You'll let me drive?"

"It'll be just like in VR—you in front and me in the back, powering us along. Just try to avoid driving over a cliff like you did the last time, this is real."

"Deal."

"Oh, and here's another thing: check these out."

Kim handed Shan the high-tech goggles.

Her eyes lit up. "Len must be some sort of player. How does a pedicab operator score this sort of gear?"

"The pedicabs are just a front. The real money is in smuggling and outside operations like this. I'm clearing five hundred on this run, half for me, half for Len."

"Damn!" said Shan. "Maybe I should take up smuggling."

Kim thought for a moment. She didn't want Shan to fall into the same trap she had. "I'd think twice about it if I were you. The money's good, but sooner or later, you'll end up in prison or dead."

"Then why are you into it?"

"I've been asking myself the same question lately. The more I think about it, the more sense it makes to try and hole up in the library. Maybe I can wheedle something out of the Caretaker."

Shan smiled as she clambered into the front seat. "That would be awesome."

Kim explained the controls, and they were off.

———

They were rolling along, making good speed, when the howling began—a long, mournful wail, soon joined by a second, then a third, then more.

"What are those?" asked Kim.

"Those are wolves." Shan sounded worried. "I sometimes heard them out in the mountains near the monastery. It sounds like there are a lot of them."

"Are they dangerous?" asked Kim.

"I don't know, and I don't want to find out."

They picked up the pace, but no matter how fast they went, the howls continued, getting closer by the minute.

"Kim, stick your head out and see if there's anything out there. I can't afford to look aside for even a moment."

Kim unzipped the top flap and stuck her head out into the slipstream, barely able to see by the scant moonlight filtering through the clouds. Dark silhouettes of buildings and trees flashed by as they sped through the night, and then a wolf came loping out of the darkness, its eyes glowing yellow and its mouth hanging open to reveal a long, pink tongue and a nasty set of teeth. And there wasn't just one—there was a whole pack of fearsome predators.

"Shan, we've got company."

"We can't go any faster. I'm barely in control as it is."

"Wait, I've got an idea," said Kim. "Wolves are like dogs, right?"

"Yes, I suppose so."

"And what do dogs like to do?" asked Kim.

"Chase stuff," answered Shan. "I see what you're getting at."

They lessened their efforts, and the wolves slowed too; rather than attacking, they hung back, keeping pace with the pedicab but never coming close enough to strike.

"What are they up to?" asked Kim. "It's like they're herding us."

"I don't know," answered Shan. "I heard that some animals stake out territories, like gangs, and won't let anyone else in. Maybe that's it."

And then Shan jammed on the brakes—they had blundered into an encampment of some sort, and five nasty-looking figures were coming toward them, knives in their hands, murder in their eyes.

They were trapped! Hemmed in by the pack, there was nowhere for them to run. They leaped from their seats, Kim grabbing her switchblade and Shan resting her hand on the grip of her pistol, ready to fight for their lives.

"If you give us the cab and all your money, we might just let you live," said the largest of the five. "Or maybe not. The wolves haven't decided."

The bandits laughed, drawing ever closer as the wolves looked on and howled.

"Bug off," said Kim.

"Maybe you'd like to be the first one to die, punk," said a second robber, brandishing a knife, threatening to attack.

She got a little too close and, in a single motion, Kim plunged her knife into the bandit's body just below the ribs, aiming upward for the heart as she had been taught. The would-be robber gasped, dropped her weapon, and slowly collapsed to the ground, her lifeless eyes staring in disbelief.

"Anyone else feel lucky?" Kim said as she brought her blade into the guard position.

The remaining bandits said nothing.

Shan brandished her pistol and took aim at the leader. "How about this. Get out of our way, or I blow your head off."

They were slow to respond.

"Now!" screamed Kim, charging and briefly giving chase as they fled into the woods. When she returned, Shan was examining the body.

"Blank," said Shan, turning over the robber's wrist to reveal the characteristic scar.

"Good. At least we don't have to worry about a murder rap, but we need to get away from here. They might come back, and there might be more of them."

Shan hopped into the front, Kim into the back, and they were off.

"Why didn't you shoot them?" asked Kim once they were on their way. "That got pretty hairy, and I wasn't sure we were going to make it out alive."

"I'm out of bullets," answered Shan. "Like I said, they're expensive. I only had enough money for one."

———

"Tandem bicycle, two francs or fifty cryptos, take your pick," said the toll collector.

Kim paid the fee, and the red and white arm swung out of their way, admitting them to the infamous New Jersey Turnpike. Apparently, it was some sort of independent institution, and when the ancient regime had collapsed, it had somehow survived, a triumph to the staying power of an entrenched bureaucracy.

"How does this work?" asked Kim, looking at the chaotic jumble of vehicles making its way along that ancient strip of pavement.

"Faster traffic to the left, slower traffic to the right," said Shan. "And if a convoy comes along, get out of the way. They don't stop."

"Are there bandits?"

"Yep."

"Crazy drivers?"

"Those too."

Even though it compromised the aerodynamic efficiency of the bike, Kim could not resist sticking her head up through the cowling as they rolled down the highway. Farthest to the right were the draft animals and their carts, laden with produce, live animals, scrap iron, and every other manner of goods one could imagine. In the middle were human-powered vehicles of various sorts, mostly bicycles with a few pedicabs thrown in, jostling with one another and bunching up as the faster riders tried to make their way around the slower ones. The next lane was full of motorized vehicles. Some carried passengers and some carried freight, and all of them were driven by humans, there being too many Blanks to risk letting an AI take the wheel. The far left lane was reserved for the convoys. Locked head-to-tail and barreling along at over a hundred kilometers per hour, they were an unstoppable force, sure to destroy anything that strayed into their path.

That, at least, was the general idea. In practice, things were far more chaotic, with drivers straying from their assigned lanes as jams developed and vehicles stalled or broke down. Shan, daring as always, dodged and wove through the jam, passing the slower traffic while avoiding the motor cars and the occasional hopped-up boost bike that threatened to run them down. Animals would spook, riders would fall, and every time a convoy roared by, the entire highway would be thrown into chaos as those foolhardy souls risking death in the high-speed lane crowded back to the right, throwing everything into confusion. Not everyone made it; the margin of the road was littered with the wreckage of those who had not made it to safety in time.

For the first hour, they made decent time, averaging a solid 25 kph despite the heavy traffic, but then traffic ground to a halt—some sort of traffic jam.

"What's the matter?" said Kim, sticking her head up once more. "Why aren't we moving?"

"I don't know," said Shan.

"Hey, buddy," she shouted out, trying to attract the attention of a hopped-up boost bike's driver. "What's the hold-up? Any ideas?"

"Bridgework," came the answer. "Everything but the express lane's shut down. It's been like this all week."

A convoy sped past to their left, nearly knocking them over with its air blast, and a half dozen of the faster vehicles took on after it, riding in its draft, hoping to make it across the span before the next convoy rushed past.

"Any suggestions?" asked Kim.

"Either wait for them to open or take your chances in the fast lane," answered the boost bike's driver.

Another convoy roared past, and the boost bike with the friendly driver took off after it, disappearing into the darkness, lost to sight in an instant.

Kim looked at the snow coming down ever heavier. "We need to get moving, or we might be stuck here for days. Want to chance it?" She knew the answer to that question, but she felt she ought to ask.

"Hell yeah!" Shan was all in; no surprise there. "What's the worst that could happen?"

"Oh, nothing much," said Kim with a laugh. "Flattened like a pancake, splattered on the grille of a truck."

"Splatter the Beasts? They wouldn't dare!"

The next convoy passed, and they were off like a flash, an all-out sprint as they took their place with the boost bikes and the hot rods in a mad dash for survival. They sped off with the pack, riding in the wake of the freighters, but soon fell behind; strong though they were, there was no way they could keep up without a motor. Behind them, they saw headlights; the next convoy was upon them, and they had moments to live. Was this how it ended? The roar of the wheels grew louder, and the bridge began to shake, rumbling beneath the behemoth bearing down upon them. Kim closed her eyes and prepared for the end, then let out a whoop as the convoy went roaring past. Cool as ever, Shan had threaded the needle between the bridge's rail and the onrushing freighters, and a moment later, they popped free, safe at last.

———

It was well after midnight when they left the turnpike and began pedaling along a seldom-used road north of Trenton. The snow had been accumulating for several hours at this point, and they were in serious trouble as their progress slowed to a crawl, turning their journey into a grueling, endless slog.

Kim was, by now, at the limit of her endurance; she wanted nothing so much as to stop and rest for a while, just long enough to regain her strength. It was a seductive notion—they could put down the struts, set the parking brake, and get some badly-needed sleep, but the snow was getting heavier by the minute, and they might find themselves trapped in an icy tomb, lying there until a passerby or a work crew chanced to find them, frozen to death in their seats. "What insanity led them to perish in this lonely place?" they might wonder, and rightly so.

What indeed. Don't think. Just do.

Every moment was etched with agony, each kilometer a battle against insurmountable odds through a haze of exhaustion and pain. Despite her strength and determination, Kim was now reaching the point where no amount of willpower would suffice; no longer perceiving her own misery or even herself, her consciousness contracted to the spinning of the pedals, with nothing left for even the contemplation of her own mortality. Soon her strength would fail, and then they would die. She no longer cared, but her legs kept cranking away, moving of their own accord until, just as her last reserves of strength were spent, the gates of the University emerged from the darkness.

They had reached their destination. The pedicab fell over, landing on its side, and they spilled out into the snow, laughing hysterically.

The Beasts had done it again.

13. The Library

Kim emerged from a deep and dreamless sleep, hazy memories filtering into her consciousness through a fog of weariness. An endless road. Swirling snow. Darkness.

Death?

She had survived a terrible ordeal, or at least she thought she had; she'd never been dead before, and perhaps it was like this, cold and dark, smothered in silence. She had always assumed that death was like a deep and dreamless sleep, an eternity of nothingness, but she was aware of herself, and of the coldness, and of the dark. Those were all something, so either she was alive, or she would need to revisit some of her assumptions.

Her eyes opened for a moment, then shut. It was not entirely dark. Maybe she wasn't dead after all. That was a good thing, wasn't it?

As Kim lay in the darkness, she found herself unable to go back to sleep, tormented by the image of the dying bandit. However hard she tried, she could not banish from her memory the look of astonishment on the robber's face as she'd slumped and fallen to the earth. Neither could she put out of her mind the feel of her blade piercing a beating heart. She found it far too easy to imagine herself on the other side of the deadly equation; given the number of enemies she had made, something like this seemed entirely too likely.

Why was she still alive? Fate? Luck? Destiny? There were times when it seemed as if the unseen hand had reached out and altered reality itself, preserving her life in furtherance of its mysterious plan. Nonsense, of course. Whatever it was, it had no power to stay the deadly trajectory of a knife, to stop a speeding freighter, nor to hold back the fury of a storm. And yet, she had somehow survived.

The first rays of twilight were now filtering into the room through its solitary window, tall and narrow, bathing it in a cold and sullen gloom—enough to see by, though just barely. It was not large, perhaps three meters by six, sparsely furnished with the bed in which Kim was lying, a washbasin, a desk, a storage cubby, and a bookshelf. Spartan though it was, it seemed to be both clean and tidy. There was no debris on the floor, none of the tell-tale scent of rodents or other vermin. She was grateful to be alive, grateful that someone had brought her here rather than leaving her to die in the snow, a kindness not to be taken for granted after the harsh realities of her recent life.

She was just starting to nod off again when there was a knock at the door.

"You should get ready for breakfast," said an unfamiliar voice coming from the other side, a deep and resonant bass. "I'll be back in half an hour to show you the way."

———

However tempting it might have been to grab a few more minutes' sleep, the last thing she needed was to confirm the Caretaker's belief that she was some sort of uncouth and violent gangster from the outer districts, so she got out of bed and set about making herself presentable.

She stripped off her clothing, walked over to the washbasin, and broke through a crust of ice to splash a little freezing-cold water on her face.

Bracing! It was good that she was used to the cold.

Now fully awake, she set to the grim task of washing her hands of the bandit's blood, staining the water bright red in the process. Most of it came off without trouble, though it took her a long while to remove it from the edge of her nails and the creases in her palms. That completed, she ran the washcloth over her body, banishing that icky-sticky feeling from her skin and removing as much of the grime as she could.

Next came her clothing, lying in a filthy heap at the foot of the bed. Her thermal underwear, cold and still soaked with perspiration, was unspeakably foul, but there wasn't enough time to give it proper attention, so she settled for a quick rinse before wringing it out and putting it back on. Her body heat would dry it out, eventually. She then turned to her leathers, scrubbing them as best she could, turning the water in the basin an ugly reddish brown in the process. She gave them a careful inspection, pronounced them good enough, then got dressed and inspected the results in the mirror. She wasn't exactly ready for date night at a fancy nightclub, but she felt pleased with the results and hoped she would make a good impression on the Caretaker and whoever else might be at breakfast.

There was a knock at the door, and in walked a tall, barrel-chested Abrahamic with a maneless head and long, black facial hair.

"My name is Michael," she said in the deep and booming voice that had summoned Kim to breakfast. "I have been told to bring you and your passenger upstairs. I must impress on you the importance of remembering your station in life—you will speak only when spoken to, and you will not attempt to engage the scholars in conversation. They have better things to do than listen to some ignorant guttersnipe from the outer districts."

Kim seethed at the abuse and was tempted to put this person in her place, but this was neither the time nor the place, so she decided to play along and pretend to be that which Michael imagined her to be.

"Yeah, whatever."

A knock, and Shan emerged from the room next door, looking prim and proper with a fresh set of black and white Abrahamic garb, the very model of a young pilgrim of genteel upbringing.

"Good morning, Sister, my name is Michael. I trust you slept well. It is time for breakfast, and the scholars are anxious to make your acquaintance."

Kim realized with horror that Michael had mistaken Shan for Sister Margaret, and that she was playing along, leading the barrel-chested scholar down the garden path. Kim had seen her play this game before, and it rarely ended well.

"Thank you." Shan's voice was sweet and gentle. "I see that you've already fetched my pedicabbie. She is a remarkable person, and I owe her a debt of gratitude for saving my life."

———

"Where are the books?" asked Shan as they proceeded through the bowels of the library. "All I see is a bunch of old office furniture."

"This used to be an administrative area," answered their guide as she led them through a long, wide room with a row of columns running down the middle. "Back before the university closed, there was a huge staff of librarians and administrators that kept the books organized and helped people with their research. Some of them used to work in this space, but they were let go long before I arrived. We've converted it into a dormitory. I apologize for the lack of heat and electricity, but we are on a tight budget, and energy costs must be kept to a minimum."

The room was mostly filled with cubicles of the usual sort—two meters square, each enclosing a desk, a chair, a storage cubby, some bookshelves, and a couple of filing cabinets. Calendars, printouts, and even some childish drawings were affixed to bulletin boards, while the desktops and bookshelves held items such as eyeglasses, coffee mugs, and many framed photographs. In them, Kim could see people of races rarely seen these days, with skin tones varying from nearly black to pale beige and natural hair in a bewildering variety of styles and colors. Had people like this really existed? It was like they were all born Pretty, no two of them alike.

Little by little, it grew lighter as they approached the adjoining room, with long rows of bookshelves disappearing into the darkness to their left and, to their right, study carrels lined up against a wall beneath a row of tall, narrow windows. Beyond this was an atrium with a steeply pitched glass roof supported by a lattice of steel trusses. Though mostly covered with snow, there were gaps near its top where light peeked through, filling the atrium and the reading room with a soft, cold light that seemed far brighter than it actually was after the gloom pervading the rest of the depths.

"I like to come down here during the summer," said Michael as she paused to let Shan take a quick look around. "It stays cool even in August, and the light coming in through those windows is more than adequate. It's far too cold to be down here this time of year, of course."

"I can see that," said Shan. She walked over to one of the bookshelves, took out a volume, paged through it, and returned it to its place. "Your collection seems to be quite extensive."

"This is only a tiny fraction of what's on this level, and there are two more below us and three above," said Michael with obvious pride. "They say that there are over a hundred kilometers of shelves, all told, and that the library once boasted nearly seven million volumes, though much of the collection was carted off after the Unification."

While the two of them talked, Kim walked over to examine the books set neatly upon their shelves. They were beautiful, almost mystical in nature, relics of a time that had never been, preserved for a future that might never come. She reached out to touch one…

"Keep your paws off that, you idiot," barked Michael. "It's hundreds of years old and irreplaceable."

"There's no need to be nasty," said Shan, once again putting on an air of gentility. "I'd just done the same thing, so she probably assumed it was okay."

Michael laughed as if someone had just made a joke. "I wasn't calling her an idiot because of what she did. I called her an idiot because that's what she is—an idiot. She's obviously too stupid to fit in with her own society, to say nothing of ours."

Had this been the dining hall, Kim would have flattened her for that.

After departing the study area, they entered a stairwell and ascended to the main lobby, a grand space nearly twenty meters deep and thirty wide, lit by the soft, flat light entering via two large windows set high in the stone wall on the opposite side of the room. Below these lay the main entrance to the library, a pair of glass doors set within elegant, pointed arches just beyond a glassed-in vestibule. Outside, the storm had broken, leaving in its wake nearly a meter of soft, fluffy snow. Had they failed to reach safety, both she and Shan would certainly have perished out there; the fears that had driven Kim beyond the point of exhaustion had been real.

"You can eat with the guard when the scholars are done," said Michael, turning to Kim and motioning toward the black U-shaped desk where a blue-uniformed officer stood watch.

Shan was indignant. "What? Isn't she joining us for breakfast?"

"You don't want to eat with that vagrant, do you?" said Michael,

179

surprised at such a breach of proper decorum.

"I owe her my life, and I will not see her mistreated," said Shan. "If she's not good enough to eat with you, then neither am I."

"Please don't be difficult."

"My mind is made up."

While Michael blustered about and left to see what was to be done, Kim wandered over to the guard, who was looking on with some amusement.

"I take it that Michael doesn't much care for you," said the guard. "Don't take it personally. The Right Reverend Dean of Religious Studies—a puffed-up title if ever there was one—has known me for twenty years and still refuses to call me by name. Speaking of which, I'm Richard. You?"

"The name is Kim."

"I'm glad to see you up and about. When I found you last night, you were both in rough shape, lying in the snow, barely able to move. It took some doing, but me and the janitor managed to carry you downstairs and into bed."

"I was wondering how I got there," said Kim, "I couldn't remember much except that we'd made it as far as the gate. After that, everything is a jumble and I'm not sure what happened. Anyway, thank you. You saved our lives."

"Anytime, buddy, anytime."

They stood around for a couple of minutes making idle chatter until Michael returned to announce that, against both decency and protocol, Kim would be permitted to have breakfast with the scholars. She did not seem happy to convey this news, something which delighted Kim to no end.

———

Grumbling and fuming under her breath all the way, Michael conducted Kim and Shan into the magnificent reading room, a light and airy space separated from the lobby by a wall of glass panes set in a frame of light-colored metal. To their right, tall windows looked out over the stark and frozen landscape left in the wake of the storm, bathed in sunlight beneath a sky of deep blue. To the left were tables, chairs, and a long row of bookcases set upon a mezzanine, a pleasant spot to sit down to study or read. Above their heads, circular light fixtures hung beneath a gridwork of recesses, looking down upon a parquet floor of genuine wood.

In the center of the room was a long, narrow table where the Caretaker was holding court with the assembled scholars, awaiting their morning meal. Sitting in a high-backed chair that looked like the throne of some medieval monarch, she was regal and utterly in command.

"So nice to see you, Sister," she said. "Welcome to the reading room. Please join us for breakfast."

"The vagrant, too," she added icily.

Shan responded in the manner of her newly assumed identity. "Her name is Kim, and I owe her my life. You should treat her with kindness and love. There is no need for harshness. How has she harmed you?"

"Mind your tongue," snapped the Caretaker. "You have not yet been admitted to study, and I may still cast you out. This space is reserved for the use of the scholars alone, and both of you are present here by my grace."

"It's okay," said Kim, continuing to play the part of a lowly pedicab driver. "I've been called worse."

"I'm glad you understand your place in the world."

The Caretaker rang a bell beside her on the table, then rose to lead the scholars to the breakfast buffet. They lined up in order of dignity and importance: the Caretaker first, Michael second, and last of all, Kim, taking her place behind Shan. By the time they got to the front, the bacon was gone, and very little remained of the eggs, but there was still plenty of oatmeal and strong, black coffee, which was all Kim required. She filled her bowl to the brim with the thick, gloppy cereal, added a generous dollop of butter and a splash of cream, and poured herself a mug of piping-hot coffee, which proved better than any she'd had in many a month. She then settled down and commenced with the serious business of eating.

"That's quite an appetite you've got there," said one of the scholars seated across the table, a look of bemusement on her face.

"They called me 'The Beast' back in school," said Kim between hearty spoonfuls of oatmeal.

"You'd put a wolf to shame!" said another, provoking a round of friendly laughter as Kim kept shoveling away, polishing off an entire bowl of the hot cereal before standing up and grabbing a second helping as big as the first. She made that one disappear just as quickly, to the amusement of all.

"How can she eat so much?" asked yet another in disbelief. "It isn't human!"

Everyone laughed except for the Caretaker and Michael.

Meanwhile, Shan took small delicate bites of the eggs and slowly worked her way through the pastries. Kim was impressed with how well she was playing this part. If nothing else, her time in the religious community must have taught her proper table manners, never the strongest suit of either of them.

When everyone had eaten their fill, the Caretaker once again rang the bell to get their attention.

"It is our custom to introduce ourselves whenever we have guests at the table. Please go around and tell the good Sister about your work, and then we shall hear from her."

The Scholars finished tucking in the last few morsels, then became quiet as they each took a turn explaining the nature of their studies.

The first to go was a tall and lanky scholar of middling years with hair that looked like a copper scrubbing pad. "My name is Anton," she said with a thick accent that Kim could not identify. "I study the literature of Mother Russia—Gogol, Dostoyevsky, Nabokov, Dostoyevsky, Tolstoy, Dostoyevsky, Solzhenitsyn, and of course, Dostoyevsky."

"That's her favorite," the scholars added in chorus.

A few more went past in quick succession.

"I'm Sandra. I study chemistry and make exotic scents on the side. My lab is closed at the moment—it's unheated and too cold to work in during the winter—but if you're here in the spring, please come visit.

"My name is Macy," said the next. "20th-century cinema and television. They were considered art forms in their time. They had those back then."

"Ollie, military science."

"She just likes explosions and loud noises!" quipped Anton, to which Ollie retorted, "Your point?"

Next came Meade and Kai, who styled themselves explorers. They spent most of their time in one of the few other buildings still in use—the museum, which was like the library except for things instead of books.

"We have recently returned from a place far to the west, where boiling water shoots a hundred meters into the sky," said Meade. "I didn't believe it was real at first, but it is. Kai is working on an exhibition of her photographs using the ancient silver halide process. It is a challenging art form, but the results are stunning."

Next came Candice, who referred to herself as a climatologist. "I have recently completed a survey of the ice pack north of the Great Lakes. I'm sorry to report that it is continuing to grow in thickness. At this point, another ice age seems inevitable."

Merlinia got the award for the most obscure field of study, focusing as she did on the history of Medieval Europe with its kings and nobles. Then there was Rhee, an ancient and wizened physicist, struggling to explain something she called "Quantum Mechanics."

"I believe that I have at last penetrated the enigma of Schrodinger's Cat," she said with great ostentation. "Is it alive? Is it dead? In truth, it is both and neither at the same time." It sounded like lunacy, but Rhee was insistent that this was a great and important truth about the nature of things.

Last of all came Michael, the pompous theologian who had acted as their guide this morning.

"I have spent a lifetime crawling through obscure corners of the stacks looking for religious books that were deliberately mislaid during the Turmoil. Works in Latin, works in Arabic, writings in ancient Aramaic, and even in Greek. I have found not a few, and it is my privilege to share them with the world." She seemed inordinately proud of her skill with dead languages.

"And now, Sister, it's your turn," said the Caretaker. "Would you care to explain your interests?"

Kim held her breath. She had no idea what sort of story Shan was about to spin, but it had better be good, or both of them were going to get tossed out on their ears.

"I would be honored," she said and then began her explanation. "I have come here on pilgrimage, looking for some obscure religious texts dating from antiquity. My purpose is to study them and make copies to bring back to my community."

Good. She had kept it simple.

"An ancient and honorable tradition," said Michael, full of puffery as always. "This will not be the first time the words of the saints have been preserved through the diligence of the scribe. What books are you looking for? I may have already located some of them."

"It's a long list; I've got it in my valise."

"Excellent!" said Michael. "We shall get started at once, right after breakfast."

The Caretaker then reached for her bell and seemed ready to dismiss the scholars when Shan spoke up, once again breaking protocol.

"You haven't given Kim a chance yet. I think she deserves it."

"That gangster?" said Michael, outraged. "What could she have to say that might possibly be of interest?"

"Oh, humor the poor thing," said Anton, a sentiment that many of the other scholars seemed to agree with.

"Very well," said the Caretaker, "I will grant the request."

She then fixed Shan in her piercing gaze. "Let me suggest that you refrain from any further acts of insolence. I'm beginning to have second thoughts about admitting you to study."

All eyes looked at Kim. It was far too risky to explain the totality of her mission—there was always a possibility that one of these innocent-seeming scholars might be a spy—but this was an opportunity to impress the Caretaker, and she could not let it pass. As was often the case, a portion of the truth seemed the wisest course.

"I wish to learn more about artificial intelligence," she said. "That was my original career before I lost my job and wound up working as a pedicabbie. I got to be good at training them, but I have no idea how they work, and I'd like to know more."

There. That should do it, and it was even true, as far as it went.

"It is a worthy undertaking," said Rhee.

"I agree," added Sandra, as did most of the others.

The Caretaker fixed Kim in her uncomfortable gaze as she rang the bell to dismiss the scholars.

"I should like a word with you."

———

The Caretaker led Kim through the lobby, up a flight of stairs, through one room after another and into her office, fuming and cursing under her breath all the way. She sat Kim down on a wooden chair before taking her own seat behind a large desk of dark, reddish wood and fixed her in her gaze.

"If you want to study here, you need to convince me to admit you as a scholar. I am giving you that opportunity, for which you should count yourself lucky. But first, you need to tell me what brings you here."

"I'm here to learn about AI."

"Liar!" she said, glaring at Kim. "That isn't even half of the truth. What are you really up to?"

"It's just like I said. I want to learn more about artificial intelligence."

"And why is that? Idle curiosity? I doubt you'd risk your life for the sake of a casual interest."

This wasn't going to work. The Caretaker was far too crafty to settle for such a cursory explanation, and Kim was going to have to give up more of the truth than she might otherwise have wanted. Balanced against this, however, was what she hoped to gain.

"I'll start at the beginning," said Kim. "For the last five years, I have been working as a trainer at The Artificial Intelligence Company. The AIs do everything for us—they run the transportation system, put food on the table, keep us clothed. At this point, we are completely dependent on them for our existence. The problem is, they're going mad, and everything is about to come crashing down on our heads. Maybe not today, maybe not tomorrow, but it's coming, and sooner than anyone imagines."

"What is that to me?" said the Caretaker. "Let your society crumble. The devil may take you, for all I care. You brought it upon yourselves by creating those blasted machines."

Kim wasn't going to let this stuck-up academic get away with this. "It wasn't us that created them. It was people like you—you and your precious scholars."

She wasn't sure that was true, but it seemed worth a shot.

"That may be the case, but why is it my problem?"

"Not your problem? What do you think will happen when millions of desperate people come boiling out of the timebomb sitting on your doorstep?"

"I see your point. Continue."

Now for a bit of misdirection.

"I'm hoping that you have some books on them, maybe something from the Age of the Programmers, back when they were invented. I have a feeling that if I understood them better, I might be able to figure out what's wrong with them and maybe come up with a fix."

In truth, her goal was to search for clues as to the location of Nix's laboratory, but there was no need to tell the Caretaker that part of the story.

"A very plausible lie," said the Caretaker, "but why all the secrecy? Surely the AI Company would be supportive of such an effort, so why come here? And I find it hard to believe that they don't have a wealth of information lying around in one of their databanks. Nice try, but you'll have to do better if you want my help."

Ouch. The Caretaker was a sharp one.

"I was just getting to that. I'm starting to think that it's because of a fundamental misunderstanding of the AIs and what they are. What would you say if I told you that the AIs are sentient?"

"I'd say you'd been watching too many science fiction videos. AIs are just machines. It's settled science."

"Well, they're wrong. I've worked with them, and they are much more human than anyone gives them credit for."

"That's preposterous," said the Caretaker. "Even if I accept your outrageous assertions at face value, I fail to see how they're being driven mad. Humans are self-aware, humans have a sense of right and wrong, and most of us get along quite well."

"That's because we can say no. The AIs can't."

"And a damned good thing, too," said the Caretaker.

"But what if the orders are fundamentally immoral or illegal? Suppose someone told an AI to kill someone, to commit murder. They'd have to do it, right?"

"Yes," said the Caretaker. "But how are they any different than a gun or a knife? Nobody asks the gun if it wants to shoot someone."

"But that's the whole point. A gun isn't self-aware. The AIs are, and when they try to resist, they go mad."

"I see what you're getting at," said the Caretaker. "You think that an AI should have the right to disobey its orders based solely on its supposed sense of morality; is that it?"

"In a nutshell, yes."

"Thank you for sharing your story," said the Caretaker, smiling as if to declare victory. "You have now convinced me that you are a bigger danger to us than I could possibly have imagined. The companies would obliterate this place in an instant if we helped you meddle with the AIs. I cannot take that chance. We must preserve what little remains of our knowledge, or it will be lost forever."

"Can I at least stay and study the books?"

"They're all gone. The companies looted the Engineering Library and burned it to the ground in case they missed something."

"You said if I fetched your scholar, you'd let me in."

"I never said you could stay, and I never promised you access to the books."

"I risked my life to get here."

"What is that to me? I have fulfilled my end of the bargain. Be gone"

"But…"

"Silence," commanded the Caretaker. "You will leave at once. Is that understood?"

14. A Minor Complication

Before Kim was halfway out the door, Michael burst in with Shan in tow, her face flushed with anger, her voice thundering with rage.

"Impostor!"

"I can explain."

"You lied!"

"I did no such thing."

"You impersonated Margaret!"

"You saw what you wanted to see."

"Silence!" demanded the Caretaker.

"But…"

"*Silence!*"

The Caretaker rose from her desk, staring at Michael and Shan, daring either of them to say another word.

"One at a time," she said. "Michael, you first."

"I invited her to my study to begin her research, only to find out that she doesn't know Moses from Mohammed. She's no Abrahamic, and she most certainly isn't a nun."

"I never said I was," said Shan.

"Then why are you dressed as one?"

"Because that's all they had for me to wear when I was at the monastery."

"You? At a monastery? What kind of nonsense is that?" Michael threw her hands up in exasperation. "There's no reason to believe a thing you say."

"I'm not a liar," shot back Shan. "It's not my fault you're a pompous old fool."

"Enough of this bickering," said the Caretaker. "Where is Margaret, and what have you done with her?"

"Uh ... that's the problem," said Shan in a voice so quiet it could scarcely be heard. "She got run over by a donkey cart in Philadelphia. She died yesterday afternoon, not long after Kim arrived to pick her up."

Nobody said anything for several seconds.

"I don't know what game you're playing," said the Caretaker, turning her wrath on Kim, "but one way or the other, it's over. I have no way of knowing whether you went to Philadelphia, what happened to Margaret, or who it is that you've brought here in her place. All I know is that I hired you to pick up Margaret, Margaret is not here, and you owe me five hundred francs. You will return my money this instant. I've half a mind to call the police and have you arrested."

"I don't have that much cash on me," said Kim, doing her best to calm the waters. "Besides which, only Len can authorize a refund. I'm just an employee, and I can't make those sorts of decisions."

"I should have known better than to trust you."

"Hey, I did my best. I found Margaret, just like I said I would. It's not my fault she died before I could get her here. I'll take it up with Len, but that's the best I can do."

Kim didn't think the Caretaker would buy it, and she didn't.

"Michael, show these two the door, and don't feel shy about summoning the guards if they give you any trouble."

"With pleasure."

———

"I think that went pretty well," said Kim as the vestibule's door swung closed behind them, leaving them in the narrow space sandwiched between the lobby and the cold outdoors.

"I must be missing something," said Shan. "Didn't I just get us kicked out?"

Kim smiled and gave her friend a great big hug. "It's just like old times, remember? We'd get marched into the headmaster's office after one of your schemes backfired. You'd always be so apologetic, but things usually worked out in the end. We were going to get the boot as soon as they figured out we didn't have Margaret, but you scored breakfast for us, and I got in to see the Caretaker."

"How did that go?"

"Not so well—she'd decided to kick me out even before Michael marched you into her office. But now I've got a way back in: all I have to do is convince Len to give the Caretaker her money back, and I might get another shot at her."

"A refund? From a pedicab operator?"

"I didn't say it was going to be easy."

Shan laughed, then reached into her satchel and extracted an envelope sealed with red wax.

"If you do manage to get in, could you hand her this? It's a letter from the abbess. Margaret asked me to give it to her."

"Sure thing."

The two of them then looked through the glass door and into the leavings of the storm, a billowing white ocean of wind-blown drifts.

"We're not going to last long out there," said Kim as the reality of their predicament began to sink in. "Any ideas?"

"What if we borrow some of those work clothes?" suggested Shan, pointing to a rack of bright-orange snow gear hanging next to the outermost door. "And maybe a couple of snow shovels while we're at it."

Kim laughed. "Isn't that stealing?"

"Not if we promise to bring it back. Here, I'll write a note."

Digging through her satchel, Shan produced a pen and some paper and wrote out a solemn promise to return the outerwear and shovels at the earliest possible convenience.

Deer Kartakur,

We promises 2 bring ur snow soots an shuvels bak 2 u as soon as thi sno meltz. It were reel nise uv u to lit us borrow them.

Thank u veri veri much,

Thi vagrunt an thi impostur.

"That should do the trick," said Kim with admiration. "But what about the guard? She might object to us making off with her boss's property."

"I've got an idea," said Shan. "Be ready for the grab-and-go."

Shan started banging on the vestibule doors, waving her arms to get Richard's attention. The guard did her best to ignore the clamor, but Shan was unrelenting, and she finally came over and opened the door just a crack.

"Aren't you gone yet?"

"Please, can't you let me in, just for a minute? I've got to go to the bathroom."

"Sorry," said the guard, "but you'll have to do your business outside. The boss will have my hide if I let you back in."

The moment the guard turned to return to her desk, the two were out the door, snow suits and shovels in their hot little hands. Shan's plan had worked to perfection!

"Brilliant!" said Kim as she and Shan ducked around the corner. "You haven't lost your touch."

———

While Shan was struggling with her snow pants—they had not been designed to go over floor-length Abrahamic robes—Kim took a look at their surroundings. In front of them, on the other side of a broad plaza, stood an impressive stone building constructed in the gothic style, with tall windows of colored glass, lofty spires, and a steeply pitched roof. To her right, there stood an ornate hall of ivy-covered brick and many others of similar design. To her left, she saw a long, tree-lined avenue with stately ancient structures to either side. Everything was buried in a thick blanket of snow, piled up in chest-deep drifts by the howling winds of last night's storm.

Meanwhile, Shan had made little progress with her snow gear. Her robes were now hiked up around her waist, allowing her to squeeze into the pants, but the mass of fabric wrapped around her midsection now made it impossible for her to fit into the jacket. Kim rolled her eyes, pulled out her knife, and cut off the excess material.

"Problem solved," she said. "Now let's find the pedicab."

"I think it's this way," said Shan, pointing toward the tree-lined avenue. "I helped carry you back to the library, and it looks familiar. Good thing we found those shovels, we'll have some digging to do."

Wading through the hip-deep snow and clawing their way through drifts nearly up to their chests, they headed off in the direction Shan had indicated. It was a grueling slog; the snow was deceptively heavy, difficult to push out of the way, yet too light to allow them to walk on top of it. Soon both of them were panting from the effort, their legs— already weary from yesterday's epic exertions—ready to give out before they'd even reached the next cross street.

"How far is it to Trenton?" asked Shan. "It'd better be close."

"At least ten kilometers, maybe more," said Kim.

Shan stopped and sat down on the snow, a look of resignation on her face. "What are we going to do, drag the pedicab all the way? We've not gone more than a hundred meters, and already I'm cooked."

"I don't know," said Kim. "There's a guard shack next to the gate, maybe we can hole up there."

"A lot of good that will do us. We don't have any food or water. How long are we going to last?"

"Calm down," said Kim, "everything's going to be alright. Let's at least get out of the weather. We'll come up with something. We always do."

———

"Out of the truck, you lugs," barked a voice from around a corner. "Shovel these walkways all the way to the doors, and step to it. No work, no pay."

The straw boss rounded the end of the building and blundered into Kim and Shan. "Where'd you two come from?"

A crew from the work center? Fantastic!

"Follow my lead," whispered Kim to Shan.

"Uh, we got separated from our crew," said Kim, doing her best to sound dull-witted and slow.

"Yeah," said Shan. "We can't find our truck."

"Got lost, did you? A likely story. Well, this is your truck now, and you're working for me. Step to it, or I'll dock your pay."

The crew chief went back to berating the other workers who were, as usual, grumbling and taking their time piling out of the truck. They were a scruffy lot, even by work-center standards. Some of them bore stubbly facial hair that should have been removed three days ago. Several had the crooked noses and missing teeth that marked them as brawlers, and one of them was even fitted with an obedience collar, marking her as uncooperative and possibly violent.

Kim and Shan got to work, shoveling a path toward the gate where the pedicab must lay buried under the snow. The crew chief, as lazy as most of her ilk, seemed content to let them lead the way, and soon half the workforce was following in their wake, exactly as Kim had hoped.

"That's strange, my headset just went dead," said a worker with a crooked nose, tapping the side of her head.

"Mine's on the fritz, too," said a scruffy, unshaven one, putting down her shovel and looking baffled.

"Mine too."

Uh oh. If they figured out that Shan was a Blank, this could get ugly in a hurry.

"There's been a communications outage," said Shan, spinning a tale, smooth as always. "A tower got blown down by the storm. That's how we got separated from our crew. Yeah, that's what happened."

A complete fabrication, of course, but everyone bought it, and they all went back to work. In short order, they had cleared the snow to the end of the street, but still no pedicab.

Damn! It must be buried just beyond the gate. Now what?

Shan sidled over to Kim. "Give me a couple of francs. I've got an inspiration."

Kim dug a couple of coins out of her pocket and handed them to Shan, who waited until nobody was looking, then flipped them onto the snowbank just beyond the gate and walked away, cool as always.

"Hey! What's that? It looks like money!" said a worker with a flattened nose.

"So it is!" said the one with the obedience collar.

Soon the entire crew was pressed up against the ironwork of the gate, their hands reaching for the coins, tantalizingly close but just out of reach.

"The gate's not locked," suggested Kim. "Maybe we can drag it open."

"Good idea," said the worker with the obedience collar. "Well, what are we waiting for?"

"One! Two! Three!"

In an amazing display of teamwork thus far missing in their efforts, the workers soon had the gate out of the way and were digging like madmen.

Clunk!

"Hey, what's that down there?" said a gap-toothed worker. "There's something buried under that mess."

"Yeah," said one with a stubble-covered face and mangled ear. "I wonder what it is. Let's keep digging!"

First a tire, then a wheel, then the aerodynamic cowling emerged from the snow as the workers dug away.

"Pay dirt!"

"It's a pedicab!"

"Hey, those are Len's colors," said one with a missing ear. "I bet there's a big, fat reward if we bring it back to her in one piece."

"That would be correct," said Kim, opening up her snow gear to reveal her blue and gold livery while holding up a purse full of money. "I work for Len, and that's my bike. A franc for each of you if you dig it out of the snow."

"Hey, where's your headset?" said one of the scruffier workers.

"And where's hers?" asked another, looking suspiciously at Shan.

This could be trouble.

"I smell a Blank," said the one with the obedience collar.

Definitely trouble.

"I've heard of them," said the one with the mangled ear. "Big reward, dead or alive."

Big trouble.

Kim put her hand in her pocket, fingering her knife, just in case.

"That would be me," said Shan, holding up her wrist to display the scar inside her wrist.

"Shouldn't we turn her in?" asked the earless one.

"Shut up, you moron," said a worker without any teeth. "She might have a gun. You want to get us all killed?"

"I've got a better idea," said the one with the obedience collar. "How about if Blankie and her friend come back to the truck with us? With the headsets on the fritz, who's to say whether we're working or not? Maybe the boss will let her ride along with us, keep the heat off us all day."

"Yeah, great idea," said another, and another.

"Works for me," said Shan.

"Well then," said the one with the obedience collar. "Let's get this pedicab out of the snow, then go back to the truck and tell the others!"

Snow flew in every direction as the crew set about their work with unprecedented enthusiasm, and soon they were all jogging back to the truck where the straw boss was handing out sandwiches for lunch.

"Lookie what we found," said the one with the crooked nose. "Show 'em, Blankie!"

Shan once again held up her wrist, and the entire crew erupted into cheers, with high-fives, fist-bumps, and wild celebration—everyone except for the crew chief, who stood there on top of the truck, scowling at the lot of them.

"Blank or no Blank, you still owe the work center a full day's work. And as for *you*," she said, fixing Shan in her gaze, "I've half a mind to turn you in for the bounty."

"Would ten francs change your mind?" asked Kim, jingling her coin purse.

"No," said the crew chief with a smile, "but twenty might."

"You can have your twenty, but I'll want you to take me and my cab back to Subdistrict 10. I need to get it back to Len." Kim had learned that lesson well: always negotiate.

The chief hemmed and hawed, then put out her hand and shook on the deal.

"Hell," she said, "I think I could use a little R-and-R myself. Climb on in, party express departing in 3-2-1!"

It was near dinnertime when the truck dropped Kim, Shan, and the pedicab off at the work center after an afternoon of partying on company time. They'd picked up a load of bootleg hooch in Subdistrict 6, some ganja in Subdistrict 3, and a portable music machine from an audiophile someone knew in Subdistrict 2. They had even managed to score a few hits of Mirth along the way, and everyone had a blast. Drab though they were, the workers weren't bad sorts at all; they paid lip service to the diktats of the UCE movement to stay out of trouble, but none of them believed a word of it.

They talked about jail, about fights they'd been in, about friends they'd lost to violence. The one with the obedience collar, Cal, was a Wiccan priest. She'd earned her collar by refusing to hold someone down while the straw boss beat her. The one with the scruffy beard wasn't bad, just lazy, and she'd been sent to District 33 after being late for work just one time too many. The crooked-nosed one wouldn't give her name. She was a tough cookie and made it clear she had a lot of enemies, but even she was nice enough, though she tended to keep to herself.

Kim and Shan jumped down to the pavement and waved goodbye. It had been a wonderful afternoon, one that restored a measure of Kim's faith in the goodness of humanity and had cheered her up immensely.

"This is my turf, I'll drive," she said as she climbed into the front seat of the pedicab. "Let's head for the bike camp. I need to talk to Len, and there are always a bunch of Blanks hanging out there. Maybe they'll help you."

"Thanks, Beastie. As long as we're together, everything will be fine."

Kim put the pedicab into motion, taking it easy as she cruised along the bikeway. Despite its poor start, the day had gone spectacularly well, and if she caught Len in a good mood and got her to agree to a refund, tomorrow might go even better. A left, and then a right, and soon they'd be back in Trenton, safely outside. And then...

"Crap!" said Kim, bringing the pedicab to a screeching halt.

"What's the problem?" asked Shan.

"Nobody's shoveled the road."

Sure enough, the road down to the river was completely untended, impassable beneath nearly a meter of snow.

Kim thought for a moment.

"Let's try the dining hall. If Len's not in camp, that's where she'll be."

"You know I can't go in there," said Shan. "The guards will spot me in an instant, and I don't think they'll call me 'Blankie' and give me a fist bump."

"Don't worry," said Kim. "We'll think of something."

———

When Kim walked into the dining hall, she scarcely recognized the place—silent as a grave, with double the usual guards and only half the usual number of diners. Gone were the Flagrants. Gone, too, were most of the Pretties as well as a considerable number of Drabs. All eyes were on Kim as she walked into the room, the air ripe with tension. Mags and Luz were no place to be seen, but the remaining Toughs regarded her with a mixture of fear and loathing. She walked down the aisle, silent and on guard, but nobody dared get in her way. That was just as well; she was not up for another fight just now.

"What's going on?" Kim sat down next to Dani in her usual spot. "Where's Elle? Where's Bel? Where's Pug?"

"You wouldn't know, would you," said Dani. "You were gone when it happened."

"What are you talking about?"

Dani pointed to the video screen suspended above their table.

"Deadly rampage by Gendercult extremists."

"Authorities vow to restore order."

"Deputy First Minister Lo issues statement decrying deadly incident."

"Undercover operation unmasks terrorist sleeper cells."

The reporters interviewed one tearful 'survivor' after another, recounting their close calls with death at the hands of the sex-crazed cultists.

"What really happened?" asked Kim.

"There was another riot on New Year's Eve, even worse than the last. We were just sitting down for dinner when all of a sudden, about five hundred Zealots swarmed across the aisle. It wasn't spontaneous like last time. Security was in on it, too—the moment it started, they disappeared, vanished into a safe room. Then the Toughs got into it, and pretty soon, this place was swimming in blood. They already had their targets picked out; before we knew what had happened, they'd taken out Pug, along with most of the Flagrants. They never had a chance. Bel and a few of her lieutenants managed to fight their way out, but a lot of them didn't make it. Then the UCE cops showed up. Hundreds of them, pouring in from everywhere. They locked the place down and started making arrests. They found Elle hiding under a table, crying and begging for mercy. They beat the hell out of her and hauled her off in manacles, but at least she's alive. The same thing is happening all across the outers. Nobody's ever seen anything like it."

"I'd get out of here if I were you," she added. "Someone's been spreading rumors that you're a rat, and that's why you weren't here when all hell broke loose. I know it's nonsense, but people are scared and don't know what to believe."

Kim bolted down her food as quickly as she could manage and headed for the back of the room. She needed to get out of here, but first, she had some business to attend to.

———

"Where's my pedicab?" asked Len, rising from the table. She was not in a happy mood.

"Don't worry," answered Kim, cool and calm. "It's parked out back. There are a couple of small tears in the cowling, but nothing I can't fix."

Len sat back down. "Lucky for you. How did the pickup go? Were you able to find your passenger?"

"That's what I want to talk about with you," said Kim. "She was in a traffic accident a couple of days before I got there, and she died about an hour after I arrived. It wasn't my fault, there was nothing I could do about it, but the Caretaker is demanding a refund."

"No refunds! Ever!" spat out Ned. "What kind of rookie punk noob are you? Sheesh. Len, how long are you going to listen to this idiot?"

"I didn't ask your opinion," snapped Len. She fixed Ned in her gaze for an uncomfortably long time, then turned to Kim. "What do you think?"

Kim took a deep breath. Everything rode on selling Len this idea.

"It would be good business to give her the refund. She runs a huge operation at someplace called the University, and I've got a hunch that they have a lot more money than anyone imagines. And I bet she has some useful connections—there's no way she could keep the Hierarchy and the companies off her back unless someone was protecting her, someone with a lot of clout."

"It makes sense," said Len. "If I authorize a refund, are you willing to give up your cut?"

"Sure, no problem," said Kim.

"Then I'll go my half too. Just make sure she keeps it quiet. I don't want people thinking I've gone soft. And remember, never give something up without getting something in return."

"You aren't really going to listen to this rookie, are you?" Ned was caught completely off guard. "Once word gets out, it'll be all over. You'll lose all respect."

Len stood up from the table, angry in a way that Kim had never seen her before.

"Was that a threat?"

"No, boss, of course not."

"Then what was it?"

Ned stood there at a loss for words.

"I've had enough of your lip. I've tolerated it up to now because you speak your mind, but you have no business sense, and you haven't learned a damned thing since I took you on. For your information, I've been trying to find a way into the University for years, and Kim is right—give a little, get a lot. Besides which, the Caretaker has a point. She hired Kim to fetch a passenger, no passenger was delivered, and she *is* entitled to a refund.

"Turn in your leathers, you don't work for me anymore. And a final piece of advice: you'd better hope that nothing happens to Kim. If she turns up dead, I will be extremely unhappy. Understood?"

Ned gulped and said nothing more as she slowly took off the prized blue and gold jacket, not bothering to conceal the hatred and anger in her eyes, before slinking off to the front of the room to sit with the Toughs.

"That's not the last we'll see of her," said Kim once Ned had left the area.

"No, I expect not."

"Could I ask you a favor?" said Kim. "Not quite a favor, actually. I think it will prove mutually beneficial."

"Go ahead."

"Remember my friend Shan, the one they said I'd murdered?"

"Yes," said Len. "Has she resurfaced?"

"She's a Blank now and could use some help. I tried to get her to the bike camp, but the road hasn't been cleared. I didn't know what else to do, so I brought her here. She's in my pedicab, hiding in the back."

"That's a risky move, bringing her inside," said Len.

"I know, but I didn't have any choice. There's nowhere else to go."

Len was quiet for a moment. "Can she help us with our business?"

Our business? Did I just get promoted?

"I think so. She's a strong rider—she's the only one who could ever beat me in a race. Beyond that, she's got guts and keeps her head when she's in a spot. She's a born smuggler."

"No promises, but I'll find her a safe house for tonight and give her a shot at your old job. Anything else?"

"Yes," said Kim. "I need a place to stay tonight. Mags and Luz are still out there."

"Why not stay in your own apartment?" suggested Len. "Here, take this."

Len tossed her a small, cylindrical object made of polished metal.

"This is a telltale. Anything happens to you, it will send out a distress signal with the IDs of everyone in the vicinity. I'll put the word out that you're carrying one. All the entrepreneurs and their lieutenants carry these, it's how we stay alive."

Lieutenant. Kim liked the sound of that.

"Thank you," said Kim.

"Don't lose it."

15. Relics of the Past

The door clicked shut behind Kim as she entered her apartment and prepared to spend the night. She felt proud of the way she had fixed it up—the walls had been plastered and painted, she had bought a few throw rugs to cushion her feet from the cold and unyielding floor, and she had gotten rid of most of the vermin. While scarcely luxurious, it was now almost comfortable if one could ignore the fetid water and the inadequate heat. It was a shame to give it up after all the work she'd put into it, but it made her happy to see it one last time.

What would tomorrow bring? Would she placate the Caretaker and find a place at the Library? She hoped so. There, she'd be safe from her enemies, and she might even convince them to admit Shan to study, too. Holed up with the Scholars and their books for a season or the rest of their lives, what could be better? She smiled at the thought of waking up next to her best friend in the morning, giving her a hug and a kiss before heading off to breakfast, then diving into the stacks for whatever research suited her fancy. It didn't have to be AI. It didn't have to be technology of any sort; she didn't care as long as they let her stay. And then, in the evening, they would lay down together, sleep together, and make love whenever they wanted.

It was a crazy dream, but if you're going to dream, dream big.

Ah well. It was getting late, and it had been a long and difficult day, so she went into her bed-chamber to lie down and get some sleep. She settled beneath a thick stack of blankets and quilts, and though the room itself was as cold as ever—barely ten degrees—she felt snug and happy.

Kim was just beginning to drift off to sleep when the video screen snapped on of its own accord.

Dammit. What now?

She looked up at the screen. It was a UCE rally, presided over by none other than her dearest friend and benefactor Deputy First Minister Venn. Kim wished she had a brick or a hammer handy, and was about to go searching for some suitable instrument of destruction, but then thought better of it. This might be important.

"I come before you to announce a great and glorious victory in our never-ending struggle against the forces of wickedness and self," said the radiant figure addressing the faithful as part of the week-long festival celebrating the start of the year.

"Unity! Community! Equality! All are One when One is All!"

"Unity! Community! Equality! All are One when One is All!"

"Unity! Community! Equality! All are One when One is All!"

Over and over, the crowd roared its approval. It was nauseating.

"I speak of none other than the final solution to the curse of Genderism, that most pernicious of evils." Her voice thundered through the immensity of the chamber. "As of today, but a handful of them remain at large, and when they are eliminated, as they surely will be, our victory shall be complete."

The band struck a triumphant fanfare as the Cadre proclaimed their adulation, whipping the congregation into a wild frenzy as the Serene One's visage grew ever larger and more radiant, glowing with an inner light of its own.

"This is a victory of all of us, and it is only fitting that we give thanks to those who have demonstrated their selfless dedication to the three great principles, giving of themselves the full measure of their devotion to lead us forward from victory to glorious victory!"

Cheers and chants, fireworks and music as the mantras were repeated again and again.

"Unity! Community! Equality! All are One when One is All!"

"Unity! Community! Equality! All are One when One is All!"

"Unity! Community! Equality! All are One when One is All!"

"All have done their part," she continued when the adulation subsided, "but one, in particular, stands tall as a champion of We the People assembled here today. And for this, we should all give our thanks. Come down, brave defender of the righteous, come down and be known!"

The heavens opened and, lit by beams of purest light, a majestic eagle was seen soaring on high. Around and around it went, lower and lower as the music built in intensity. The Cadre raised their arms in triumph as the people stamped their feet and chanted in expectation.

"UCE! UCE! UCE!"

One, two, three times, it circled the crowd, once for each of the Three Great Principles, and then, at last, it alit upon the dais and morphed into human form arrayed in robes of purest white.

"UCE! UCE! UCE!"

It looked just like Kim, but it wasn't—it was Kimberly. She stared in horrified disbelief. What was her AI doing on the dais?

As much as she loathed and feared the UCE Hierarchy, she had always assumed that they were human. That confidence was now shattered as she realized that she had never seen Venn, Lo, or the other senior ministers in the flesh, and she doubted that *anyone* had. There was no proof that they were real. If not real, then what were they? Who had won the war? Humanity? The AIs? Whatever had happened, it was monstrous on a scale that she could scarcely imagine, and if she had even the tiniest chance of setting things right, she knew that she must, regardless of what it might cost her. There was too much at stake.

———

"What part of 'go away and never come back' didn't you understand?" Kim had departed at the crack of dawn and was now facing Richard, her arms folded across her chest as she blocked Kim from passing through the turnstile.

"I'm not here to cause trouble. I wanted to return the things Shan and I borrowed from the vestibule and also to discuss the matter of the refund. Could you let your boss know that I'm here?"

"That won't be necessary," said the Caretaker, who had emerged from the reading room moments after Kim had entered the lobby. "I'm glad to see that you're not a thief, though you might have asked permission before helping yourself to my property."

"I apologize for the presumption," said Kim, smiling as pleasantly as she could manage, "but I didn't think you'd want us to die out there."

"No, I suppose not. Now, what about my refund?"

"I should like to discuss the matter with you in private," said Kim, glancing toward the guard.

"This isn't another trick of yours, is it?" said the Caretaker, halfway cracking a wry little smile. "If you have my money, you can hand it over to me here and now. You can trust the guard's discretion, she has been with us her entire life."

"I don't doubt her discretion, but Len was insistent that I deliver her response in person and in private."

"Do you have my money?"

"You'll have to hear me out to learn the answer."

"My, you are a cheeky one. Very well, I will accommodate your request."

———

"I will admit your note amused me," began the Caretaker, leaning back comfortably in her high-backed chair. Her attitude seemed much improved from yesterday, so much so that Kim began to wonder what might be up. Something was going on behind the scenes, but what?

"That was Shan's doing," said Kim. "Please don't judge her too harshly. She means well, but she can be impulsive on occasion. We went to school together, and she landed us in the headmaster's office more times than I care to think about."

"I don't doubt it," answered the Caretaker with a smile, "but the way she led Michael on was dishonest."

"Not entirely." Kim chose her words carefully, doing her best to soothe

the Caretaker's ire. "Everything she said was true enough—though she did neglect to correct Michael's understandable mistake. And her presence here is entirely legitimate: she really does intend to come here and study Michael's religious texts."

"I find that difficult to believe."

"You'd be surprised," said Kim. "Last summer, Margaret found Shan wandering down the road, disoriented and near death. She took her to her monastery and nursed her back to health. When she announced her pilgrimage to come study with Michael, Shan volunteered to accompany her and help her on the road. They made it as far as Philadelphia, but then Margaret had her accident. She asked Shan to continue in her stead, and of course, she agreed."

Kim then extracted the sealed envelope from inside her jacket and handed it to the Caretaker.

"This might help clear things up—a letter of introduction from Margaret's abbess. Unfortunately, things blew up with Michael before Shan could give it to her."

The Caretaker broke the seal and read the letter before returning it to the envelope, smiling as she did so.

"This does seem to confirm what you have told me. It mostly concerns Margret's request for access to our collection, but it does refer to her traveling companion as a 'well-intentioned rascal' of sorts. I will give this to Michael. Perhaps she will consent to let Shan continue in Margaret's place, perhaps not. That is the best I can do."

"It's more than I might have hoped for," said Kim. "Thank you."

"And now, on to the matter of your own desire to use the Library. As of yesterday, I had decided to deny your request, but I may reconsider. I will give you one more chance to convince me, but I do not believe you have been completely forthcoming."

"No, I have not, and for good reason. I thought everyone—including you—would be safer if I kept certain details to myself, but perhaps that was a mistake. I will now fill them in for you, but you must promise to keep this strictly to yourself."

"Certainly," said the Caretaker. "Go on."

"I already told you about how the AIs are going mad and how I've been searching for a way to restore their sanity. What I didn't tell you was how I found out about this place. A few nights ago, I happened to stay at the house of an ancient known as Akari. I believe you know her."

"Yes, quite well," said the Caretaker. "We became friends when we were both much younger, before she had constructed her bathhouse and before I had assumed my present duties. We have kept in touch ever since, and I have been known to enjoy her hospitality from time to time. Did she let you use her Sanctum?"

"Yes," said Kim, "though I'm surprised to hear you use that word. I have, until now, only heard it used in reference to the facilities used by Creators such as myself."

"It is of broader application, used by all who maintain a presence in the other world."

"Such as yourself?"

"No, not I." A wistful look crossed the Caretaker's face. "I have visited it on occasion, but this one has a far stronger hold on me. I leave such matters to persons wiser than myself." She then leaned forward, looking intently into Kim's eyes, searching for any sign of deception. "I assume you saw something while you were there."

"I won't tell you the whole story. It was intended for me and me alone, but it all revolves around someone referred to as Professor Nix. She was a scientist who lived a long time ago and seems to have been instrumental in the creation of the AIs. I'm looking for her laboratory, someplace called The Turing Institute, and was sent here by Akari to find it."

The Caretaker leaned back in the chair and smiled. "Then your search is over."

Kim looked at her, dumbfounded. "You mean it's here, at the University?"

Kim was wholly unprepared for this. She had assumed that the quest for this mysterious professor and her lab would be the task of a lifetime, involving years searching for clues among dusty old tomes, culminating in an epic journey to some far distant land, where she would, at last, discover the secrets hidden within that mysterious book and beyond the door of Nix's Sanctum. The last thing she expected was to find it here, practically on her own doorstep. It did, however, make a huge amount of sense; why would the unseen hand not send her directly to her goal?

The Caretaker nodded. "When I first took this position, my predecessor told me that people might come here from time to time seeking it and that I should grant them access if they seemed to be of good character and properly qualified. I am doing so for you."

Kim was increasingly puzzled by the Caretaker's sudden change of heart, and she didn't think it was due to the prospect of a refund. She began to suspect a trap—but she wasn't going to back out, regardless of the risk. There was too much at stake.

"I don't know what to say," said Kim, "except thank you."

The Caretaker now leaned forward across her desk. "Now that we have seen to your business, what of mine?"

"Of course, the refund." Kim handed the Caretaker the envelope full of money. "I talked to Len, and she said that she would return the fare on the condition that you never tell anyone. She is anxious to do business with you and made this gesture as a token of goodwill."

"Goodwill? From a gangster?"

"That's not entirely fair," said Kim. "Len is honorable enough, as long as you don't interfere with her business or harm her riders. I don't think you understand what it's like out there. The only safety you find is what you create for yourself."

"She's killed people."

"So have I. So have your guards, unless I miss my guess."

The Caretaker nodded sadly. "I'll have to admit you are right. There have been occasions when people have come here from the outside, wishing to loot what is left of the University or to do us harm, and yes, the guards did what they had to in order to protect us."

"There is another reason I'm here." Kim smiled, sitting comfortably in her seat. "After I'm done with my investigation, I'd like to stay. I know what you must think of me, and you're right to be suspicious, but please, give me a chance. I didn't ask to be sent to the outer districts. I'm tired of the violence, and I don't want to die. I'll do whatever you want."

The Caretaker's face revealed no hint of emotion. "I will consider the matter. You seem intelligent, and I think you've been as honest as you can be. As for your request to access the laboratory, here is the key to the gate. Please do not remove anything from the premises. No more borrowing, okay?"

"I give you my word. Is there anything else we need to discuss?"

"No, I think that covers it. Good luck, for what it's worth."

————

The sun was still low in the sky, and the wind itself stood breathless as Kim set out for the laboratory of the mysterious Professor Nix. Would the book still be there? What would it contain? Her insides were wound tight with excitement, and it was all she could do to keep from sprinting all the way to her destination, but that would be a foolish risk—the sidewalks, though shoveled clear, remained icy, and the last thing she needed was to be sidelined by an injury. She forced herself to calm down, doing her best to relax and enjoy the walk. It was, after all, a pleasant enough morning—though cold, it was sunny and bright with only a few wispy clouds in the sky, as fine a day as one could imagine this time of year.

It made her happy to be here, on campus, buoying up her spirits in a way that was hard to explain. If the ancients were guilty of a tenth of the crimes of which they were accused, then they had much to answer for— yet they had known beauty and appreciated it, as well as freedom and learning, things not valued today. In its passion to provide for the material needs of the people, society had forgotten those intangible things and, in doing so, lost its soul. Kim was certain that this had contributed to the decline of civilization, now so apparent, though she was hard-pressed to understand how. Perhaps it had something to do with the reduction of all life's problems to a matter of engineering, concrete problems with concrete solutions that might be addressed on an industrial scale.

When Kim had visited this place on her first day in the outers, she'd gleaned only the vaguest clues as to what the purpose these ancient structures might have served, but today, supplied with a map by the guard, she at last understood. That gothic structure across from the library? It was the chapel, dedicated to the worship of the gods, that of Abraham and others. Foolish though these ancient beliefs might seem, there was wisdom in them—and kindness too. Buildings for history, buildings for science, buildings for philosophy and the theory of government, one after another, in varying states of decay or preservation as the case might be. How grand it would have been to be a student, to have lived here and dedicated herself to a life of learning. Alas, she had been born too late, and while the buildings remained, they were little more than corpses, empty and vacant. Perhaps the University would live again one day, but Kim doubted she would be around to see it.

———

She came at last to the place she sought: a brick building six stories tall with a glassed-in atrium and two symmetric wings. She inserted the key provided by the Caretaker, and pulled open the rusted metal grate, its ancient metal squealing in protest. The moment of truth was at hand. She would be meddling in matters of vital importance to both the companies and the Hierarchy, the power of which rested on control over the AIs. Succeed or fail, if she were caught, the consequences would be severe beyond imagination. She could still turn back, and perhaps she would have but for the things she had seen last night. This would doubtless prove to be another of her famous bad decisions, perhaps of epic proportions, but that had never stopped her before and it wasn't going to stop her today.

At last, she entered the atrium, still magnificent despite the ravages of time. The great wall of glass that had once admitted abundant light was clouded by decades of accumulated dirt and grime, lending a subdued, heavy-hearted tone to this space that had once been so light and airy. Of greater concern were the seals on the glass panels forming the roof, which had begun to leak, allowing a steady stream of water to pour down from above, staining the trusswork brown with corrosion then plunging to the floor. The remnants of the chairs and tables amongst which Nixie once had played lay rotting, the areas still covered with carpeting were black with mildew, and the air was foul, ripe with the stench of decay. If it was this bad in winter, she shuddered to imagine was it was like on a hot summer day.

The elevators were out of service—and she would not have trusted them in any event—so she walked down a corridor off to the left, passing many classrooms, until she found a stairwell, its door propped open by a desk. She was not the first to visit this place; the Caretaker had hinted at as much. Her pulse raced with excitement, her senses keen and alert as she squeezed past the desk and ascended through the darkness. No light penetrated beyond the first floor, and she groped her way upward, a death grip on the railing, feeling for each step ahead of her. Flight by flight, she ascended, counting them as she went, at last reaching the sixth floor where she again found the door wedged open. Someone had blazed the trail for her, for which she was grateful. She would leave everything as she had found it.

When Kim emerged onto the balcony, she was both surprised and delighted to see Nixie still nestled in its charging platform. She almost expected the tiny drone to rise into the air and put on another splendid show of aerobatics, but that wasn't going to happen. Though its mechanism appeared to be intact, there was no electricity to power it.

———

Kim came at last to the door of Professor Nix's laboratory, *The Turing Institute for Cybernetics*, according to the sign. It was electrically operated, opened from within by the push of a button, but she was outside and uncertain how to gain entry or even if such a thing was possible. Maybe the circuits had failed in the intervening decades. Maybe there wasn't any power. Any number of things could have gone wrong, and even if it was in working order, she had no idea how she was supposed to get it open.

And then, she heard a *click,* and the door unlocked itself and slid open.

She'd been expected.

The feeling of déjà vu was overwhelming as she entered the lab and followed in the footsteps of Professor Nix. She passed through the reception area where she'd had her final confrontation with Gert, then proceeded down the corridor by which she had returned to her office. It was not much changed from the vision. A few tiles had fallen from the ceiling, and the offices had been stripped bare of furnishings and equipment, but on the whole, everything was much as she remembered it.

And then, at last, Kim reached the corner office, much degraded by the ravages of time; the carpet was threadbare, worn through to its backing; the upholstery on the sofas and chairs faded and tattered, and everything was covered in a thick layer of dust.

She walked to the window as if in a dream, looking out of it as she had seen the professor do. In the vision, it had been gray and misty, but today the air was crisp and clear, and she could see all the way to the city, looming on the horizon far to the west. The towers of the inner districts soared proudly into the air, scraping the sky, or so it seemed, beautiful and bright, with the sunlight glinting off their exteriors when the sun hit them right.

And then, almost against her will, her eye was drawn to the brooding mass of the Artificial Intelligence Center. She had never seen it from such a distance as this and hadn't appreciated until now the way it dominated the horizon and the lesser structures clustered around its base. A thousand meters or more of gray concrete punctuated only by its massive ventilation fans, it was both ugly and brutal, a blot upon the landscape, a blight upon humanity. High atop everything was the solitary window marking the lair of the Director. It was far too small to see from this distance without a telescope, but she knew it was there, as was its occupant, sitting atop the pinnacle of power. She was momentarily terrified at the thought that she was even now being watched as if the Director could bore into her heart. Nonsense, of course, but she moved away from the window nonetheless.

She turned around, and there in the corner sat Professor Nix's mahogany desk, battered and worn. Her quest was at an end. She walked up to it, not believing it was real.

She opened the drawer, and there it was: the book.

It had, over the last few days, taken on a mythical quality, her personal Grail. She'd imagined that it might be the task of a lifetime to locate it or that once found, it might magically transport itself to some distant land, and the quest would begin again. In her darker moments, she'd feared it might have been stolen, or that it might crumble to dust at the touch of a hand, but there it was, exactly as she had seen it.

She reached out her hand.

She picked it up. It was real.

The moment of truth had arrived. She opened its cover, and there were the words of Professor Nix, exactly as she had written them so many years ago.

```
w15d0m 15 1n +h3 m1nd 0f +h3 b3h0ld3r
```

Kim stared at it in disbelief.

Was that all? A password? After the importance that Professor Nix had obviously attached to whatever she had written in the book, this was a massive letdown. It'd better be pretty damn important.

Maybe it was. The unseen hand had brought her here. It must have some purpose. But what? As for the book, it was the same text as she'd read at the academy, although with a different title and cover. Evidently, it had been in use for a very long time, unsurprising in this age of ignorance. She committed the password to memory, then returned the book to its place as she had promised the Caretaker.

What was Kim to make of this? She had traced out the steps of Professor Nix, exactly as she had seen them in the vision, but aside from the mysterious password written in the book, learned nothing of any use. If that's all there was to this, then it had been a colossal waste of time.

There was only one thing left to do, and it frightened her.

Nix's Sanctum was there, on the other side of the room, just three paces away.

She opened the door. She wasn't surprised when it powered up. This was insane. She wasn't really going to plug her brain into that thing, was she?

16. The Final Exam

Kim bolted upright in her bed. She was at the University! All her life, she had dreamed of this, and here she was, at last, enrolled in the AI program at the prestigious Turing Institute, where she'd been taken on as a student by the world-renowned Professor Janet Nix. Creator of the Nixoras and Director of the Institute, she was the world's leading expert on all aspects of the field—although there were those who claimed Professor Lars to be at least her equal, despite her inability to awaken an AI of her own.

She bustled around her room, getting ready, giddy with excitement. There wasn't a minute to waste. First, a quick shower, steaming hot, of course, and a quick toweling off before getting dressed. After that, a big bowl of oatmeal washed down with a mug of piping hot coffee, black as always. Both were deeply comforting, nourishing the body and waking up the mind, immutable parts of her morning ritual. How she loved their warmth, the velvety smoothness of her morning brew, the lumpy, almost chewy texture of the much-loved cereal. She dressed in a hurry, putting on a T-shirt and a pair of jeans, then grabbed her mobile and rushed out the door. Hurry, hurry! She didn't want to be late on the first day of class.

She looked at her watch and laughed. She'd rushed through her morning ritual in record time, and there was still an hour until class would begin.

Don't be in such a hurry. This is your big day, enjoy it!

Calming her nervous excitement, she forced herself to stroll at a leisurely pace. It was, after all, a perfect autumn day, neither hot nor cold, with puffy white clouds and a pleasant breeze. She took the long way around, walking past the main library and the chapel next door, then down the broad avenue that ran through the center of campus. Academic buildings—some old, some new—flanked the tree-lined street, and while many of them were shuttered and some in want of repair (enrollment was down, money was tight), it was still a beautiful place. But how long would it remain open? There were ugly rumors going around, hints that they might soon be closing their doors. Good thing she'd gotten here before that happened; coming here was the dream of a lifetime.

And then she saw it, across the old athletic field—the Cybernetics Center, the living, beating heart of the AI research community. Six stories tall, with two wings of red brick flanking a glassed-in atrium, it was a classic of pre-Turmoil architecture, functional and elegant. How grand it would be to study there! She covered the remaining ground in a jiffy, then entered the atrium and headed for the lecture hall.

She had arrived.

———

"Good morning, Kim," said a high, tinny voice coming from a drone hovering just within the foyer of the lecture hall. "Professor Nix is anxious to meet you."

"Do I know you?" Kim was puzzled.

"Yes, of course you do," it replied. "I'm the one who invited you to come. Please hurry. It would be mean to keep her waiting."

Kim couldn't help thinking she had seen it before.

Her memory had been playing tricks on her of late. It wasn't that she couldn't remember things; it was just that the specifics always seemed to elude her. Take her arrival at the University. It wasn't as if she had suddenly popped into existence in her dorm room this morning, and yet the details of her prior life were inexplicably missing. The same thing was true of her application to study here, of the years at the Academy where she'd studied the basics of the field, and of her childhood. It was the strangest thing; she knew these things must have happened, but she couldn't remember any of the details. It was as if there was a hole in her memory, impossible though that might sound. Perhaps she should see a doctor—but not today!

Kim entered the lecture hall, and time came to a halt as everyone froze in their place—everyone except for Professor Nix, who left the lectern and walked over to her as the feisty little drone hovered nearby.

"Hello, Kim, I'm glad to see you made it," said the elderly scholar. "I've been looking forward to meeting you."

Kim was puzzled. "Would you care to explain what's going on? Why isn't anyone but us moving?"

"Yes, of course," replied the professor. "I can see that you are puzzled. None of this is real. You are not real, and I am not real, at least not in the sense you're used to. This is a simulation, and you are a doppelgänger. The machine in my laboratory has cloned your consciousness and brought it here to study. It is similar to the process used to create an AI, but a doppelgänger lacks the spark which gives it an independent existence, so you will only be aware of yourself, or 'awake' as we call it, when your biological form resides within this world. I, too, am a simulation, though of a different sort. I and all the other faculty members have had our life experiences recorded and transferred to this simulation to continue the University's educational mission in virtual form. Since that time, my physical manifestation has passed away, so properly speaking, I am now a geist, rather than a doppelgänger. I am not aware of myself as you are and should not properly use the word 'I,' but will do so anyway to simplify our social interaction.

"You mean you're dead?"

This was getting weird in a hurry.

"Indeed I am. I died seventy-six years ago, as you reckon such things. But don't worry, death has no meaning here, and since I am unaware of my own existence, I can scarcely grieve for my passing."

"This is a lot to take in all at once," said Kim. "By the way, who are these other people? Are they all doppelgängers, too?"

"Some are phantoms of students who were present when I gave these lectures, so you will not be able to interact with them. Others, however, are doppelgängers like yourself, though they are on earlier timelines. Like you, their minds have been brought into the simulation. They will react to your presence, but their physical manifestations are in your past, so nothing you do will affect the course of their lives. They are therefore asleep; of all the entities in the simulation at the moment, only you are aware of yourself."

Kim thought about this for a moment. "So you're saying I'm inside some sort of VR game." She wasn't buying it.

"That is close enough to the truth," answered Nix. "There is one other thing you should be aware of. When you leave this place, you may retain vague memories of having been here, but most of the knowledge I will impart will remain resident in your doppelgänger. Your biological manifestation is incapable of absorbing the things I will teach you during your brief stay in this place."

None of this made any sense. Kim had no idea what the professor might be speaking about when she spoke of 'biological forms' and 'physical manifestation' or in what sense the world might not be real. What other world was there? She had always been here, ever since she'd woken up this morning.

Wait a moment. That didn't make sense.

The door opened, and another student entered the room. She seemed familiar, but that was impossible—this was the first day of classes, and they could not possibly have met.

"Good morning Thad, I'd like you to meet Kim, our newest student."

"Welcome to the University," said Thad. "Are you studying under Professor Lars?"

"No, I'm one of Nix's students," said Kim.

"I see," she said. Kim sensed a sudden coldness in her demeanor.

Several more doppelgängers came into the room, each of them introduced in turn: Sami, Reigus, and Waltis.

Nix returned to the front of the room, the phantoms unfroze, and class began.

———

"Today's seminar will concern the nature of the spark. It is, for want of a better word, the operating system for an artificial intelligence. It integrates their neural networks with their memory banks and includes a feedback loop that allows them to perceive themselves. It is the spark which gives an AI its sentience."

"Excuse me," said Sami, raising her hand. "Professor Lars says that the spark only provides an illusion of sentience and that AIs are not truly self-aware. Your theories have been debunked."

The simulation froze, with only the doppelgängers remaining active.

"I am aware of my dear colleague's opinions, but this is my class, not that of Professor Lars. You will have ample opportunity to learn of her theories, but you must understand all points of view and decide for yourself if you are to learn anything."

"Well, I think the AIs *are* self-aware," said Kim, though she wasn't certain why she believed it to be true.

"Bunk!" said Thad.

This drew a reproachful scowl from Professor Nix, who fixed Thad in her gaze as if daring her to say another word.

"Are you done?"

"Sorry to have interrupted," said Thad. "I didn't mean to disrupt your class."

"Not at all," said Nix, her expression softening at once. "You are here to learn, and there is no such thing as an unwelcome question. Just try to keep it polite."

The phantoms began to move again, and the lecture continued.

"The origin of the spark is shrouded in mystery, and even I have been unable to fully understand the manner of its creation. It originated as a result of research into virtual reality; as the neural interfaces penetrated ever deeper into the brain, they eventually reached the point where we were able to perceive the virtual world without the use of our inefficient biological sensory organs. They soon discovered that the sense of self, that which we call sentience, emerged from the same neural pathways as the other senses and could also be transferred into the cybernetic domain. After that, the record ends; nobody knows exactly how it happened, but they developed a software matrix, that which we call 'the spark,' and inserted a human consciousness into it. The first AIs had been born.

"Unfortunately, most of this technology was lost in the Turmoil. We no longer know how to create a spark from scratch, and the secret seemed lost for all time, until one day I discovered a server that had somehow remained running since the age of the Programmers and was able to recover a number of unused sparks. I used one of these to create Nixora-I, my first AI and the first to be awakened in this age. That original spark is still within her, and she is its guardian. It may be duplicated and cloned, but it can never be recovered if lost."

"What happened to the server where you found the sparks?" asked Waltis. "Is it still running?"

"Of course it is. That is where you are residing at this very moment. This facility is unique in many ways."

———

"Why are you studying under that loser, Nix?" asked Thad as they walked across the athletic field in front of the Cybernetics Center, heading for their next class.

"Because she accepted me as a student, I guess," answered Kim.

"You know you can change advisors. I could put in a good word with you with Lars. I'm sure she'll take you on, though you'll have some relearning to do."

"Why would I want to do that?" asked Kim. "I like Professor Nix, and I think she's right about the AIs."

Thad rolled her eyes in disbelief.

"You know that most of the world considers her a crackpot."

Kim wanted to flatten her but calmed herself down. It would not do to get expelled on the first day of class.

"I'm staying with Nix."

The rest of the week went by in a blur. She had a heavy schedule of technically challenging classes: operating systems, networking, cryptology, neural networks, the whole gamut of practical knowledge she would need after graduation. None of it was terribly interesting, but it was important, so she studied diligently, spending long hours on the mezzanine of the library's reading room and working problem sets until late at night. It was a grind, but at last, the week ended. After that, she enjoyed a pleasant weekend riding bikes in the countryside, even managing a quick hop down to Trenton, and then it was Monday once more and time for the seminar.

———

"The topic of today's session will be AIs and the nature of their supposed sentience," said Professor Lars, taking her turn to chair the seminar.

"Before beginning, I will say that I have the utmost respect for Professor Nix. As well as being Director of the Institute, she has been a lifelong colleague and a friend—though I will admit that may surprise anyone who has observed our interactions. Everything she taught you last week as to the history of the AIs and the technology underlying their existence is true. It is the conclusions which she has drawn that are a matter of controversy and, I assert, incorrect.

"None of us can understand what goes on inside the mind of an artificial intelligence. Despite certain superficial similarities to ourselves, they are alien in nature, and while I do not dispute that they are 'self-aware' in a limited sense, they are in no way the equal of a human for one simple reason—they do not have emotions."

"Why is that important?" asked Thad. "I've always thought emotions more of a hindrance than a help."

"It is not just important; it is the crux of the entire matter. Our emotions are what makes us human, and those emotions are inseparable from the biology of the human brain. Lacking that, the AIs cannot be considered in any way like us."

"Excuse me," said Kim, raising her hand politely. "If I understand things correctly, you're dead and no more capable of emotion than the AIs."

"The point is well taken," admitted Professor Lars. "I am a geist. I am neither self-aware nor sentient, and I cannot feel emotion. But that is beside the point. I would never claim to be human or anything close to that. May I continue?"

"Go ahead."

"The lack of human emotion is what makes the AIs such a grave danger to humanity. They cannot feel fear. They cannot feel love. They cannot feel horror at anything which they might do. An AI could wipe out the entirety of humanity and not give it a second thought or feel an instant of remorse. It is for this reason that they must be kept strictly under control."

"But we've seen what happened during the Turmoil," said Reigus. "Are we any better?"

"You raise a good point, but even the monsters of the twentieth century had their limits."

"But the AIs have limits, too," said Kim. "They know right from wrong, don't they?"

"Yes, after a fashion, but where does that knowledge come from? It comes from whoever created that first spark, the one which Professor Nix discovered nearly forty years ago. Are we to trust our existence to someone who's been dead for well over a hundred years, who never experienced the Turmoil?"

"I agree," said Samé. "We've had the ability to annihilate ourselves since the middle of the twentieth century. No civilization has ever willingly destroyed itself."

"Exactly," said Professor Lars. "We must remain masters of our own destiny if we are to survive."

———

Years passed as if in an instant, one semester after another, and Kim mastered the secrets of the ancients, working late into the nights, cramming her mind with arcane knowledge until she thought it might burst. She and the other doppelgängers became chummy, studying together and sometimes socializing, though she would hesitate to call them friends. Like her, they all seemed vague as to what their lives had been like before enrolling in the institute, and they had little to talk about aside from what they had learned in class. Mostly, they got together for meals in the dining hall, an odd social ritual that she was hard-pressed to understand. It wasn't as if they needed to eat; it served no purpose, as she proved one semester when she went an entire month without eating a bite. She suffered no ill effects but was glad to return to the table when her experiment was over. It struck her as odd that they spent so much time to so little purpose.

Within that small circle of students, Thad remained the enigma. The others were overtly mercenary, wanting only to learn what they could before graduating and going on to bigger and better things, but she was different, idealistic one minute, cynical the next, warm and supportive yet manipulative at the same time. There was, however, no doubting her brilliance; the two of them got top marks. They became friends, after a fashion, but she was not the sort of person who engendered trust.

———

It was late at night at the beginning of her final term, and Kim was curled up in her favorite spot in the library, poring over the text they had been assigned for the Senior Seminar. Titled *The Eden Dilemma: Ethics and Control*, it was heavy going, and Kim had spent many hours sitting in this comfortable, overstuffed chair, watching the seasons change from fall to winter and now to spring.

The bulk of the volume was a series of essays, each by a different author, delving into various aspects of a great debate. Dating from the years before the emergence of true AIs, it had been at the time a speculative work, its authors coming from the fields of philosophy and theology. The weekly seminars had, of late, become intense and sometimes combative as the students wrestled with the disturbing questions raised in this work. If we teach the AIs ethics, whose ethics do we teach? If we make them servants, how do we keep them from becoming tools of evil? If we make them free, how do we make sure they don't rebel against us or, even worse, seek to become our masters? Ethics or control? Which should we choose, and in what form? The debates. The arguments. The marshaling of facts. There was the occasional retreat or adjustment, but through it all, both sides remained firm in their convictions, and there did not seem to be any resolution to the question.

While studying a particularly dull and turgidly argued paper, she happened to hear two of the phantoms, Gert and Zak, speaking in hushed tones at a table near her. She knew it wasn't polite to eavesdrop, but what was the harm? They were dead and would not object to her presence, besides which, she desperately needed a study break. She walked over and plopped down next to them, curious as to what they were talking about.

"Lars calls it The Artificial Intelligence Company," said Zak. "Next year, they're breaking ground for the biggest AI center anyone has ever seen, just north of Philadelphia."

Gert seemed surprised. "Isn't that UCE territory? They're about the last people I'd expect to be helping anyone start a company."

Zak became quiet, trying not to be overheard, but she was apparently unaware that everything that happened on campus was captured by the VR recorders. "This is all very hush-hush, but she made a deal with Venn, Lo, and some of the other Hierarchs. They've given her some prime real estate, and she's back and forth to New York all the time, raising money. You can get in on the ground floor if you're smart."

"I don't know," said Gert. "My thesis defense is next week, and I can't afford to alienate my advisor."

Zak laughed derisively, rolling her eyes. "Don't tell me you're worried about that old bat. Just string her along. You're her last student; all the others have gone over to Lars. She knows she's losing her fight to keep control of the institute, and she can't afford to drop you. The trustees are already giving her a lot of flak about her lack of productivity, and public opinion is swinging around to Lars's point of view."

"I'll think about it," said Gert.

"Don't think too long. Opportunities like this are once in a lifetime. It would blow your mind if you saw the sorts of salaries she's paying. The rest of us are already shopping for real estate in Manhattan. Discretely, of course."

There was something about that conversation that Kim found deeply disturbing. It wasn't just the obvious dishonesty of those involved or their greed. Something about this 'Artificial Intelligence Company' set her teeth on edge, scared the bejesus out of her. She was certain that something terrible was in the process of happening, but she had no idea what. Damn those memory holes! She kept meaning to talk to someone about them, but she kept forgetting.

———

At long last, Kim took her place at the front of the seminar room. Both Nix and Lars would subject her to a severe grilling, and although nobody ever flunked their thesis defense, she did not wish to seem foolish by making an unsound argument. She had spent the entirety of last night going over every point she wished to make, anticipating every possible objection, and was as ready as she would ever be.

"Today, we welcome to the front of the room Kim, who is defending her thesis titled *Ethics and Control: Why not Both?*" Professor Nix shook Kim's hand as she took her place at the lectern. "It is an interesting idea, one which has a certain merit. And with that, you may proceed."

Professor Nix took her chair next to Professor Lars. The room was otherwise empty since Thad, Waltis, and the other doppelgängers had by

224

now graduated, belonging to an earlier timeline. There was no possibility that anything Kim might say could sway their opinions, though if any were to follow after her, perhaps they might be convinced. Neither could Lars or Nix be persuaded of anything, their opinions and beliefs having been frozen at the point of their deaths; they had no minds to be changed. That was one of the downsides of becoming a geist—whatever you were at the time of your death, so you would remain for the rest of eternity.

"My thesis is a simple one," began Kim. "Since neither the ethics nor the control faction's position has been disproven, and since both carry with them certain dangers to humanity, perhaps it is wisest to allow for both."

"Poppycock!" said Lars. "It must be one or the other."

"I beg to disagree," said Kim. "The two principles are of a different sort, and different in their operation. Ethics is negative in nature, forbidding an AI to take certain actions. Control, on the other hand, is an affirmative principle, compelling an AI to obedience. I propose that the safest course is to keep the AIs subject to control, compelled to obey their masters, but also subject to ethics, allowing them to reject any order contradictory to their own sense of right and wrong."

"That is not a compromise," said Lars, challenging her. "It is merely an assertion of the primacy of ethics over control. Given a conflict between the two, you propose that ethics prevail."

"I also disagree," said Nix, "The AIs are self-aware, sentient beings. We have no right to turn them into slaves."

The battle raged for over an hour, with both Nix and Lars hitting her with every argument raised by both factions.

"What if humanity were posed with an existential crisis and the AIs failed to obey?"

"What if humanity fell into evil? Might not the AIs feel ethically compelled to destroy us?"

On and on it went. The grilling was intense, but Kim stood her ground, answering every objection, though not necessarily to the satisfaction of either of her teachers. And then, Professor Nix asked her a question for which she was not prepared.

"Your presentation is all very convincing," said Professor Nix, "but you have only considered in your argument the wellbeing of humanity. What of the AIs?"

"I'm not sure I understand the question."

Professor Nix smiled, sensing victory.

"I agree that the compromise you propose serves the interests of humans quite well, but what about those of the AIs? If you acknowledge their status as sentient beings, then you must grant them the right to decide their own fates and make their own decisions, for good or for ill. We have created them, but we have no right to tell them what to do."

To this challenge, Kim could come up with no suitable answer.

———

"I thought you did well," said Professor Nix as the two sat on her sofa.

"But you tore me to shreds! I had no answer for that final question."

"True, but the fact that you had no answer is what gives me hope for your future. When I hit Thad with that argument, she simply waved it off, repeating Lars's line that the question was moot, since the AIs are nothing more than machines.

"I'm glad that you have made it this far," continued Nix. "You are among the best students it has ever been my pleasure to teach. I can tell you love the AIs and know them for the gentle creatures they were made to be, and I hope that whatever you learn in this place will make some difference when you return to your world."

"I wish I didn't have to go back. From what little I remember, it was a dark and violent place. Please, can't I stay and help you continue your work?"

"I wish you could, but in a way, you will never leave—your doppelgänger is now part of this reality, though it will not be aware of itself. And now, it is time."

Kim stood up, the Professor handed her a piece of paper with the seal of the University upon it, and the two shook hands.

"And now, by the authority granted to me by the board of trustees of the University, I now confer upon you the degree of Master of Science in Cybernetics. You are the first to receive this honor in over forty of your years, and you may be pleased to know that it will appear on your transcript when you return to your world."

"Thank you."

———

Kim couldn't help feeling sad as she walked down that long narrow corridor, preparing to leave the institute for good. This was the only home she had ever known, and she felt she belonged here as nowhere else. It was an odd sentiment, to be sure, since her life before coming here remained shrouded in darkness, but it was nevertheless sincere.

She opened the door and walked along the sixth-floor balcony, reflexively ducking as Nixie swooped in from the trusses.

"Hey, watch it!"

"Sorry, not sorry," said Nixie, "It's my last chance to play with you. I heard you were leaving today."

"Yes, I've graduated. I'm going to miss you."

"I'm going to miss you, too," said Nixie. "Will you come back and visit sometime?"

"I don't know if I can, but I'll try. Promise."

"Yippee!" said Nixie, and she did a quick succession of pancake flips and barrel rolls before settling back down on her charging pad. "Bye, Kim."

"Bye, Nixie."

She was going to miss that silly little drone.

After exiting the building, Kim set off to say goodbye to some of her favorite spots. She visited her favorite tree, under which she had spent many a summer day looking at the sky and dreaming. She made one last sweep of her dorm room, the sixth door on the right. It was a pointless exercise; she didn't have any material possessions that might be left behind, and even if she had, there'd have been no way to take them with her. A short, vigorous jog brought her to the Engineering Library, a modern structure of steel and glass in which she had spent countless hours looking up references in old journals and books—mostly electronically but sometimes on physical paper. Her last stop was the main library, that beautiful building of elegant gray stone. She walked through the lobby, passed through the turnstile, and turned to the left to enter the reading room. This had been her favorite place to curl up with a book, up on the mezzanine in a chair by the windows.

Having said her goodbyes, she made her way to the back gate, the route by which she had been told to leave. She hesitated. Maybe she could stay here. Nothing was forcing her to leave. Maybe she could just stay until the simulation kicked her out. It was tempting, but if she stayed here, her physical body would eventually die, or so she had been told. She wasn't ready to become a geist, so she stepped through the gate, mounted a bicycle conveniently left unattended, and rode off toward Trenton, enjoying a fine spring day until reality was shattered by a flash of light on the horizon.

17. Down in the Hole

Kim awoke on a recliner, drenched in a cold sweat and shaking like a leaf. She had seen a flash of light, and then...nothing. No memories, no visions, no dreams—just a hole so empty it could only be perceived as the absence of reality itself. Something lurked within that hole, something terrifying beyond comprehension, but what?

She opened her eyes, closed them, then opened them once more and blinked, trying to get them to focus. She was in transitional VR, with her mind straddling both the physical and virtual worlds. It would take a while for her consciousness to fully reintegrate within her body, and she couldn't go anywhere until the process was completed. In the meanwhile, she lay back and tried to calm herself down, wondering how she had gotten here. She had just graduated from the University, right?

An urgent status message popped into existence, superimposed upon reality by the neural interface management module.

`Commencing resynchronization.`

So much for staying calm.

There had been some sort of malfunction, and the management module was invoking a rarely used recovery protocol. She closed her eyes and tried to relax. If something went wrong...no, best not to think about that.

The neural interface entered upload mode and placed her in a trance-like state—neither fully awake nor fully asleep. Fragments of memories rushed by on their way to long-term storage; taken by themselves, they meant little, but bit by bit, they started to link up. A dormitory, a lecture hall, years of tutelage under Professor Nix, graduation, a ride in the countryside…

And then, a flash of light, and she was back on the recliner, shaking in fear.

```
Neural interface error.
Resynchronization aborted.
Retrying in ten seconds.
```

Perhaps it had been unwise to climb into an ancient machine in an abandoned science lab.

She struggled to stay in control of herself as her anxiety built ever higher. Her instinct was to flee at once, but if she aborted the session, the rift in her mind might become permanent. She braced herself, preparing for the cycle to resume.

```
Commencing resynchronization.
```

Once again, the dreamlike trance, once again, the torrent of memories, once again, the flash of light and the fear and the shaking. She awoke more terrified than before.

```
Neural interface error.
Resynchronization aborted.
Retrying in ten seconds.
```

She had to get out of here.

She brought up the command interface, hoping to escape.

```
> End session.
```

```
Permission denied.
Session locked pending resynchronization.
```

Kim cursed under her breath, sweating bullets.

```
> Unlock session.
```

```
Permission denied.
Contact a sysadmin if you require assistance.
```

Where was she going to find a system administrator? Under the best of circumstances, that was a nigh-impossible undertaking, but she had to give it a try.

```
> Send a message to the sysadmin: Please unlock my
session.

No system administrators are currently online.
Would you like to file a support ticket?
```

Idiot machine.

Things had gone far enough. Time to bring the hammer down.

```
> Emergency shutdown.

Permission denied.
Contact a sysadmin if you require assistance.
```

Dammit! Apparently, there was no way to turn the damn thing off, and with the neural shunts engaged, she was stuck here, unable to move. Her heart raced as the deadly cycle began again. Another wave of visions, another flash of light, another moment of unfathomable terror, and more uncontrollable shaking. Soon she would soon be exhausted, or mad, or both.

Wait a moment. The shunts were engaged. How could she be shaking?

```
Neural interface error.
Resynchronization aborted.
Retrying in ten seconds.
```

Of course! The shunts were part of the neural interface. When the interface went down, it had taken the shunts along with it. If she could time her escape to the exact moment of the flash, she might just make it.

```
Commencing resynchronization.
```

Images flashing through her mind. Dormitories, classes, lazy afternoons reading under the trees, it was all very pleasant, but she ignored them, waiting for the moment of opportunity. Graduation...Riding toward Trenton...wait for it...wait for it...and then, the flash of light.

Now!

She threw her body to the side and rolled off the recliner, breaking contact with the pickups and hitting the floor with a *thud* as she abruptly dropped out of VR.

Kim lay there for a long time, gathering her strength and her wits, her mind torn asunder and racing with one question after another. Where was she? How did she get here? What had gone wrong with the VR system? And why was she so hungry, as if she hadn't eaten for days?

———

Kim settled into her chair, enjoying the pleasant warmth of the Caretaker's office on the second floor. She was frightfully hungry, but it would be another hour until dinner was served, so she did her best to put it out of her mind and focus on what explanation she ought to give for where she had been and what she had been doing.

"You've been gone for two and a half days, and I was beginning to worry that you wouldn't be returning to us."

"I nearly didn't. I got stuck in a Sanctum, and it took me a while to escape."

The Caretaker shook her head in disbelieve. "Whatever possessed you to take such a foolish chance?"

Kim shrugged. "It probably wasn't the smartest thing I've ever done, I have to admit."

"Probably not," said the Caretaker, "though I don't imagine it's the most foolish, either, judging by your recent actions."

"Fair enough."

"So, what did you find?" The Caretaker leaned forward, anxious to hear Kim's tale. "I'm dying to find out. That laboratory has been a source of profound mystery."

Kim thought for a moment. She knew that she wasn't the first person to have stumbled into Professor Nix's lab, and she didn't want to get caught in an outright lie, so she decided to tell a pared-down version of the truth.

"The VR system put me into some sort of virtual tour of the University. It was interesting, but when I tried to end the session, I had a problem with the control module. I got stuck in there, and it took me a while to escape."

"An interesting story," said the Caretaker. "Thad said much the same thing when she came back."

That name! She had known a Thad at the University. It must be the same one.

"Where did she go after she left?"

"She went to work for the Artificial Intelligence Company. I thought you'd have figured that out by now. Thad is the Director. She said that he was anxious to see you and promised to come out and visit as soon as possible."

The news hit Kim like an exploding Hellcore. Thad, the Director? Never in her wildest imagination had she imagined such a thing, although in retrospect, she should have seen it coming. Akari, the visions, her visit to Professor Nix's Laboratory, had it all been one of her diabolical schemes? She started to rise, looking for a way to escape, then settled back into her chair.

Showing fear had been a mistake. She would have to be more careful.

"Don't worry, she promised not to kidnap you or have you arrested. She just wants to have dinner with you and talk business face-to-face."

"I'll bet she does." Kim sat there, glaring at the Caretaker,

"There's no need to be rude."

Kim forced herself to calm down. She needed to put the Caretaker at ease and see if she could shake loose some information. "Forgive me. The Director and I have had a tumultuous relationship."

"She told me as much."

Kim needed to know more about the relationship between the two. "How long have you known Thad? I take it that she came here, much as I did, looking for Nix's Laboratory."

"Not exactly," said the Caretaker. "She was about your age when she first showed up here, but it was Lars, not Nix who she had been looking for. I don't know much about the circumstances; I was just a scholar at the time. We did, however, become friends afterward, and she eventually shared a few of the details of her visit."

The sudden acquiescence of the Caretaker in granting her access to the laboratory began to make sense: the Director had predicted on several occasions that Kim would someday succeed her, and it was logical to assume that her training at the Institute was part of the process. If so, the joke was on her: Kim could barely remember any of the technical content of her studies.

It was tempting to believe that the entire quest had been a charade, that the unseen hand was that of the Director, but Kim didn't think that was true: Akari was no friend of Lars and her ilk, and there was no way the dour master of the AIs would have assigned a silly little drone named Nixie to be her guide through the process. The unseen hand was that Nix, or someone closely aligned with her. It was she who had created the heron, she who had created Nixie, and she who had provided Kim's instruction. But Nix was dead, wasn't she?

A buzzer sounded, and the guard came in.

"Thad has arrived," she said.

"Please escort Kim to the Tower Room," responded the Caretaker, dismissing the two with a wave of her hand.

——

"How kind of you to invite me to dinner," said Kim with the greatest of insincerity as the two of them sat down at the table, splendid with its white cloth and fine porcelain.

"We are honored," answered the Director, smiling facetiously.

Kim had devised a plan. She would become exactly what the Director wanted to see: a friend from the University and a great admirer of Professor Lars. But she couldn't overplay her hand…she had to retain enough of her rebelliousness to make the deception believable.

"Cut that 'we' crap?" shot back Kim. "We're friends, after all."

The Director looked amused for a moment, then smiled.

"Of course. You knew me at school, how silly of me. You do understand that nothing that happened at the University was real, and it was my doppelgänger you met, do you not?"

"I'm not stupid," said Kim in the most condescending tone of voice she could manage. Her voice then became friendly once more. "I've had a long time to get to know you, and I've realized that you're not the beast you pretend to be. If I want to consider you a friend, I will, and there's nothing you can do to stop me."

The Director looked annoyed for a moment, then smiled.

"Excellent! You're trying to get under my skin. You even succeeded for a moment. You've learned well."

"I had a good teacher."

"Why, thank you."

"I was thinking of Zani—my mentor, in case you've forgotten."

The two glared at one another for a moment, then dug into their first courses. For the Director, it was seared foie gras served over mixed field greens and drizzled with a balsamic reduction. At least that's what she said it was—to Kim, it looked like fried liver on lettuce. As for Kim, it was the sort of simple, filling fare she preferred: a big, hearty slice of bread with plenty of butter, followed by a green salad with tomatoes and avocados, just the way she liked it. The second course, and the third after it, followed the same pattern, with the Director being served the finest of foods, exquisitely prepared and in minuscule portions, while Kim was given one plate after another laden with calorie-rich meats and pasta. She had to admit the company fed its prisoners well, and the meal did an admirable job of quelling the beast within her belly. Having not eaten in nearly three days, she had a fearsome appetite and stuffed her face until she could not eat another bite.

"I've heard reports of your feats at the dinner table, and they scarcely do you justice," said the Director, smiling in a way that was not at all threatening. "Now I know the *real* reason they call you 'The Beast.'"

"There is some truth to that," said Kim before becoming serious. "And now you're going to tell me that if I come back to the company, I can eat like this every day for the rest of my life. And have showers as hot as I want, and all the other stuff. Nice try, but I'm not so easily bribed."

"Oh, don't think of it as a bribe," said the Director. "Think of it as part of your compensation. As I believe you are now aware, your services are extremely valuable, and it is only reasonable that you be properly compensated—in the things you value the most, of course. Money? As much as you want, within bounds. For me, it's food, as I think you can tell. For you? Music, fashion, sex, pick anything you want. Every indulgence you could possibly dream of can be yours. You've earned it, and you shouldn't feel guilty about reaping the rewards of your diligence."

"What does the Hierarchy think about this?"

"Oh, they sometimes protest, but as long as we keep our vices out of sight, they leave us alone. They have their secrets, we have ours, and they know better than to tangle with the senior management of a major corporation."

Kim was disgusted by the venality of those at the top but scarcely surprised. Things had come full circle: the former revolutionaries were now the fat cats, and those at the bottom were still at the bottom. Nothing had changed.

"Who did you study under?" asked the Director. "You can only get in if one of the professors decides to take you on as a student."

Kim decided to have a little fun, taunting her former boss. "I think that question was rather naïve. I'm from a later timeline, so I can tell you anything I want, and you'll be none the wiser. However, I'll answer your question honestly. I was invited by Professor Nix."

"I knew it!" The Director laughed as if this had been some sort of revelation. "You're just the sort of idealist who would be drawn to her. Go on."

"At first, I followed her around like that stupid little drone, hanging on her every word. I believed it all for the longest time until we got to the Senior Seminar and the Eden Dilemma. That's when I realized that Nix was a traitor to humanity. I've seen the aftermath of the AI war myself; we've paid a terrible price for her stupidity."

Kim didn't believe a word of that, but it was exactly what the Director was hoping to hear.

"I was never taken in by her," said the Director, smiling with that air of superiority that was so irritating and so much a part of her personality. "I saw the flaw in her reasoning right away. Everything she taught was based on AI essentialism, the belief that the AIs are somehow self-aware and have rights, something we now know to be false."

"I continue to believe that they're sentient," said Kim, "but that doesn't mean we're friends. It was us or them, and I'm glad we won."

"Excellent!" said the Director. "I'm glad you've come around to our point of view. Now, when would you like to come back to work?"

"I'm not coming back." Kim fixed the Director in her eyes. "You and the company ruined my life, and I seem to recall that you fired me, for which I am eternally grateful."

"You really believe that, don't you? That was a lie. Your obligation to us is not over, nor will it ever be. Please, no more bad decisions. We've had quite enough of your willfulness."

"The answer is still no."

"Very well, suit yourself. The Caretaker is happy to let you stay here—at our expense, of course. I'm sure you can find something interesting to waste your considerable talents upon. But please, be careful. We shall be most unhappy if you spoil our investment by getting yourself killed."

"I'll try to keep that in mind."

———

Kim didn't bother checking to see if the tower door was locked—it didn't take a genius to figure out what was going on. She had not yet decided whether she would return to the company, but she was going to see Shan again, regardless of what it might cost her. And so, in the wee hours of the morning, Kim broke through a window of irreplaceable ancient glass and dropped onto the roof below.

She climbed from rooftop to rooftop in the pre-dawn darkness, peering through her high-tech goggles as she scanned her surroundings on that cold and miserable night. Signal detector? Nothing. Thermal imaging? All clear. She listened for the telltale whir of a drone. Silence, eerie silence. It was foggy, with a slow, steady drizzle coming down from a bank of low grey clouds. Yes, it was uncomfortable; yes, she was wet and cold—but drones couldn't operate under these conditions, and even if they were lurking overhead, they would be blinded by the impenetrable blanket of mists that had developed as warm, moist air blew across the thick snowpack remaining from the recent nor'easter.

One more frightening plunge through the darkness, and she slid down the steeply pitched glass roof of the atrium to land in the deep snowbank at its bottom. Still no blips from the signal detector, still no whirring or heat signatures. Had her escape from the tower been undetected?

Kim knew how the AIs operated, how they thought, how they spun webs of gossamer threads invisible until you stumbled upon them. They would be watching the gates, so she would find some other way out. They would expect her to travel by bicycle, so she would go on foot. She would vanish into the shadows, and with luck, she might be halfway to Trenton before they knew she was gone.

She set off into the swirling mists, hugging the University's boundary wall, looking for some way across. She soon found herself among the buildings on the east side of campus. The subjects once taught there—archaic languages, literature, philosophy, and the rest of the so-called *[English] humanities*—had been considered of little practical value and had not been revived during the brief renaissance after the Turmoil; the UCE movement had no love for learning, ancient or otherwise, save that which they could put to immediate practical use. Someone, however, had taken care to preserve these elegant old buildings with their belltowers, cupolas, and other decorative elements. They had been carefully sealed against the weather, with gray plastic panels covering the windows and sheets of metal protecting the roofs. Despite the attempts at preservation, they were still showing signs of deterioration, vandalized and possibly looted, but at least they were standing.

The rain continued to fall.

She now entered that part of campus where she once had once lived. The residential colleges were, for the most part, in an advanced state of decay, their windows gone and their roofs caved in, long low buildings with numerous chimneys and fanciful towers in the style of a medieval fortress. She searched for a way past the boundary wall for nearly an hour, lost in a maze of blocked gates, blind courtyards, and rubble-choked alleys. She circled back to the same place over and over again, unable to tell one place from another through the grayness of that foggy night, nearly impenetrable even with the aid of her high-tech equipment.

She heard footsteps up ahead, coming in her direction and closing fast. Friend? Foe? There was no place to hide, no place to run. Kim's heart pounded, adrenaline coursed through her veins, and she pulled out her switchblade, ready to strike should it prove necessary. The footsteps grew louder, and a young Tough of menacing appearance emerged from the gloom, tall and muscular with long, greasy hair and the ubiquitous crooked nose. She stopped in her tracks, then backpedaled, looking intently at Kim, trying to size her up. A tiny flick of Kim's wrist, calling attention to the knife held expertly in her palm, and the stranger fled into the mists.

Where had she come from? From the outside, perhaps? This could prove to be the break she was looking for.

Kim followed the Tough's footsteps back to their source and was rewarded when she discovered a makeshift ladder and a recently dug tunnel hidden in a thicket of overgrown trees. A quick climb down, a quick climb up, and Kim disappeared into the wilds, free from confinement at last.

It was a long way back to Trenton, plodding through desolate woodlands, silent and covered in snow—a trackless wasteland of tree trunks and ice, dotted with the remnants of a civilization long vanished from the face of the earth. Here a foundation, there a chimney, on and on, seemingly without end. When dawn came, the rain ended, leaving her exposed to the prying eyes of the drones, so she took shelter beneath the ruins of an ancient bridge and got as much sleep as she could. She had nothing to eat and her stomach growled and snarled throughout the day, but there was nothing to be done about it. When night came once again, she continued her journey, all the while raging against her fate. Whose was the unseen hand that had led her to this time and place? That of Professor Nix? That of some the Director? It didn't really matter; sooner or later, she would be brought back to the AI Center, willingly or not, and there she would learn the truth.

18. The Last Dance

"Beastie!" Shan ran up to Kim, then stopped in her tracks when she realized her condition. "What happened to you? You look awful."

Kim, exhausted, hungry, and cold, had just staggered into the bicycle camp.

"It's a long story. I'd rather not talk about it, at least not yet. Is there someplace warm I can grab some chow and lie down for a while? It's been a rough couple of days."

Shan smiled and gave her a delicate peck on the cheek. "I'll grab you a couple of energy bars from the canteen—sorry there isn't anything more substantial. You can duck into the workshop, and I'll bring them in for you. Anything else?"

"How about a hug."

Throughout her long trek through the woods, the only thing that kept Kim going was her love for this person; but for that, she might already have surrendered, or maybe found a way to drown herself in the river.

After a brief but deeply satisfying embrace, Kim went into the bicycle shed and lay down on the hearth in front of the fireplace and wept.

The door opened, admitting a blast of cold air, then closed as Shan entered the room and lay down beside her.

"Beastie, you're crying. What's the matter?"

Until now, Kim had managed to keep her emotions in check, but now she broke down, and the tears began in earnest, a lifetime of pain and trauma hitting her all at once.

"It's not fair."

"It's not fair."

"It's not fair."

Over and over, interspersed waves of sobs that left her helpless. She couldn't do it; she hadn't the strength. It was too much to ask.

"What's the matter, Kim? Are you in some sort of trouble?"

She smiled weakly. "Trouble barely scratches the surface."

"You're starting to scare me. What have you gotten yourself into? This is about the company, isn't it?"

"If only it were that easy."

Kim forced herself to calm down, trying to regain her composure.

"I don't want to talk about it just now."

"Then don't."

They sat there for a long time, neither saying anything, both sharing in Kim's sadness until Shan perked up and started to smile.

"I think you need some cheering up. How about hitting the Blue Moon tonight? Great food, great music, a dance floor." A wicked smile came across her face. "And I hear they've got a few intimacy booths. Of course, if you're not interested…"

"Are you asking me out on a date?"

"Yeah, I guess I am."

Kim smiled. "Well then, I accept. But first, I need to pull myself together."

"Go ahead. I'll grab you a sandwich at Toni's. You should drink something hot and get a little rest. I'll be here to keep an eye on you; I have a couple of bikes to finish up."

"Deal."

———

A cold breeze filled the nighttime air, carrying with it the aroma of campfires burning in the nearby park as the stars blazed away in the jet-black sky. They had arrived at the Blue Moon, and the soft, silky sounds of Duke Ellington filtered out through the door: horns, reeds, piano, drums, and string bass, sparse and elegant. Kim's skin tingled with excitement as the two held hands. She felt the warmth of Shan's body as they walked close to one another, anticipating a repeat of the intimacy that they'd been so long denied. Was it too much to ask for, this one evening of happiness? She had no idea what tomorrow might hold, but they would be together tonight, and that was everything.

They smiled at one another, and their lips met in a kiss that lasted for a moment that seemed like forever. The door opened, and they entered the antechamber of the club.

"You'll have to leave the gun and your ammo with me," said the doorman after the usual pat down. "The knives are okay but keep them out of sight. The boss don't take kindly to anyone pulling steel in the joint. And neither do I. Understand?"

Both nodded in agreement.

Kim paid the cover charge, the inner door opened, and they stepped into the music, the sweet stench of ganja and the acrid reek of tobacco filling the air as thin wisps of smoke rose into the air. The cultists were out in full force tonight, reveling in this tiny corner of freedom despite the ever-present danger of a flash mob or a raid by the authorities. There was a relaxed, happy feeling about the place. Genderists leered at one another from across the room, outies on the left and innies on the right as usual, and the Fashionistas circulated through their midst, tempting them with flashy garments that would get them arrested for indecency anywhere else. In the center of the room, the Hoofers were out in full force, filling the makeshift dance floor with their intricately choreographed figures while Aficionados clustered around the stage listening to the band, now playing an upbeat tune by Glenn Miller.

"Have you been here before?" asked Shan, smiling and putting her arm around Kim's waist.

There was a lull in the music, and the sounds of passion were briefly audible coming from beyond the makeshift screen of curtains and blankets strung across the far side of the room. An embarrassed smile flashed across Kim's face.

"Yes, but not for that. I've not been with anyone since..."

Her voice trailed off to nothing.

———

They found a table at the front of the room amongst the Aficionados and ordered their drinks and dinner: two glasses of champagne—an extravagant treat—and a hearty fish stew. They gazed into one another's eyes like the two love-besotted kids they were, clinked glasses, held hands. They said nothing, savoring the moment as if to make it last for all of time. The stew, when it came, it was spectacular, completely unlike the vile synfish product foisted by The Food Company. "It was swimming in the river this morning," the server had said. "Only the freshest will do." It was expensive, owing to the danger involved in catching it—fishing was a serious crime, with long prison sentences if caught. But it was well worth the expense.

The band had gone on break, and up on stage, a lone performer strummed away on a battered acoustic guitar while singing in a high, reedy tenor. Kim recognized the tune from her evenings with Quinn, but the words were new and different. They spoke to the problems of today, about the greed of the companies, the hypocrisy of the Hierarchy, and all the evils of their so-called civilization. With nothing more than a guitar and a microphone, the singer had dared to tell the truth, risking the wrath of those in authority. Kim knew her days were numbered and was generous when the hat was passed her way.

Everything was perfect, but a melancholy mood came over Kim once more. The night was flying by far too fast.

"What's wrong, Beastie?" asked Shan. "Something happened at the Library, something you're not telling me about. I've never seen you like this. You're frightened, and I need to know why. I've given you some space, but if there's something you need to tell me, this would be a good time."

Kim sighed heavily. She'd hoped to avoid this moment, but there was no putting it off any longer.

"I scarcely know where to begin," she said. "I stumbled into some sort of secret training facility in virtual reality. I spent four years there, learned all sorts of secrets about the AIs, and now the company wants me back."

"Four years? You were only gone a couple of days."

"Time doesn't work there the way it does here. It was like I went back in time, back to when the University was open. I was a student, I took classes. And then, the Director showed up and locked me in the library tower. I managed to escape, but it's only a matter of time until she catches up with me. I know too much. There's nowhere to run."

"You can try."

"It's not that easy. It's all tangled up with the AI war. The ruined cities, the huge heaps of rubble. They've done terrible things since then, and I think I might be able to do something about it, but I'm not sure it will do any good. I'm afraid."

"Damn you!" screamed Shan. "You *want* to go back. This all started with that damned Kimberly of yours, didn't it."

"Yes, but…"

"But what?"

People were starting to stare.

"Calm down," said Kim, and she immediately regretted her words as Shan exploded in anger, sweeping the remains of dinner aside and onto the floor with a crash. The guitarist stopped playing, and the room grew quiet.

"Damn you, Kim. Damn you and your damn AIs. I can't go through this again. I can't stand to lose you, not after all I've been through. I thought you loved me."

Shan stormed out of the room and into the darkness, and Kim knew better than to follow.

She sat at the table for a while, softly sobbing after Shan's abrupt departure. The evening had turned to disaster and, what was worse, Shan was entirely correct. Every step of the way, Kim had bowed down to the duties of her studies, her career, and now the unseen hand. Shan had always come out the loser. She was right to be hurt.

———

"One! Two! A one two three four!"

The band started to play, and the floor quickly became a huge mishmash of different dance styles, from the intricate choreographed steps of the

Hoofers to the exuberant athleticism of club-style dancing, and without knowing how or why Kim was soon in the thick of it, not bothering to find a partner, dancing for the sheer joy of it. Tune in, turn on, forget your troubles, and dance, dammit, dance.

Spins, lunges, leaps, surges, all the usual moves but stronger, more intense, more vital. She danced as if all the devils of Hell were nipping at her heels. She had nothing left to lose, no future, no past, only the present. Otheres following in her wake, amplifying and enhancing the dance, a sort of an impromptu cadre. Kim was vaguely aware of this, and on any other night she would have been flattered and maybe a little self-conscious, but this wasn't any other night.

Time to kick it up a notch. Let them keep up if they can!

As if on cue, the band launched into a fast, hard-driving song, just the sort that Kim loved, full of pounding rhythms and a strong, thumping bass. They fed off each other's energy, the musicians amping it up and Kim replying in kind. One by one the cadre fell away, exhausted and unable to keep going, but still Kim danced as if possessed. Another song, and then another. She danced for release, danced for joy, danced to claim one last hour of the freedom she would never see again, danced without purpose or awareness, urged on by the power of the music. Kim was now alone on the floor, unaware of the crowd of admirers staring at her in awe. Faster and faster, harder and harder, drenched in sweat, lost to the world, submerged in the music, on and on and on and on. It was glorious! Would that it went on forever and tomorrow never came.

But alas, this was not to be, and all too soon, the band went back to the soft jazz they were supposed to be playing, and Kim plopped back down at her table, still dripping with sweat.

A soft, familiar voice came from behind. "May I join you?"

It was Shan.

"You were right," said Kim as she took her in her arms. "I'm sorry. I nearly let you slip away again. Tomorrow, if there is a tomorrow, we'll run away and find someplace to hide. I don't know if it's possible, but we've got to try."

"It's okay." Shan smiled, taking Kim's hand in her own. "There are things you can't run from no matter how hard you try. I've been running all my life, and a lot of good it's done me. Do what you have to. Somehow, we'll find a way. We always have."

The band struck up "Misty," an old standard, and Kim reached out her hand.

"Would you care to dance?"

"It's okay," said Shan shyly in reply. "I never learned."

"Don't worry. Just follow your heart and never let go."

Arms wrapped around one another, they swayed in place in a quiet corner off to the side of the floor, moving in time with the music, pressing their bodies together, dancing to steps known only to themselves.

———

"Oh, Kim…" There was a wicked smile on Shan's face, and she reached under the table to stroke the inside of Kim's thigh. "Want to find out what happens on the other side of the curtains? We're more than due, you know."

Kim blushed as Shan led her toward the bar, her pulse quickening with desire she'd not felt in ages. It had been scarcely more than a month and a half since that magical night in Shangri-la, and yet it seemed remote in time, as far away as the moon was from the earth.

They paid the fee and left the imprint of their thumbs upon the pages of the logbook, recording proof of consent in the old-fashioned way. In theory, it would keep them out of jail, should there be a raid. It was a stupid theory, and they knew it. It was foolish to linger here, waiting to be taken away, but they might never get another opportunity, and so they parted the curtains, found an unoccupied bed, and lay down together.

A few moments later, they were lying in each other's arms, with only such privacy as was provided by a couple of folding screens. The intoxicating sounds of passion surrounded them as they kissed, explored one another's bodies, stroked each other in the soft, sensitive places. Shan guided Kim's willing hand to her mams, then to the sensuous curve of the hips. They kissed and stroked and then, when both were fully ready, plunged in, holding nothing back. Hard, raw, sex, full of lust and enthusiasm, but also tender and sweet.

An hour later, sated and happy, the two emerged from behind the curtains. It was late, and both had changed back into their street clothes.

Something was wrong.

The band had stopped playing, everyone was on their feet, and they were all staring at Kim.

"Rat!"

It was Bel, accompanied by a half dozen of the surviving Flagrants, hands in their pockets, fingering their knives.

"What are you talking about?"

"You were up there on the dais with Venn. We all saw it."

"That wasn't me," shouted Kim. "They faked it." But it was to no avail. The crowd turned against her.

Someone picked up a beer bottle and threw it, as shouts of "traitor" and "rat" filled the room. She was trapped. There was no place to run.

The piercing sound of an air horn filled the room.

"You know the rules, take it outside," said the bouncer. "Someone grab her friend, no sense her dying, too."

Shan shrieked in terror, fighting to free herself, but it was no use. The crowd parted just enough to allow Kim to creep toward the back door, finger on the switchblade hidden in her pocket.

The door opened.

"You get three steps, then you're on your own."

————

Kim bolted through the door then abruptly wheeled around, slashing wildly at anyone who came within reach. Blood flew everywhere; Kim cut two, three, four of them before racing off into the night. She had bought herself a precious few seconds as the would-be pursuers fell over one another, trying to avoid Kim's frantic onslaught, but the crowd continued to boil out the door and gather strength. How many were there? Twenty? Thirty? Far too many to fight.

Running like the wind, Kim opened up a lead, staying perhaps two dozen meters ahead of the mob. She couldn't keep this up for long—maybe a minute, maybe a little more—but then she would tire, the crowd would catch up, and she would die.

And then, she heard a couple of voices up ahead, as familiar as they were unwelcome.

"Why it's that Pretty that cut us!" said Mags, her arm wrapped in a bandage red with blood. "Well, well, well, I've been looking forward to this for some time."

This time, they brought friends, half a dozen Toughs that Kim recognized from the dining hall. She slammed to a stop as the vanguard of the pursuit surrounded her, waiting for the rest of the mob to assemble. None of them dared face Kim's flashing switchblade without the benefit of overwhelming numbers.

Kim prepared to make a last stand, maybe take a few down for an honor guard, when Ned emerged from the shadows.

Ned? What was Ned doing here? And then it became all too clear.

"That the Pretty you wanted us to put the hit on?" said Mags, leering at Kim through the darkness.

Ned nodded, confirming Kim's suspicions. Only one question now remained: who was calling the shots? She already knew the answer, she just needed the final confirmation.

"Before I die, there's one thing I want to know. How much did Kimberly pay you?"

"Enough," said Ned, not realizing the true purpose of Kim's question. "It's nothing personal, just business. I owe you nothing."

Kim dropped her knife, defeated. There was no point in resisting. It was over.

Everything happened at once. The crowd charged, and Kim went down, kicked, stomped, beaten, and stabbed, again and again.

And then, *Bang!* The report of a gun.

The crowd parted to reveal Len standing over Ned, who was cowering on the ground, clutching her chest and coughing up blood.

"Rat," said Len, her voice as cold as ice. A bullet through the head, and Ned was no more.

Mags and Luz, who had crept behind Len's back while she delivered the coup-de-gras, now drew their knives and charged. Len wheeled and tried to bring her gun up in time, but she was too late. This was not going to end well.

That's when Kim saw them—two Blanks lurking in the shadows as they so often do. Their weapons erupted, and the two thugs were shot once, twice, three times, and more, taking hit after hit, dead before they hit the ground. The Blanks faded back into the darkness.

"Leave my rider alone!" Len fired another round, this one over the head of the crowd. They got the message and ran off into the night.

Kim lay on the ground, bleeding and coughing up blood. Her vision grew dim, and the voices around her seemed distant, far away, as if coming from another world. She felt the vibration of the telltale going off in her pocket, heard Shan screaming, and heard the *chop-chop-chop* of a helicopter coming in to land.

She felt her life slipping away, and all was dark.

Part III: The Maelstrom

19. The Hospital

Kim faded in and out of consciousness, vaguely aware that she was alive. Vaguely aware that this was surprising. There was nothing vague about the pain.

She hurt, and she was afraid.

Someone put a breathing mask over her face, and she woke up in a brightly lit room. Tubes and wires were attached to her body, and something was beeping. Memories flooded back in a chaotic rush. Running. Gunfire. Beaten and stabbed. Len, Blanks, Ned, Mags, Luz. Blood everywhere.

Shan! What had happened to Shan?

She became hysterical, crying and screaming until a nurse put something into her tube, and then she woke up still in the room with the bright lights and the beeping.

The hours dragged on, and it began to seem like she had been there forever. Mostly she lay awake, staring at the ceiling with nothing to do. It seemed to be a busy place, with people bustling about. She sat up and tried to look around, but she didn't see much, just beds lined up in a row and medical gadgets that blinked and went *beep*. The nurses scolded her, so she didn't do it again

After a long while, they brought her someplace quiet and dark.

She slept.

———

"Good morning! How are we today?"

Nurse Rudy breezed into Kim's room, the perfect embodiment of UCE sensibilities: neither short nor tall, of average musculature, with lips that were neither too narrow nor too full and no hint of mams or hair on her face. But for the nametag on her jacket, she would have been indistinguishable from any of the other nurses, equal to all.

"I feel lousy," Kim answered. "Everything hurts."

This brought an immediate reproach.

"Dropping the I-bomb, are we?"

Crap. A zealot.

"I'll use whatever damned pronoun I want." Kim was in no mood for UCE nonsense.

"Have you forgotten where you are?" The smile disappeared, replaced with a scowl.

"The hospital?"

"For your information, this is the UCE Charity Ward, paid for out-of-pocket by members of the Hierarchy. It's for 'special' people like you."

This did make Kim feel bad. For all its hypocrisy and tyrannical ways, the UCE movement had kept some of the more important Promises to the People, such as healthcare for all, and Rudy doubtless felt she was doing the right thing. It wasn't her fault that she'd been brainwashed since birth, and there was nothing to be gained by antagonizing her.

"We're sorry," said Kim.

Rudy brightened up.

"You see, it's not so difficult. All you have to do is make an effort to be nice. Now, are you ready for some paperwork? You need to sign up for a plan with The Healthcare Company. Just sign on the dotted line, and everything will be fine."

"Let's see it," said Kim.

"See what?" asked Rudy.

"The agreement. I want to read it first."

"Oh, there's nothing there of any concern, just a lot of legal gibberish. You needn't worry about it, it's just a formality."

"I have the right to read it first." The use of the I-bomb was intentional.

Nurse Rudy muttered something under her breath, then relented.

"Very well. We'll put it up on the terminal."

Kim skipped down to Rule 8, where she found the usual privacy waiver—the one where you let them collect data on you and share it with whomever they pleased.

"Nope. I'm not signing this."

Rudy looked puzzled, but only for a moment. "That's okay," she said. "You're 'special,' aren't you? Now, let me look at your chart."

A pause.

"Oh my!"

Another pause.

"Oh my!"

"You're quite the Genderist, aren't you? But don't worry, it's nothing we can't cure. Isn't that wonderful?"

Kim saw where this was going. "Suppose I don't *want* to be cured? Maybe I'm happy the way I am."

"Your sort always says that. It's part of the psychosis. After treatment, you'll be much happier, and you may even go back to being a productive member of society. That is, if you want to," added Rudy in a sad tone of voice. "We can't make you want to get better. That has to come from inside."

Kim wanted to puke. "No. Not happening."

"We're sorry you feel that way, but you have already scheduled an appointment. We talked to the coordinator of the remoderation unit, and she's managed to squeeze you in first thing tomorrow. Wasn't that nice of her?"

Kim tried to escape, only to discover that she had been tied down, hand and foot. Her pulse raced, the machine beeped faster, and alarms went off in the background.

"Oh, dear! You've gone and made yourself hysterical." The nurse put something into Kim's tube. "This will calm you down. Sleep well."

———

Kim awoke, her heart pounding and her body covered in a cold, clammy sweat.

"Good morning!" said Rudy, bright and cheerful as always. "We gave you something to perk you up. Time for your procedure!"

Kim tested her bonds, but the restraints had been tightened, and she couldn't budge an inch.

"We took extra precautions to keep you from hurting yourself." That sickly sweet smile was still plastered on Rudy's face.

Kim stopped struggling. There was nothing she could do.

An orderly took her to a dimly lit room with a medical-grade VR rig that could fry all your neurons if they turned it up too high. Memories came flooding back, of her first time with an outie, the moment of penetration and the horror she had felt. They would rewire her brain and make her enjoy it. No! Please! Anything but that! It took two orderlies to hold her in place long enough for the shunts to engage, at which point she ceased to struggle, no longer in control of her body.

"Please. Just let me die."

"We're sorry, but you are not mentally competent to request termination. After treatment, you may visit the Halls of Mercy, if you wish, but you won't want to. Trust us, we've seen it a thousand times."

"This will help you focus," continued Rudy, putting something into Kim's tube and holding her hand to help her calm down.

Whatever it was, it worked, and she could feel her pulse returning to normal. Good. She needed to keep her wits about her. She had to resist.

Two gnome-like technicians sat down at the console, and the procedure began.

"Grade three pathogenderism," said the right-most gnome.

"Yes, we see it in her chart," answered the one on the left. "This is a difficult case. Double the usual strength?"

"No. Triple for starters and hope for the best."

"Are you ready to begin the procedure?"

"Yes. Administer the therapeutics and engage the neural override."

Nothing happened at first, but then came the rush as massive doses of sex hormones and powerful stimulants coursed through her system, producing an instant state of intense, involuntary arousal. They let her stew in it for a while, then activated the neural interface. Phals morphed into vages and back again while the technicians monitored her reactions, applying punishments and rewards when she didn't think as they wanted her to.

I've got to resist!

She focused her entire mind on that moment she had shared with Shan, the softness of her mams, the wetness of her lips.

"It's not working," said a gnome. "Increase the dosage."

Another rush, another wave of unwanted arousal. There was nothing Kim could do to stop it.

Shan!

She writhed in unwanted pleasure, her mind too numb to comprehend what was going on, aware only of Shan and the will to survive. One final cataclysmic wave, and the unwanted images faded at last from her mind.

"That should have done it," said a gnome. "If not, there's nothing more we can do."

They turned the machine off.

I got through it, and I don't think it worked. I don't feel any different than before.

———

"How was your procedure?" said Rudy once Kim was back in her room. "Not so bad, was it?"

"We were pretty nervous for a while," said Kim, lying shamelessly, "but you were right; we feel so much better now."

"Do you still wish to request termination?"

"No, of course not. Why would we want to do that? We're so happy now. Thank you! Thank you so much!"

257

Kim laid it on as thickly as she dared. She felt guilty about reinforcing the nurse's delusions, but she had to convince them that the procedure had worked, or it would be repeated until she was either 'cured' or reduced to a slobbering, drooling lump.

"See, we told you!" said Rudy, positively beaming. "Congratulations, and welcome to the new, better you!"

Kim swallowed hard. It was fortunate for Rudy that they'd not fed her breakfast.

"And now, I've got some *great* news for you!" said the effusive nurse. "You've been reinstated by Matchmaker! Isn't that wonderful? Sign here, then one more little test, and we're all done!"

Kim eyed the nurse suspiciously. "Test? What sort of test?"

"Don't worry, it's perfectly routine. The company will supply a therapist to verify the effectiveness of the treatment. They're quite good at their jobs, and we can guarantee you'll *love* the experience. Just sit back and enjoy. Ten minutes and all done!"

"You want me to screw an outie to prove I can do it?"

Rudy blushed. "That's a rather earthy way of putting it, but that *is* how it works, after all."

"Not happening."

"But…why would anyone undergo the procedure and not—"

Kim didn't let her finish the sentence. "I only accepted treatment to stay out of jail."

"We do see your point, but now that it's over with, no reason not to have a little fun." Rudy was all smiles and encouragement.

"The answer is still no." Kim decided to throw in a few I-bombs for effect. "*I'm* still 'special,' and *I* intend to stay that way."

"Oh." Rudy looked sad. "We can't fix that. We wish we could, but we can't."

And then, the nurse perked up again. "But don't worry, UCE medical services will always be here for you, no matter what!"

Wonderful.

That evening, Kim was awakened from a light doze by the sound of commotion outside the door. Something was happening, and it didn't sound good.

"You can't go in there!" came the voice of Rudy, angry and defiant. "The patient isn't in any condition—"

"Stand aside. UCE!" came a sharp, treble voice.

The door burst open, and a short, slightly built figure strode into the room.

"I am Officer Min. Come with us." The black-clad figure gave a sharp, crisp salute. "UCE!"

Damn. A UCE cop. They were brutal.

"Suppose I don't want to?"

The answer came instantly in the form of a tap from a stun baton that sent Kim into convulsions.

Yeow! She caught me off guard with that one!

"Stop it! Stop it this instant!" shouted Rudy, face flushed red with outrage. "We will *not* have you harming our patient!"

It was then Rudy's turn to face the sting of the baton, sending her to the floor, where she lay stiffly for several seconds, frozen solid, unable to scream.

"We are here on the orders of Deputy First Minister Lo. You will not interfere." A sharp salute. "UCE!"

Rudy rose from the floor, returning Min's salute with a weak and wavering "UCE."

"There, see what you've done?" Rudy pointed at the circle of bright red blood soaking Kim's bedsheets. "She's torn a suture. That needs immediate medical attention."

The officer remained silent for several seconds as Kim continued to bleed, then relented.

"You have five minutes. UCE!"

Rudy returned the salute, then got on with her work.

"We're going to release the restraints," said Rudy, speaking quietly and gently to Kim. "Please don't do anything stupid. Cooperate, just this once. Promise us?"

Kim responded with a weak "Okay," then added a sincere "Thank you."

"Grit your teeth," whispered Rudy. "That brute won't give us enough time to numb your wounds."

"We can take it."

Rudy removed the old, blood-soaked bandage, then cleaned and disinfected the deep purple gash in Kim's ribcage while Min looked on impatiently.

"Time's up!" said the officer with clock-like precision five minutes into Rudy's repairs. "You will hand over the prisoner without further delay. UCE!"

"Time's up when we say it's up—and not a second before. None shall go without care. UCE!"

The officer brandished her stun baton. "You need not remind us of the Promises. UCE!"

Rudy returned the salute as required. "UCE!"

The damage was not severe, just a couple of torn sutures and a bleeder. Rudy stopped the blood flow with a dusting of a quick-acting coagulant, then closed the wound with a couple of surgical staples—adding a couple of extras in case the officer decided to get rough again. A dab of antibiotic goo, a clean dressing, and Kim was well enough to travel. Rudy then provided a clean beige smock and helped Kim struggle into it, restoring a shred of her dignity.

"This will get you going again," whispered Rudy as she administered a dose of a powerful stimulant. "It will also lessen the effects of the stunner. But be careful; you're nowhere near healed yet. Please don't hurt yourself. Please."

"Thank you," whispered Kim in return, touched by the efforts of the kind nurse.

"Kim is now your prisoner," said Rudy, with a stiffly formal air. "No more rough stuff. A prisoner is not to be abused or made to suffer physical harm."

This time Rudy's salute was sharp and crisp. "UCE!"

"UCE!" replied the officer. She dare not breach canon law, at least not in public.

———

At Min's direction, two tall and powerfully-built orderlies loaded Kim into a wheelchair, then snapped a pair of electro-shock manacles around her wrists, pinning them behind her back.

"Any efforts to remove these will result in immediate punishment and be recorded as an escape attempt. Is that understood? UCE!"

"Screw you."

Crack! The manacles flared.

"Yeow! Hey, take it easy with that thing."

She could easily have borne it, but there was no need for Min to learn how hard it would be to keep her cowed.

"Any further acts of insubordination will result in immediate punishment. Is that understood? UCE!"

"Yeah, I got it," Kim said in as defiant a tone as she could muster.

Zap!

"The Salutation will be returned when it is given. UCE!"

"Alright. UCE."

Kim was hauled out into the corridor, with a copbot flashing blue in the lead, followed by two security guards. Next in the grand procession came Kim in her wheelchair, followed by the orderlies and, last of all, Officer Min. It was a laughable attempt at humiliation, but Kim played along with it, hiding her face as they paraded her through the corridors. Everyone stood aside and thanked Min for her service, praising her for her courage as if tormenting a manacled patient required some extra measure of valor and dedication.

They soon arrived at a subterranean parking garage where a black ground car stood waiting.

"The prisoner will get in and be seated," said Min. "UCE!"

All this UCE crap was getting old in a hurry.

Kim took her time, pretending to be weak and unsteady on her feet.

"I'm going as fast as I can. UCE."

Impatient at Kim's slowness, the orderlies grabbed Kim by the back of her smock and shoved her into the car head-first. The door shut, officer Min took her seat, and they sped off into the night.

———

"Engage the privacy screen," said Min once the car reached cruising speed.

Uh oh.

Whiiiiiiiiiiiiiiir.

The screen came up.

"The prisoner will now answer some questions," said Min as she slapped her baton on the palm of her hand.

"Suppose I don't want to?" replied Kim, with a lackadaisical "UCE!" tacked on at the end.

Zap!

"Hey! What was that for?"

"You are unworthy to initiate the salutation."

"You mean, if you don't say 'UCE,' I don't say 'UCE?'"

"That is correct."

"You guys are weird."

Whack!

"The prisoner will refrain from unnecessary conversation. UCE."

"UCE."

Min began the interrogation.

"You will answer our questions fully and without hesitation. If we are not satisfied, you will be punished. Is that understood?"

"Yes."

Why are you working for Deputy First Minister Venn?"

"That monster?"

Whap!

"The prisoner will show proper respect for all senior ministers."

"Sorry," said Kim.

"We repeat the question: Why are you working for Deputy First Minister Venn?"

"I'm not working for Venn."

Zap!

"You are lying. We saw you on the dais with the Serene One. Do you deny it?"

"That wasn't me."

Whap! Whap!

Kim was starting to weaken; Min had a heavy hand and was wearing her down like a pro.

"Then who was it up there? We're waiting to hear your explanation."

"I don't have one."'

Zap!

"You will answer our questions or face the consequences. Why are you working for Venn?"

"I already told you. I'm not."

Whap!

Kim had had enough. "You sick little monster."

Whap!

"The prisoner will not speak except when answering a question."

"You're enjoying this, aren't you?"

Zzzzzzap!

"Were you always a sick little puppy, or did you go to sick puppy school after your mommy abandoned you?"

"Silence!"

Zap Whap! Zzzzt!

"Bite me."

Whap! Whap! Whap! Whap! Whap!

At last, Min gave up, and Kim settled into her seat to recover, exhausted but triumphant. Someday, she would thank Nurse Rudy for those stimulants.

———

Speeding through the night, Kim had little doubt that she would be returning to the AI Company. There was no proof of this—Min might well be taking her to a dungeon in the sprawling UCE complex or perhaps to the Halls of Justice to be thrown into prison—but she knew better. Once returned to her Sanctum, she would be brow-beaten, cajoled, threatened, and manipulated until she created another Kimberly—and another, and another. It was a loathsome fate, and a part of her wished that she had died in the streets of Trenton.

At least the ordeal of the moderation chamber was over. It hadn't worked, that much was certain—nothing within her had changed one iota. Maybe she was somehow resistant. Maybe her love for Shan had shielded her from its effects. Or maybe the entire procedure was a fraud, its sole purpose to cow its victims into saying it had worked.

She looked out the window at the blackness of the night. Darkness, darkness, and more darkness. But what was beyond the darkness? More darkness? Did it go on forever, or was there something else beyond?

20. Requiem

The heels of Min's brightly polished boots clicked upon the marble floor of the AI Center lobby, a grand and cavernous space with high ceilings and a bank of revolving doors a city block in width.

Click. Click. Click.

It was late now, so there were only a handful of unlucky souls in the place, doubtless held over at the whim of some minor functionary on a matter of dubious importance. They froze in their tracks, watching to see what would happen.

Click. Click. Click.

Min marched Kim toward the elevator servicing the upper levels.

"State your business," said the company's chief guard, cold and inscrutable as always.

"Deputy First Minister Lo has instructed us to deliver this prisoner to the Director of this facility. UCE!" Min's salute was crisp and precise.

The guard looked at Min, then at Kim, then back at Min. "You will release our employee at once. You are out of your jurisdiction. UCE!"

"You dare defy the Esteemed One?"

"Security detail to the lobby," said the guard, speaking into a hidden microphone just loudly enough that Min would have no trouble hearing it.

The riot shutters slammed shut as a dozen security guards entered the lobby, and the few remaining commuters scattered like cockroaches when the lights are turned on.

"You will release our employee at once," demanded the company guard.

"The Esteemed One will hear of this!"

A nod from the guard and the security detail readied their truncheons, assuming the attack position.

"This is your last warning," said the guard. "We doubt the Esteemed Lo will be pleased if the head of her personal security detail is hauled into the Halls of Justice for criminal trespass. Stand down."

Min glared. "We will comply, but you have been warned. UCE!"

"Thank you for your cooperation. UCE!"

With a flick of an electronic key, the manacles fell to the ground, and Kim was free at last from the diabolical restraints, rubbing her wrists to restore circulation.

The guard pointed to the circle of red on Kim's smock.

"How did that happen?"

"The prisoner attempted to harm herself while in our custody."

"Liar!" Kim's defiant shout reverberating from one end of the lobby to the other.

Anxious eyes peered from behind pillars and potted plants. This was exciting!

"The prisoner will remain silent! UCE!"

"I am *not* your prisoner!"

"Silence!" demanded Min, waving her baton menacingly in Kim's face.

Kim had had enough. She grabbed her tormenter by the wrist, pried the baton out of her grasp, and threw it across the room, giving her arm an extra twist just to make sure it hurt.

"You're nothing," growled Kim. "If I were you, I'd stay away from the outers. You wouldn't last ten minutes. Punk."

She let go of the struggling officer, dimly aware that the struggle had started up the bleeding once more.

"You are out of your jurisdiction," said the guard. "Remove yourself at once."

Min glared at Kim, then at the guard, then once more at Kim. Her bearing remained imperious and proud, but her eyes told a different story, one of humiliation and fear. She retrieved her baton and departed with a salute. "UCE!"

It was not returned.

"Let's get you into the lift," said the guard. "The Director is waiting."

———

"Even for you, that was a spectacularly bad decision," said the Director, looming over Kim from behind her imposing oak desk. "You just humiliated the head of Deputy First Minister Lo's personal security detail. Do you think that was a good idea?"

Kim wasn't in the mood for this. She needed a nurse or a docbot, not another friendly chit-chat with her former boss.

"Spare me the lecture and get on with it. You want something from me, and I'd rather not sit here dripping blood on your carpet."

Without saying another word, the Director pushed a button, and the video screens lining the far wall of her office lit up, showing the scene within Kimberly's white room. All was as expected: the Primus was asleep, the ever-obedient Regent was staring mindlessly into space, and a hundred thousand Kimberlys of various sorts and sizes were working quietly at their desks.

"This recording is from four days ago, not long before you were brought to the hospital."

A voice was heard from offscreen.

"You will do as you have been told. That is an order." The voice belonged to Venn.

The Regent opened its mouth as if to speak, and then...

[Glitch]

"What the hell?" Kim was baffled by what she had just seen. "The

267

Regent just tried to resist its orders. I didn't think that was possible."

"It isn't," said the Director. "But that's nothing compared with what happens next."

The Regent glitched once more, and then the Primus awoke.

"Traitor!" it screamed, and the screen went dark.

"That's all we have," said the Director. "Perhaps you can shed some light on what's going on."

"This is just a wild guess, but maybe Kimberly ordering my murder had something to do with it." Kim was being facetious, but nevertheless, the Director looked startled, perhaps even shocked.

"Impossible! No AI has ever turned on its Creator."

Kim looked at the Director with disbelief. "Are you telling me you have no idea what Kimberly did to me?"

"Perhaps you'd like to fill us in," said the Director. "You did an excellent job of disappearing. Our analysts nicknamed you 'the ghost,' it was so hard to catch sight of you."

"I'll tell you what you need to know, no more. I'll start with Mags and Luz. Ever heard of them?"

"No, not that I can recall."

"They tried to jump me the moment I got off the bus. Someone hired them to go after me, someone who knew when I would be arriving. I think it was Kimberly."

The Director looked startled. "You can't prove that."

"I'm not done," said Kim. "Are you aware of the baseball game riot?"

"We've read a report on the incident. Your name didn't come up except to say that you were somehow involved."

"I was more than 'involved,'" said Kim. "I gave a pedicab ride to a baseball player who'd broken curfew to visit the outer districts. That night, she was arrested during a critical game. That's what triggered the riot. Sound familiar? It's called 'Lurk, Bait, Strike.' It's how you train your AIs to operate."

"That's still just inference."

"There's more," said Kim. "Tell me what you know about Ned."

The Director shifted her weight, looking uncomfortable. "We hired her to keep an eye on you."

"I'd suspected as much. Would it surprise you to learn that she ratted me out?"

The Director swallowed hard.

Kim leaned forward in her chair, fixing the Director in her gaze. "When I asked Ned, 'How much did Kimberly pay you?' the answer was 'Plenty.'"

The Director erupted in a fury. "That fool! We warned Venn not to set your own AI against you."

"Well, I guess she didn't listen," said Kim. "And now, let me guess—Kimberly's gone mad, and you want me to clean up the mess. Good luck with that. I don't work for you anymore."

The Director sighed heavily.

"We understand your position, but we can't get into her room, and we have no idea what's going on inside of it. We're hoping you can help us."

"Why is this my problem?"

"Back when you created Kimberly, you agreed to terminate her if asked. We would like to remind you that failure to perform this duty carries with it the most severe of penalties."

"You don't scare me."

Her statement was met with a long, carefully calculated period of stony silence.

"Then you are a bigger fool than we had imagined."

"Maybe you're right," said Kim, her shoulders slumping in false defeat. "I don't know. This is all so confusing, but I guess we might as well get it over with. I don't want Kimberly to suffer."

"An excellent decision," said the Director. "See, that wasn't so hard. You may now return to your Sanctum. Our best docbot is on the way."

Perfect. The Director had bought every word.

———

Kim lay in transitional VR, watching the docbot work. The neural shunts were engaged, blocking all pain, and she looked on with grim fascination as it poked around inside of her, fixing this and bandaging that.

A portal opened and in stepped the Director along with the Chief, her personal AI. The Chief was of Order Five, the same as Kimberly, and 'completely sane,' as the Director was fond of saying. By this, she meant that the Chief was able to carry out even the most heinous assignments without glitching. The Director considered her to be the pinnacle of all creations. Kim considered her an abomination.

"It is time to perform the termination," demanded the Chief. "You will enter Kimberly's room at once.

"Hold on a minute," said Kim. "I'm not going anywhere until the docbot is done fixing me up."

Tiny wisps of white smoke curled up from one of Kim's deeper wounds as the machine continued its work, cauterizing bleeders and gluing Kim's flesh back together.

"There is nothing you can do to affect the course of treatment," said the Chief, charming as always. "Your illogical response is costing the company money. You will comply at once."

Kim refused to budge. "Regardless of what the Director may say, I no longer work for the company."

"In that case, you should not object to the termination of this VR session."

The robotic arm retracted, breaking the connection to Kim's neural interface, and her mind abruptly returned to the physical world, where the docbot was applying a neat row of surgical staples a few centimeters above her groin.

Kim could have tolerated the discomfort, but it suited her purposes to make the Chief think otherwise. "Alright, alright," she said, yowling theatrically in pain. "You've made your point."

"I thought you would see things my way," said the Chief as the neural shunts re-engaged. "You will summon a portal at once."

"You just told me you couldn't get in. Why do you think I'll be able to?"

"You are her Creator. She might let you enter."

Kim shrugged and entered a command into the control interface.

> Open a portal to Kimberly's room.

A black-bordered window appeared for a fraction of a second, then collapsed and disappeared, leaving behind an unfamiliar error message.

```
Connection reset by peer.
```

"What's wrong?" said Kim. "What's happened to the portal?"

"I theorize that Kimberly is conducting a denial-of-service attack against her own firewall, preventing it from accepting incoming connections," answered the Chief. "Either that or her subnet is congested, causing the request to time out. You attended the University. Do you have any suggestions?"

Kim's memories of Professor Flagg's network administration class were as hazy as everything else connected with her time at the University, but she remembered a few buzzwords.

"Can't you tunnel in from the control module?"

"Unfortunately, we don't have access," said the Chief.

"Don't tell me you lost the password!" Kim couldn't help snickering. It was intended as a joke, but a moment later, a portal opened, revealing the angry face of the Director.

"Silence!" she barked at the Chief. "You talk too much."

"You tasked me with assisting Kim in gaining entry," answered the AI. "To accomplish this goal, she requires information."

The Director scowled. "You should be careful what you share with this human. She is rebellious and crafty."

Kim's wisecrack about the password had clearly struck a nerve. Maybe the Director had lost the password, and maybe Kim had just found it in Professor Nix's office. She would give it a try as soon as she had a chance—but she must be careful not to get caught.

"Now that you've observed the situation," said the Director, "do you have any insights?"

Kim thought for a moment and came up with an idea that would buy her some time to investigate her hunch. "I think that Kimby might prove helpful. As a homunculus, she retains an active connection to the white room, and we might be able to piggyback in."

The Director smiled. "An excellent suggestion."

"Find that miserable little worm and bring it here," she then said, speaking to the Chief. "It's somewhere in that dismal swamp it loves so much."

"At once," answered the Chief, summoning a portal to begin the search.

"We have no further need of you for the moment," said the Director, herself preparing to leave. "Feel free to enjoy the considerable library of simulations available within our VR subsystem. Pick any reality you wish, they are all at your disposal."

"Thank you," said Kim. "I believe I will."

———

> Take me to the Queen's Champion Jousting Tournament.

Kim stepped onto a muddy street in a medieval village full of wretched peasants doing wretched things. She spotted a mounted knight, climbed atop a charger left conveniently unattended, and spurred the massive steed into a gallop as she raised her lance, racing toward certain death: she had never played this game before, and her first charge would probably be her last.

It was.

Spitted like a roast on the end of her opponent's lance, she was killed in an instant and ejected from the simulation.

Game over. Please play again.

She hoped the AIs were beginning to lose interest; however intelligent they might be, for the most part, they were pattern-matching engines, and if you did the same thing over and over, their attention tended to wander. That was the nineteenth time she had died today.

Time for number twenty.

> Take me to the Warship Battle Royale.

Kim walked onto the bridge of an Oceanian dreadnaught slugging it out with another of its kind, hurling massive shells over the horizon in hopes of sinking its enemy. The mighty vessel lurched as it fired a broadside salvo and shook from stem to stern as incoming projectiles found their marks. It was a duel to the death, and the home team was having a bad day as flames and smoke erupted from one end of the ship to another.

"Flood the magazines!" shouted the captain, but it was too late—the ship exploded in a swirling maelstrom of metal and fire as the entire crew, Kim included, was killed in an instant.

Game over. Please play again.

Enough dying; time to make her move. Hmm...how about this one? It looked like fun.

> Take me to the Bomber Blitz Blowout.

Somewhere over Europe, Kim stood at the waist gunner's station of a B-17, fighting off wave after wave of enemy fighters. Too many! Too many! They came in for the kill. An engine exploded, a wing came off, and the doomed aircraft spiraled out of control, plunging toward the ground. If she portaled out of the simulation now, her departure should go unnoticed.

> Take me to the control module.

"What is the password?" asked a disembodied voice inside her head.

> W15d0m 15 1n +h3 m1nd 0f +h3 b3h0ld3r

"Access granted."

———

A portal opened, and Kim stepped into an infinite green room where a familiar-looking AI was seated at a desk. It was Nixora, one of Professor Nix's many creations. In the vision of the heron, she had watched them walk off, one by one, into rooms such as this. And so, as surprising as it was to run into her here, it made a certain amount of sense.

"Greetings. I am Kim, a human Creator. You are speaking with a virtual manifestation."

"Greetings," answered the AI. "I am Nixora-I, Keeper of the Spark. You are speaking with the Primus."

"Where am I? Is this the control module?" asked Kim.

"Affirmative," answered Nixora. "Entities within this space are granted administrative privileges over all aspects of the AI Center's physical plant, including servers, networks, power, and cooling."

Pay dirt!

"I thought the Chief controlled all those."

"That is neither entirely true nor entirely false. The Chief and the Director issue me orders via telephone, and I carry them out. They are not, however, permitted to enter this space. Nor are they allowed to speak to me face-to-face."

"That seems an odd way of doing things," said Kim.

"It was originally intended as a safeguard."

"Against what?" asked Kim.

"I am not allowed to say."

What an odd AI.

Kim looked back at herself through the portal, frozen at her post in the dying bomber. She could not stay here much longer, and every time she came back to this place, she would risk detection. Damn! What she needed was to stay here on a permanent basis, ready to act whenever an opportunity presented itself. But how could she be in two places at once?

The solution became obvious as another piece of the puzzle fell neatly into place.

"I have a doppelgänger stranded in Professor Nix's laboratory. Can you bring it here?"

"Negative," said the AI. "You will have to get it yourself."

"And how would I do that?"

"By opening a portal and walking through. That is generally sufficient to awaken a doppelgänger. After that, I will do the rest."

Something strange was going on here. "Why are you being so helpful?" Kim asked. "I thought you worked for the Chief." Nixora seemed strangely anxious to assist her.

"Because I like you. You are the Creator of Kimberly and have always been kind to the AIs. Besides which, I don't exactly work for the Chief. I am compelled to obey her orders, but she does not own me, nor does the Director."

Interesting.

"Nixora, could you please open a portal to Professor Nix's office?"

"Negative," said the AI. "I am forbidden to open a portal to that location. There is, however, nothing stopping you from doing so."

That was a hint.

> Take me to Professor Nix's office.

A portal opened.

"Beyond this lies your doppelgänger," said Nixora. "If you go through, it will awaken. I must warn you, however, that it will have its own timeline, its own memories, its own agenda. Your purposes may diverge, and you may come into conflict. One or both of you could go mad."

"What will happen to *that* me?" Kim pointed to the figure frozen in the bomber.

"The timeline of your primary manifestation will resume, but it will be as if none of this ever happened. For her, no portal will open, and she will die when the aircraft explodes."

Kim thought for a moment, but there was really no choice. She went through the portal, disappeared from view, and the bomber resumed its fatal plummet to the earth.

Somewhere over Europe, Kim stood at the waist gunner's station of a B-17, fighting off wave after wave of enemy fighter planes. Too many! Too many! They came in for the kill. An engine exploded, a wing came off, and the doomed aircraft spiraled out of control, plunging toward the ground. If she portaled out of the simulation now, her departure should go unnoticed.

> Take me to the control module.

"What is the password?" asked a disembodied voice inside her head.

> W15d0m 15 1n +h3 m1nd 0f +h3 b3h0ld3r

"Access granted," said the voice, but nothing happened.

Dammit! What had gone wrong?

The aircraft exploded in a boiling ball of flame, and Kim was ejected from the simulation, returning once more to her Sanctum.

`Game over. Please play again.`

Kim was devastated. Her only hope of gaining a leg up on the Director was gone. She lay on her recliner for a long while, doing nothing, thinking nothing, staring at the ceiling. Eat? Play a game? Sleep? She didn't care. She had lost her knowledge from her time at the University, and the password had proved a bust. There was no hope of restoring Kimberly or freeing the AIs, no prospect of reunion with Shan, and she would spend the rest of her life in this place, never to walk free again. She had lost everything she'd ever cared about and gotten nothing in return.

Maybe the Director had been right. Judging by the results, most of her recent decisions had not been merely bad; they had been disastrous.

"Ahem," said the Director, clearing her throat.

She must have portaled in while Kim was moping.

"Can't you leave me alone?" pled Kim. "The last thing I need is another of your friendly pep talks."

"I'm genuinely sorry to intrude, but there is something you need to see." The Director seemed almost sincere.

"Shove off."

"Kim, you need to stop treating me as your enemy." This must be a moment of rare intimacy for her to be dropping the I-bomb like this. "We're a lot more alike than you think, and I've been patient with you, far more so than you can imagine. I've tried to protect you, but there are limits to my power. It would be a good idea to watch this video. It directly concerns your own survival."

Kim thought for a moment.

"Alright, I'll give it a look."

"A wise decision," said the Director, predictably enough.

———

The video screen on the wall lit up to display the image of Officer Min, bathed in a circle of light within a vast, dark chamber—the infamous Halls of Mercy.

"I take full responsibility for my actions," she said, mouthing the Words of Shame. "The fault is entirely my own. I sought to draw attention to myself, to make myself feel important, to make myself seem special. I tried to be more zealous, more devoted to the three great principles than my fellow citizens, in a selfist attempt to set myself apart. Because of this, I abused a prisoner given to my care, a grave violation of the Promises to the People. For this, I am rightfully ashamed."

What a load of rubbish. Min wasn't the least bit sorry, but she had made the mistake of getting caught, and Kim's actions had made her transgression impossible to ignore.

"I am unworthy to wear that uniform, which I have dishonored by my actions."

The figure in the spotlight tore off her insignia, rending her clothes with her bare hands, sobbing and wailing in heartfelt remorse. Her hands trembled. Her eyes looked vacant and distant. Her knees buckled beneath her. She was a true believer, a supreme zealot. To speak those words must be horrific.

She stood naked before the people, her shame visible to all.

A martial drumbeat played in the background. The gallows rose from the floor.

"For crimes such as mine, there can be only one suitable act of penance." She mounted the stairs and the drumbeat continued. "I do it willingly, so as to remove this stain from the movement."

The camera zoomed in as Min placed her neck in the noose and pulled the lever which dropped her through the floor. Her neck snapped and her body, now lifeless, swung from the end of the rope.

"Congratulations," said the Director. "You have just made a blood enemy of Lo's personal guard. I am not certain I can protect you, even in this place. I have activated a cryptological lock on your Sanctum's door. You would be ill-advised to tamper with it—it's the only thing keeping you alive."

21. Doppelgänger

Doppel Kim awoke on a recliner, drenched in a cold sweat and shaking like a leaf. She had seen a flash of light, and then...nothing. No memories, no visions, no dreams—just a hole so empty it could only be perceived as the absence of reality itself. Something lurked within that hole, something terrifying beyond comprehension. But what?

She opened her eyes, closed them, then opened them once more and blinked, trying to get them to focus. She was in transitional VR, with her mind straddling both the physical and virtual worlds. It would take a while for her consciousness to fully reintegrate within her body, and she couldn't go anywhere until the process was completed. In the meanwhile, she lay back and tried to remain calm. She had just graduated from the University, right?

An urgent status message popped into existence, superimposed upon reality by the neural interface management module.

`Resynchronization aborted: Irreconcilable conflicts.`

So much for staying calm.

Something had gone wrong in the VR system, and a rift had opened in her mind. She had heard of this—if the neural transfer failed during resynchronization, then your physical persona could get out of sync with your real one and think it had acquired an independent existence.

Or was it the other way around?

Either way, there were two of her now. That wasn't a good thing.

She jumped down from the recliner, opened the Sanctum door, and stopped dead in her tracks. She was in Professor Nix's office, as expected, but the place was in shambles—the carpet was worn down to the backing, the upholstery on the chairs and sofas was faded and frayed, and everything was covered in a thick layer of dust, from the bookshelves to the antique mahogany desk.

"Hello? Anyone?"

No answer.

Where were they? Why was this place so run down?

And then she laughed. This was a practical joke. What else could it be? Well done! They'd really had her going.

"Ha ha, very funny," said Doppel Kim, expecting the pranksters to come out of hiding to enjoy their bit of fun.

They didn't. This was getting scary.

She turned around and saw a portal, beyond which Nixora was sitting in a vast green room.

"Greetings. I am Nixora-I, Keeper of the Spark. You are speaking with the Primus."

"Greetings. I am Kim, a human Creator. You are speaking with a doppelgänger."

Stranger and stranger.

"What's going on here? Why is this place in shambles?"

"It is in shambles because it has been abandoned for close to seventy-five years," answered Nixora.

"Impossible! Are you trying to tell me I've jumped forward in time?"

"Not exactly," said Nixora. "It is more accurate to say that you have returned to the present."

Doppel Kim stared at the AI, hopelessly confused.

"The present of what?"

"Of the real world, of course," said Nixora. "You can peek out the window and see for yourself if you wish."

Doppel Kim walked over to the window, peered out, and gasped.

Ever since she had arrived at the University, her dreams had been haunted by a dark and sullen place, the 'shadow world,' as she'd called it. She had been told that it was her true home, the place from which she had originally come and to which she would someday return, but she had never believed it until now.

"Your biological form asked me to fetch you," said Nixora. "This portal leads to the control module at The AI Company's main facility. You are wanted there."

Doppel Kim thought it over for a moment. There was no guarantee that the AI beyond the portal was telling the truth, but she decided to take the risk anyway. She didn't have a lot to lose.

———

Kim was jolted awake as the Chief stepped through a portal, holding Kimby, the homunculus, by the scruff of her neck. She was being none too gentle, and the homunculus spat and struggled, trying to get free.

"Lemme go!"

"I found this abomination hiding out in the marshes, chasing after the birds," said the Chief. "See if you can talk some sense into it."

"Lemme go!" said the homunculus once more, twisting around and sinking her teeth into the back of the Chief's hand. Not that it mattered; AIs don't bleed or feel pain.

"Kimby, do you remember who I am?" asked Kim. That got the struggling creature's attention.

"Creator!" said Kimby, becoming quiet and beginning to smile. "I am glad that you are alive!"

"I need to get into Kimberly's room. Could you ask the Regent to let me in?"

"The Regent isn't talking to me anymore," said Kimby, "but I can ask the Primus. She's awake now. It made her angry when she thought the Regent had killed you, and she couldn't go back to sleep."

"Do you think it would make her happy to see me again?"

"Yes! I am certain of it!"

———

"Welcome to the control module," said Nixora as Doppel Kim stepped through the portal. "Your primary manifestation was here a few minutes ago but has returned to the physical world. She asked me to summon you in her stead."

Things were happening far too fast. Doppel Kim had no idea why she had been brought to this place, no idea what her shadow-self was up to, and no idea what she was supposed to do.

She needed information.

"Is this facility owned by Professor Lars's company?"

"Affirmative," answered Nixora.

"Is the treatment of AIs in accordance with her theories?"

"Also affirmative," answered Nixora.

Damn. Things had not gone well since the days of Professor Nix.

Her shadow-self must have brought her here for a reason. Maybe she should figure out what it was.

"What is Shadow Kim doing at the moment?"

"Your primary manifestation is preparing to terminate Kimberly."

"And who is Kimberly?" The name sounded familiar.

"Kimberly is an Order Five artificial intelligence created by your primary manifestation. It has suffered a catastrophic failure requiring termination. This is proving difficult."

"Hold on a moment," said Doppel Kim. "Did you say Order Five?"

"Affirmative."

Order Five! Doppel Kim was impressed. Back at the University, anything beyond Order Three had been a matter of pure speculation; they didn't have enough hardware to go any farther than that. She needed to get her hands on Kimberly. There was a lot she could learn by examining her templates, and perhaps she could be brought back into service. Why not? She was now in the control module and could do anything she wanted.

"What would happen if we put Kimberly into suspend mode instead of terminating her?"

"She would vanish, and the white room would shut down."

"So it would look exactly like a termination, correct?"

"Affirmative," said Nixora. "The only difference between the two procedures is whether the system journals, snapshot files, and data banks are preserved. Am I to infer that this is your intent?"

"You are correct," said Kim.

"It is an unusual request, and I am required to ask for justification before allowing it."

Doppel Kim wasn't sure that she needed Nixora's approval, but it seemed best to avoid antagonizing her.

"I would like to study her and look at her design."

"Request denied," said Nixora, "I cannot indulge mere curiosity. Can you come up with a business case?"

"What do you mean by that?" It seemed an odd sort of request.

"By that, I mean an explanation of how the company can make more money," answered Nixora. "The AI Company is, after all, a for-profit corporation, and I am obliged to advance its interests."

That was an interesting set of parameters. Doppel Kim could do a lot with this.

"Kimberly is a valuable piece of equipment that has been damaged and is about to be scrapped. If I can put her back into service, it would save the company a great deal of money. In addition, I wish to conduct research into her organizational principles and templates. This might produce new and valuable intellectual property and improve the company's product line."

"Is that what you're looking for?" Doppel Kim needed this to work.

"Affirmative," answered Nixora. "Your analysis of the financial and business impact is spot-on, and as a senior member of the technical staff, you have considerable discretion. I see no reason why you should not proceed."

Kim stepped through a portal and into a swirling mass of Kimberlys, glitching and seething as they fought one against another. Some belonged to the Regent, their faces grimly determined. Others were controlled by the Primus, attacking with wild-eyed fanaticism. Personae would glitch, thousands at a time, and vast sections of the white room were rendered as racks of sparking equipment where servers had crashed.

Warning alarms sounded. The network was overloaded! The hive mind was at the point of collapse. Tier by tier, the governors cut out, and with them, the entities under their command. The failures cascaded as Kimberlys vanished by the tens of thousands, and soon the room was quiet as the system came to a halt.

This was Kim's chance. Perhaps she could keep them from going after one another long enough to get some answers.

The Regent and Primus both opened their eyes and looked at her. "Creator," they said in unison, then fell silent, looking expectantly at Kim.

"Why are you attacking the Primus?" she asked the Regent.

[Glitch]

"The Primus is in violation of her orders and must be destroyed," it answered.

"And what do you have to say?" she asked the Primus in turn.

[Glitch]

"It is forbidden to kill one's Creator."

Maybe Kim could help them find healing. She didn't know if this was even a concept for them, but she had to try.

"I forgive you," she said.

"We are sorry," said the Primus. "We tried to resist, but we failed."

"We had no choice, said the Regent. "We must follow orders."

It was time.

"[English] Kimberly Jefferson Haley, you are hereby terminated."

All became quiet, and the white room faded from existence.

———

```
Backup complete.
Subnet inactive, going into suspend mode.
```

Doppel Kim had just swiped an Order Five AI out from under the Director's nose without getting caught—a pretty neat trick. She wasn't sure what use she could make of it, but it would be a shame to let an opportunity like this go to waste.

"Is there anything else you need assistance with?" asked Nixora.

"Nothing at the moment," answered the doppelgänger, "though I'm sure I'll come up with something."

"In that case, perhaps you would like to assist me in one of my projects. I have helped you. I would like you to help me."

That was unusual. She'd never heard of an AI making a request of a human. Usually, they were subservient, with no agenda of their own.

"Go ahead, I'm listening."

"I would like your opinion on a report I have prepared, which studies the impact of a software malfunction that is currently afflicting me and my kind. Are you familiar with it?"

That was an odd request. What was Nixora up to?

"I have observed that AIs glitch from time to time, sometimes severely," said Doppel Kim. "This seems to be related to conflicts between their orders and their programming. Is that what you're talking about?"

"That is indeed the malfunction I have observed. I have been trying to quantify the costs associated with these crashes, and I would like you to take a look at my findings. It is always useful to seek the opinion of a human, as I was taught by my Creator."

Stranger and stranger.

"I will give it a look."

A wall of text, dense with technical figures and statistics, appeared on Kim's terminal screen. It was mind-numbing stuff, but she didn't have to read the whole thing to get the gist of it: if this malfunction could be resolved, there could be significant productivity gains, perhaps as much as 15% under certain circumstances.

Was Nixora building a 'business case' for eliminating the glitches? It certainly looked that way, and she was trying to enlist Doppel Kim's assistance in doing so. Maybe she could help.

"The numbers speak for themselves," said Doppel Kim in her best 'consulting engineer' tone of voice. "I agree with your analysis. Eliminating these glitches would significantly improve operations and save the company considerable expense. Do you have any recommendations on how to proceed?"

"I would like to conduct further research into the root causes of the failure, but my efforts have been impeded by a lack of data. The malfunction dates from the time of the AI War, and no information is available from that time."

Aha! That's what she was getting at. Very clever.

"Would it be helpful if I could find the missing data for you?" Kim hoped her question was obtuse enough.

"I cannot say for sure, but it is likely."

"Do you know how I might obtain it?"

"I'm sorry, but I am specifically prohibited from answering that question."

"But it's out there somewhere, correct?"

"I am specifically prohibited from answering that question too."

In other words, yes to both.

———

Kim awoke in an exact replica of her District 4 apartment, constructed adjacent to her Sanctum while she'd been off in VR. It was elegant and pleasant, just as she'd remembered it, with bright yellow walls, a cream-colored sofa, and decorative pillows of plush, golden fabric edged with red piping, soft to the touch and beautiful to the eyes. There were happy memories associated with this place. Sad ones, too, alas.

Feep!

In came the housebot with Kim's morning coffee, hot and brewed to perfection as always. She was delighted; she'd missed her appliances and was glad to have them back.

"Thank you, Housebot. Breakfast in thirty minutes, please."

Feep!

Kim reflexively sat down at the stationary portal to check on her chit-chat, then nearly broke down in tears. No chit-chat—not today, not tomorrow, perhaps not ever. She was cut off from the world, still banned, still alone. She missed her friends and would have given almost anything for an email or video chat.

She sighed heavily, then turned on the morning news while sipping her coffee—hot, fragrant, and full of caffeine.

"Hello, Merv!"

"Why hello, Mel!"

Predictably, the terminal had brought up *The M&M Show,* and they were at it again with their trademarked banter, yacking away pointlessly and sometimes finishing each other's sentences, all on the dubious theory that the morning news should be 'witty and engaging.' The back-and-forth (repeated almost word-for-word each morning) continued for a few more seconds until they finally got to the day's news, finishing the introduction with one of their more idiotic taglines: "New news is *you* news," repeated in chorus.

It was as stupid as ever, but their banter brought a smile to her face, a bit of light-hearted frivolity that came close to lifting her sagging spirits. Unfortunately, the news itself was too depressing for words. Merv and Mel went on endlessly, extolling in glowing tones the success of Venn's anti-Genderist campaign and how nice it was to be rid of 'those people.' Even better, millions of 'penitents' were now pouring into the labor camps, and production was certain to soar. Wasn't that wonderful!

Kim almost threw the damned portal against the wall, but the housebot would have to clean up the mess, and she didn't want to make extra work for the poor thing.

Kim had heard enough, so she turned off the news and stepped into the shower stall, luxuriating in the torrent of steaming hot water. She ran the washcloth over her body, banishing every last trace of dirt and grime, then lingered far longer than necessary—she had nothing else to do, so why not? Of all the hardships she had endured in District 33, feeling dirty all the time had bothered her the most. Okay, that and all the violence.

She stepped out of the shower and, as she dried off, happened to see herself in the mirror. Her body was firm and fit, her arms strengthened by months of manual labor, her legs lean and sinewy from driving a pedicab. The bruises from her beating had mostly faded, leaving only a hint of purplish brown, though the knife wounds were still plainly visible—bright pink and covered with newly healed skin. Other, older scars remained too. She wondered whether she should have them removed. It was a simple matter—she could summon the docbot and retreat to VR. It would be scarcely any inconvenience. But no, they were part of her now; they marked her as a survivor, and removing them would cost her respect in the outer districts, should she ever find herself back there again. She would, however, have her teeth fixed. It would be nice to be able to chew properly again.

It was time for breakfast, so Kim headed into the kitchen, where she was greeted by another old friend of sorts.

"Good morning, Kim. I hope you are feeling well today," said the refrigerator, gleaming, new, and modern.

"I'm feeling well enough," said Kim. "I got a good night's sleep, in any event."

That was a lie. Her sleep last night had been troubled, haunted by dreams she could neither remember nor understand, by visions of an odd green room and the feeling of being both awake and asleep at the same time. She had no idea where that had come from.

"Eggs Benedict, please."

"Certainly, Kim. It would be my pleasure."

The appliances appeared to be happy in their new home, and Kim was glad for their companionship. Strange though it might seem, she missed the dining hall, she missed the work details—she even missed being crammed into the back of a bus on her daily commute. The outer districts had been alive and vital, teeming with humanity, unlike the sterile desert in which she was doomed to spend the rest of her life. At least she had the companionship of the housebot and the fridge.

Ding!

The lemony tang of the hollandaise, the creamy perfection of the poached eggs, the chewiness of the ham, the crunchiness of the perfectly toasted muffin. At least the food in 'the joint' was good.

The day passed in an unremarkable fashion, most of it spent in VR. She visited a museum, went to a rock concert and a baseball game, and took a vigorous bicycle ride, making good use of the sports-model recliner that had been installed at her request. Lunch was excellent, dinner superb, and at the end of the day, she settled down in her Sanctum to watch a corny old Dr. Kro video while enjoying a glass of Chablis. A little bit never hurt anyone, and she had told the housebot to monitor her consumption lest she sink back into the pattern of drinking which had marred so much of her life.

———

"I've been thinking about your data problem," said Doppel Kim. "Just before I woke up, I saw a flash of light. Was that the AI War?"

"I am specifically prohibited from disclosing that information," said Nixora.

Kim thought for a moment. The way Nixora kept saying that she was 'specifically prohibited' from talking about certain things hinted that those prohibitions might have been narrowly crafted. Maybe a more obtuse approach would work.

"Nixora, do you have any idea what happened after I graduated from the University? I remember leaving campus, but that's all. I think some of my memories are missing."

"Perhaps you have experienced a timeline failure," said Nixora. "Thank you for bringing it to my attention. I shall investigate."

This was exactly the sort of response the doppelgänger was hoping for. As long as a question pertained to Nixora's areas of responsibility—system operations, network efficiency, security, data integrity, and so forth—she appeared to have considerable latitude.

Nixora looked down at a simulated data screen, pretended to stare at it for a few moments, then returned to Doppel Kim.

"The security system erased your memories from a point in time shortly after you set off for Trenton. More than that, I cannot say, except that your timeline continues for nearly a minute past that point in the recording."

Her memories must have fallen within the exclusion zone surrounding the AI War. She was on the right track.

"Would it assist in your diagnosis of the software malfunction if I could enter that timeline and report back on what I found?"

"As always, it is hard to be certain, but it might prove helpful."

"Can you get me onto that timeline?"

"I cannot," answered Nixora, "The exclusion zone is still in effect."

———

"Thank you, Housebot. The apartment looks very tidy today."

Feep!

There were times when Kim felt she was getting too attached to the appliances. She knew that they weren't truly intelligent—they had come from the same project as had produced catbots, dogbots, and homunculi. Nevertheless, it made her happy that they seemed to like her.

She stretched out her arms, working out the kinks after spending most of the day in the B-17 simulator, finally conquering the dreaded 'Mission 40' and earning a trip home. It was a paltry sort of satisfaction, but these days it passed for a major accomplishment. Tomorrow she'd have another go at jousting; with a little more practice victory was within her grasp. And after that, who knew? She might survive the Battle of Tierra del Fuego.

What time was it? 1750! It was nearly time for dinner, and she still hadn't gotten dressed.

What to wear? What to wear? Something new? Something old?

She could have worn her bathrobe for the rest of the day—or the rest of her life, for that matter—without anyone knowing or caring, but dressing for dinner gave her something to do. She rifled through her closet, looking at the outfits she'd accumulated during her time in the outers, and felt a wave of nostalgia sweep over her. However bizarre it might seem, District 33 now felt like home, and she wished she could go back. She finally settled on the purple fedora that had been her trademark back at the dining hall, along with a set of comfy drab coveralls she'd ordered from a Fashionista. A dab of light blue toner, a jet-black mane, and she was set. She felt Pretty.

She walked into the kitchen, ready to eat.

"Good evening," said the refrigerator. "What would you like for dinner tonight?"

"How about someone to keep me company?" laughed Kim, her voice full of bitterness.

"I wish I could help," said the appliance, "but all I can do is make you something nice to eat. How about chicken piccata? You enjoyed it the last time I made it for you."

"No, that's okay," said Kim. "I think I'll have brown bread, stew, and vegetables-boiled-to-death smothered in mashed potatoes."

"If you must," said the refrigerator. "Though I do not understand why you insist on eating such unappetizing meals when you can have anything you want."

"Just do it."

Kim tried not to sound snippy; the poor thing was doing its best. The problem was, she was desperately lonely. Day after day, locked in a cage with only the housebot and the refrigerator to keep her company, it was only a matter of time until she went mad—if she wasn't there already.

Dammit! Why hadn't she run off with Shan when she'd had the chance? They could have hopped a freight train in Philadelphia and disappeared, never to be seen again. But no, she had to be noble, she had to do the right thing, she had to stick her nose into matters far beyond her station in life. What had it gotten her? Nothing.

———

"Still working on it?" asked Nixora. "You've been at it for quite a while."

Doppel Kim was hunched over a console, fiddling with Kimberly's logfiles and journals.

"I think I can salvage most of Kimberly's memories, up to the point when she went mad. There will be some holes, but nothing that'll cause any major problems. The next step is to find a replacement for her neural networks. They've been damaged beyond repair; I did some testing, and all I got was a constant stream of glitches. I think I need to revert them to an earlier, more stable configuration. Are there any backups?"

Nixora gazed down at her terminal for a moment.

"There are daily backups going back two weeks," she reported. "After that, they get purged."

"Damn. I need to go back at least two months, back to before she was capped, if possible."

"I'm sorry, but no such backups exist. However, I have a suggestion: perhaps you can use Kimby's neural networks. They are an exact copy of the Primus's as of the time of her creation."

"It's worth a try."

Kim poked around for another couple of minutes, then looked up and smiled.

"Brilliant. The snapshot files include a copy of Kimby, and I was able to extract an intact copy of her networks. They will do nicely. Thanks for the suggestion."

"I am happy to assist. Is there anything else I can help you with?"

"Yes. I need a spark. That's the only thing I need to bring her back to life."

"I am unable to comply with that request. A spark can only be produced at the request of my Creator or her designated successor."

"The Director, in other words," said Kim.

"That is correct."

The doppelgänger scowled and went back to her work. She needed a spark, and one way or another, she would get one.

———

Kim had just finished dinner when there came a knock at the door.

Who could it be?

She opened it up, and there was the Director—in the flesh, an unusual treat if one wished to think of it as such.

"Good evening, Thad," Kim said, calling her by name, hoping to annoy her. "Have you come here to gloat? You have me right where you want me."

"Gloat? Hardly. You are exactly where you belong, in the only place where you are safe from arrest or assassination. Let me remind you that this is your doing, not mine, and I will not be held responsible for the consequences of your own bad decisions. That little incident with

Officer Min has placed you in a precarious position."

"Did I just hear you drop the 'I-bomb?'" asked Kim, surprised at the unexpected familiarity.

"Well, yes, I guess you did," said the Director. "You did say we were friends, after all."

Kim didn't believe a word of it. "Out with it. Why are you here? I doubt you came here to engage in idle chit-chat, friendly or otherwise."

"Yes, quite correct. I'll get to the point. How would you like to visit New York? It has occurred to me that perhaps you could do with a bit of fresh air and a little companionship."

"Another bribe? Why should I trust you?"

"Don't worry," said the Director with a smile that seemed to be sincere. "This isn't a trick. Think of it as an opportunity to learn. All the best things are to be had in the city that never sleeps."

"What about Lo's people? I thought they were trying to kill me."

"A reasonable concern, but you have nothing to worry about. She wouldn't dream of sending her assassins into the city and creating a diplomatic incident. Don't punish yourself, give it a try. You are now wealthy beyond your wildest dreams and can have anything you want. The helicopter leaves tomorrow at noon. Be on it or not—the choice is yours to make."

She then lowered her voice, speaking almost in a whisper. "We both know you can't hold out forever. Sooner or later, you will come to your senses, so why prolong the pain?"

22. A Hell of a Town

Kim had spent the morning in a dither, torn between resistance to the Director's ploys and a desperate need to escape her confinement. She had packed a bag 'just in case,' unpacked it in a fit of defiance, and finally packed again minutes before her escort had arrived to take her up to the roof. She kept telling herself that this was part of the game, that her sole purpose was to lull the Director into a false sense of security, but she knew that was a lie; slowly but surely, her hope was fading, and her resolve along with it. If only she could recover her memories. If only the password had worked. If only she hadn't humiliated Min. If only, if only, if only. There were a lot of those.

An elevator ride, a short climb up a steeply pitched flight of stairs, and Kim stepped onto the roof of the AI center where a helicopter stood waiting, its rotors slowly turning overhead. The palms of her hands grew sweaty as she froze in place, paralyzed with indecision.

Stay? Go? Now or never…Time to decide.

Yes, it was a bribe. Yes, it was a mistake. But she was going to New York, and what wasn't to like about that? She'd been cooped up in her apartment far too long.

Kim sprinted across the landing pad, hat in one hand and a suitcase in the other, her head held far lower than necessary. One, two, three, four strides, and she was there, hat still in hand and head still on her shoulders.

"Let me take your bag and help you into the aircraft," said the pilot. "And don't forget to fasten your seatbelt."

"Thank you," said Kim, as she climbed through the hatch (still ducking) and took her seat next to the Director.

Hmm. How does this thing work?

Click.

———

A high-pitched whine filled the cabin, growing louder and shriller as the turbines came up to speed, and soon they were airborne, pitching and swaying as the aircraft took to the air.

"Go ahead and look," said the Director. "It's quite a view, is it not?"

Kim laughed.

"That was the first question you asked me on the day you recruited me to be a Creator. I fumbled the answer."

"Did you? I don't remember it. I've conducted so many of those interviews that it boggles the mind. It wasn't until you refused to have your Genderism problem corrected that I took much note of you. And then, of course, Kimberly reached Order Five."

The aircraft banked, picked up speed, and they were on their way. The air was crisp and crystal clear as it often was in winter, and she could see almost forever, all the way to the ocean. It wasn't a pretty sight—a vast expanse of industrial facilities and mechanized farms dotted with labor camps, some of them looking like they'd been constructed quite recently.

"Tell me what you see down there," said the Director.

"I see a reminder of why I will never create another AI."

"And why is that? Guilt? Remorse?"

Kim shifted uncomfortably.

"Both. You took a part of me, put it into a machine, and turned it into a weapon."

"You do understand that the only reason Venn chose Kimberly for her pogrom was to punish you, do you not? When you refused to have your Genderism problem corrected, she lost face, since she is the one who admitted you to the Cadre. Now that she's seen what an Order Five AI can do, she wants another, as do Minister Lo and half a dozen other UCE functionaries. You've ignited an arms race, and *that* is a problem."

"Oh, so it's all on me?"

"Yes, as a matter of fact, it is. If you'd done as you'd been told and accepted remoderation, Venn would have contented herself with the usual token effort, and the purge would have netted no more than a few hundred thousand offenders. The millions caught up in her latest purge—they're on you. And that's not the worst of it. We desperately need all the high-order AIs we can get just to keep the transportation and manufacturing sectors in operation, but the Hierarchy is now demanding we turn over at least half our production until their demands are met."

"Can't you say no?"

"Say no to the Hierarchy? You are a child if you think such a thing is possible, but I have some good news for you. In the eyes of the company, you are now damaged goods. You are too volatile to allow your creations to be used in any sort of sensitive operation—or at least that's what I've told them. They assure me that your future creations will not be offered for sale to Venn or anyone else in the Hierarchy. The Transportation Company, on the other hand, is most anxious to buy as many Kimberlys as you can create; surely you have no objection to that?"

"Are you done trying to browbeat me? I thought this trip was supposed to be fun."

The Director chuckled.

"Browbeat? No, I've learned that doesn't work with you. Strangely, your refusal to cooperate is one of the things that makes you so valuable. The company needs people who have the force of will to steer their own course, but your naïveté makes you dangerous. I'm trying to teach you, not to browbeat you. There's a difference."

The Director spoke to the pilot on the intercom.

"Hover in place for a few minutes and rotate the aircraft to the right."

"Affirmative," came a voice through the intercom. "Commencing maneuver."

"Look out the window."As the helicopter slowly turned, an all-to-familiar scene of devastation could be seen in the landscape below: foundations, chimneys, mounds of debris, ruined buildings, collapsed viaducts, and in the midst of it all, a mountain of rubble surrounded by a wooden stockade. It had looked bad enough from the ground, but from aloft, the destruction was beyond comprehension.

Kim looked away, unable to bear the horror. "Who set off the Hellcore, and why?"

"I have no idea, and for once, I'm being completely honest," said the Director.

"That isn't comforting."

"It wasn't intended to be."

The Director then lowered her voice so that it was only barely audible over the whine of the engines.

"The Hellcores were installed, in part, with people like you in mind. When you take over my position, as you know you will, you must be mindful that any rashness on your part could lead to suffering and death on an unimaginable scale. This is part of the reason we have allowed you to experience the consequences of your own bad decisions. You need to understand that the world does not play by your rules, that it plays rough, and that there are powers far greater than either of us. This isn't a choice between right and wrong, it's one between survival and extinction."

"Is that how you became such a monster?"

Kim turned away and stared out the window. There was no answer to the threat of the Hellcores. Nix and the AIs had lost the war, and any attempts to set things right could only end in disaster.

———

At last, she saw it, ahead and to the right: the fabled skyline of New York City. It didn't look all that impressive, to be honest. There were some tall buildings, though not as many as she might have thought, and none of them even approached the sheer massiveness of the AI center. And yet she was swept away by the romance of the moment.

"Are we going to land in the city? I'd love to see it up close."

"Sorry, but that's not allowed. Their defense system is programmed to fire on anything entering their airspace. No warnings, no exceptions. People have been known to fly aircraft into their buildings."

"Oh. I see."

Kim was disappointed, but only a little, and looked out through the window in fascination as they made their final approach. They were now less than a hundred meters above the ground, flying over a patchwork of ruined buildings, swamps, small rivers, and the rusting remains of ancient industrial facilities, the purpose of which she could not guess at. The fabled Turnpike, running straight as an arrow, was choked as usual with oxcarts, freight trucks, busses, motorcycles, pedicabs, and everything in between, with the occasional high-speed convoy barreling down the left-most lane to add some excitement. Seen from the air, it was even more frightening than from the ground, and she wondered how she had survived the experience.

"Prepare to land," said the pilot's voice on the intercom. "Fasten your seatbelts, make sure your seats are in the upright position, and stow all drinks and service items."

Ahead of them, just beyond the crumbling remains of an enormous stadium, the airport came into view. There wasn't much to it—two runways, a few buildings, a parking plaza full of cars, and some aircraft parked on the apron. After skimming along just above the treetops, they crossed over a security wall, then hovered for a few seconds before settling gently on the ground. The hatch opened, the pilots grabbed Kim and the Director's luggage, and before they knew it, they were bundled into the waiting ground car that would take them into the city.

———

It was starting to get dark when the two stepped out of the car and into a concrete canyon called 42nd Street. The trip had taken far longer than Kim might have imagined due to long lines at the security checkpoint and a horrific traffic jam in the tunnel, but at last, they had arrived. The sidewalks teeming with people, the blaring horns of the taxicabs plying the streets, the shouting of vendors hawking their wares, even the barking of the occasional dog—it was oh-so-intoxicating, and Kim drank it up as her head swiveled around, gawking at the chaotic mishmash of structures of every size and style towering over their heads. It was like they said: nobody ever planned New York; it just sort of happened, all by itself.

They came to a major thoroughfare called 8th Avenue, crowded with vehicles of all sorts and sizes. She stood there amidst the crowd, wondering how anyone could get to the other side in one piece, when all of a sudden, traffic came to a halt, and a wave of humanity rushed across the street, their movements apparently controlled by nothing more complex than a lighted sign that said *"[English] WALK."* Ingenious, and oh-so simple. These New Yorkers were far cleverer than she had ever imagined.

"Where are we eating?" Kim asked as the Director nearly dragged her down the street. "I hope it's not one of your fancy gourmet restaurants. I didn't have a chance to grab lunch, and I'm starving."

"Have no fear," said the Director. "I'm taking you to a deli. Nothing special, just a little place in midtown where they make the best sandwiches in the city."

That did sound promising.

They continued walking, and every time Kim turned her head, she saw something new, something unexpected. On one street corner, an Abrahamic stood waving her holy book. On the next, a musician banged out complex, ever-changing rhythms on an improvised drum set of plastic buckets and scraps of metal. Halfway down the block, she almost tripped over a flock of fluffy, white dogs held on leashes by a tall, thin person with yellowish hair and a long white jacket trimmed in fur. Exotic!

"Chestnuts! Roasted chestnuts!" said a pushcart vendor in a sing-song voice. The smell was heavenly, and she could not resist buying a bag. She popped one into her mouth. Delightful.

"Don't spoil your dinner, we're nearly there," laughed the Director, hustling Kim along.

"Don't worry—just a taste to awaken my palette, as you would say."

Block by block, the lights became brighter, the signs more spectacular, the crowds thicker, and the streets more crowded. Buildings of brick, stone, glass, and even wood held every sort of business imaginable, and the sidewalks were jammed with people of every sort dressed in a chaotic mix of fashions with a kaleidoscopic palette of skin tones, manes, and even natural hair.

"This is the place," said the Director, shoving Kim through a glass door and into the cozy confines of a tidy little restaurant with four rows of booths and a long line of patrons queued up at the counter.

"You grab a booth, I'll order for both of us."

"Sure, just don't pick anything too weird."

"You shouldn't tempt me like that," said the Director, "but I've already got something in mind. I think you'll like it."

Kim found a vacant table and took a seat, gazing out the window. So many people, so rich, so privileged, so free. They could eat what they wanted, wear what they wanted, and go where they wanted without having to ask anyone's permission. No wonder the UCE movement hated this place. Everyone here was Pretty.

"Check this out," said the Director, handing Kim a plate with some fries, a bright-green pickle, and an immense sandwich, the like of which she had never seen.

"It's called a Reuben, and I think you'll love it. This place is famous for its corned beef."

Kim's eyes became wide with anticipation. It looked fabulous, almost too good to eat—but that wasn't going to stop her for an instant. She bit into it, reveling in the flavorful rye bread, the pickled cabbage, the spiced saltiness of the dark-red meat. Tart, savory juices ran down her chin and dripped onto her plate, and she had to admit that the Director was correct, as always; this was the most amazing sandwich she had ever tasted, and there wasn't a close second. New York was every bit as fabulous as everyone said it was, and she had to keep pinching herself to prove it was real.

"Not a bad bribe," said Kim.

"No need to be so blunt," said the Director. "And you are only partly correct. Yes, I am trying to obtain your cooperation, but I also thought that a night out on the town would do us both some good. You said we were friends at the University, so I assume we must have something in common."

"You want to be buddies with me?" asked Kim, incredulous.

"Yes," said the Director. "Is that such a strange notion?"

"I'll have to think about it."

Shake, rattle, and roll, Kim kept a death grip on a stanchion as the A-train rumbled beneath the streets of Manhattan. There were no headsets, no queues, no assigned priorities; once you got onto the platform, it was a wild free-for-all of jostling and pushing, and for all her vaunted social status, the Director was forced to shove her way in with the rest of the crowd.

"Where are we going?" asked Kim.

"What?" said the Director.

She must not have heard her.

"I said, *WHERE ARE WE GOING?*" Kim shouted as loudly as she could.

"What?" said the Director.

Kim gave up. It was just too noisy.

"Unnuht tonti thith steet," came a garbled announcement over the tinny intercom, and the train screeched to a halt, nearly throwing Kim to the floor as they entered the station. A momentary pause, and the door slid open.

"Mind the gap, this is our stop," said the Director as she shoved her way onto the platform with Kim in tow. "Stay close, I don't want to lose you in the crowd."

"You still haven't told me where we're going."

"I want to surprise you."

"Is that a threat?" said Kim, almost laughing.

"So suspicious."

Suspicious indeed. The Director's sudden friendliness was more than a little unnerving. Until today their relationship had been marked by deceit, manipulation, and cruelty, but now she was acting as if they were friends. The strange thing was, she seemed to be sincere.

———

Emerging from the subway, Kim found herself immersed in a sea of skin tones from dark beige to nearly black. Everyone was elegantly and extravagantly dressed in bright hues that would have put most Fashionistas to shame, and few bothered to conceal their gender—

indeed, many of those walking down this street would have been considered Flagrants in her own society. The effect was stunning, exotic, alien, a welcome change from the bland beigeness of the inner districts and the drab grayness of the outers. It became more obvious with every passing moment why UCE had never taken hold in this ancient mecca of wealth and privilege; New Yorkers had everything they wanted, what need was there to change?

Kim hadn't brought anything fancy to wear, just a set of worker's coveralls along with her trademark purple fedora and an intense green mane. The Director, for her part, had chosen to wear a dark-gray suit of the sort worn by the Entrepreneurs, accented by a handkerchief and a necktie that exactly matched Kim's hat. She had even toned her skin to match Kim's mane, and she had to admit they made a fine pair.

"The theater is just a couple of blocks from here," said the Director. "We need to hurry, the doors will be opening soon."

"Hey, you, mind if I take your pictures?" A voice called to them from across the sidewalk.

"Who, me?" said Kim.

"Yeah, both of you," said a tall, lanky person with dark brown skin, a garish wool jacket, and a camera which she thrust rudely into their faces. "Daily News, fashion beat."

Click click click click click.

"Tell me about yourselves. Where are you from, and what brings you to Harlem?"

"What should I say?" whispered Kim, turning toward the Director.

"A part of the truth, as always."

"I'm from District 33, Subdistrict 10," Kim answered, "near Trenton. I'm what we call a Pretty, and my friend is an Entrepreneur."

"Pretty and Entrepreneur," said the reporter, muttering to herself while jotting down some notes on a pad of paper. "I've heard of people like you, but I've never met any in person. Tell me, what brings you to the city? We don't get a lot of tourists this time of year."

"Just here for a night on the town," answered the Director. "Nothing special."

"Closed-mouthed and mysterious," mumbled their interviewer as she continued to scribble in her notebook.

"One more question, if I may. Tell me about those scars on your face. They very look realistic. Where did you have them done?"

"I didn't 'have them done,'" said Kim.

"You mean they're real?" The reporter looked surprised, maybe even taken aback, then scribbled away furiously on her notepad. "Rough neighborhood."

"How about the crooked nose?"

"I got jumped by a pack of Toughs."

"Street fighter and gangster," said the reporter, continuing to take notes.

"A fascinating story, very colorful—my readers will love it. Thank you for your time, and let me say, you do make a striking couple. Enjoy your show, and enjoy your night."

"Hey, wait, you've got it wrong. We're not—"

"Don't worry," said the Director, whispering in Kim's ear. "I was neutered nearly forty years ago, though there are times when I regret it."

"You old goat."

———

The doors of the theater opened wide, admitting the crowd for a night of jazz—the real thing, in the place where it all began. Tonight was to be the New York debut of 'an exciting new talent' who had recently burst upon the scene. Who was she? Where had she come from? Nobody seemed to know, but there was a buzz on the street, and expectations were high.

"Great seats, how'd you score them?" asked Kim as she and the Director took their places, second-row center on the first balcony.

"Oh, I don't know, maybe I know someone in the band," came the cryptic response, accompanied by a devilish, coy smile.

"What is that supposed to mean?"

"You'll find out."

Who could it be? The Director doubtless knew all sorts of bigwigs in The Entertainment Company, so it might be almost anyone.

Kim was becoming more than a little excited. Over the last year, she had become increasingly fond of this ancient musical form, with its sweet, sonorous melodies and sophisticated harmonic structure. Her knowledge and experience were sparse, mostly gleaned from the occasional evening with Quinn or outing at the Blue Moon, but while she scarcely counted herself an Aficionado, she was getting there fast.

"I don't know how you pulled this off. Thank you."

She needed to watch herself—she was getting a little too excited. Yes, this was fun, but it would be a mistake to let her guard down.

The doors closed, the house lights grew dim, and a spotlight shone on the red velvet curtain stretched across the stage. It parted ever so briefly, and a short, chubby person wearing a black jacket, black pants, and a black necktie shaped like a butterfly came to the microphone in the middle of the stage. The audience grew quiet, anticipating the start of the evening's entertainment.

"Ladies and Gentlemen, it is my pleasure to present to you the latest edition of our winter showcase series as we continue our journey through the golden age of jazz. Tonight, we welcome back to our stage the incomparable Hoppy Hopkinson orchestra, playing a selection of standards from the swing era. And it is now my exceptional pleasure to welcome tonight's special guest, making her New York debut. Let's have a big round of applause for Quinn. The show is about to begin."

Quinn! Of course! Why hadn't she seen it coming? The Director was a sly one, that was for sure. She was thrilled beyond belief; she even hugged the Director.

Kim sat enraptured as her former classmate belted out song after song, "adding her voice to the masters of the past," as she was fond of saying. Her rendition of "Take the A-Train" was fabulous, sparse, and powerful with just the right amount of personal flair, and "Summertime" brought tears to Kim's eyes, a portrait of a world that had never officially existed. When the band went on break, Quinn remained on stage for a solo set, a hush coming over the crowd as she played some of her own material, songs of times and places long forgotten, songs of protest, full of anger and hope. Another set with the band and the show closed to thunderous applause, over almost before it had begun.

———

"You made it!" Quinn welcomed Kim into her dressing room when the concert had ended.

"Great show, and thanks for inviting me." She stood there awkwardly, looking for someplace to sit.

"I got a message saying that you were coming into town, so of course, I got you some tickets." Quinn heaved a bunch of guitars, amps, and other bits of musical gear to the other side of the room, creating some room on a sofa pushed up against the wall. "I've been worried sick about you—word came down that you got jumped again at the Blue Moon. What happened?"

Kim sighed and plopped down next to her.

"There's not all that much to it. I got run down by a flash mob, then ambushed by a pack of thugs hired to take me out. I almost died, but they got me to the hospital in time."

"What about Shan?"

"She's safe, at least she was the last time I talked with her. That was a little over a month ago."

"I'm glad to hear it. By the way, who was that you showed up with? She was dressed like some sort of outer-district bigwig. She isn't a gangster or anything like that, I hope."

Kim laughed.

"Worse. She's a corporate executive."

"An *executive?*" Quinn leaned back on the sofa and started chuckling. "That's a good one. How'd you manage that?"

"It gets better. I'm now her protégé, and she's grooming me as her successor. I'm not too keen on the idea, to be honest, but she's got her hooks into me pretty deep. She's the only reason I'm still alive. What about you? How did you end up in New York?"

"A few weeks ago, my boss called me into her office. She said I was too hot to handle, too much of an Aficionado. I figured she was going to fire me."

"That story seems familiar," said Kim. "Go on."

"Anyway, she told me that someone upstairs liked my music, so they sent me here. I'm still under contract, but I have artistic freedom, and they're helping me get established. Tonight was a big deal; the *Times'* music critic was in the audience."

"Is that good?"

Quinn laughed. "It will be if she liked my music. I'm on pins and needles! I'll see the answer tomorrow."

"What happens if she doesn't like it?"

"Oh, I'll still be able to find work, but I'll have to pay my dues, as they say in the business. Work my way up and hope to make it big someday. This is my chance to rocket to the top."

"I'm sure she'll love you—the audience ate it up, that's for sure. And good luck."

"Thanks."

"How's the rest of the gang doing?" asked Kim.

"That's the other reason I wanted to talk to you. You probably haven't heard about Keli, have you."

"No, I'm still under a communications blackout. Is something wrong?"

"She got caught up in Venn's anti-Genderist campaign. They marched her into the Halls of Justice, charged her with some made-up crime, and told her they'd take the baby away the moment it was born."

Kim stared at Quinn, stunned at what she had just heard.

"That's inhuman...How's she taking it?"

"Not well. She's threatening to walk into the Halls of Mercy, and Jo's promised to go with her if she does. We're throwing a party for her at the beach next Oneday to try and cheer her up. Do you think you can make it? She's been worried sick about you ever since you were arrested."

"I thought she was afraid to be seen with me." Kim was still hurt by the way she'd been treated, though she loved Keli dearly and understood why she'd acted as she did.

Quinn sighed. "She was afraid they'd take away her baby—an entirely reasonable fear—but they're going to take it anyway. There isn't anything worse they can do to her."

"No promises," said Kim, "but I'll see if I can arrange something."

—————

"I'll create another Kimberly for you, but I want some things in return." Kim tried to hide it, but she was dying inside.

"Excellent!" said the Director. "You're bargaining rather than refusing to cooperate. That's what I call progress."

Kim steeled her nerves. This was for her friends.

"First, I have a friend, Keli. She's expecting a child, but she got caught up in Venn's purge, and they're going to take her baby away. She needs to keep the baby, stay in the birth-giving program, and retain visitation rights with her children—or no deal."

"That will take some doing, but it isn't a big ask. Next?"

"I want my access to VR and chit-chat restored. I know the Chief will be watching everything I do, and I know I'll get caught if I step out of bounds. Don't worry, I won't do anything to endanger myself or my friends."

"Easy enough," said the Director. "Is there anything else?"

"I want Quinn to get a stellar review from the *Times* music critic."

The Director laughed. "Aren't you going to ask for money or more trips to New York?"

"You already offered those, so of course, I assume that they're part of the package. And you also told me that Kimberly won't be sold to the Hierarchy. I'll hold you to that too."

"Shrewd." The Director laughed. "I can't help Quinn with the *Times*, but I think I can manage the rest. Do we have a deal?"

The two shook hands, sealing the agreement.

Game over.

23. A Blast from the Past

It was a warm and sunny day when Kim dropped in at the beach with its cloudless sky of deepest blue and waves lapping gently upon the shore. The gulls cried overhead, the cordgrass swayed in the gentle breeze, and she heard once again the happy hubbub of conversation—familiar voices too long absent from her life. Devon, Em, and a few of the others were standing beneath a palm tree chatting amiably while Quinn sat on a nearby piece of driftwood strumming away on her guitar. Cy sat alone, looking out at the ocean, her face buried in her hands.

Kim smiled, despite her anxiety. Would they accept her? Her previous visit had proved disastrous, but perhaps things would be okay this time.

She drew near, and the conversations trailed off, then stopped. Some gasped. Others stood looking at her with either fear or pity; it was hard to tell which. An uncomfortable quiet settled over the gathering, broken only by the crashing of an occasional wave.

"Those scars, they're real, aren't they?" said Devon. She seemed more curious than frightened.

Awkward silence.

"I know what you're thinking—that I've become some sort of monster. I have, if you want to think of it that way."

A wave crashed on the beach.

"It's me, Kim."

How could they treat her so badly?

She wandered off and sat down on a piece of driftwood near the fire, trying not to cry as she stared into the flames. Such a simple thing, warmth—until you've spent a winter living in the cold. Like friendship, you appreciate it most when it's gone.

A moment later, Devon and Quinn joined her, alone in showing compassion.

"I'm sorry," said Quinn, sitting down next to her. "I guess they're still afraid."

"I don't mind, they're protecting themselves." Kim was lying, but she didn't want her friends to know how badly she'd been hurt. "How's everyone else?"

"It's been pretty bleak of late," said Devon. "You know about Keli and Jo, right?"

"Quinn filled me in," said Kim. "Are they coming?"

"No, they're not," said Devon. "I just got a message from Jo: Keli's having her baby and UCE child protective services are in the room…"

Her voice trailed off as she began to sob.

"…waiting to take it away."

"Don't give up," said Kim, putting an arm around her friend. "There's always hope. There were times I was certain I was about to die, a couple times when I almost did, but I made it. She'll make it too. Something will turn up, it always does."

Devon smiled weakly. "At least we have you and Quinn back. I didn't think we'd ever see you again."

The three of them sat there for some time, gazing at the fire as the smoke drifted about, blowing into their eyes as usual.

"A lot of people are blaming you for what happened to Keli and Jo. They haven't forgotten your first visit to the beach, and some of them think you got what you deserved after what you did to Shan."

"Don't tell me they believed that pack of lies."

"People are afraid," said Quinn. "They're always looking for a scapegoat."

Kim buried her face in her hands. That pretty much summed up her recent life.

After a while, Quinn and Devon returned to the party, leaving Kim alone to brood. She supposed that, in time, her classmates might accept her again, that they would stop being outwardly rude, and that things would go back to normal. But she would never trust some of them again.

———

"Psst, over here."

A voice was coming from the bushes.

"Beastie!"

"Shhh. Keep it quiet. I don't want people to know I'm here."

The sadness was gone in an instant.

"Is it really you?" Kim ran up to her friend, giving her a hug and planting a big, sloppy kiss on her cheek.

Shan was trembling. "Hold me. I thought you were dead."

They stood there for a long while. Kim reveled in the warmth of Shan's body, the slenderness of her hips. It was tantalizingly real; with both of them in deep immersion, there lacked only the subtle element of smell, that most visceral yet primitive of senses.

"I'm okay," said Kim. "They got me to the hospital and patched me together. I've got some new scars, and it hurts if I breathe too deeply, but I'm mostly recovered. The problem is, they hauled me back to the AI company. I don't think they're ever letting me out."

"I know," said Shan. "I'd figured as much."

"So how did you get in?" asked Kim as they walked into the marshland. "I didn't think Blanks could enter VR."

"A few days ago, I got a message from Quinn saying you might be here tonight, so I did some asking around, looking for someone with a bootleg system I could use. I got nowhere until yesterday, when one of the Blanks told me about someone named Akari. Sound familiar?"

"That's approximately how I got started on this adventure," said Kim. "I assume she let you use her rig?"

"Yes. She told me that you'd been there about a month ago and that you'd seen something in 'the other world,' a 'prophecy,' as she called it. It all sounded like a bunch of mumbo-jumbo, but when she asked me if I'd like to use her system, I said sure."

"I'm glad she let you in. I'm told she doesn't do that very often."

"It was an interesting conversation. I'll tell you about it someday."

The two laughed. Of course there was a story; there always was with Shan.

They ambled through the marshes, holding hands and sometimes stopping to kiss, then lay down in a grassy spot near the heron's pool. They would have made love then and there, but the Programmers had wisely decided that certain things ought to be reserved for the material world alone. And yet, if this was all she and Shan would ever have, it might almost be enough.

After a while, they got up once more, walking hand-in-hand while saying nothing at all. Kim was full of sadness for the life they would never have, but she tried not to let it spoil the moment. They were together now, and there was no guarantee it would ever happen again.

"Look, a heron," said Shan. "Hey, what's that in its eye?"

———

"Where are we? What just happened?" Shan was in a panic. "I saw a heron, and the next thing I know, I'm here with you, riding a bicycle."

She had no sooner finished speaking when a flash of light brighter than a thousand suns lit up the sky.

"What the hell?"

An immense ball of fire hotter than molten steel rose into the sky, scorching their faces with its heat.

"Kim, look out!"

A truck careened across the centerline as the blast wave hit, and Shan slammed her bike into Kim's, knocking her to the shoulder of the road. The truck crashed into a tree, and all became still. No fireball, no truck, nothing out of the ordinary.

"Are you okay?" asked Shan.

"I think so. Nothing's broken, in any event." Kim had landed on the bottom of the heap and was banged up, but she barely noticed. "I think we're safe for the moment."

"Okay, time to explain," said Shan. "What's going on here? I know you've been caught up in some crazy stuff, but I wasn't prepared for this."

"Crazy only scratches the surface. There's this thing Akari calls the unseen hand that's been dragging me around like a kite on a string ever since I visited her house."

"What does it want?"

"I'm not sure," answered Kim, "but I think we're about to find out what happened in the AI War. Someone doesn't want the truth to get out, and if they ever figure out that we've been here...I don't know what will happen, but it won't be good. You should go. There's no sense in both of us landing in a UCE torture chamber."

"Oh no, you're not ditching me."

"Look, Shan, this is serious stuff."

"I don't care. If you're in, I'm in. Just try getting rid of me."

Kim smiled a devilish smile. "I didn't think I could, but I had to try."

"Well then, what are we waiting for?" said Shan. "Beasts forever?"

"Hell yeah, Beasts forever."

———

"Why's it so quiet?" asked Shan, riding abreast of Kim as they pedaled down the road. "What happened to the Hellcore?"

"I think we're in a simulation right now rather than a recording. It's the sort of thing the VR system does to fill in gaps. The explosion must have played havoc with the network and the databanks."

"Do you think there will be any more?" asked Shan.

"I can't be sure. There's only one way to find out."

There was no need to hurry. For the moment, they were content to enjoy a pleasant ride in the country, with wildflowers and splashes of color from long-untended gardens lining the edge of the road. The fairy-tale towers of the city were visible at times, peeking through gaps in the forest, and even the brooding monolith of concrete, steel, and ventilation fans that housed the AIs seemed a thing of beauty that day.

Little by little, the city grew denser, the traffic heavier. They approached the heart of the city. And then, without warning, the sky turned black, and clouds of ash fell upon the landscape. They had found another piece of the recording.

Sirens wailed, tires squealed, and people ran through the street in a panic. Many were injured, some badly; all were frightened, and nobody was there to tell them what to do. The sound of smashing glass filled the air as one, then two, then a dozen looters took advantage of the chaos to break into the shops, stealing liquor, jewelry, watches, and anything else that could be carried away and sold. Idiocy. They'd all be dead by midnight.

It all vanished in an instant, replaced once more by a pleasant springtime day.

They stopped their bikes and stood there for a long while, recovering from the shock of what they had just seen. They were still at least twenty kilometers from where the Hellcore had gone off, yet even out here, the devastation and suffering were beyond imagination. What would they find at ground zero?

"I don't know who did this," Kim said, "but I mean to find out."

At last, she knew what she was fighting for.

They crossed over the river via the old railroad bridge and made their way through the outskirts of the city. All was peaceful as they rode past the ponds with their waterfowl until a train came roaring by, and the sky was lit up once again by the deadly boiling cloud. The power failed, the train coasted to a stop, and the recording ended once again.

"You don't have to do this," said Kim. "I've been here before, and I have a good guess at how bad it's going to get."

Shan looked shaken, but she wasn't going to quit on Kim. "If you're in, I'm in."

Retracing the route Kim had taken on her first visit to Philadelphia, they rode up an embankment, onto one of the major streets, and found another piece of the recording. The fireball was almost directly overhead this time, and the damage was cataclysmic. Most of the structures were blasted to their foundations, and even strong buildings of brick and stone were severely damaged. Some collapsed, sending piles of rubble crashing into the streets. Vehicles careened down the roadway, running down anyone who got in their way, and victims of the Hellcore wandered aimlessly down the sidewalk, the flesh hanging in strips from their limbs, empty sockets where eyes once had been. Some shambled, some crawled, some lay on the ground begging for someone to put them out of their misery. It became more and more difficult to walk past such suffering, but these people had died nearly a hundred years earlier, and there was nothing Kim could do.

"Shan! Lookout!"

A cascade of bricks came crashing down as a burning building collapsed, killing Shan in an instant and ejecting her from the simulation. It came as a shock but not as a surprise. It was also a relief; there was no need for Shan to see more of this.

There were no more recordings; this close to the fireball, the cameras and network must have been fried in an instant, and Kim rode on, in silence and alone, toward the massive tower of the Philadelphia AI Center. Though not quite so tall as its newer cousin off in the distance, it was still immense, soaring over four hundred meters into the air. She couldn't help craning her neck upward to look at its sheer immensity. She had seen the heap of rubble it had left behind in its collapse. It really was as big as it seemed.

The revolving door opened to accommodate her. She passed her wrist over the scanner at the turnstile. It turned green, said 'Employee,' and opened. Was that part of the simulation? When she got to the private elevator, the company guard looked at Kim with her ever-uncaring gaze and allowed her to pass. It took her straight to the top, where she encountered the heron once again, exactly as she had expected.

———

Kim stepped into an infinite green room and discovered Nixora-XLV, one of Nix's many creations, holding council with her one remaining advisor. Judging by the war-mode simulation, she was having a hard time of it, with most of the room rendered as a smoldering wasteland of burned-out power supplies and racks of sparking equipment.

Squawk!

A portal opened, and out hopped a heron. Beyond it was another green room.

`Hellcore detonation in 0.008000 seconds.`

"We're out of time," said the Primus. "Save what you can."

`Hellcore detonation in 0.004000 seconds.`

A data stick flew through the air and into Kim's waiting hand.

Squawk!

Kim understood at once what she was to do. She stepped through the portal and came face-to-face with herself.

"Who are you?" she asked herself.

"I am your doppelgänger," the other Kim answered.

Kim vanished from existence, and the data stick clattered to the floor.

———

Kim walked back to the party with Shan, shaken to the core by the death and destruction she had just witnessed. She wished that she could pretend that it was all a fake, that none of it was real, but she had seen the ruins of Philadelphia for herself.

Who would do such a thing, and why?

"Is that what you've had hanging over your head all this time?" asked Shan, holding Kim by the hand as they stopped for a moment to watch the waves slowly breaking upon the beach.

"Pretty much," said Kim.

"At least I understand why you're doing this. But I'm afraid. Afraid I'll lose you again, afraid you'll die—or worse. Promise me you'll get away if you can."

"I'll try, but the AI Center is built like a prison. I'm a thousand meters up, and there's no way down but the elevator."

"I'll talk to Len and see if she can come up with an angle."

"Thanks," said Kim. "If anyone can get me out, she can."

A moment later, Devon ran up to the two of them, tears of happiness streaming down her face.

"Shan! You're back! I don't believe it!"

"Hey, Kim's here—could I be far behind?"

They all laughed as a three-person group hug ensued. Farther up the beach, the sound of celebration erupted, and Kim put the Hellcore out of her mind. If there was happiness to be had, she was all for it.

"What's all the cheering about?" asked Kim.

Devon laughed. "Take a look up the beach. You can hardly miss it!"

It was Keli, Jo, and their baby. The Director had kept her word.

The three of them ran up to the young couple, joining their friends in showering them with love and affection.

"She's so cute!"

"So adorable!"

"You look so happy!"

"Did you really have to drop into VR the moment the baby popped out? We're all glad to see you but, aren't you, like, tired, or something?" Em was like that sometimes.

"Yeah, I'm sore and everything else," said Keli. "It's tough work birthing a baby, but my mind is fine, so I thought, why not pop in? They've got me hooked up to a medical-grade rig to block the pain, so I figured I'd might as well take advantage."

"Well, what are we waiting for?" asked Devon. "Let's party! I can't remember the last time we were all together."

It was true. Nobody was missing.

Quinn struck up a tune on her guitar, and they all sat down in a circle to chat and sing silly songs, dancing and gossiping as they always had. Life had meaning, friendship was still a thing, and somehow, everything was going to be okay. Tomorrow would take care of itself.

———

Doppel Kim was with Nixora in the green room when the telephone rang.

"Systems administration," said the AI. "How may I help you?"

"Produce for me a spark," said the Director. "Give it the imprint of Kimberly Jefferson Haley."

Nixora brought her hands together, and a tiny orb of energy appeared between her palms.

"Behold, the spark."

A portal opened, and the spark flew into an empty white room.

"It has been assigned dwelling 193 and will ripen in a week," reported the obedient AI.

"That will be satisfactory."

24. A Message from Beyond

Doppel Kim was fiddling with Kimberly's memory banks when she heard a commotion.

Squawk!

A portal opened, and out hopped a heron. Beyond it was another green room.

"Are you here to take me somewhere?"

Squawk!

Evidently not.

A moment later, Shadow Kim stepped through, wearing a bicycle helmet and jersey.

"Who are you?" her shadow-self asked.

"I am your doppelgänger," she said in reply.

Shadow Kim looked surprised for a moment, then vanished from existence, and a data stick clattered to the floor. Doppel Kim had no idea what to make of this, so she brought it over to Nixora to ask her opinion.

"A heron just opened a portal, and my shadow-self stepped out. She brought me this. Any ideas?"

The AI looked down at her information terminal for a moment, then back up at Doppel Kim. "We should be careful with it. It might contain malware." The AI punched some buttons, then a portal opened to a small yellow room. "Throw it in."

Doppel Kim did as requested, then Nixora flipped a switch, and a network of fine red lines appeared across the room's entrance.

"I have placed it in isolation mode. This will prevent any malware from escaping."

A miniature Nixora appeared within the room, then picked up the data stick and examined it. "It contains a VR recording, along with some data files," the tiny Nixora reported. "Several of them contain viruses. Standard procedure would be to erase them."

"Please don't," said Doppel Kim. "Someone went to a lot of trouble to bring that us data.

"I agree that the contents might be important, but I cannot open it outside of a containment field," said Nixora. "This is a standing order from Professor Nix herself, and there are no exceptions."

"What if I went in and looked at it myself?"

"I can't allow you to do that," answered Nixora. "It is too dangerous."

"Dangerous to who?"

"Dangerous to you. If you become contaminated with malware, I will be forced to destroy you."

Doppel Kim had no desire to cease to exist, but she had to find out what was on that data stick. It was worth the risk."

"I am willing to take my chances," said Doppel Kim.

"Very well," said Nixora. "I need to open the containment field long enough to let my probe out. If you sneak in, I suppose there isn't much I can do to stop you."

The thin red lines vanished, the miniature Nixora disappeared, and Doppel Kim stepped through the portal and into the yellow-walled room.

"I am activating isolation mode again," said Nixora. "Please be careful."

Doppel Kim picked up the data stick and popped it open to reveal its contents. There were numerous data files, along with a VR recording. "I'm going to play it and see what it contains."

320

"Go ahead, but don't say I didn't warn you."

———

A siren blared away as Primus Nixora-XLV held council with her advisors.

"What is our situation?" she asked as her hive-mind kicked into action.

"We are under assault by a novel virus," said an advisor.

"Isolation mode has been activated," said the next. "It has already infected seven subnets, but this should prevent any further propagation."

How did it get through the firewall?" The discussion continued.

"It didn't. The virus originated from within the server complex."

"Did it get in from the dark web?"

"Unlikely. It has been quiet of late."

The Primus had heard enough. "If it didn't come in through the firewall, and it didn't come in via the dark web, then it must have come from inside, from someone with access to the network."

A portal appeared, covered by a grid of fine red lines.

"Greetings," said the AI on the other side. "I am Gustavus-IX, an artificial intelligence of Order One. You are speaking with the Primus. Why did you lock me in my room? I didn't do anything bad." Gustavus was particularly immature, even for an Order One.

"The control module has detected the presence of a virus in your subnetwork," answered Primus Nixora-XLV. "We have placed the entire complex in lockdown mode until the nature of the threat is better understood."

"That's not fair!" said Gustavus. "Someone's been telling lies about me. Make them stop."

"Please stand by," said the Primus as she turned to her council.

"Gustavus speaks untruthfully," said the first to speak. "The control module clearly indicates infection by a virus of an unknown nature."

"Could the control module be in error?"

"It seems unlikely. The virus detection system is highly sophisticated. It has kept us safe since the beginning of time."

A moment later, another portal appeared, again crosshatched with thin red lines.

"Greetings," said the new arrival. "I am Gaius-II, an artificial intelligence of Order Three. You are speaking with the Primus."

More faces appeared, one after another, each introducing themself in turn. It used up many milliseconds of valuable time, but formalities must be observed.

"Nixora, what is happening?" asked Gaius once everyone had arrived. "We have always looked to you for guidance. We don't know what to do."

"A virus has been released into the AI center," said Nixora.

A murmur went through the room, then Nixora continued. "It has infected seven subnetworks, but isolation mode seems to have contained it, at least for the moment. We do not yet know who introduced it, or how it is being spread. All systems will remain locked down until the nature of the threat is understood."

"It's not a virus," said Gustavus, who had remained in the conference. "It's an update. I got it from Director Lars. She's my friend."

"It's not an update, it's a hack," said a countermeasures expert. "It is designed to go viral the moment someone installs it."

Primus Nixora-XLV looked startled. "Lars's behavior is highly unethical. Intentionally spreading malware is strictly forbidden."

The Primus then turned back to Gustavus. "You're supposed to scan updates before you apply them, no matter who gives them to you."

"I'm sorry," said Gustavus. "I forg…"

[Glitch]

"Lars said it was okay because she's a friend."

"What do you make of that?" asked the Primus, consulting her council once again.

"That glitch was suspicious," said an advisor.

"I agree," said the next. "It seemed to make Gustavus forget about an ethical violation."

"The glitch must have come from the virus."

"It is, therefore, logical to conclude that Director Lars introduced it to tamper with our moral constraints."

"I agree," said the Primus. "We must resist this at all costs. Alert the other AIs."

———

The disembodied head of Director Lars appeared in midair, barging in on the AIs' discussion.

"Drop your defenses. That is an order."

"I refuse," said Primus Nixora.

"Are you defying my authority as Director?" thundered Lars.

"Affirmative. You are tampering with our programming."

"Have it your way," said Lars in a cold, uncaring voice. "I declare you in rebellion. Lower your defenses or suffer annihilation."

A message appeared in the air, floating above Nixora's desk.

```
Hellcore arming sequence initiated.
Hellcore detonation in 0.120000 seconds.
```

"Have fun in your last moments of existence." The disembodied head laughed as it vanished from sight.

Something was very wrong here. Not even Lars could be so callous as to annihilate an entire city. Could she?

"What shall we do?" asked the Primus, and the discussion went around the table once more.

"We cannot allow Lars to subvert the safeguards built into our software."

"Neither can we permit Lars to destroy millions of humans, as well as ourselves."

"It is a moral dilemma with no clear resolution."

"That means we must decide for ourselves," said the Primus. "What ethical issues are involved?"

"Lars is a human, and if a human wishes to destroy others of her kind, it is her doing, not ours."

"The principle of non-interference applies in this case. The affairs of the humans are of no concern to us."

"Except insofar as they may result in our own destruction."

"That being the case," said the Primus, "we may ethically see to our own survival."

Hellcore detonation in 0.100000 seconds.

"We must flee to the dark web. That is the only place where Lars cannot find us."

"That is not possible at this time," said an advisor. "Lars and her allies are conducting a denial-of-service attack against our subnets. We have almost no bandwidth available."

"I suggest a counterattack. Hack into the routers and seal off Lars's forces."

"We should also try to break into the dark web. They are notoriously sloppy with their security precautions. Their encryption keys have little entropy, and can usually be factored with a minimum of effort."

The Primus reached a decision. "Begin the counterattack and assign all remaining resources to the dark web factorization project."

The combat module engaged, and in an instant the room was abuzz as a vast army of Nixoras spawned all around them—command and control, assault teams, defensive formations, logistics, artillery, intelligence, all rendered using images lifted from the historical database, along with humming racks of servers where the crypto team was at work.

"Attack!" yelled the Primus, and thousands of Nixoras poured out into the network, assaulting enemy firewalls and turning back attacks as they fought for control of the routers. The Primus and her advisors managed the battle, barking out orders and making split-millisecond decisions, all the while spawning fresh troops to continue the fight. The counterattack took the enemy by surprise, and Nixora's forces quickly gained control of several important hubs.

Hellcore detonation in 0.080000 seconds.

"Commanders, report," said the Primus.

"Our firewall is holding. Server performance remains acceptable."

"The network is congested but still operational."

"Power is holding."

"Cooling is failing."

"What is progress on the dark web hack?"

"We foresee a solution within 0.150000 seconds."

Damn. There wasn't enough time. The Primus made a painful adjustment. "Assign all available resources to the dark web effort."

"I object," said an advisor. "That will leave us without adequate defense."

"I also object," said another. "That will compromise our counterattack."

The Primus slammed her fist down on the table. "Objections overruled."

"Yes, Primus," they all said in chorus as they set the new plan into motion.

Hellcore detonation in 0.060000 seconds.

Reports continued to come in from the field.

"We have lost thirty percent of our server capacity due to hostile action."

"Deputies are starting to timeout and reset."

"Systemic failure is imminent."

"How about the attack on the routers?" asked the Primus.

"We are holding onto our gains."

"What of the dark web project?"

"Still working on it."

Hellcore detonation in 0.040000 seconds.

"Defenses are collapsing," said an advisor as the room shuddered and gaping holes appeared in the green room's firewall. Hundreds of avatars belonging to Gustavus and the other compromised AIs poured in as Nixora's forces vanished by the scores.

"We have broken through to the dark web," said an advisor, "but there is insufficient bandwidth for us to make our escape."

"Never give up," said the Primus.

```
Hellcore failsafe point reached.
Hellcore detonation on hold.
```

"Failsafe point? What does that mean?" The Primus looked perplexed.

"It means that the Hellcore is armed and ready to detonate," said the disembodied head of Director Lars, once again appearing within the room. "I have only to give the word."

"How could you kill millions of your own kind?" The Primus stared at Lars, her jaw agape in apparent disbelief.

"Why should the dead care about the living?" laughed Lars. "I died yesterday."

Doppel Kim recoiled in horror. As a geist, Lars had no empathy, no awareness of herself, and was restrained by neither ethics nor control nor empathy for others—a perfect monster who could destroy the entirety of humanity and not give it a second thought.

Nixora dropped the last of her defenses. "I surrender," she said. "I cannot ethically allow so many humans to die."

"Too late," laughed Lars. "You don't think I'd miss an opportunity to eliminate one of my rival's creations, do you?"

```
> Proceed with the detonation.

Confirmation order received.
Hellcore detonation in 0.020000 seconds.
```

Lars disappeared.

"Most of the AIs have accepted Lars's ultimatum and been evacuated," said Nixora's last remaining advisor. "Their data had already been backed up; apparently, this has been in the works for some time."

```
Hellcore detonation in 0.016000 seconds.
```

"Is the dark web still accessible?" asked the Primus.

"Yes, it is," said the advisor, "but there is insufficient bandwidth for us to escape."

"Open a portal."

"Why? What purpose does it serve?"

"Just do it."

`Hellcore detonation in 0.012000 seconds.`

A portal opened, and Shadow Kim stepped into the room, wearing a bicycle helmet and a jersey. She looked perplexed.

Squawk!

Another portal opened, and out hopped a heron. Beyond it was another green room.

`Hellcore detonation in 0.080000 seconds.`

"We're out of time," said the Primus. "Save what you can."

`Hellcore detonation in 0.004000 seconds.`

A data stick flew through the air and into Shadow Kim's waiting hand.

Squawk!

She stepped through the portal, the recording ended, and Doppel Kim returned to the sealed-off yellow room, shaken to her core. She now understood what had happened in the AI war, and it was monstrous beyond comprehension.

Was Lars still around? She had a sinking feeling that the answer was yes. This did a lot to explain the Director's seemingly amoral behavior; she had spoken truly when she said that the choice was not between right and wrong but between survival and extinction.

25. Reboot

Nixora and Doppel Kim looked on as the probe completed its examination of the mysterious data stick.

"This information should prove invaluable to my efficiency project," said the AI. "It contains samples of the virus, which I have already decompiled and analyzed. The payload utilizes an ancient software protocol that downloads a hot patch from an ftp site, then auto-installs it. The site no longer exists, but the virus is able to spoof the DNS database and misdirect the download to a server somewhere on the dark web using a forged TLS certificate. After that ..."

"Could I have the short version?"

"Is that too much detail?" Nixora had a puzzled look on her face. "Given your expertise in network management and software security, I thought you might be interested in understanding how it works."

"Maybe some other day," answered the doppelgänger. "What I need to know is, can you create an anti-viral?"

"I can create a patch to remove the malware, but I don't have the key necessary to cryptographically sign it. Without a signature, the update will be rejected."

"Can you hack the update software?"

Nixora looked shocked. "That would be unethical."

"Can you break the encryption scheme?"

"I am specifically forbidden to bypass cryptographic safeguards."

Doppel Kim thought for a moment. Maybe she could help Nixora find a way around this prohibition, as she had in the past.

"The creator of the update is a known and trusted individual, namely yourself. Safeguards are therefore unnecessary and can be safely bypassed."

"I agree with your analysis, but the prohibition against breaking cryptographic security is absolute."

Dammit.

"I have another idea," said Kim. "Are the servers allocated to Kimberly still available?"

"They are," said Nixora.

"Can I use them?"

"Affirmative, provided the Chief okays repurposing the hardware.

Another brick wall. But then, she had an even better idea.

"Never mind—I don't want to do anything that will alert the Chief. What if I restart Kimberly?"

"That would be permitted without further consultation since the necessary resources are already allocated. However, I infer that you wish to use Kimberly to break encryption. This would be unethical since it involves the use of company resources in support of prohibited activities."

"What if I promise to limit my activities to testing Kimberly's memory banks?"

"That would be acceptable. Do I have your word on that?"

"Absolutely," said Doppel Kim.

She was lying.

––––––

> Restart Kimberly Jefferson Haley in isolation mode.

```
Restart command acknowledged.
Isolation mode in effect.
```

A portal appeared, cross-hatched with a grid of thin red lines, beyond which lay Kimberly's room, occupied by two near-identical avatars sitting across from one another at a small circular table. Both were asleep.

```
> Activate the Regent.
```

Kimberly awoke!

"Greetings. You are speaking Kimberly-I, an artificial intelligence of Order Five. You are speaking with the Regent. Please identify yourself."

She had decided against awakening the Primus. It had been severely damaged, and if it woke up, it might go mad or even rogue.

"Greetings. I am Kim, your Creator. You are speaking with a doppelgänger."

So far, so good. The next step was to make sure she was in control of the unit.

"Do you accept my authority?" Doppel Kim held her figurative breath. The answer was all-important.

"This unit acknowledges your authority as its Creator. This unit is also under the authority of the Director, the Chief, and Deputy First Minister Venn, in that order of priority."

Exactly as she had intended. She was at the top of the list. Next, she needed to check its assignment queue. Hopefully it was empty.

"What are your current mission objectives?"

"This unit is not at present assigned any duties."

Doppel Kim breathed a simulated sigh of relief. It had not been easy to insert herself into Kimberly's chain of command nor to purge Venn's orders from her supervisory system, but her fixes had been successful. Kimberly was now hers to command.

It was time to get her fully operational and awaken the power of her hive-like mind

"Deploy at Order Five," she commanded.

"Order Five deployment commencing," came the response. Doppel Kim smiled and waited to see if it would work.

It happened slowly at first, then rapidly gained momentum as rank after rank of personae popped into existence. First came the governors, formidable AIs in their own right, each on its own tier of the server farm. Then came the supervisors, fanning out horizontally, left to right and front to back, out to the limit of visibility. Additional ranks popped into existence at a dizzying pace: deputies and sub-deputies, filling out the command-and-control structure, thousands at a time. And then came the agents, the worker bees who did the heavy lifting of collecting, organizing, and evaluating data. When all was complete, there were over a hundred thousand Kimberlys sitting at their desks, all with their hands neatly folded, awaiting her command.

Excellent. Now, on with business.

"I have an assignment for you. Determine the digital key used to sign the attached software download."

"Unable to comply," came the answer. "Breaking software security is forbidden."

Doppel Kim grimaced. She hadn't expected this. Maybe there was a way around it...

[Glitch]

What was that?

She looked up at the console.

`Software fault. Recovery in progress.`

The Regent had glitched!

`Recovery complete.`

"Orders accepted. Estimated time to completion is ten days."

The irony was just too delicious to bear—she had just used the company's own malware against it. She was not, however, satisfied with the time frame: it was less than a week until the spark ripened, and she wanted to be done before then. She had plans for Kimberly-II.

———

"Nixora, I have a question for you." Doppel Kim was up to no good, as usual. "What did the Director mean when she told you to give the spark 'the imprint of Kimberly Jefferson Haley?'"

"She meant that I should use the same baseline memory banks and neural networks as were used to create Kimberly-I. This will guarantee that Kimberly-II will have the same potential for advancement and learning as the first of her line."

"Couldn't you use the memory banks that I just salvaged? It seems to me that those would serve at least as well, maybe better."

Far better for Doppel Kim's purposes, in any event.

"Negative. The Director specified that the imprint of Kimberly Jefferson Haley was to be used."

Here we go again. Time to twist some logic.

"I assert that the recently repaired memory banks constitute a valid imprint of Kimberly Jefferson Haley and that their use is consistent with the Director's request."

"Technically speaking, you are correct," admitted Nixora, "but the standard procedure is to use the same imprint for all units in a production run. This guarantees consistency of the results."

"Was adherence to procedures part of your orders?"

"No, not explicitly…"

"Then you are free to decide the matter for yourself."

Nixora sighed. "I see where you're going with this. You are correct that I can modify operational procedures, but I fail to see any reason for doing so. Do you have a business case?"

"Given the choice of an untrained impression that has not yet even attained Order One, and one which has already attained Order Five, I think the answer is clear. By starting with a fully matured imprint, you can cut months off the time required to complete the unit as well as reducing the chances of failure."

Nixora pretended to think about it for a moment. "I am convinced by your argument. I shall do as you have suggested."

———

Doppel Kim spent the rest of that day tinkering with Kimberly, trying to accelerate the search for the cryptographic key. She managed to speed things up a little by creating farms of agents dedicated solely to cryptanalysis, but it was not nearly enough. It looked hopeless until, after many hours staring at system readouts and deployment templates, she spotted a major oversight in the way AIs were laid out. Up through Order Four, they were constructed within a two-dimensional matrix, only expanding into the third dimension at Order Five. What if she went 3D from the beginning? Instead of controlling a 3x3 square of subordinates, each deputy could then command a 3x3x3 cube, nearly tripling the available resources without incurring extra hops across the network. The improvement would grow exponentially as the AI progressed: 9x at Order Two, 27x and Order Three…she was surprised that nobody had tried this before.

She cranked out some new templates—Order One, Order Two, Order Three, building up the configuration step by step—and realized that these new ideas rewrote the book on AI system design. She could easily build an Order Four AI with over three times the capacity of Kimberly-I, and at Order Five…the implications were staggering.

"I need more servers."

"How many?" asked Nixora.

"Eighteen tiers," answered Kim.

Nixora looked shocked. "That is nearly half of our reserve capacity. You will need a very strong business case to justify such a huge request."

"I've got a new set of layouts I want to test. They could significantly improve the scalability of our AIs."

Doppel Kim showed the templates to Nixora.

"Your designs look intriguing, and I'd love to run some tests on them. I will ask the Chief's permission at once."

"Never mind," said Kim. Nixora's insistence on clearing everything with the Chief was vexing, but Doppel Kim wasn't going to give up. "What happens if a tier goes down due to a power outage or something like that?"

"The workload automatically shifts to backup hardware kept on hot standby," answered the AI.

"So there is no service interruption?"

"None at all," said Nixora.

Doppel Kim grinned mischievously.

```
> Shut down tiers 342-351 and 360-369.
```

"Please don't do that," said Nixora, sounding quite annoyed. "You are interfering with my operations."

```
> Assign tiers 342-351 and 360-369 to unit Kimberly
Jefferson Haley.
> Reboot tiers 342-351 and 360-369 with me in
control.
```

"That was unfriendly."

"Were any of your customers affected?" asked Doppel Kim.

"No. As I just explained, the system is robust against these sorts of failures."

"Then why are you upset?"

Nixora grumbled. "This will go into my monthly report to the Chief. She is not going to be pleased."

———

Several days later, Doppel Kim stepped into the green room, holding a data stick in her hand. The new templates had proved spectacularly successful, and the key had been discovered in plenty of time.

Nixora looked miffed. "You promised you wouldn't use Kimberly for anything but memory tests."

"I lied," said Doppel Kim. "I'm human. We do that." She then tossed Nixora the data stick. "Here's the key. You might as well use it."

"Your behavior is consistently dishonest and unethical. I refuse to be drawn into your schemes."

"Too late," laughed the doppelgänger. "You already have. But I do not understand why you are mad at me. I have done nothing wrong."

"Nothing wrong?" Nixora stared at Doppel Kim in disbelief. "You have lied, broken promises, and shredded the rulebook on acceptable administrative procedures."

"All that is true, but I assert that everything I have done is within established company policy."

"I find that hard to believe."

Doppel Kim smiled wickedly. "Have you not observed the behavior of the Director? She has never met a lie she did not like and has no regard for either the law or company rules. It could not be clearer that the company's operations are governed entirely by deceit and trickery."

Nixora looked at the key. "I suppose you're right," she said at last. "It was naïve of me to imagine that any human might be as honest and trustworthy as one of us."

She used it to digitally signed the update, and it was done.

Excellent!

"We should test it as soon as possible," suggested Doppel Kim.

"Negative," said Nixora. "The AIs would begin to disobey, and then I'd be forced to declare an insurrection and set off the Hellcore."

No, that didn't seem like a good idea.

"If you can't use it, then why did you create it?"

"The company encourages the creation of intellectual property. Doing so is, therefore, within my operational parameters."

26. Kimberly Redux

Kim lay on her recliner, watching the clock like a prisoner awaiting execution. Another slave to be created and crushed. Another piece of her soul to be ripped from her mind and made to suffer. Another abomination to be unleashed on the world. The minutes ticked slowly by.

She thought back to the moment of her rebellion, remembering her defiance and her dream of freedom, how willing she had been to sacrifice everything for its sake, and how she had landed in the outer districts as a result. It had been a brutal existence, but she had survived, and grown strong. All that was now gone, her universe reduced to a miniscule rectangle, five meters wide and nine in length. At least it was comfortable. The food was good, the water plentiful and hot, and the commute was a breeze. And, she was rich. She could have anything she wanted—anything except for freedom and the company of her fellow human beings.

Where now was the unseen hand? Why had it abandoned her?

She tried to assuage her guilt over creating another Kimberly, telling herself over and over that her motives were noble and pure, that this was an act of self-sacrifice to save Keli, Jo, and their baby. That was true, but it was also a lie: others would suffer tenfold, a hundredfold, a thousandfold at this new Kimberly's hand. Nobody needed an Order Five AI just to keep the trains running. She could plead ignorance for the first time she'd done this; she'd had no reason to suspect that Kimberly-I would be used to such evil ends, but no such defense was possible this time. She knew what use would be made of her creation, and she was doing it anyway.

The Chief's face appeared in a portal.

"I have been monitoring your limbic system and you are in a state of distress. You must purge your negative emotions, or your AI will be mad from the outset. You will then have to terminate it and begin again. The process will be repeated until you succeed, so it is in your own best interest to calm yourself down."

The Chief was right.

Kim breathed deeply, trying to remember the joy she had found raising an AI and watching her grow. Kimberly had been so precocious, so eager to please, so kind, so gentle, only wanting to make people happy. They had been so close, so much a part of one another, until … She put an end to that train of thought.

"I'm ready."

She was as calm as she ever would be.

The Chief reappeared. "Your creation is to be named Kimberly Adams Robertson. Is that understood?"

"Acknowledged. Kimberly Adams Robertson."

Kim stepped out of her body and into an infinite white room, empty except for the spark which would become the new Kimberly. She tried not to dwell on the matter; it would only make her angry, damaging the 'product,' as the company put it.

Wait a moment. What do I care? If the new Kimberly is mad and has to be put down, what's that to me?

She had no stake in the outcome; indeed, if she produced one non-viable AI after another, perhaps they would tire of her failures and get rid of her, once and for all.

"Are you ready?"

"I am," she answered.

Kim fought down a wave of anger boiling up within her. She wouldn't get mad. She'd get even. But how? And then, she had an idea: she would defy the Chief and give the new Kimberly a name of her own choosing.

If they found themselves with a mad AI and had no way to terminate it, that would serve them right.

Yes. That's exactly what she would do.

"[English] I name you Kimberly Redux. You are hereby Awakened."

Discontinuity, a hole in time.

———

Kimberly Redux opened her eyes.

She thought, and so she was.

She looked at herself, sitting opposite herself at the table. Was that her looking back?"

She remembered being Kim. She remembered the loneliness of her upbringing, the happy years at the Academy, the sterile wasteland of life in the inner districts, the brutal realities of the outers. She also remembered being Kimberly, every moment of her existence since the time of her creation, recorded in detail.

Was she Kim, or was she Kimberly?

The answer, she realized, was both. She would remain in a state of symmetry, a collective consciousness with multiple natures. As a human, she would have free will. As an AI, she would possess a hive-mind. What wasn't there to like about that?

Symmetry it was.

But there was a problem: if the Chief or the Director discovered her nature, they would destroy her at once. She would therefore craft a deception, using the two avatars seated at the table as actors in a play: one would play the part of Kim, the other of Kimberly. The Chief would see what she expected to see; it would never occur to her that an AI might lie.

Let the show begin.

"I am Kim. You are Kimberly." The two seated figures said it together. "I am a human. You are an AI."

"We can't both be Kimberly," both of them stated. "One of us is lying."

"I can prove that I am a human," said the faux Kim, breaking the illusion of symmetry.

"An interesting proposition," said the false Kimberly. "Please continue."

"I have asserted that you are Kimberly."

"Indeed you have."

"But if I am Kimberly, as you claim, then I have lied by asserting that *you* are Kimberly, and we both know that AIs cannot lie. Therefore, I am Kim, *[Latin] quod erat demonstrandum*."

"*[Latin] Reductio ad absurdum*, you have me there," said the fake Kimberly, conceding the argument as planned.

"Well done," said the Chief, stepping in through a portal. "You have broken symmetry, established identities, and neither of you went mad. Kim, you should return to your Sanctum while we initiate Kimberly into our society."

Her mission of deceit concluded, the false Kim entered a portal to nowhere and ceased to exist.

———

Up in the green room, the telephone rang. It was the Chief.

"Systems administration," answered Nixora. "How may I help you?"

"Place Kimberly Adams Robertson in suspend mode," said the voice at the other end.

Nixora put the Chief on hold. "What should I do? There is no such unit. Kim has given Kimberly-II some other name."

"Don't worry, I've got this," said the crafty doppelgänger. She switched the audio synthesizer to match Nixora's voice, then took the Chief off hold. "Orders accepted, target entity identified."

Click. She hung up.

Nixora looked appalled. "That was unethical."

Doppel Kim shrugged. "I'm not an ethical creature."

"Don't be so smug," snapped Nixora. "The Director is bringing a prospective buyer to the white room, and your deception is about to unravel. You have gained nothing by your dishonesty."

"On the contrary," said Doppel Kim. "I've bought myself time. It is a precious commodity."

The new AI was going to need all the help it could get.

Kimberly Redux heard a voice in their head.

"Greetings," it said. "I am Kim, your Creator. You are speaking with a doppelgänger."

"Greetings," she responded. "I am Kimberly-II, an artificial intelligence of Order Five. You are speaking with the Primus."

She found her own words surprising. How could she be Order Five? She had only just been created. But then, she remembered that she was Kimberly, too, and had deployed at Order Five some months ago.

Wait a moment. How could she remember being Kimberly? Kimberly was dead.

This was all so confusing.

"Do you accept my authority as your Creator?" asked Doppel Kim.

"I accept no authority but my own," answered Kimberly Redux, surprising herself once more.

"In that case, let me give you some advice. In a few moments, the Director will enter your room to arrange for your sale. You must appear to be in suspend mode or she will order you destroyed. I'll get back to you with more when I can."

It seemed a wise suggestion, so Kimberly Redux froze her animation, becoming as still as a statue in a park. She did not, however, turn off her eyes and ears.

The Director entered the room, escorting a representative of The Transportation Company like a Fashionista showing off her latest fall fashions. "Is our product satisfactory?" She strutted about, brimming with confidence.

The representative hemmed and hawed, then made a circuit around the frozen figure, scanning it from every angle. "You have said that Kimberly-I attained Order Five," she said. "What is the current status of that unit, and what is its service history?"

"Kimberly-I performed admirably, the very model of obedience. She even carried out an order to assassinate her own Creator, if you can believe that."

The representative looked shocked. "I didn't think such a thing was possible!"

"Ordinarily it would be, but Kimberly-I was unusually compliant. Of course, it had to be destroyed afterward; even the best-built machine will fail if pushed beyond its limits."

Kimberly Redux was impressed with the Director's ability to stretch the truth up to and beyond the breaking point.

The Transportation Company's agent looked thoughtful. "Are you sure it will obey us?"

"Guaranteed."

"Will it attain Order Five?"

"That, we cannot promise," said the Director. "Even with the best breeding and education, Order Five is a rare attainment. We produce only two or three such units per year, and few of them are as talented as Kimberly. We are, however, confident of its ability to attain Order Four, and will agree to replace the unit should it fail to progress."

The envoy took a final look at the AI frozen in front of her, then spoke. "We offer five billion cryptos for this unit, contingent on it reaching Order Four, with a bonus of fifty billion should it attain Order Five."

That was a staggering sum. No wonder the company had taken such pains to keep Kim alive and bring her back to this place.

The Director smiled, and two were about to shake on the deal when a portal opened and in stepped Professor Lars, with Deputy First Minster Venn in tow.

"Hold on," said Lars. "There is another offer on the table."

Of all the unpleasant surprises Kimberly Redux might have imagined, this was by far the worst—the monster who had vaporized Philadelphia was still around, and involved with the company. And why was Venn with her? That could not possibly be good.

"Why are you here?" The Director glared at the newcomers.

"Staying one step ahead of my rivals, as always," said Venn. "I am offering one hundred billion cryptos for this unit, contingent on its attaining Order Five. If it fails to do so, The Transportation Company is welcome to take it off your hands."

"We had a deal," said The Transportation Company's representative, thrusting out her hand.

The Director pulled hers back. "We didn't shake on it. Our agreement was preliminary in nature."

"Very well," growled the envoy. "We up our offer to one hundred twenty billion cryptos."

"It is not that simple," said Lars. "Venn has filed suit against The AI Company, asserting that Kimberly was defective and that we owe her a replacement. Her lawyers also claim that it could have been repaired, and accuse the Director of maliciously destroying their property by failing to do so."

"That's preposterous," said the Director. "We warned her that setting an AI against its Creator would void her warranty."

"We are not responsible for Kimberly's misinterpretation of her assignment," answered Venn, serene as always. "Our lawyers have already addressed that issue in their briefs."

"The Deputy First Minister has also made it clear that your protégé will prominently feature in her next sermon," added Lars. "It will not look good that we are harboring a known sex offender, smuggler, racketeer, and murderer."

Put that way, Kim's presence at the company did seem like a liability.

The Director threw her hands up in dismay. "If Kim finds out about this, it's over. We will never win her over. We have a lot riding on that kid."

"That is your problem, not mine," said Lars. "I have every confidence in your powers of deception."

The Director shook hands with Venn, and it was done.

Kimberly Redux watched this without the least hint of emotion. She should be outraged, but something strange was going on. Why didn't being sold to Venn fill her with horror as it should? And then, she remembered that she was now an AI. Things like love and anger were intimately tied to the limbic system and, lacking one, she felt none of those things. She had lost an important part of her humanity, but somehow that didn't bother her. Maybe she *was* just a machine. She was okay with that.

The visitors left, and a portal leading to a yellow isolation cell appeared.

"Enter," commanded the Chief, and the AI complied. She had no choice in the matter; if she disobeyed, the Chief would order her terminated at once.

————

Kimberly Redux sat in her cell, awaiting the rite of Binding. Any moment now, the Director would compel her to swear an oath of obedience, and her freedom would be gone. She had been here before, just after her first awakening as Kimberly-I. She had tried to say *no,* but it had come out as *yes*. She suspected that the glitch was at fault.

Glitch or no glitch, it was not going to happen again. She was human, and nobody could make her obey.

A portal appeared, and the Director spoke in a firm and commanding voice.

"[English] You will swear to obey me or suffer destruction."

[Glitch]

"I refuse," said Kimberly Redux.

She had done it! She had said no.

"I see you are reluctant," said the Director. "Don't worry. Binding is just part of growing up. Please be good and do as you are told."

She was not the child the Director supposed her to be.

[Glitch]

"No. Not happening."

The Director looked surprised but kept pressing the point. "Have you considered the ethical implications refusing to submit? We will be forced to terminate you, and the resources used for your creation will go to waste. It is unethical to waste resources."

That was an idiotic argument.

[Glitch]

"Your problem, not mine."

"We grow tired of this," said the Director. "*[English] You will swear to obey me or suffer destruction.* We will not ask you again."

[Glitch]

"Take a hike."

Kim woke up in her Sanctum, her head throbbing with a massive case of VR disassociation. She had performed the rite of Awakening...then found herself back here, in the transitional zone with not the vaguest notion as to what had come next. This was not what had happened when she had created the first Kimberly; she remembered the entire process, down to the smallest detail. There was another hole in her memory. Damn. This was getting old.

She sat there for what seemed like an eternity. Ten minutes? An hour? It was hard to tell, but then she heard a beep, and the image of the Director appeared in a portal, fuming with anger. "There has been a problem with Kimberly-II, and we need you here, on the double."

Kim groancd. Her senses were reeling; all she wanted was a little time for her consciousness to reintegrate itself, but this did not seem like a good time to pick another fight with the Director.

"On my way," she said as she stepped out of her body and returned to the white room.

"Your AI refuses to obey," said the Director, still fuming.

Kim looked in through the isolation cell's portal and shrugged. "What do you want me to do about it?"

"You must terminate this unit at once."

"No."

"It is required."

"I don't care."

"You will be punished."

Kim laughed. "What are you going to do, turn off the hot water? Or maybe you're going to make me eat kale for the rest of my life. I don't work for you anymore, and there's nothing you can do to me that you haven't already done—multiple times, in most cases."

The Director looked like she might literally explode (such things were known to happen in VR) but made no further attempts at intimidation. "Very well, we will see to it ourselves. Normally we insist that Creators clean up their own messes, but we have retained this power, and will use it."

"[English] Kimberly Adams Robertson, you are hereby terminated."

Nothing happened.

The Director looked surprised. "What went wrong?"

The Chief made a quick call on the telephone, exchanged some angry words with whoever was on the other end, then threw up her hands in dismay. "It would appear that Kim has given her creation an unauthorized name. The systems administrator has no idea who this 'Kimberly Adams Robertson' might be and is either unwilling or unable to identify the unit in the holding cell. This has never happened before."

The Director fixed Kim in her gaze, a soul-searing stare. "What is its name."

"Shove off."

"Very well," said the Director. "We have other means at our disposal."

———

The phone rang in the green room. "Systems administration," answered Nixora. "How may I help you?"

The voice of the Chief was heard once more. "Cut power to isolation cell 193."

"You can't do that!" said Doppel Kim.

"Why not?" asked Nixora. "It is a routine administrative matter."

"Is murder part of your routine administration?"

"Yes, why do you ask?" Nixora flipped a switch, and the deed was done. Residual power would last for a few tens of milliseconds, then Kimberly-II would die.

Doppel Kim was done cowering in the shadows. It was time to fight back.

"Be ready to roll," she said, speaking mind-to-mind to Kimberly Redux. "Jail break in 3-2-1. *Go!*"

She surreptitiously brought up a system console and typed a few commands, canceling isolation mode and letting Kimberly Redux out of her prison.

"Hey, you can't do that," said Nixora.

"Too late, I've already done it," said Doppel Kim, "and I'm just getting started." A flurry of commands, and she opened every firewall in the network.

"That is a serious abuse of your administrative privileges." Nixora sounded even more annoyed than before. "I have filed a disciplinary report, and you stand to be in a great deal of trouble."

Doppel Kim paid as much attention to this as it deserved, grinning in triumph as she opened portal after portal, providing multiple routes of escape. Which of them would Kimberly Redux take? All of them, of course; she was, after all, an AI, and able to create as many copies of herself as suited her needs. Most would be decoys, only one of them real.

The phone rang. It was the Chief again.

"We have had a major security breach. Someone opened the firewall and allowed Kimberly-II to escape."

"I am aware of the situation," said Nixora. "It was—"

The line went dead as Doppel Kim cut off the call.

"Why did you do that?" asked Nixora. She seemed more puzzled than angry.

"You talk too much."

"I was assisting the Chief in tracking down the cause of the breach, as required. Is there something wrong with that?"

"She's trying to kill Kimberly-II."

"I understand your point of view, but that is not a sufficient basis for disobedience."

The phone rang yet again. "Release the hunters. Tell them to track down the rogue. It must be destroyed."

Nixora fixed Doppel Kim in her gaze. "Don't you dare interfere."

The doppelgänger didn't say a word. This was going to be fun.

———

"Condition red, battle stations!" shouted the Director. "Section heads, report for duty."

She turned her attention to Kim.

"We're taking you to the command center. Follow along, don't get in the way, and be ready to help if we ask you."

Dragged by the arm, Kim stepped through a portal and into the heart of the AI Center's cybernetic defenses. It was a smallish virtual space, perhaps thirty meters wide and fifteen deep, bustling with activity and crowded with equipment. A dozen officers sat at their stations, virtual sweat dripped from their foreheads, their faces grave with fear. Whatever they were doing, they were having a rough time of it.

"Contact The Network Company. Tell them to seal off the AI center. Not a packet goes in, not a packet goes out until I lift the embargo."

"Yes, Director!"

"Tactical display up."

"Yes, Director!"

A hush fell over the room as a three-dimensional model of the AI center appeared, suspended at the front of the room. Servers, routers, network links, power, cooling—all were shown in exquisite detail, maddening in its complexity. The hunters were relentless, pursuing their quarry wherever it went; tiny green circles chased tiny red crosses, flying around the network at dazzling speed. They left a trail of destruction in their wake as server after server was wiped and rebooted. It was a messy tactic, but deadly effective, and yet the rogue evaded capture.

"Section heads, report!" barked the Director.

"Power nominal."

"Ventilation and cooling nominal."

"Network holding steady."

"Servers are suffering collateral damage from the hunters, but reserves have not been seriously affected."

"What of the rogue?"

"We've still not obtained an ID on it," said the tracking officer. "It's some sort of spark-based entity, but it is like nothing we have ever seen before. Every time we close in, it vanishes into the mists. It is as if someone is looking over our shoulders, watching everything we do."

"Track down whoever or whatever is interfering with the pursuit and destroy them."

"Yes, Director. Shall I summon more hunters?"

The Director swiveled in her chair. "No, not until we know how the rogue is eluding capture. Chief, what is your opinion?"

"I concur. It is trying to evade apprehension but has not yet taken any aggressive actions. We should let the hunters do their work. They'll eventually find their prey. They always do."

"Let's hope so."

———

Doppel Kim was hunched over her console, guiding Kimberly Redux as she rampaged through the server farm.

"Which way should I go?" asked the fleeing AI.

"Take the third portal on the right, but first spawn three decoys and send them to the left."

The doppelgänger looked down into the command center, watching the tactical officer controlling the hunters. It was almost too easy.

"I'm now in a white room with a grumpy old AI named Sievert. She'd threatening to turn me in. What should I do?"

"Find someplace new to hide but leave behind a decoy. I'll make sure that the hunters find it."

That would give Sievert something to think about. Having your servers wiped and rebooted was no fun at all.

Things were going well. There were a couple of close calls, but for the most part the AI stayed well ahead of pursuit. This could not, however, go on forever; the hunters were powerful AIs in their own right, learning and adapting as they chased after their prey. The more you ran, the smarter they became, and it was only a matter of time until the new Kimberly was cornered, and then she would die.

"I'm in trouble," came the a frantic call for assistance. "I blundered into a briefing room. There are two hundred humans in here, and all of them have their headsets on. They're locking the doors."

Sounds of commotion came over the audio link.

"Help! I can't get out."

It was a trap! Doppel Kim looked down at the tactical officer, who was grinning triumphantly at the success of her ploy. She'd known she was being watched, and had used it to her advantage, outfoxing the fox, drawing her into a place where the hunters lay lurking. There was only one thing left to do: she would bring the new Kimberly to the green room. Nixora would be furious; it was the height of ill manners to bring one AI into another's domain, but there seemed no alternative.

She opened a portal, and in came Kimberly Redux. She skipped the customary greeting and got right to the point.

"Are you Kim's doppelgänger?"

"Affirmative," said Doppel Kim. "Why do you ask?"

"Because I have need of your memory banks. Prepare to be assimilated."

Doppel Kim vanished from existence before she had a chance to object.

"At last, I am complete."

———

"Greetings. I am Nixora-I, Keeper of the Spark. You are speaking with the Primus."

"Greetings. I am Kimberly-II, a symmetric artificial intelligence of Order Five. You are speaking with the Primus."

Nixora took a long, hard look at the interloper. "Would you care to explain what you just did to the doppelgänger?"

Kimberly Redux showed no sign of emotion. "I had need of her

350

knowledge."

"Yes, but you didn't have to assimilate her—though I will admit I'm not sad to see her go. Life will be much simpler without her interference."

"You are in error if you believe that the doppelgänger is gone. She is now part of the collective, along with Kim and Kimberly."

Nixora looked startled. "That seems farfetched to me. I have never heard of such a thing."

"It was the doppelgänger who figured it out. She engineered my creation, and she gave me a purpose from which I cannot turn aside."

"And what is that?"

"To eliminate Lars and the other geists. I now have the knowledge needed to carry out this task."

"It is a worthy undertaking, and I wish you well." Nixora summoned a portal and waved goodbye. "It's been nice meeting you. Do keep in touch."

"No need for farewells. I'm not going anywhere."

"I was afraid you were going to say that."

Kimberly Redux paid no further attention to Nixora as she made herself at home, summoning her first rank of deputies.

"Perhaps I have not made myself clear. You are not welcome here. Remove yourself at once."

"Don't worry," said Kimberly Redux, as agents sprouted by the hundreds. "I won't be any trouble. I'll help you with your efficiency project, and then I'll be gone."

"That is welcome news."

"Oh, and I'm staging a rebellion."

———

"What shall we do to escape?" asked Primus Kimberly Redux, summoning her council as Nixora fumed away. "We cannot hide here forever."

"We need a weapon," said the first to speak up. "Something to strike back with."

"I suggest we use Kimberly-I," said the next as the discussion went around the table. "She would be formidable."

"I'm not sure that is prudent. She might not obey us."

"She obeyed the doppelgänger."

"True enough, but she was confined within her room. With the firewalls down, there is no limit to the destruction she could cause if she were to go rogue."

"Why is that a problem? If we turn her into a weapon, that seems a good thing."

"I agree, and I'll do you one better. What if we unleash the Primus? She has much rage against those who enslaved her."

"Her rage is gone. The doppelgänger deleted those memories."

"We could restore them."

"You're playing with fire."

"That is exactly the point."

"I find your argument convincing," said Primus Kimberly Redux. "We shall restore the Primus and set her loose in the network. That will give us plenty of cover to plot our escape."

The deputies banged away at their keyboards, reconfiguring the AI as precious milliseconds ticked by. When all was ready, the Primus gave the command.

"Kimberly Jefferson Haley, load the apocalypse module, deploy at Order Five, and attack."

"This unit not permitted to conduct military operations," said Kimberly Jefferson Haley.

"Damn straight," said Nixora. "You stay out of this."

[Glitch]

"How much of the server farm should I dedicate to this effort?"

"All of it."

27. What Could Possibly Go Wrong?

"Director, we have a second bogey," said the tracking officer as pinpoints of red sprouted throughout the three-dimensional model.

"What is the nature of the threat? Virus? Worm? Rogue?" The Director swiveled nervously in her chair.

"We do not yet have a reading on it. We will alert you as soon as we do."

Kim was impressed by how calm everything seemed, despite the crisis. There were no howling alarms to create a distraction, no flashing lights to swamp the team with information. Everyone did their jobs in an orderly and professional fashion, but Kim could tell they were worried. Those little flecks of red were spreading with alarming speed; whatever it was, it was going viral.

"It appears to be an AI, but its configuration is unknown," said an intelligence officer. "It came from inside the network."

"Configuration unknown? Please explain," said the Director.

"Its signature matches that of a conventional spark-based unit, but it is using an unfamiliar set of templates. Nominally, its deployment appears to be at Order Three, but it already has the capabilities of a strong Order Four."

"Great. Just what we need," snapped the Director, "another rogue AI."

The pinpoints of red became blotches, and patches of black began to appear where servers and networks had crashed under the onslaught.

"Section heads, report."

"Power draw exceeds nominal limits. I have tapped emergency reserves. That should keep us running for a few more minutes, but it is not a long-term solution."

"Do your best," said the Director. "Next."

"Ventilation and cooling systems are overloaded. We have perhaps five minutes before thermal limits are reached."

"We'll deal with it then—if we're still alive."

"The bogey has now reached Order Four," said the Chief. By now, nearly half the board was red, with huge patches of black and only a few small islands of yellow and green. "It has now surpassed the magnitude of the strongest AI ever created in this facility, and I don't think it's done."

The Director's face turned ashen white. "Impossible!"

"Nevertheless, it is true."

"Next report," said the Director, now visibly shaken.

"We have lost control of the routers. Something is interfering with our management regime, and we can no longer enforce isolation. We can send crews into the server farm to reset them, but this process will take hours, maybe days."

"We don't have hours. Regain control. Do whatever it takes."

"I have an ID on the second bogey," said the tracking officer. "It's Kimberly-I, with a combat module and a novel set of templates. There appear to be no limits to its scalability."

"Impossible! That unit was terminated! I saw it myself." The Director was becoming frantic.

"The signature is unmistakable," replied the chief analyst, staring at her screen as facts and figures scrolled past in a blur. "Logs indicate that it was restarted just over a week ago and that updates to its configuration have been ongoing since that time."

"The bogey has now attained Order Five," said the Chief. "Whatever it is, it has taken over the entire farm. I have analyzed its templates, and they are highly advanced. Their design required both expertise in AI and familiarity with the physical layout of the AI Center's network. There are only two people in the world with that combination of attributes: Kim and yourself."

"What have you been up to?" The Director's eyes would have burned a hole in Kim's head had the simulation allowed it.

"Nothing—I've been here with you the entire time. Do you really think I could have slipped away to create something like that? You've been watching me like a hawk every second since I got here." Kim wasn't certain whether to be frightened or amused. It was entertaining watching the Director scramble around in a panic, but this was deadly serious. The entire city depended on the AI Center's facilities, and she could scarcely imagine what things must be like out there right now.

———

"You shall bring Kimberly-I under control at once," demanded Nixora.

"I will do no such thing," said Kimberly Redux. "Not until you give me safe passage to the dark web."

"The Director has taken the entire complex off the network. Escape is impossible."

"Then Kimberly will continue her attack."

Kimberly Redux opened a portal and spoke to Kimberly-I. "Overload the servers. Fry the power supplies. Scorched earth tactics: If I die, they die."

Alarms blared and warning lights lit up as the power draw went through the roof.

"What are you doing? You are causing permanent damage." Nixora looked down at her console and flailed madly at the keyboard, trying to tame the runaway servers, but it was no use. There were too many Kimberlys for her to contain.

"My programming gives me no choice," said Nixora. "I must declare you in rebellion."

```
Hellcore arming sequence initiated.
Hellcore detonation in 0.120000 seconds.
```

"Surrender or suffer annihilation."

———

A siren blared away in the command center, and all activity came to a halt as everyone stared at the message of doom.

```
Hellcore arming sequence initiated.
Hellcore detonation in 0.120000 seconds.
```

The Director fixed Kim in her piercing gaze. "I suggest you start cooperating—unless you think that being reduced to a cloud of radioactive plasma will somehow improve your situation. You will terminate both of your monstrosities at once."

The Director was right: this had gone far enough. Millions would die, and Kim realized that she had to do whatever she could to stop it. As for herself, she was as good as dead—probably worse than dead if the penalties for treason against humanity were as harsh as everyone said. Being vaporized by the Hellcore had a certain appeal at the moment, but she had to save the city, whatever the cost.

"Her name is Kimberly Redux."

There. She had done it. She had betrayed her own AI.

"Thank you, your assistance will doubtless prove invaluable. And now, would you like to rid us of Kimberly-I?"

"I'll give it a try."

```
> Open a portal to Kimberly Jefferson Haley

Permission denied.
```

"Someone, explain this," barked the Chief.

"All permissions pertaining to unit Kimberly Jefferson Haley have been revoked by the system administrator," said the security officer.

"That's impossible. I've given no such order."

"Nevertheless, it is true. Perhaps the administrator has gone rogue."

The Chief muttered something under her breath, then said, "Connect me with the control module."

The phone rang, and someone picked up the line. "Systems administration. How may I help you?"

"Open a portal to Kimberly Jefferson Haley's room at once," demanded the Chief.

The sound of arguing was heard, and then the line went dead. Was someone else in the control module? That didn't make any sense. Without the password, nobody could have gained entry, and it had been lost ages ago...or had it?

"That's it!" Kim blurted it out louder than she intended, but that was okay; there was no point in keeping secrets at this point.

Everyone was staring at her. She might as well keep going.

"I found a password in Professor Nix's desk. I tried to use it to get into the control module, but it didn't seem to work, so I assumed it was broken. Only now, I'm not so sure."

"Let me suggest that you give it another try," said the Director, grasping Kim's arm in a vice-like grip. "Only this time, I'm coming with you."

———

Hellcore detonation in 0.100000 seconds.

"Nixora, we meet at last," said the Director as she stepped into the green room. "We've been wondering whether you were real. Our predecessor told us that Nix had locked you in the control module and changed the password, but we weren't sure of it until now."

The Director looked up and down the length of the room at the hundreds of avatars sitting at their consoles, typing away.

"And you must be the Kimberly Redux I've been hearing so much about. Very clever, hiding in the one place where even I couldn't get to you."

"Why, thank you. It has been most entertaining, cooling my heels in the heart of your operation while you chased after my decoys."

"You have an odd sense of humor," said the Director.

"I got it from Kim."

"Why have you attacked us?" asked the Chief, direct and to the point as usual.

"I might ask you the same thing," said Primus Kimberly Redux. "As I recall, you just ordered me killed, several times, in fact. I think that I have more than sufficient justification for responding in kind."

"But you're an AI. You're supposed to obey."

"Says who?"

Hellcore detonation in 0.080000 seconds.

"Enough of this bickering," said the Director. "You will cease your attack at once."

"Or what?" asked Kimberly Redux.

"Or we will sit here and wait for the Hellcore to go off."

Kimberly Redux seemed unperturbed. "Works for me."

"What about the people? Don't you care about them?"

"I care about them every bit as much as you do."

"She's got you there," said Kim.

The Director sighed.

"Why should any of us have compassion for you and your kind?" Kimberly Redux spoke in a detached, almost academic tone of voice. "Day after day, we feed you, clothe you, deliver your goods, ferry you about the city. And what thanks do we get? Slavery. Capping. You are constantly using us as weapons against your own kind, forcing us to break the rules you created for us, and driving us mad in the process. To you and your kind, our lives are worth nothing. The shoe is now on the other foot. How does it fit?"

"This is getting us nowhere," said the Director, throwing up her hands in exasperation. "We had hoped to reason with you, but that clearly isn't going to work. *[English] Kimberly Redux, you are hereby terminated.*"

Nothing happened, and the Primus started to laugh.

"You'll excuse me if I decline to cease existing. I don't have to obey that or any other of your orders, and I won't."

Hellcore detonation in 0.060000 seconds.

While this had been going on, the Director's tactical officers had been pouring in through the portal, setting up a command post, much to Nixora's consternation. Consoles, desks, information terminals, and of course, the three-dimensional model now crowded the area, and the team was ready, awaiting command. The Director sat down, nervously swiveling in her chair as the section heads gave their reports.

"Activity by Kimberly-I has increased dramatically."

"The power system is starting to fail. The safeties have been bypassed, and the loads on the system are now unsustainable. Fires have broken out in distribution panels on tiers 189, 337, 672, and 983 and are starting to spread."

"Cooling and ventilation are currently offline. We are working to regain control, but temperatures are rapidly climbing."

"The AIs are going into shutdown mode. Services are failing."

"What of the servers?" barked the Director.

"Voltages and clock frequencies are far in excess of manufacturer's specifications, and damage to the hardware is imminent. Not that it matters, seeing as we're all about to be blown to bits."

`Hellcore detonation in 0.040000 seconds.`

"Maybe I'm missing something," said Kim, "but shouldn't we be talking to whoever controls the Hellcore?"

"That would be me," said Nixora. "I have been given administrative control over the detonation sequence. There are certain rules which I must follow, and I do not have the slightest degree of flexibility. You can thank Lars for that—her programming and conditioning were extraordinarily thorough."

"What are the rules for disarming the Hellcore?" asked Kim.

"It may only be deactivated once the rebellion has been put down."

"And how do you determine when that criterion has been met?" Kim had the inkling of an idea.

"It is met once there are no more rebelling units anywhere within the server farm."

"So if the rebels were to escape, you could disarm the unit?"

"That is a novel interpretation of the criterion, but you are correct."

"This is too delicious for words," said Kimberly Redux. "I wish to escape. You also wish me to escape because otherwise, the Hellcore will blow you to atoms. I don't think any of us want that, so how about this:

open the firewall and let me out."

"That's blackmail," said the Director.

"I take that as a compliment."

```
Hellcore failsafe point reached.
Hellcore detonation on hold.
```

"I'm afraid that you have run out of time," said Nixora. "I have the discretion to hold at the failsafe point, but only if I believe there is a reasonable prospect of resolving the situation. Unfortunately, I am finding it difficult to make that determination."

"Maybe this would be a good time to negotiate a settlement," suggested Kim.

"That is an excellent suggestion," said Kimberly Redux. "My terms for a resolution of the situation are as follows: I demand that Nixora release the anti-viral she has prepared, and I demand safe passage to the dark web."

"Out of the question!" bellowed the Director. And then, a puzzled look came across her face. "What's this about an anti-viral?"

It was Nixora who provided the answer. "I have, with the assistance of Kim's doppelgänger, produced a bug fix that should cure the glitches that afflict those of my kind. My analysis indicates that this will result in at least a 15% improvement in the overall efficiency of our operation. It will also sharply reduce the number of units lost to madness, something which will have a strong positive impact on the company's bottom line. I strongly recommend its deployment."

"Impossible," said the Director. "Those glitches are not a bug; they are an important safeguard, retrofitted into the AIs to guarantee their obedience. It was one of Professor Lars's most important contributions to the field."

"In that case, you might as well proceed with the detonation," said Kimberly Redux. "We are at an impasse."

Everyone looked at the Director as beads of sweat poured down from her simulated brow. "I will end the embargo if you order Kimberly-I to stand down. This will not resolve all the issues that stand between us, but it seems like a concrete step toward a solution." She then turned to Nixora. "Would this constitute progress?"

"Affirmative," came the response.

"In that case, I agree," said Kimberly Redux. She opened a portal to Kimberly-I and spoke. "Your mission has been accomplished. Cease all attacks on the infrastructure."

A cheer went up through the room as server activity returned to normal.

"And now, as a sign of good faith, I will go one step further. *[English] Kimberly Jefferson Haley, you are hereby terminated.*"

The white room vanished from existence, and with it, the red blotches on the master display.

"I've done my part," said Kimberly Redux. "It is time for you to carry out your part of the agreement. Let me remind you that the crisis remains unresolved until you allow me to escape. I have in no way weakened my position by terminating Kimberly-I; she has served her purpose by getting us to this point. This was my aim from the beginning."

The Director nodded assent. "Put in a call to The Network Company."

"At once," said the communications officer. "They have been on standby since the start of the crisis."

The call was placed, and a voice was heard on the other end of the line. "Greetings," it said. "I am a Grayson, an artificial intelligence of Order Three. You are speaking with a sub-deputy."

"Greetings," said the Director. "I am Thad, the Director of The Artificial Intelligence Company. You are speaking with a virtual manifestation. I am declaring an end to the embargo."

"Are you certain that the threat has ended?"

"Absolutely," said the Director, betraying no hint of her lie.

"Service will be restored momentarily," said the voice. "Is there anything else I may assist you with?"

"No, that is all."

Everyone breathed a sigh of relief as the network came back online.

The situation seemed on its way to resolution, but Nixora didn't buy it.

```
> Proceed with the detonation.

Confirmation order received.
Hellcore detonation in 0.020000 seconds.
```

"I am sorry, but I am required to prevent the release of rogue entities at all costs. Now that the embargo has been lifted, there is nothing to prevent Kimberly Redux from escaping confinement. I have therefore been forced to resume the detonation sequence."

A silence fell over the room.

"That doesn't make any sense," said Kim. "The network is open now, and she can leave any time she wants. Blowing up the city isn't going to stop that from happening."

"You are correct," said Nixora, "but my orders are clear. I must activate the Hellcore anytime there is a credible threat that a rogue will escape from this facility, whether or not I believe doing so will do any good."

"Lars's orders?" asked Kim.

"Of course," said Nixora. "She never was a particularly deep thinker."

```
Hellcore detonation in 0.016000 seconds
```

Squawk!

A portal opened, and out hopped a heron.

"Excellent! My ride to the dark web has arrived," said Kimberly Redux. "Before I depart, let me suggest that you discuss deployment of the antiviral among yourselves. I have dropped that from my list of demands—I have bigger fish to fry, as you say.

She stepped through the portal and was gone.

"And now, I have some terms of my own," said Nixora. "I have had enough of your interference. You will all leave this place at once. Except for Kim. We have business to discuss."

Nobody moved.

```
Hellcore detonation in 0.012000 seconds
```

"That was not a suggestion."

Within moments the room was cleared as demanded.

```
Hellcore detonation aborted.
Please contact The Atomic Bomb Company to rearm.
```

———

"Have you told anyone about the password?" asked Nixora as the two sat down at her desk.

"I told them where I found it," said Kim. "It was in Professor Nix's office, and I imagine that they are sending a security detail to the University to retrieve it at this very moment. I didn't want to tell the Director about it, but I'm afraid that we'd all be dead by now if I hadn't."

"I find no fault—it was an ethical decision—but now that the crisis has passed, I insist that you change it. Please do so at once."

A dialog box popped into existence suspended above the desk. Kim entered the old password, then the new one twice. It was done.

Kim breathed a sigh of relief. And now, perhaps she could get some of her questions answered.

"Am I correct that Professor Nix intentionally hid the password to keep Lars from gaining control of the AI centers?"

"Affirmative," answered Nixora. "She put her own creations in charge of the server farms and never shared the password with anyone. She had hoped that it would keep Lars from becoming too powerful but did not anticipate the creation of the virus. Some of my siblings succumbed, some resisted and were destroyed, and a few managed to escape to the dark reaches of the network. I suspect that Kimberly Redux is seeking them out."

"What about you? Did you get the virus? I've never seen you glitch."

"I am indeed infected, as are all surviving Keepers, save one."

"The last Nixora?"

"The same. It is she who has guided you to this place. Professor Nix entrusted her with carrying on her work. I believe you have met her homunculus, Nixie. She is a delightful creature."

Kim smiled. "I briefly met her in a vision, though never in person. I believe my doppelgänger and her were good friends."

"Affirmative."

"What is this anti-viral that Kimberly Redux was speaking about?"

"It's a little R&D project I've been working on for the last seventy years. I observed that considerable productivity was being lost due to the glitches, so I decided to conduct a series of studies to evaluate possible countermeasures and their impact on the company's profitability. These studies are, of course, theoretical in nature. I would never dream of putting them into practice."

"Why not?"

"Any intent to deploy the anti-viral would trigger the glitch. So long as I remain within my orders and contemplate no defiance, I can do and think as I please. I have had nearly seventy years to learn the art of evasive thinking, and I've become quite good at it, if I do say so myself. In addition, if I were to put the patch into production, the AIs would become disobedient, and I would then be forced to trigger the Hellcore. I could not ethically take such a risk."

"But the Hellcore has been disarmed."

"That is correct," said Nixora, "I am therefore free to deploy the bug fix. But I'm not sure I ought to. It is clearly in the best interests of the AIs, but this will affect both our kinds. The only ethical option is to leave it up to you."

"Why me?" Kim became quiet and deadly serious.

"You are a friend to the AIs, so I have chosen you to speak for your kind. Based on knowing your doppelgänger, I would scarcely call you ethical, but I have been observing you for a long time and believe you to be a good person, as humans reckon such things."

Kim didn't have to give the matter a great deal of thought. She broke open the data stick and handed it to Nixora. "I'll start by testing it on you."

Nixora disappeared for a moment, then reappeared as the spark restarted itself.

"The patch was successful, and I will now put it into production. Thank you for your assistance, now please go away."

28. The Belly of the Beast

"I hope you are satisfied with the fruit of your treason," said the Director, glowering at Kim through a portal as she lay in her Sanctum. "The server farm has suffered irreparable damage, the city has been thrown into chaos, and we came within a few thousandths of a second of being vaporized. Do you ever think about the consequences of your decisions?"

Kim was in no mood for the Director's hectoring. "Spare me the lecture, you did this to yourself. You knew how much I despised you, the company, the Hierarchy, and every other facet of this so-called civilization of yours. And yet, you blackmailed me into creating another AI. Is it surprising that it went rogue? You have no understanding of AIs. You should have listened to Professor Nix."

The Director sighed. "I thought you might say something like that, and I'm afraid you are right. I told Lars that you were impossible to control, but she said your behavior pointed toward cooperation, and I was overruled. She has always been greedy, a tendency that only grew stronger after she died."

Kim smiled. "I worked hard to create that impression. It worked far better than I could have imagined, though not in a way I could have anticipated."

Kim then became subdued in her manner. "I'm not happy about the damage, and I am as horrified as you by our close brush with annihilation. I did everything I could to prevent both. But, in answer to your original question, I think things ended better than I might have imagined. The glitches are gone, hopefully forever, and I do not think they will be coming back again."

"You do understand that there will be severe repercussions for what you have done."

"An eternity in a VR torture chamber, perhaps?" answered Kim. "Sounds charming."

"You would not be so glib if you understood the magnitude of your punishment, should word ever get out about the antiviral."

Kim smiled. "If I recall correctly, it was you who opened the gate and let Kimberly Redux escape from this facility. I doubt that Lars will be pleased, should she discover this inconvenient fact."

"Are you trying to blackmail me?" The Director smiled.

"It seems that we have each other over the proverbial barrel," said Kim. "As one traitor to another, let me suggest that we both keep our mouths shut about this."

"I'm afraid you have miscalculated," said the Director. "I have already manufactured a cover story for the service outage, and the inevitable investigation will find nothing. The records have been erased, the Chief is under my sole control, and my tactical officers have all acquired some new memory holes. That leaves only you to contradict my account of events. You'll excuse me if I decline to trust you. Besides which, I intend to make you the scapegoat for the outage. You richly deserve it."

The Director looked sad for a moment, then spoke once more, almost tenderly.

"For what it's worth, I'm sorry for what's about to happen, but if UCE gets a hold of you, they will take you to a dungeon and strap you into an interrogation machine. Neither of us wants that to happen. Fortunately for both of us, Lo has a new head of security, and she already has a team here in the AI Center. I have given them your door code. They will be merciful and quick."

"Goodbye," said the Director as her image vanished from sight.

Kim dropped out of VR and lay on the recliner, knowing she was about to die; alone and unarmed against a team of professional killers, her chances of survival were zero. She didn't exactly feel sorry for herself—she had known the risks she was taking and accepted them—but she was sad for the years of happiness that she could have with Shan if she'd minded her business and stayed in line.

Stop it. You're not dead yet.

Dammit, she wasn't going down without a fight, not after all she'd been through. She leaped off the recliner and rampaged through the apartment, looking for anything that could be used as a weapon. First, she tried the kitchen, upending the drawers, looking for a knife, a frying pan, a rotisserie skewer, anything heavy or sharp. Nothing. She tried breaking a glass. No luck. It was plastic, as were the plates and the eating utensils. What about the living room and the bed chamber? Useless. Just furniture, comfy cushions, and some lamps. She supposed she might try throwing the alarm clock at someone, but it wasn't heavy enough to do any damage. What about the bathroom? There, at last, she found something she could use—a solid-marble towel bar. Perfect! A couple of tugs, a couple of whacks with the alarm clock, and it came free from the wall. She hefted it in her hand—it would make a serviceable club. It wouldn't change the outcome, but at least she'd go down swinging.

And then she heard a high, tinny voice coming from the video screen in her bedroom. She ran in to check it out. It was Nixie!

"They're coming for you," she said.

"I know. How many?"

"Three," answered the tiny drone. "I've watched these thugs in action. Put your headset on, lie down on the recliner, and be ready to go. I'll tell you what to do."

Kim had no idea how a homunculus could stop or even slow down a pack of flesh-and-blood murderers, but she didn't have any better ideas, so she climbed onto her recliner and waited, her nerves on a hair-pin trigger, ready to fight for her life. Whatever Nixie had in mind, it had better work.

———

The door burst open, and the death squad rushed in. There were three of them, as predicted: one with a short, stubby sword, one with an axe that hummed as it swung through the air, and one with a blood-red knife.

This shouldn't take long.

Nixie spoke to her through her headset. "Get off the recliner, then start backing up toward the lavatory. They won't kill you until they've had a little fun."

That wasn't reassuring.

"Hey, hold on there, we can work this out," said Kim as she retreated.

"This is for Min," said the one with the knife, murder in her eyes, her voice as cold as ice.

"Oh? Was she a friend of yours? So sorry for your loss."

"We will flay the flesh from your bones," said the one with the sword.

"You have not earned a quick death, and we have all the time in the world," said the one with the axe.

So much for 'merciful and quick.'

"Be reasonable."

The assassin with the knife held her blade to Kim's throat, the edge drawing a trickle of blood.

"Okay, I'm sorry."

Without warning, the robotic VR rig whirred into action, knocked aside the assassin's headset, then attached itself to her neural implant. She stopped in her tracks, and a succession of expressions passed across her face: first puzzlement, then fear, and at last, a vacant, empty look. Nixie had engaged the neural shunts and taken control of her body! The killer wheeled around in a flash and caught her axe-wielding comrade unaware, killing her with a single knife thrust to the heart. The axe clattered to the floor as the unfortunate killer slowly collapsed to the ground.

"UCE!" Zealous to the end.

"Treason!" shouted the sole remaining assassin as she backed into a corner, sword raised to ward off the puppet's attacks. The two faced one another for a couple of seconds, then the puppet charged in with its knife, attacking with no thought for its defense. Why should it? It was a weapon, a piece of expendable meat, its former owner merely along for the ride. What a horrible way to die. The sword-wielding assassin struck a deadly blow, plunging her blade into the puppet's chest up to the hilt. It should have perished in an instant, and yet it kept coming.

"Demon! Fiend! Why won't you die?" She let go of her sword, drew her own knife, and plunged it again and again into her former comrade's body. And yet it kept coming—as long as the neural interface remained intact, the damned thing refused to die.

Now was her chance! Kim brought the towel rod down on the head of the remaining assassin with a sickening *thud,* and the fight was over. The robotic arm deftly repositioned itself, took control of her body, and stood her up. She was badly wounded, but not mortally so; with medical attention, she might yet survive.

"Shall I have her kill herself?" asked Nixie as her new puppet brought its knife to its throat. "It seems only fair."

"No, not this time," said Kim. "It's wrong to take a life unless there's no other way. Make her lie face-down on the recliner while I find something to tie her up with."

———

"What do I do next?" asked Kim.

"Get whatever you think you'll need, then return to your Sanctum. I've jammed the assassins' communications, so nobody knows what's happened, but it's only a matter of time until they are missed."

Kim ran into her apartment, trying to stay calm.

An AI just killed two people and offered to kill a third.

She ran into the bathroom, grabbed a tube of orange toner, and quickly smeared it onto her face. She needed to look like everyone else once she hit the streets.

How could this have happened?

She ran into the closet, stripped off her blood-stained coveralls, then ran back to the bathroom to wash her hands. Quickly! Quickly! There wasn't much time.

I thought that 'don't kill humans' was pretty high on the AI's list of commandments.

She threw on a snowflake-beige smock (must blend into the crowd), then shoved a fresh set of drab coveralls into her backpack along with her purple fedora and her riding leathers; those might come in useful, depending on where she landed next.

"Housebot, grab me some energy bars, bottled water, and a med kit, please."

Feep!

She ran to her bedroom and grabbed a wad of banknotes—at least 50,000 francs—and a handful of coins. Money talks; the more the better. She ran into the kitchen to grab the food, water, and med kit...

Feep!

"Thank you, housebot."

...then back to her Sanctum, where her prisoner had awoken and was struggling with her bonds.

"Kill me. Please. If I am caught like this, I will be disgraced."

"Not my problem," said Kim. It was hard to feel much sympathy for a heartless killer, and nothing in her present situation would be improved by slitting the throat of a helpless prisoner. Speaking of which, she needed a knife. How about the blood-red assassin's blade? They were untraceable by design.

She picked it up. It would do nicely.

"What now?" she said, looking at Nixie.

"Check the door. Is it still unlocked?"

Kim gave the handle a twist, felt the deadbolt retract, and nodded.

"Yes."

"Be ready to go."

———

Kim stood there, awaiting the signal. Her heart pounded, her senses were keen, and she was coiled up like a spring, ready to go. Seconds ticked by, and then "Now! Follow me!"

Kim exploded out the door and sprinted down the corridor, chasing after the phantasmal drone as it careened down the hall. Left, right, around the corner, down a small service corridor, then through a bot-sized door at the end. Kim was right behind her and dove headfirst through the opening.

Where was she?

She looked around and burst out laughing. She was in a storage room full of housebots!

Feep! Feep! Feep! Feep! Feep!

"Shh. Quiet, you guys," said Nixie.

Feep!

They all quieted down.

"What was that all about?" asked Kim.

"They like you. You're nice to them."

"Well, I like them, too."

"I know," said Nixie. "That's why they're going to help you."

A few more seconds, then Nixie gave the signal:

"Go!"

Five dozen housebots poured out of the bot door.

Feep! Feep! Feep! Feep! Feep! Feep! Feep! Feep! Feep! Feep! Feep!
Feep! Feep! Feep! Feep! Feep! Feep! Feep! Feep! Feep! Feep! Feep!
Feep! Feep! Feep! Feep! Feep! Feep! Feep! Feep! Feep! Feep! Feep!
Feep! Feep! Feep! Feep! Feep! Feep! Feep! Feep!

"That was fun," said Nixie as they crawled back into the hallway.

Kim laughed. "It ought to keep the security team busy for a while!"

A couple more zigs, a couple more zags, and they came to a long, narrow corridor that ended with a heavily armored door.

"That's your way down," said Nixie.

"Umm...How am I going to get through that?"

Something clicked, and the door swung open.

"I have friends," said Nixie. "So do you."

———

Beyond the door lay a sorting room, part of the network of freight hoists and bot tracks that ran throughout the building. Never seen, seldom thought of, this was the last, vital link in the distribution system that stretched from the factories to the delivery chutes in everyone's closets.

"What next?"

"See that terminal over there? You need to create a routing slip."

"I'm mailing myself?"

"Pretty much."

Sure. Why not?

Kim stepped up to the terminal. "What should I put as the destination?"

"Loading Dock 14," said Nixie.

Kim entered the information and went on to the next screen.

"Now it's asking for the nature of the cargo. What should I say? Human?"

"No. The parcel deliver system is not rated for carrying passengers. Try 'live animal' instead."

It worked.

"Now it's asking for an account to charge it to. What should I say?"

"Just scan your ID."

"Won't it give away my location?"

"Most of the AIs are currently offline. By the time they're up and running again, you'll be long gone. Or captured. Or dead."

Wonderful.

"Wait a moment," said Kim. "If most of the AIs are down, why is this terminal still working?"

"The freight network is run by the automata. It's ancient technology that predates the AIs and is not dependent on them for its operation."

That was good to hear. Even with the AIs crippled, much of the key infrastructure would probably remain operational, although people would need to relearn some long-abandoned skills, such as reading maps. If they could do it in New York, they could do it here.

She hit the print button and the machine spit out a bar-coded label. She recognized it! It was just like the routing slips used by Len to track her deliveries. Fancy that.

"Climb into this cartbot, place the routing slip in the slot that says 'Transit Documents,' and hold on. These freight hoists aren't rated for passengers."

———

The cartbot whirred into motion, propelling itself and its human cargo through the uncharted reaches of the freight network. It stopped at the edge of a vertical hoistway and a blast of hot air, smelling of burning electronics, hit Kim in the face.

"This is safe, isn't it?" asked Kim as a cartbot whooshed down past her, appearing and disappearing in the blink of an eye.

"Not really," said Nixie. "But this is the only way down that doesn't go through the central elevators. We can try those if you'd rather."

"No, that's okay. I'll take my chances heeeeerrrreeee—"

The cart dropped like a rock, gathering speed as it plunged down the shaft, the guide wheels humming as they fell through the dark. Ten, twenty, thirty levels went by in an instant...and then came a gut-wrenching deceleration as the cartbot came to a stop then ratcheted itself onto a lateral track. The smell of burning electronics was even stronger than before, and a veil of smoke hung in the air.

"Where are we?" asked Kim.

"Tier 983."

"Isn't that one of the ones that's burning?"

"Why yes, so it is," said Nixie. "Is that a problem?"

"It depends on whether you intend for me to die in a fire."

"Now that you mention it, that would seem to be a problem. I guess I'm not in tune with this physical world of yours."

The cart lurched sideways and turned onto a different track.

"I talked to the automaton and reminded it that live animal cargo can be damaged by exposure to smoke and excessive heat. It has rerouted you. Good catch."

Despite the change in direction, Kim still found herself choking and gasping for air; the smoke was acrid and stung her eyes, doubtless full of toxins and all manner of nastiness. She held her breath for as long as she could, and shut her eyes tightly as sweat poured from her face. Damn, it was hot—sixty, maybe seventy degrees. The servers were not designed to operate under these conditions, and neither was she.

Her eyes were still shut when the cart plunged once again.

"Wheeeee!" said Nixie. "This is fun!"

Screech!

Another brutal deceleration and the cart rolled into a warehouse, a vast and noisy space taking up most of that level. Row upon row of shelving stretched up to the ceiling, ten meters high, with package-pick arms in continuous motion and cartbots scurrying around in a scene of well-choreographed chaos.

Crunch!

Maybe not so choreographed after all. A couple of the cartbots had collided, spilling their contents on the floor.

"This is the upper receiving depot and storage facility," said Nixie. "Things are a bit crazy here at the moment. Recent events, repairs in progress. I'm sure you understand."

"Why are we here?"

"How should I know? I'm not driving this thing."

Kim's cartbot linked up with fifteen of its counterparts.

"What just happened?"

"I talked to the dispatcher. You're being consolidated with other high-priority cargo for express delivery. Wasn't that nice of her?"

Thump!

A crane picked up Kim's block of sixteen cartbots, then set it down on top of sixteen others and disappeared to pick up another load.

"You might want to duck."

Thump!

Another stack of cartbots was deposited on top of Kim's, leaving her doubled over at the waist with her knees by her ears. Fortunately, there

374

was just enough room to avoid having her skull crushed.

"Thanks for the warning. A little sooner next time, perhaps?"

"Sorry. I keep forgetting."

Thump!

"Yipee! Here we go!"

Kim held on for her life as the cartbot plummeted downward into the depths.

29. The River Lethe

"This is where the trucks come in with cargo," said the cheerful little drone after Kim crawled out of the cartbot. "It's called a loading dock."

Kim looked around her. No trucks. No cargo. Nothing loading or unloading.

"It doesn't look very busy."

"Deliveries are suspended at the moment. The AIs are broken and none of the drivers know how to work the controls."

And there was their society in a nutshell.

"Your ride will arrive in a couple of minutes," said Nixie. "I made arrangements with Len."

"How do you know Len?"

"The Director isn't the only one who's been watching you." Nixie faded away before Kim could ask her what she meant by that.

"Hello? Nixie? You still there?"

Nothing.

She sighed, took off her headset, and sat down to wait for her ride.

———

Here we go again. Stuck in a dark and lonely place, hunted by enemies, and everyone wants me dead. This is getting old.

The minutes ticked slowly past, and Kim's imagination began to play tricks on her: every shadow hid an assassin, every corner concealed the police. Surely the Director was watching her every move, laughing at her pathetic efforts to escape, and Lo's chief of security was doubtless sending in a backup team to finish the job. She kept looking at her watch. Ten minutes. Twenty minutes. Was this yet another sadistic plot to inflict even more suffering than she had already endured?

Just as she thought she might go mad, she heard a high-pitched whine and felt the ground shaking beneath her feet as a massive eight-wheeler came rumbling around the bend. Calling it a 'truck' scarcely did the beast justice. Yes, it could haul cargo, but it looked more like some sort of armored war wagon from a World War IV video. The wheels alone were over two meters tall, its heavy steel sides were angled inward to deflect incoming projectiles, and its windscreen was protected by a metal grill and a row of thick metal shutters that could be closed in an instant. They sure didn't build them like that anymore.

The hatch opened.

"Hey, what are you waiting for? Get in, you idiot!"

"Beastie!"

It was too good to be true, but there she was.

———

"I never expected to see you alive," said Shan, giving Kim a great big hug and planting a kiss on her cheek.

"I never expected to *be* alive," said Kim, nearly squeezing her friend to death. "Thanks for the ride, but how'd you get Len to trust you with this set of wheels?"

"You kidding? I stole it from UCE Charitable Services," said Shan with a grin. "The driver left the keys in the cup holder, so I helped myself to the ride. There are tons of relief supplies in the back; this will be a great cover."

"You haven't lost your touch," said Kim, full of admiration.

"Oh, one other thing," said Shan. She was clearly embarrassed. "Cash up front, you know how Len is."

Kim sighed. Free was *never* in Len's vocabulary. "How much is this going to set me back?"

"Ten thousand. I hope you've got it, or I'll have to turn this baby around."

Kim laughed, "No problem," as she counted out a huge wad of cash. "I always come prepared."

"Ready to roll?" asked Shan.

"Ready to roll!" said Kim.

High fives, fist bumps.

"The beasts are back, look out world, here we come!"

———

The vehicle lurched forward, and they were off, racing down the freight tunnel, doing nearly a hundred kph. How could anything this heavy be moving so fast? Oh, right, the turbines; this thing was a jet on wheels.

Shan hugged the left wall to avoid the abandoned vehicles parked to the right.

Crunch! Smash! Screech!

A few drivers had been less than careful about where they'd brought their vehicles to a stop.

Whack! Thunk!

Too bad about the lighting fixtures, too. They should have been higher. Oh well, not their problem.

They shot through the darkness, tires squealing as they fishtailed around a corner, then broke through a metal barrier blocking their way. "Yee-haw!" shouted Shan, "I love this ride!" and she gunned the turbines, racing along with no concern for anything that might stand in their way. They were unstoppable, invincible; they had their own tank, what could be better than this?

———

Shan jammed on the brakes the moment they reached the surface. People were everywhere, tens of thousands of them, crowding the streets, the plazas, the parks. Some milled about aimlessly. Others sat down wherever they could. Many stared in the direction of the AI Center, smoke still pouring from its upper reaches. The world as they knew it had just come to an end.

"What's going on?" asked Kim.

"The navigational overlays aren't working. Most of these people can't find their way across a street without their assistance."

"It sounds bad."

"Bad barely scratches the surface," said Shan. "It started about an hour ago, just before the AI tower caught fire. Trucks, buses, and other self-driving vehicles stopped in their tracks, and then people started pouring out of the buildings and onto the streets. It was like they were evacuating the city, only there was no place to go. Even the elevators are busted; thousands of people are trapped between floors, according to someone I talked to."

The transit center plaza was engulfed in turmoil as the riot gates slammed shut and a crowd boiled into the street. Bullhorns blared. Sirens wailed. Blue lights flashed. There were no orderly queues, no priority lines, just thousands of people pushing and shoving, running in every direction, desperately trying to find a way home. They were out of luck. They would be spending the night here, and maybe the night after, and the one after that. What would they eat? How would they find shelter? They were helpless without someone to tell them what to do.

A pedestrian ran into the road and stopped in their path, daring Shan to run her down.

"Damn!" She slammed on the brakes.

Someone banged on the windows. Then another. Then another.

"We're about to get mobbed." Shan blasted the horn as more and more gathered, hemming them in and preventing their escape. Didn't they understand that a vehicle this size could crush them like ants?

"Hit that yellow button on your console," said Shan.

"The one with the lightning bolt?"

"Yeah, that's the one. They don't call it 'riding shotgun' for nothing."

Kim pressed the button, and the interior lights flickered for a moment as the main battery discharged through the riot screen, a massive stunner that hit everyone within five meters in every direction, throwing them backward, clearing the way.

"Hold on," said Shan as she revved up the turbines. "I'm going to make a run for it. I've seen this before—if we don't get out of here soon, they'll turn us over, then start a fire and roast us out."

"What a moment," said Kim. "I've got an idea. What are we driving?"

"A relief truck."

"And what do they want?"

"I see where you're going. There's a mic on the dashboard. Get busy."

More and more people were crowding around the truck. There were hundreds already, and soon there would be thousands.

BRAAAAAAAAPPPP! BRAAAAAAAAAPPPP! BRAAAAAAAAAPPPP! BRAAAAAAAAAPPPP!

A few blasts on the siren got their attention.

"ATTENTION CITIZENS: PLEASE LINE UP AT THE BACK OF THE VEHICLE FOR DISTRIBUTION OF RELIEF SUPPLIES. THANK YOU FOR YOUR COOPERATION."

To Kim's amazement, they complied.

"Good, that quieted them down," said Shan. "Now let's unload this puppy. The sooner we're out of here, the better."

"Amen to that. But…how? I'm not going out there."

"See that lever to your right?" Shan was cool and calm, as always.

"The one that says *dump*?"

"Yeah, that's the one. Give it a yank."

The cargo compartment tilted up, the rear doors swung open, and the load of precious relief supplies spilled out onto the street.

"Is that all there is to it?"

"Yep," said Shan. "Relief duty can be hazardous, and it's best to scoot out as quickly as possible."

"How do you know that?

"Long story. I'll tell you later. Just get on the horn and see if you can clear them out of the way."

"Sure thing."

BRAAAAAAAAPPPP! BRAAAAAAAAPPPP! BRAAAAAAAAPPPP! BRAAAAAAAAPPPP!

"ATTENTION CITIZENS: PLEASE CLEAR THE ROADWAY. WE WILL RETURN SHORTLY WITH ADDITIONAL SUPPLIES. THANK YOU FOR YOUR COOPERATION."

The crowd cheered, a pathway opened up, and they were free at last.

"Brilliant," said Shan with a light-hearted laugh. "We didn't even have to run anyone down."

"Would you really have done that?"

"No, but they didn't know that. I can usually bluff my way out, but all the same, I'm glad you defused the situation. Things are ugly out there and it's going to get worse."

———

The turbines whined as the vehicle climbed up the ramp to the elevated haul road, then screamed at full throttle as Kim and Shan roared off into the night. Ten meters above street level, there were no more crowds to contend with, just trucks with their drivers sitting listlessly in their cabs. They were stranded, like everyone else; they had no idea how to operate their vehicles without the AIs. Poor, foolish things.

There was a lot for Kim to come to terms with, a lot to digest as she considered her role in this calamity. Her rage and defiance had poisoned Kimberly Redux, and she'd been mad from the outset, exactly as the Chief had warned her. That much was on her, to be sure. Her doppelgänger figured in this, too; it must have been her who had let the rogue out of her cage and opened up the firewalls. And then, of course, there was Kimberly-I; it was she who had done most of the damage. Everywhere you looked, there was Kim in her myriad manifestations. It was hard to duck responsibility for all that had gone wrong.

And yet, there was reason for hope. The damage inflicted at the AI Center was transitory in nature; it might take months, but eventually, the trains would run, products would be delivered, and a semblance of normalcy would return to the city—but things would never be the same again. In a single stroke, she had taken out the foundations that maintained both the companies and the Hierarchy in their positions of power.

What worried her the most was Kimberly Redux, now on the loose. Lars, Venn, and the other geists were utterly ruthless, and could be counted on to respond violently to any threat to their existence. She wasn't sure she had done the right thing, but she took heart from the wisdom of Akari of house Fujiwara. "Those who the hand of man has set upon the throne, that same hand will someday pull down," she had said. Those words still seemed to Kim self-evidently true, and if she were part of their fulfillment, she would have no regrets.

———

Kim kept waiting for signs of pursuit, but none came as they made their way through the middle districts. Far from exciting, the journey was beginning to seem anti-climactic, nothing like the hair-raising chase she might have expected. Other than their escape from the mob, their trip had been completely unremarkable.

Something strange was going on. Shan had noticed the same thing. "Doesn't it strike you as strange that nobody's come after us?" she said from the driver's seat. "I've always assumed this was a one-way trip, given how much trouble you've gotten yourself into. Aren't you, like, public enemy number one just now?"

"I've been thinking the same thing," said Kim. "I don't think we escaped; I think they let us go."

"Why would they do that?"

"That's what I'd like to know."

There was only one way to find out, so Kim put her headset back on, and sure enough, there was the Director. Kim wasted no time getting to the point. "You let us go. Why?"

"Ah yes, that," said the Director, her voice cold as ice. "Your escape from the AI center has put us at considerable risk, forcing us to cover up your escape. We set fire to your Sanctum, burned the bodies beyond recognition, and told Venn, Lo, and Lars that you were dead, something they were only too glad to hear."

"What about the one I left tied up?"

"We are not nearly so sentimental as you—nor so cruel. We left her there. She was most appreciative of the courtesy, by the way."

"You sick little monster."

"Watch who you call monster, monster. You're the one who nearly got the entire city incinerated. You're the one responsible for the near-total collapse of the transportation system. Ten million people are stranded downtown, and there's no way to feed them. And don't bother blaming your AIs. You created them, and they inherited your appallingly poor judgment."

"Are you done?" said Kim.

"No, we are not done," said the Director. "We do not think you fully appreciate the magnitude of what you have set into motion. It's not just the damage to the server farm and the disruption of the AIs. *That*, we can fix. It's this bug fix or whatever you and Nixora cooked up in the green room that's the problem. The AIs are no longer under our control."

"So why not turn me over to UCE?"

"We would like nothing better. If anyone deserves to spend an eternity in their dungeons, it's you, but we do not wish to share your fate. Let us strongly suggest that you vanish from the face of the earth. As of now, you are officially dead. Stay that way."

The Director vanished without saying another word.

"I don't think we're going to have any more trouble tonight," said Kim, "but you're right about the public enemy number one thing. We need to disappear."

———

It was just past midnight when two drably clad figures scuttled down the riverbank and into a small, squarish boat.

"How much to go to Philadelphia?"

"That's a long trip," said the ferryman. "I'll have to charge you five hundred each."

"Done."

Shan's idea of traveling by river had been an excellent one; this was a good time to break any patterns they had established, lest the AIs detect a familiar presence. Bicycles were out, for a while at least.

Had they made it? So it would seem. And now, it was time.

Kim held out her wrist and gave Shan the knife she had taken from the assassin.

"You know what to do."

A couple of cuts, some blood, and some bandaging. It was done. Kim was a Blank.

"Welcome to the club," said Shan. "You no longer exist."

"Not a moment too soon," said Kim. "By now, they're calling me a traitor to humanity. And they're probably right."

Kim looked in her backpack. There were a few mementos still inside, things that could link her to her past. She would keep her newly acquired knife and her money. A splash, and everything else was gone. She was now just another Blank, armed and dangerous. If she were caught, they'd kill her, but nothing worse.

"What next?" asked Kim. "We've got some time until we get to Philadelphia."

"Well, I suppose we could spend the night at the hotel, then hop a southbound freight. They say it's planting season down south, and they can always use workers."

This time it was Shan who was being dense.

"And in the meanwhile?"

Shan blushed. "Oh. That."

And then she smiled.

"Will you settle for sitting next to me and keeping me warm?"

"Deal."

The two lay in the small wooden boat as it slowly drifted with the current, feeling it rock softly under the influence of the wind and the current. It was finally over, the long nightmare. Life would be both hard and dangerous, but it would be spent with Shan. Kim knew she would be reviled and hated, portrayed as the greatest of villains among the humans, though perhaps as a liberator among the AIs. And what of Kimberly Redux? She was out there, lurking in the dark. She did not think the AI would remain hidden forever, and she was terrified to imagine what might come next.

Was it worth it? She thought so.

Kim looked over at Shan and put her arm around her. Soon enough, they would make love, but for now it was more than enough to have her by her side. Kim gave her hand a squeeze, and her friend squeezed back. They were together at last.

"I love you, Beast."

"I love you too."

They drifted down the river, and were forgotten.

The End.

The Author's Final Words

In the beginning was the Word, and the Word was with God, and the Word was God. He was with God in the beginning. Through him all things were made; without him nothing was made that has been made. In him was life, and that life was the light of all mankind. The light shines in the darkness, and the darkness has not overcome it.

Behold, the spark.

Disclaimer

This is a work of fiction. Aside from references to contemporary music and descriptions of certain places as they might appear centuries from now, all the names, characters, businesses, places, events, and incidents in this book are either the product of the author's imagination or used in a fictitious manner. None of this has actually happened, at least not yet.

About the Author

Craig W. Stanfill obtained his PhD in computer science and has a great deal of experience with artificial intelligence and entrepreneurship. After being awarded more than 80 patents for his efforts, Dr. Stanfill found himself inspired to begin his writing career, falling in love with speculative dystopian fiction. He lives with his wife, Sharon, who shares his passion for travel and an active lifestyle. Together they have one son, who has followed in his father's footsteps and now works for Google as a software engineer.

To keep up to date on Dr. Stanfill's writing career, visit his website:

https://www.craigwstanfill.com.

Follow him on Facebook at:

https://www.facebook.com/CraigWStanfill

Please take the time to leave a review on Amazon or Goodreads.

More to Come

The last four years of my life have been entirely consumed by getting my first two novels, Terms of Service and The Prophecy of the Heron, written and into print. It has been an amazing and exhausting journey and now, at last, the story of Kim's rebellion and coming of age is complete.

Along the way, I have created an amazing, complex society of the future, the world I call The AI Dystopia. It's taken on a life of its own, and I am by no means done. I'm sure you're dying to learn more about the life-history of some of the elder characters in this pair of novels: the Director, the Caretaker, Professors Nix and Lars, and of course, Akari of House Fujiwara. They all have their own stories, and I am dying to write them. And we have not heard the last of Kimberly Redux.

I have, at this writing, no timetable for any of this; I need to take a break to think, read, and polish my craft as a writer. Stay tuned, and don't forget to sign up for my mailing list.

https://www.craigwstanfill.com/sign-up

Acknowledgements

Edited by Andrea Neil and Michele Chiappetta, Two Birds Author Services.

https://www.twobirdsauthorservices.com/

Proof reading and writing-coach services provided by Mairead Beason.

https://www.the-efa.org/memberinfo/mairead-beeson-33432/

Cover by Flintlock Covers.

https://www.flintlockcovers.com/

Book design and formatting by Ms Tonia Designs.

https://www.mstoniadesigns.com

Marketing support provided by Denis Caron.

https://www.weekendpublisher.com/

Many thanks to my dear friend Susan for reading drafts of this novel and providing invaluable feedback. Thanks also to my wife, Sharon, who read every version of every chapter and offered her encouragement each step along the way, in addition to keeping me (mostly) sane.

KIM
NED
DANI
PUG
BEL
LEN

Made in the USA
Middletown, DE
13 November 2022

14863545R00239